THE CULT OF
LOVING KINDNESS

THE CULT OF LOVING KINDNESS

Paul Park

WILLIAM MORROW
AND COMPANY, INC.
NEW YORK

Library of Congress Cataloging-in-Publication Data

Park, Paul, 1954-
    The cult of loving kindness / Paul Park.
      p.   cm.
    ISBN 0-688-10574-2
    I. Title.
    PS3566.A6745C85   1991
    813'.54—dc20   90-19167
                                                       CIP

Printed in the United States of America

First Edition

1 2 3 4 5 6 7 8 9 10

BOOK DESIGN BY BERNARD SCHLEIFER

FOR JMC

THE CULT OF
LOVING KINDNESS

MR. SARNATH

A man had been arrested at the port of Caladon. His disembarkation papers had been smudged with sweat. Further investigation had revealed a false bottom to his suitcase.

Sulky, unimpassioned, he stood on the veranda of the customs shed, where the deputy administrator sat behind his desk. Around them the dark night was full of noises. Insects buzzed around the lamppost in the yard.

The deputy administrator leaned forward in his chair. He balanced one pointed elbow on the blotter of his desk, and with the fingers of one hand he combed delicately through a pile of small copper medallions. Each one was stamped with the image of the shining sun.

Under the desktop light they seemed to glow. The deputy administrator rubbed his eyes. It was the fourth hour after sunset; behind him in the shed, the senior deputy director was already drunk, asleep and snoring. At intervals his liquid grunts would seep out past the curtained doorway, mixing with more subtle forest sounds.

"Please sit down," said the deputy administrator. He indicated a wooden stool and the smuggler sank onto it, his knees spread apart. His fat face held no expression. His hair, plentiful upon his neck and hands, was thin on top. His scalp was slick with perspiration.

Next to the pile of medallions a small statue was lying on its side. It was the second part of the smuggler's consignment; the deputy administrator lifted it in both hands and set it upright underneath the lamp. Though only nine inches tall it weighed several pounds, a copper statue of St. Abu Starbridge standing erect, his hand held out in front of him. The tattoo on his palm was inlaid with a plug of solid gold.

The deputy administrator was a judge of craftsmanship. He ran his fingers over the folds of the saint's copper cloak, admiring the work. "Jon Blox," he said. With his left hand he turned over the pages of the smuggler's passport.

The man nodded. A mosquito had landed on the crown of his head. The deputy administrator watched it drink, and swell with blood, and drift away.

"Do you have anything to tell me?" he asked. "You must admit you're in an intricate position."

The smuggler stared at him briefly and then turned his head. He looked out over the wooden balustrade. Something was scrabbling in the bush on the other side of the yard. After a moment a badger waddled onto the perimeter and pressed its naked face against the fence.

The deputy administrator rubbed his eyes. These devotees were hard to break, for they were buttressed in their faith by the example of their saint, who never spoke to his tormentors even when the fire was around his feet. "You could make this simpler for yourself," he said. "Simpler and more complex. But as it is, you have neglected to fill out any of the proper forms. These items, though proscribed for the general public, nevertheless may have legitimate artistic and educational uses. I have seen a statuette just like this in the cultural museum in Charn."

A tremor of interest passed over the smuggler's face. He turned back toward the light. His voice was low—"What do you mean?"

"I mean that there's no reason for despair. This case may be more complicated than you understand."

He had the man's attention now. The soft pucker of a frown appeared between the smuggler's brows. "What do you mean?" he asked again.

The deputy administrator took a paper from his desk. He read a few lines from the back of it and then looked up. "You are accused of smuggling these items of religious contraband," he said, indicating the pile of medallions and the statue of the saint. "But perhaps we might consider entering a lesser charge, under the right circumstances. For example," he continued, "Customs Regulation 412ao forbids the export of all artifacts without a license from the Bureau of Antiquities. If you prefer, Regulation 6161j forbids the use of precious metals in the decorative arts. It is a question of a modest fine."

The smuggler shook his head. "I know the penalty for what I've done."

"I'm suggesting you may not. Your offense may be more trivial than you suppose."

Five wooden steps descended to the yard from the veranda of the customs shed. Two soldiers slouched on these, their backs to the administrator. Occasionally as they turned their heads, he could see the glow of their marijuana cigarettes and catch flickers of their conversation. Now one got up. He ambled over to the perimeter and knelt down by the fence.

"What do you want from me?" demanded the smuggler, his face suddenly alive, contorted with disgust. "Aach, I know your kind. Bureaucratic parasites!" He brought some saliva into his mouth as if to spit, then paused, then swallowed it again. He leaned forward on his stool, placing his fat fist upon the desk. "Let me tell you now, I have no information. No addresses. Not even a name."

At the fence, the soldier reached into his pocket and brought out part of a candy bar. The badger stood opposite him on its hind legs.

The deputy administrator shrugged. "You misunderstand me. But I appreciate your fears. Perhaps you are familiar with certain worst-case scenarios. Perhaps involving relatives or personal friends." He smiled—a wasted gesture, for the lower part of his emaciated face was covered by a veil.

"Let me explain," he said. "Some members of my department do what they can to discourage certain activities, which they interpret to be linked to superstition and idolatry. They feel the truth of man's condition can be better understood through reason than through faith."

Again the smuggler's face seemed to have shut down, and settled into stolid impassivity. The deputy administrator tried again: "Let me explain. Our function here is not only to prosecute. It is to inform. These objects"—here he waved his hand dismissively at the pile of medallions—"these objects have no meaning. They are the relics of a bankrupt church."

On the steps, the remaining soldier slapped his neck and swore. And at the fence across the yard, his comrade got up from his knees. He was looking up into the sky.

The lights from the compound overwhelmed all but the brightest stars. But now the moon was rising, its pale edge gleaming among the tallest trees. The smuggler studied it in silence until the arc of its great rim rose unimpeded over the forest canopy. Then he bowed his head and stared down at the floor between his knees. "I guess I'll never leave this place alive," he said. The new light gave his face a new composure.

The deputy administrator rubbed his eyes. "Your position is more favorable than you suspect. You have not begun to think about your options."

The smuggler made no reply, only stared at the floorboards underneath his boots. No man is so stupid that he cannot learn, reflected the administrator. But it takes time; he clapped his hands. "We are both tired," he said. "And I am explaining myself badly. Even so, please think about what I have said. And I will speak to my superiors." He looked down at the appointment book upon his desk. "In the meantime," he said, "I have you scheduled tentatively for next Friday. That's the thirty-fourth."

The soldiers took the man away. In a few minutes one of them returned to the porch bearing refreshments—crusts of bread and cheese, and a tin basin full of water. He deposited them on the desk and then withdrew.

After he had gone, the deputy administrator sat by himself for a long time. He switched off the small light upon his desk. Now the moon was rising, showing its silver belly in a sea of darkness.

He left the food untouched. He sat listening to the mosquitoes and the cautious stir of animals beyond the fence. In the distance, at the limit of his senses, he could hear occasional noises from the port—steam whistles from the packet boats and once, the clang of a buoy on the gentle sea. Occasionally the air was stiffened by the smell of salt. Behind him in the customs shed, his director had turned over and was still.

A gekko lay watching a spider on the balustrade near his right hand. Tendrils of flypaper, twisting gently in the humid air, hung from the ceiling of the porch. On one of them a moth had lighted and was stuck.

It was a luna moth, with iridescent wings as big as a man's hand. The deputy administrator sat back in his chair. He admired the composure of the creature, how it declined to hurt itself in futile struggles against fate. Its great wings scarcely moved. In a little while he took a pair of scissors from his desk and stood up behind his chair.

For several minutes he did nothing. From his changed position he could no longer see the moon directly. It was cut off by the overhanging roof. But instead, he could observe its entire shape reflected in the basin on his desk. The light spread over the plane of his desk, and fell especially on the image of the saint, and touched the star-shaped plug of gold upon his palm.

The statue depicted an episode from the saint's later life: how he calmed the mob below the Harbor Bridge when Chrism Demiurge was lord of Charn. His sad copper smile was full of wisdom and compassion.

The insect rustled its bright wings next to the administrator's head—the faintest susurration on the midnight air. How long did it have to live? Not long, not long, even in the best of times. He raised the scissors. Holding the cartridge of the flypaper in his other hand, he stretched it tight, and with single-minded care he cut the insect loose, amputating its five feet next to the glue.

Suddenly free, the moth folded its wings and dropped tumbling to the desk. It dropped onto its side in the middle of the basin, troubling the water, scattering the light.

Now the moon was rising. The deputy administrator stood looking out over the deserted yard. At midnight precisely, the light from the lamppost was extinguished, and the silver moon washed unimpeded over the black grass.

After half an hour the deputy administrator untied his tolliban. He stripped the long gauze veil from around his mouth and head, revealing features that were almost human. That night he felt supremely sensitive to every sound; leaning out over the porch's wooden balustrade, he stood listening to the air in the tall grass. He heard the bell buoy on the sea ring once, twice. He heard the prisoners breathing in their cells, the sentries sleeping at their watch, the sodden dreams of his superior in the shed.

He wadded his veil into a ball. Turning, he dropped it onto the center of the blotter on his desk. Next to it, next to the basin and the drowned moth, lay his appointment book. It was a record of interrogation stretching far into the past, far into the future: thousands of names penciled in at half-hour intervals, the faded marks glowing silver in the moonlight.

A ledger of unhappiness and waste—the deputy administrator stood with his hand over the open book, his finger on the page for the next day. Only a few hours away—he had planned to spend the night in meditation, perhaps dozing for twenty minutes at the end. But now the page felt harsh and rough under his hand; he closed the book. He lined it up along the edges of the blotter, and then weighted down its cover with the statue of the saint.

From a cardboard crate on the floor beneath his desk he pulled a change of underwear and two pairs of socks. These, together with his veil and the untouched bread and cheese, he tied into a bundle, which he could carry over his shoulder. He picked up one of the saint's copper medallions from the pile on his desk.

Due to the success of his department, the market in religious contraband—and especially these emblems of the Cult of Loving Kindness—was lucrative on both sides of the border. In Caladon the smallest trinket, for a sweeper or a guard, was worth more than a month's pay. The deputy administrator, with this coin, hoped to bribe the sentry at the gate to let him go. Holding it in the center of his palm, he stalked across the floor and down the steps, leaving his post for the first time in seven months.

The customs compound—six rectangular buildings surrounded by barbed wire—occupied a wooded ridge above the port, and was connected to it by a metal tram. The deputy administrator stalked across the yard. The grass was thick under his shoes. Expecting to be challenged, he slunk between two buildings, keeping to the shadows. But he saw no one. And when he reached the outer gate, the sentry in the box was fast asleep. So he slid the coin into the pocket of his trousers, and ducked under the crossbar.

A paved road led southeast from the gate. He followed it

for half a mile until he found a bare place in the trees. Here the road descended sharply toward the port two hundred feet below; from the crest of the ridge the deputy administrator could see the hands of the breakwater stretching out into the bay, pallid in the moonlight, each decorated with a single jewel. And there were lights, also, on the packet steamer by the dock, and a single shining ruby on the bell buoy out to sea. The deputy administrator listened for the sound—a muffled clanging on the small east wind. He heard it, and heard something else, louder, more insistent, closer, and he stepped aside into the grass. Below him at the bottom of the hill, the shuttle started on its hourly circuit from the port to the compound and then back.

He squatted down in the long grass. Soon he could hear the rattle of the car as it labored toward him up the slope. Soon he could see it—empty, brainless, fully lit, its wheels sparking on the steel rail that ran beside the road. He crouched down lower as it gained the slope, and he could read the advertisements in the empty compartment, and smell the singed metal as it hurried past.

Then it was gone. The deputy administrator stood up. For a minute he stood looking back the way he had come. Then he stepped out onto the road, continuing downhill for another hundred yards before he turned aside under the trees. A narrow track led away south along the ridge. It was the footpath over land, due south to the border and beyond, scarcely used now that the packets made the journey twice a week from Charn.

The forest closed around him after a dozen paces, and the dark was monstrous and loud. To the right and to the left, beetles quarreled in the underbrush, while high above among the jackfruit trees, tarsiers grabbed bats out of the air. Furry creatures, stupefied by moonlight, stumbled up against his ankles.

He walked almost for half an hour before the border came in sight: a small white cabin set adjacent to the track. East and west, a strand of luminescent wire sagged off into the trees, interrupted by the cabin and a wooden barricade. Placards in five languages were posted to this barricade, though only the boldest headings—PAPERS PLEASE, FORM SINGLE LINE, EXTINGUISH PIPES—were visible by moonlight.

Officially, the gate was open. But tongueweed licked at the administrator's shoes as he came up the track. He stood studying the placards; to his left, a single lantern glimmered on the cabin's porch.

By its light he could distinguish the gatekeeper sitting cross-legged on a table, his shoulders hunched, his head bent low, his hands clasped in his lap. It was an attitude of meditation; a kerosene lantern on the desk in front of him flickered in the humid wind, and it shone upon his narrow face, his naked scalp, his veil. He was staring deep into the flame.

Standing on the porch's lowest step, the deputy administrator watched him carefully. He took pleasure in watching him, in examining his meager arms and legs, for the old man was a member of his own race, living, like him, in a world of strangers. Old and thin, the man was still quite supple, and his spine still made a graceful curve. Clearly he had crossed the seventh boundary of concentration, and was beginning to perceive the essences of small inanimate objects. An inkwell, a pebble, and a leaf lay before him on the tabletop, grouped around the base of the lantern.

The deputy administrator waited. After several minutes, the old man raised his head. His eyes glowed bright with comprehension. "Please submit your documents face down upon the corner of the desk," he said. "Are you carrying liquor or illicit drugs?"

His voice was creaky and disused. Instead of answering, the deputy administrator climbed the steps until he stood inside the circle of the light. The old man stared at him with luminous eyes. And then he shook his head. "Sarnath," he exclaimed. "Sarnath Bey."

Mr. Sarnath took his bundle from his shoulder and lowered

it to the floor. He pulled a chair up to the table and sat down. Leaning forward with his hands over the lamp, he indicated the three objects on the tabletop. "What do you see?" he asked.

The old man shrugged. "Three different kinds of death."

They spoke in a Treganu dialect, using it gratefully and tentatively after so long away from home. The old man unwrapped part of his long veil and pulled it down, so that it hung around his neck. "Why are you here?" he asked.

Mr. Sarnath smiled. With his index finger, he reached forward and touched the stem of the dry leaf. "I saw a moth drown in a bowl," he said.

"Tell me."

"No. It was as if I almost understood. Yet it was enough— I'm going home."

The old man didn't speak for half a minute. Then he shook his head, and his voice, when it came, was softer, clearer, full of sadness. "They let you go?" he said.

"I was a volunteer. And they were all asleep." Mr. Sarnath looked over the railing of the porch to the dark forest all around. "You must know what I mean," he said. "What keeps you here?"

The old man sighed, a melancholy sound. "You have all the luck," he grumbled. "Yours is the first face I've seen here in a week."

"A moth was drowning in a bowl of light," said Mr. Sarnath. "It is not the time or place that is important."

"Even so," replied the gatekeeper. He gestured toward the gate. "This can't be what the master had in mind when he told us to go out into the world. If I see seven clients in a month, I'm lucky. What can I learn from them, or they from me? But you had boatloads every day."

Mr. Sarnath shrugged. He gestured down the track the way he'd come. "They have a vacancy," he said.

There was an uncomfortable silence. Mr. Sarnath looked away, and calmed himself by studying the effect of moonlight as it pierced through the forest canopy. This night was magical and rare, for only at rare moments in the voyage of his life had he ever sensed his forward progress. Now in everything he saw the traces of a new significance, and it was lurking in the darkness like a delicate and subtle beast, vulnerable and shy of controversy.

Here and there, bright beams of moonlight fell unbroken to the ground, a hundred feet or more. Insects spiraled up them as if climbing to the stars; on a sprig of manzanita by the trail, a polyphemus fly arranged its wings. "I'll be going now," said Mr. Sarnath. He rose to his feet and retrieved his bundle from the floor.

The gatekeeper ignored him and continued to sit hunched over the lantern, staring at the flame. Mr. Sarnath made a little gesture of farewell. Then he walked down the steps. The gate was a simple one, an X-shaped cross of wood set in a wooden frame. Mr. Sarnath pulled it open and slipped through.

But he hadn't gone a half a mile before he heard a cry in back of him. The old gatekeeper was hurrying after him; he stopped and waited by the track. "Sarnath Bey!" cried the man. And then, when he got close: "Please forgive me, Sarnath Bey. Please—I wish you well."

He too was carrying a bundle, a cotton knapsack covered with embroidery. This he thrust into the traveler's hands, and then he bent down wheezing, out of breath. "Forgive me," he repeated, as soon as he could speak. "My eyes were blind from envy and self-pity."

"There is nothing to forgive."

"No, but there is." He wrapped his skinny rib cage in his arms, bent his head, and then continued: "Three thousand days I've lived there. More than three thousand, and I think that I'm as far as ever from achieving understanding. How long has it been for you? Not long—you're still a young man."

He stood up straight and reached his hand out toward the

knapsack. "Forgive me," he repeated. "I was jealous, I admit. Because I've been away from home so long. But perhaps it's my impatience that keeps me here. Perhaps if I can overcome that. . . ." His voice, eager and unhappy, trailed away. But then he shook his head. "I've brought you gifts," he said. He pulled the knapsack out of Sarnath's hands, and pulled the strings that opened it.

They were standing in a patch of moonlight. "Here's some food," he said. "Sourbread and wine—it's all I had. A flask of goat's milk. Here, but look at this." He opened a small purse and showed a handful of steel dollars, each one incised with the head of the First Liberator, Colonel Aspe. "These I confiscated from a merchant." He shrugged. "I have no use for them."

He drew out a cotton sweater and a quilt. This he spread out in the moonlight on the grass, and then he squatted down. "There's a flashlight and a pocket knife," he said. "And look."

He unrolled a length of fabric. "Look," he said. He flicked on the flashlight, and in its narrow, intense compass Sarnath could see a row of bones: the skulls and limbs and shoulder blades of various small animals, each one covered with a mass of carving.

"These I do in my spare time," said the old man. "I find them in the woods." He held up the femur of a wild dog, cut with scenes from the lives of the Treganu sages and set with precious stones.

The work was exquisite. Mr. Sarnath picked up the skull of a small child. Flowers and leaves were cut into the bone, and on the broad white forehead was engraved a single sign: the endless knot of the unravelers. "That one's for my sister," said the old man. He pointed to a piece of elephant horn, decorated with quotations from the nine incontrovertible truths. "For my mother, if she's still alive. No, take them all. I have no use for them. Give them to my friends, to anyone who still remembers me."

Mr. Sarnath shook his head. With careful fingers he separated out the food, the sweater, and the quilt. "These I'll take," he said.

The old man picked up a piece of bone. "Please take them to my friends," he said. "And this one—look."

They were squatting in the grass. The old man held the flashlight in one hand. He dropped the bone onto the others, and then he pulled a bundle of paper from the last recesses of the knapsack. "This is the finest one," he said. "It is my gift for the master. Please."

Mr. Sarnath uncovered the last bundle. There in a nest of ancient paper covered with ancient spidery writing lay another skull, with a curiously flat forehead and a curiously bulbous occiput. The eyeholes and the inside of the nasal cavity were chased with silver, the jaw rebuilt with silver and fastened with a silver hinge.

"Look at the top," said the old man. He shone the light along the cranium, so Mr. Sarnath could see that its surface was covered with new carved figures, the new lines gleaming white against the dull brown bone.

They were scenes out of the master's life. "It is my gift to him," persisted the old man. "My finest work—the skull I took from an old smuggler—the papers too. They're valuable—I know they are. The man refused to tell me what they were, and when the guards came he attempted suicide."

"It is not valuable to me," said Mr. Sarnath gently.

The old man squatted on his heels. He looked up into the darkness, and when he looked back there were tears in his eyes. "No," he said. "Of course not."

Then he stood up. He left the flashlight lying on the quilt, but he had the purse of dollars in his hand. With trembling fingers he undid the cord, and then he was throwing handfuls of currency off into the darkness, until the purse hung empty. Mr. Sarnath could hear the coins clinking against tree trunks and against stones. He could hear the movement of small animals as they dodged away; then there was silence.

The old man bent down to the ground. And then he was picking up the pieces of old bone and scattering them into the undergrowth. The small skull of the girl he tested in his palm, and then he threw it with all his strength against the trunk of a java tree.

"You were always a quick scholar," he said. "But I'm just an old man. But," he said, a tint of pleading in his voice, "you'll tell the master about me? How I threw these things away? 'All life is a journey,' " he quoted miserably. " 'The more I carry, the more difficult it is for me to move.' "

Mr. Sarnath put his hand on the last skull. It lay in the beam of the discarded flashlight, tangled in its nest of papers, staring up at him with hollow, silver eyes. "This I'll take," he said. "A present for the master. I'll tell him what you said."

"No," repeated the old man. "Leave it. You were right, and I was wrong. It's eleven hundred miles. Too long to carry an old bone."

For an answer Mr. Sarnath rearranged the skull inside its bundle, and wrapped it in the quilt. Then he took the food, the sweater, and his own few clothes, and thrust them with the quilt and the knife into the knapsack. Last of all he turned off the flashlight and slipped it into a side pocket of the pack. "Thank you," he said.

There were tears upon the old man's cheeks. "Thank you," repeated Mr. Sarnath, standing up. The old man was muttering and mumbling. Suddenly he seemed embarrassed, eager to be gone.

Mr. Sarnath slung the pack over his shoulder. The old man stood in the beam of moonlight, hugging his frail rib cage. "My master told me to give all I had," he muttered plaintively. Then he turned away. "Good-bye," he said, shaking his head, not responding when Sarnath embraced him, and kissed him with the kiss of peace.

* * *

Now the moon was rising, and the track wound gradually uphill. Sarnath moved his bag to his right shoulder. He walked quickly, for his breath was good. And toward three o'clock he broke out of the trees—a wide, sandy valley stretched away from him, and in the distance glowed the lights of a small town.

Here the wind was in his face, a cold new breeze. It came to him up from the shore. South and east between the hills a line of stars dipped low over the bay. It was a constellation known locally as "the cucumber"; beyond the village Sarnath could already see some lights upon the beach, as the fishing boats set out to hunt the most elusive of the deep-sea vegetables.

The wind blew up the valley toward him, and brought a mixture of fresh smells. After the dark and pregnant forest, Sarnath turned gratefully downhill. The air was full of salt, and there was sagebrush all around him on the valley's upper slope. And something else: some hint of poison in the soil, some alkali that kept the trees away.

It was this poison that gave the place its character. A quarter of a mile down the slope the path traversed another wider way, which stretched east and west into the hills. An ancient monument stood near the crossroads, the tomb of Basilon Farfetch. He had been the patron saint of travelers before the revolution.

As was traditional in that part of the country, the crossroads was a barren, lonely place. It was inhabited, according to the local superstition, by ghosts and spirits who had cursed the soil so that nothing grew. They were the ghosts of all those who had died by violence in that part of the country—after midnight, travelers were rare. Mr. Sarnath, coming down out of the trees, hesitated in surprise to see a light at the crossroads, the flicker of a lantern in the wind.

He looped the ends of his veil around his face, concealing his mouth. Almost he was tempted to leave the track and go down through the bush another way. This area was famous for the depredations of a highwayman, a man who called himself Lycantor Starbridge—though his real name, Sarnath suspected, was much humbler. Since the days of reconstruction, when outlaw bands of Starbridge soldiery had terrorized these hills, it had been the custom for all bandits to wear silk and jewels, and to pretend extraction from the ancient kings.

Lycantor Starbridge had carried this tradition to extremes. A handsome man, he had treated women with flamboyant gallantry. But his reputation among men was crueler; a hundred yards from the crossroads Sarnath paused again.

A lamp was guttering untended on the sand. And for the first time Sarnath heard a noise, the sound of weeping in a woman's voice, and a high-pitched cry. Then some soft words of command. Mr. Sarnath hesitated, and then moved forward, reciting in his mind the precept of his master, that fear is an illusion of the heart.

And in a few steps he was conscious of another noise, a subtle groaning in the wind and the small clanking of a chain. Wading through the sage, he came down over the last hill and out onto an open, barren place with the crossroads at its center. The tomb of St. Basilon Farfetch was on the other side, beyond the gusting circle of the lamp, and Sarnath could see the outline of the stone bulk of the tomb, and the statue of the ancient saint astride it. The stone stumps of his hands were raised up to the sky. Behind his head, the moon shone like a halo.

A gallows had been raised along the wider road that led off west toward Charn. Hidden before by some trick of the shadows, now it was visible, a twenty-foot shaft of wood surmounted by a short crossbar. The body of a man hung from this crossbar, suspended from a chain around his chest.

Ten yards away under the flank of the stone sarcophagus, a girl lay on her back, her head against the sand. The lantern cast a flickering shadow against the wall of the stone frieze; as Sarnath came close, the silhouette resolved itself into two dark bulges, one formed by the girl's upthrust knees, the other by the back of someone else who was hunched over her body. The girl turned her face into the light so that her cheek was flat against the sand. There was sweat on her face, moisture on her lips.

"Easy now, easy," came a voice. The second humpbacked shadow straightened up. Coming closer, Sarnath could see part of a face, a mass of long grey hair. It was a woman. "Easy now," she said. She was kneeling down between the legs of a young girl.

She was talking to herself. The girl on her back was beyond listening, her eyes turned backward in her head. Sudden, wild convulsions shook her body, and the middle of her spine arched off the sand. "There," said the other as the spasms quieted down "There now, there, that's all it is."

She was an old woman dressed in black. She was crouching down between the girl's knees, but when the crisis passed they lolled apart; the woman rose and pulled herself around, so that she could take the girl's head upon her lap. "There now," she said. With the hem of her shawl she wiped the girl's lips and wiped the sweat from her face. A small crescent of sand was stuck to the girl's cheek, where she had laid her cheek against the ground.

"Hush now," said the grey-haired woman. The girl's head rolled loosely in her hands. Since the crisis, all the girl's muscles seemed to have relaxed—her knees and arms lay flat against the ground.

"Can I help?" asked Mr. Sarnath. He was standing at the crossroads. Now he came forward and squatted down next to the old woman, where she sat cradling the other's head. She turned to watch him and turned back—a sharp-faced, hard-skinned woman, smelling of kerosene.

She shook her head. "No help," she said.

By contrast, the girl in her lap was beautiful, with red curls around a delicate, pale face. "No help," muttered the old woman to herself. "No help—she's almost gone."

With the vague idea of trying to find her pulse, Mr. Sarnath reached out to the girl's arm, where it lay near him on the sand. But he stood up when the woman hissed at him and pulled the girl away. "Don't you touch," she said.

The girl's legs were spread apart. There was a blanket thrust between them, partly hidden by her long red dress, which had blown up almost to her waist. Embarrassed, Mr. Sarnath stood waiting, and after a minute the old woman relented, and when she spoke her voice was softer. "Sleeping pills," she said. "Poisoned herself, because of him." She gestured with the point of her chin toward the gallows, where the corpse hung creaking in the wind.

"Your daughter?"

"No, my sister. Who are you? You're one of those officers they've got up by the border. Hunh—I've seen your face."

Around them now, the night was full of noises. Sarnath watched a centipede next to his shoe. "I'll go down to the town," he said. "I'll get a doctor there."

"No. It's good like this." The woman's hands upon her sister's cheek were gentle and forgiving, but her face was not. "She used to come up here to meet him," she continued. "Sneak out at all hours. This is where she met him. Hunh— Lycantor Starbridge. She'll be with him now." Again she gestured toward the gallows with her chin.

"Do you live near here?" asked Mr. Sarnath. "I could help you bring her home."

"No!" repeated the old woman. Again, her voice was harsh and rough, but her hands were soft around her sister's face. "No—just leave us." She nodded down the western road. "Is that your way? Two miles on the left you'll see the Forest View Motel. Tell my man to bring a shovel. He's the owner there."

Irresolute, Mr. Sarnath pressed his palms together. The girl's breath was shallow in her chest, and there was a froth of scum upon her lips, which her sister wiped continually away. How strange it is, thought Mr. Sarnath. Perhaps the soul's life has a natural end. The wise person knows when to desist, to seek out some new understanding. But to abandon life before that end, perhaps—

"Are you still here?" grumbled the old woman.

He stood watching the corpse of the highwayman, turning slowly on its chain. Then he stepped away toward the girl's legs and kneeled down. "What's this?" he asked.

The woman shrugged. "The pills caused her to miscarry. She was ninety days before her time." She pointed with her chin. "There's the father, so she claimed."

"The child is still alive," said Mr. Sarnath.

He had dropped his knapsack a few feet away. Now he retrieved it and pulled out his flashlight. Switching it on, he drew back a corner of the blanket to reveal two infants in a caul.

A movement had betrayed their presence, a small tremor on the surface of the blanket that had covered them. No cry, no noise had escaped them, though now Mr. Sarnath thought he could detect a tiny sputtering. They turned their heads away from the harsh light, a dark girl and a pale, fair boy, wrapped in each other's arms.

Their eyes were open, blue and dark, their arms were wound around each other's backs, their tiny legs around each other's hips. Sarnath noticed with surprise the boy's erect penis; he laid the light aside and then picked up the pocketknife the gatekeeper had given him, to cut the double, knotted cord that joined them to their mother.

"They're alive," he said.

"Not for long."

The cord was greasy underneath his fingers, slippery with blood. He cut it off ten inches from the mother's slack body and then held it up, pinching it tight, unsure of what to do. "What do you mean?" he asked.

She shrugged. "I've seven of my own." At that moment,

her sister started to moan softly. The old woman pulled her sister's head into her lap and cradled it in her thin arms—a fierce, protective gesture. "Take it away," she said. "Leave it on the altar—there."

By this she meant the stone sarcophagus. The image of the saint loomed over them, his hands held to the sky. Sarnath bowed his head, and with a common sense he didn't know he quite possessed, he tied the cords off on the bellies of the twins and cut them short. With a corner of a pair of underpants, Sarnath wiped the blood and fluid from the babies' faces, and removed the remnants of the caul. They stirred fretfully under his hands. And they were making noises now—wet little clucks and moans, though still far short of crying.

He wrapped them in the blanket. "I'll take them to the town," he said. He sat cross-legged on the sand. The eastern sky was pale above a line of hills.

Awkwardly, he held the children up. They were restless and squirming in the blanket. Their mother had quieted down again, and the old woman's eyes were full of tears. Then she made a sign that Sarnath barely recognized. She ducked her chin down into her left armpit and then spat into the sand—the ancient sign of the unclean. "Who'll take them?" she said fiercely. "Spirit children, look— they're one month premature. More than ninety days— they should be dead."

"What do you mean?"

"Look at them—they're healthy as a snake, while she lies dying. Big, too. They weren't so big inside her body, I can tell you. You could scarcely see."

"What do you mean?"

"Look at this place! Do you think those are her children? No, but they were conceived there on that altar."

"These are superstitions," murmured Mr. Sarnath. He was trying to find a way of holding the children that would keep them comfortable. But they were squirming and fretting in his hands. Were they hungry? He had goat's milk in a bottle.

"Superstitions! No one comes here. No one but the murdered dead." She pointed toward Lycantor Starbridge with her chin.

THE MASTER | 2

In those days the moon rose twice each season. The first time Mr. Sarnath saw it he was just a boy, living with his master in the village in the trees. It had risen for a dozen nights during the final phase of spring, the time of its least influence in the affairs of men. Then it had been a small disturbance at the zenith, a small light in a bank of clouds.

Then he had stood watching in a bare place in the almond grove, while his master raised his arm to point. But Sarnath wasn't listening. Then it had been hard even to think about the wintertime. Hard to imagine all the trees down, and the horizon all around, and the land empty. Hard to imagine how Paradise had shone like a pale sun on the pale snow, commanding the night sky, the dreams of men, the city of Charn—it seemed unreal to think of it. Winter was safe when Mr. Sarnath was a boy, a distant memory, a distant prophecy of nightmare. It was sealed in the past, sealed in the future.

Yet eleven thousand days later, when the moon rose again the night that Rael and Cassia were born, its power was already waxing. Only midsummer, yet already by midsummer the world had turned. Gradually, inexorably, new impulses were combining with ones as old as time to threaten the power of democratic Charn, born in the bloody revolutions of midspring. Not so long before—there were men alive who still remembered the tyranny of the old government, and it made them desperate to forestall the future. Desperate when they saw those old roots bear new greenness, those old sophistries and superstitions gather weight. It was for this reason that the smuggler at the port of Caladon was put to death.

In those midsummer days, forests and jungles stretched a thousand miles from the coast, beyond the borders of the old diocese of Charn. Traveling through it on his long, slow journey toward the village of his birth, Mr. Sarnath passed evidence of this new awakening. He saw the shining sun of Abu Starbridge painted on stones and on the trunks of trees. He saw the painted image of Immortal Angkhdt. And even though he had left his duties at his desk in Caladon, still he was made anxious by these new phenomena. For he was a student of history, a student also of human nature, and he wondered how the indigent and unsophisticated peoples of the forest could find anything in the old legends to attract them. Yet the Cult of Loving Kindness seemed to flourish best among the poor.

Once when the children were just old enough to walk, Mr. Sarnath had stayed a month in a small town. It was hidden in a grove of mescal bushes; on the sixtieth night he had left the children sleeping and had climbed down the slope into a swamp. Dry land in the middle of the wet, difficult of access, and there he had crouched with many others, watching a shaman of the Cult of Loving Kindness sing his song. The man had told them how Beloved Angkhdt came down from Paradise in the world's morning, and sifted gold from dirt, and threshed out corn from chaff, and raised up certain men and women to be Starbridges and kings. He told them how the rest should suffer gladly, how they like Angkhdt himself had been reborn on earth to suffer for their sins, how it was only through glad suffering that they could purge themselves of sin, until their souls rose up to Paradise again.

The shaman's face was painted white. His lips were drawn back in a grimace almost of anger as he told them of Angkhdt's journey through the solar system, through the planets of the nine hells where worse torments, perhaps, awaited them upon their deaths. And in the swamp they had sat listening with eager gaping faces as the shaman made each of them confess their own inadequacies; troubled, Mr. Sarnath had climbed back up into the town to sit with the children as they slept.

Or once when Cassia was already talking, he took a job for a few months near Cochinoor. One night he saw a traveling group of players act the passion of St. Abu Starbridge—how his hand was marked with the tattoo of privilege. How he declined to use it to protect himself. How he was put to death. How he was seen drinking in a barroom that same night, according to a dozen witnesses. How he descended into darkness, and fought there with a white-faced devil. How by his victory he spread his privilege to common folk, and loosed the chain of hell, and brought the sugar rain. How he replenished all the earth.

Or in another town, Mr. Sarnath once had been accosted by a doddering old woman, who told him stories of the wonders of old Charn before the revolution. She was toothless and she mumbled so that he could barely understand. She gripped him by the arm. A city of ten thousand palaces and shrines, she told him, ruled over by a Starbridge bishop of the golden blood, a young girl martyred by the usurper Chrism Demiurge, burned together with her wild lover. She and her wild antinomial had been taken down from her tower cell and burned. But a magic tree had grown over the pyre. Broken open in the revolution time, her tomb was empty. She was the white lily on the stump—"Wait for me among the days to come," she'd said. Also: "Once more I will be with you for a little while." Also: "I am the spark that reignites the fire."

The old woman had gripped him by the arm. Mr. Sarnath smiled at her and pulled away, sad in his heart. Yet there was something touching in this version of events. How poignant it is, he thought, that we are always eager to surrender the burden of our own power, even to people who have always tortured us. He conceived of a desire to discuss this with the master, and so he hurried from that town, and from the next. He rented a donkey for a little while. And finally in November of the fourteenth phase of summer, 00016, he found himself at last in a wet jungle of almond trees, forty miles from the nearest human settlement, eight hundred miles west of Charn. This was the site of his master's village.

In those days it consisted of twenty-seven palm and bamboo houses raised on stilts above the forest floor. The novices had dammed the stream, and in the marshy ground below the village they grew taro root and rice. On drier ground above the stream they had burned the vegetation from a number of small hilltops, and after careful management they were able to grow soybeans, manioc, yams, and even occasionally cotton. These crops, harvested communally together with small plantations of bananas, mango trees, and pawpaw, gave to the villagers a richer diet than that of any other forest race. "Strength, which is the wisdom of the body, comes from the multitude of small experience," the master said.

His house was in the center of the village. All the others were arranged around it in concentric circles, according to the spiritual progress of the occupants. In theory all the houses were identical, for they had been built according to the master's precepts. Inside they exemplified the same three principles of sparsity, simplicity, and emptiness, but outside there were differences—the novices, who themselves lived in the outermost ring, had worked hard on the inner houses. They had built elaborate roofs of banana leaf and almond

wood, painted in bright colors, all oriented inward toward
the master's dwelling. These roofs served no purpose, except
to shelter from the rain some of the open space between the
houses. Spiritually, their implication was at best ambiguous,
yet even so the master tolerated them. In those days he
tolerated foolishness that would have once infuriated him,
for he was old and close to death. Lately some people had
even started to build altars in their homes, and decorate them
with small carved images of the master sleeping, eating, talking. But if he knew of this he gave no sign.

On November ninety-second of the fourteenth phase of
summer, three travelers appeared on the outskirts of the
village: two children and a middle-aged man. This was Mr.
Sarnath, coming home after an absence of half his life. The
journey from the customs house at Camran Head had taken
more than three thousand days, for when the children were
first born he had been obliged to find employment in a series
of small towns.

The children appeared first. They came running down the
forest pathway, a big, golden-haired boy and his dark sister.
The girl was laughing and running with her brother close
behind; his face was twisted up with anger, and he was trying
to crowd her off the path and down into the ditch. A quarter
of a mile below the village they were running along the top
of a raised embankment when the boy managed to trip her
with his heel, so that she fell headlong down the dike and
down into a swamp of mangrove trees. When the first novices
arrived from the village she was lying on her back and laughing, even though she was covered with mud and bleeding
from cuts on both palms and both knees. The boy was standing on the path, and when the novices tried to restrain him
he attacked them too. His skin was slippery with sweat; he
slid inside their hands and started punching at their stomachs,
which were as high as he could reach. Startled and confused,
they fell back along the dike, which made the little girl laugh

harder than ever. She was shrieking, almost choking with hilarity by the time Mr. Sarnath arrived at the bottom of the path.

"Stop that, stop," shouted the novices. "Stop that noise!" They fell back before the fury of the boy's attack, but one of them, a small, thick-bodied man with big protruding ears, held up when he saw Mr. Sarnath. He grasped hold of a sapling that was growing by the dike, and with his other hand he pushed the boy aside. "Sarnath?" he inquired—a soft, tentative question that cleared away all other noise. The little girl stopped laughing suddenly and there was quiet, save for the boy's angry breath.

The novice was bare-chested and was dressed in baggy shorts. Despite his low spiritual condition, he was not young. His face was heavier than those of most of his race, and when his mouth broke open in a smile, he revealed a row of large white teeth—evidence of a strange genetic mix.

He pushed the boy aside. He walked slowly down the dike and stopped, and reached out his dirty hand to touch the traveler's face. Mr. Sarnath was smiling and he closed his eyes, but the old novice hesitated at the final instant, and reached instead to grasp the end of Mr. Sarnath's veil where it was hanging low around his mouth. The novice pulled the veil away completely, unwound it from the traveler's neck. Then he reached out to touch Mr. Sarnath's arm and take his knapsack from his shoulder. "How are you?" he asked, his wet lips making a mess out of the words—"How are you doing?" But his face was lit with happiness, and when Sarnath hugged him, he placed his forehead shyly on the taller man's chest. "Nice to see you," he said.

"Honest Toil," replied Mr. Sarnath.

The little girl had dragged herself onto the dike. Avoiding the boy's stare, she limped down the path toward Sarnath, and she burrowed in between him and the older man, cleaning her face against their pants. The path was wider where they stood, but not much; startled by the new contact, Honest

Toil pulled away. He gestured the other novice forward and stood holding the shoulder bag, muttering to himself and making soft, impatient noises, while Mr. Sarnath squatted down with his handkerchief and started to wipe the mud from the girl's hands and legs.

Under his fingers the bruises seemed to grow, spreading soft and yellow from her knee. The gladness that protected her from pain had dissipated; now she was biting her lips to keep from crying. Mr. Sarnath raised his head. "How far are we?"

Honest Toil was shaking his head and mumbling to himself, but when he saw he had Sarnath's attention, his face cleared suddenly and he smiled. "Oh," he said. "I would like you to meet my friend Mr. Goldbrick."

The second novice, a younger man, stood relaxed and unresistant as Honest Toil pulled him forward by the hand. "Pleased to meet you," he said, a hint of good-natured irony in his voice. Mr. Sarnath wasn't looking. He was poking at the little girl's thigh. But then, glancing up, he noticed signs of renewed consternation on Honest Toil's face, and he reached out his hand. He nodded hello; for an instant the three men's hands came together, and they seemed to generate a spark that only Honest Toil could feel. He grinned excitedly, shaking out his fingers. "One quarter of a mile," he said.

The day was hot and overcast. A little way along the path, the boy stood on one leg and picked a thorn out of his foot. A cloud of midges jiggled around Sarnath's head, and the swamp gave off a rich, fermented smell. Unctuous water stretched away on both sides of the dike.

There had been no swamp here when he was a child, no mangrove trees upon their stiltlike roots. Here had been a dry glade of anorack. Now at eight-thirty in the morning it was already hot. Cassia's skin, as he wiped it with his handkerchief, was covered with small beads of sweat.

* * *

That day was important in the history of the village because at nine o'clock the master announced to his disciples that he was leaving, that his term of life was over, that he was unable to stay longer with his students and his friends. Eight weeks before, he had broken his hip while he was working in the lentil pit. The bone had twisted when they were getting him out—he had hung suspended in the ropes, cursing steadily, and by the time he reached the ground he was unconscious. Though he had awakened in two minutes, the joint itself never reknit, and for the whole month of November he lost weight. He lay on his back in his house in the center of the village. He was not able to write, or even sit. Often before, during the days of his strength, he had been querulous and demanding, and had sometimes lost patience with his students, and called them fools and blockheads when they made mistakes. But in his final illness he achieved a new tranquillity. He spoke softly and carefully, using many small words of endearment. He answered the most clumsy questions without irony or impatience. Toward the end, even when the gangrene had spread into his leg, he persisted in refusing opium. Instead he lay immobile on his back, meditating, or else listening and talking until late into the night. Nor did he speak about his death, except to say: "When it is no longer possible for me to live correctly, then I will begin to consider my alternatives."

On the morning of November ninety-second, at the same time that Honest Toil and Mr. Goldbrick led the three travelers up into the town, the senior students of the master gathered around his bed. The novice who had been assigned to help him with his breakfast lowered him down onto the pillow and wiped the liquid from his chin. The master's plate was still half-full of broth, but he could stomach no more; he smiled and shook his head. The senior student made a gesture with his hand, a signal for the novice to take the plate away. The novice bowed. But before he could get up and leave, the master put his fingers out and grasped him by the wrist. "No," he said. "Stay with us, please."

For several minutes he lay on his back with his fingers tight around the novice's wrist. He shut his pale old eyes for several minutes, and then he opened them. "There is room for everybody here," he said.

Again he lay silent for a little while, and then he turned his head. One by one he looked into the faces of his senior students. His mat was on the east wall of his house next to the window screen and the veranda, and his students sat in a semicircle around him, in order of their spiritual precedence. It was an order they had assigned among themselves, according to their performance in certain spiritual debates, when on Tuesday nights they sat up late, arguing the master's precepts long after he himself had gone to bed. They never troubled him with the results. Only in the morning they sat around him in a certain order, and they wore cords of different colors knotted around their waists, black, blue, red, tending toward white, according to their scores. The master himself, in his days of health, would always tie his trousers with an old white belt, one of the nine objects that he owned.

On the last day of his life, four students sat around him. He looked at each in turn. Then he said to one of them, "Canan, will you please go out and tell the people? I would like to see each one."

Again the student made a gesture with his hand, a signal to the novice. Again the novice bowed. But the master's hand was tight around his wrist; he could not move, and in a little while the student rose to do the errand himself.

When he had gone, the master had his mat dragged to the center of the room, so that he could accommodate the entire village close around him. "Don't forget the children," he said. Then he closed his eyes and waited, while Canan Bey gathered the farmers from their fields, the women from their houses. This took half an hour. Worried, whispering among themselves, thirty-six more villagers came in and found their places.

And when they were assembled and the children were squirming gently in their laps, the master opened his eyes and cleared his throat. The people hushed themselves and settled down to silence while he spoke to the novice by his side, who brought his soup plate close so he could spit. A few words more, and with great labor and effort the novice propped him up upon some pillows so that he could look around more easily.

He said: "Last night as I was lying here, I understood that I was too weak to continue. I thought then that I would die. But because at night my mind has sometimes been affected by strange symptoms, I decided to hold on until the morning, to see if some new fact or condition might occur to me by daylight, that would make it possible for me to stay among you.

"But as I lay, and the sunlight came to creep across the matting by my hand, at the same time that I realized that no new fact or condition was going to present itself, I conceived of a fresh thought. And therefore, when the morning came, I requested my friend Canan that he bring you to assemble here, so that I could see each of your faces, and so that I could ask each one of you whether in all the time that you have known me I have ever said anything that is now unclear to you, either due to my mistake in self-expression, or your mistake in memory or comprehension. And if there is some part of my teaching that is now unclear to you, either through my mistake or yours, and you wish to have that part explained, then ask me to explain it now, for you will not have another chance."

There was quiet in the room after he had spoken, except for the sound of people breathing or resettling their weight. When he was talking they had strained to hear, for his voice was labored and unsteady. Now they relaxed and looked around, until he spoke again: "It is possible that some of you have questions but are unwilling to express them, either out of respect for me, or because you fear each other's ridicule. Once again I remind you that you will not have another chance. Therefore, so as not to reproach yourself later when you find that there is some piece of understanding that you cannot reach, please, ask me now, or else whisper your question to your friend, so that he or she can ask it in your place."

Again there was a silence as people looked around. Then a woman who was sitting in the middle of the floor raised up her hand.

"Sir," she said. "I have a question. I heard you answer it before and while I listened I thought I understood you. But then after a few hours I couldn't remember anymore. So I asked someone and then a few people and every time they told me, I understood less than before. So tell me now again—how can I, a simple woman and not gifted in debates, hope to understand the difference between good and evil in my life and in the world? I want to know, and sometimes it is hard."

No sooner had she finished speaking than Mayadonna Bey—one of the master's senior students who was sitting by his bed—turned toward her. "Old woman," he said, "do not waste the master's patience with your stupidity. Any child could explain to you the master's seven noble precepts for an honorable life. Anyone can explain them; I myself will cheerfully explain them at another time. But not today. This is a day for serious discussion."

When he heard this, a flicker of annoyance passed over the master's face, and in the first few words of his response his students could hear traces of his old asperity—"You are the stupid one." Ashamed, the student bowed his head. But then the master calmed himself. He closed his eyes for a few seconds, and then opened them. He made a gesture to the novice beside his head to lift him up.

Then he was silent for a little while. He frowned, and small wrinkles seemed to spread out from his eyes all over his large face. "Think of it this way," he said. "If I were to take all of you out into a field and stand before you with a jewel in one of my hands and a potato in the other, is it only the wisest student that would see the difference?"

"No," said Mayadonna Bey, bowing humbly.

"And is there anyone here who is so simple and so foolish that they would not be able to understand the difference between the jewel in my right hand and the potato in my left?"

"No."

"And is there any condition or circumstance at all that might hinder any one of you from understanding the difference between the jewel in my right hand and the potato in my left?"

"No."

"Yes," corrected the master, smiling and relaxing, so that the wrinkles around his eyes all fled away, and his face was smooth again. "There are four conditions at least. The first is if I stand before you when the ground mist rises from the fields, so that you cannot see my open hands. The second is if I hold my fists behind me, so that you cannot tell what they contain. The third is if you turn your back to me, willfully, and look away. The fourth is if you have some blindness or infirmity. Now let us examine each of these four conditions in turn, so that if in the future we might have some difficulty in understanding, we may learn first to classify that difficulty, and then perhaps to overcome it." Then he raised his head to look back at the woman who had first asked the question.

At the same time that the master was speaking, Honest Toil had led the travelers to his own hut, which was meager and humble and made of mud, thatched with banana fronds. It was separate from the rest, beyond the ditches on the south skirt of the village.

Mr. Goldbrick had left them and gone up to give the news, but he had found all the houses deserted until he reached the master's house. There he saw the screens were drawn

and friends of his were crowding the veranda, so he went up
to join them.

But Honest Toil, unaware of what was happening, poured
water for his guests. Sarnath had carried the little girl partway
along the path, but as they approached the hut she had
squirmed out of his arms and asked to be put down. In high
spirits once again, she had limped across the threshold into
Honest Toil's hut; with a quizzical expression on her face,
she had accepted a dish of water from her host's grave hands.
But instead of drinking it or thanking him, she threw it at
her brother as he stood sulking by the wall. He jerked aside;
missing him, the water splashed upon the hard-packed floor.

"Oh now stop that please," said Honest Toil. He stood in
the middle of the single room, holding an earthenware
pitcher he had made himself.

"Cassia," admonished Mr. Sarnath. He had sunk down
upon the only stool, and then he reached out his hands. The
boy stood by the entrance to the hut, but when he saw his
sister limp to Mr. Sarnath once again, whining, fretting, rubbing her knee, he ducked outside through the cloth door and
disappeared.

Sarnath never turned his head. He accepted the boy's de-
parture, knowing there was nothing he could do to hinder
it, knowing also that in an hour or a day the boy would find
them once again, wherever they had gone. And he would
be bruised and battered from running in the forest, and he
would accept no comfort, and he would not even be hungry.
Already he was as strong and fierce as other children twice
his age.

The girl sat squirming on his lap, her small head near his
head. She whimpered underneath his hands. Her skin gave
off a sweet smell.

He put his nose into the back of her neck. He was pow-
erless to help her with her bruises, and in fact she wanted
simple consolation, nothing more. In a minute she had

squirmed away again and jumped up on Honest Toil's bed, and she was examining a row of small clay objects. They were balanced on a ledge in the mud wall.

"Where is Honest Toil?" asked the master suddenly. He had closed his eyes and sunk down on his pillows, listening to a senior student, who in answer to another question was expatiating on the twenty-four subsidiary truths. The argument was a complex one, and the master had fallen back and closed his eyes with a discouraged look upon his face. Now he raised himself and looked around. "Where is my friend Honest Toil? Where is he today?"

Interrupted in midspeech, Mr. Canan bowed his head, his mouth constricted in a narrow line. He sat back on his heels and was silent. It was another of the senior students, the third in the semicircle, who raised his voice to answer: "Sir, he is not here. Forgive me, but I thought that it would serve no purpose to distress him with talk that he could never understand. Also, he finds it difficult to distance himself from his own passions. He loves you very much, and I was afraid that he might disturb the serenity of this last gathering with childish tears."

At ten o'clock the day was achieving its dull heat. The children in the room were restless; the adults fanned themselves with square pieces of banana leaf. The master's face was covered with a sheen of moisture, and also at that hour, the smell from his gangrenous leg began to penetrate to every corner of the room.

"And you," he said to the third student. "What do you feel for me?"

The third student was a small, potbellied man named Palam Bey. The knot of his belt was only lightly touched with pink. Taken by surprise, he stammered, "Sir . . . a great affection and a great respect. . . ."

"Yet you would not willingly spare yourself this moment. My friend, you cannot protect Honest Toil from my death, for I will die today, and I am dying now. It is a false compassion to protect a person from his own experience—go and get him, please. If I ask him not to cry, he will not cry."

At that, Mr. Goldbrick stood up in the back of the room next to the screen, where he was sitting with the novices. "Sir," he said. "Honest Toil and I were on the almond path and saw three people, someone from this village and two human children. Now they're at his house." But the master had turned his face into his pillows. Palam Bey got up to leave, but he lingered for a moment first.

The master put his hands together in his lap. He joined his ring finger and his thumb together on his right palm, and his left hand he made into a fist. That is the way he is represented in most statues from the period: propped up on some pillows with his face turned to the side, his fingers arranged in a way that was always associated later with a certain school of teaching, though it is unlikely that he meant much by the gesture at the time.

He said: "It is true that my friend Honest Toil is not able to appreciate much that I have told him, and there is much that is obvious to the simplest of you, which is still a mystery to him. Yet there are other lessons which he understands in all the deepest fabric of his heart, lessons which are at the center of everything that I have taught you, and which many of the cleverest of you would never understand, even if I lived forever and I told you these things every day."

After hearing these words, Palam Bey nodded his head and went out past the screen to the veranda. He went out down the steps. When he was gone, the master raised his voice. And with his hands joined in his lap he delivered his last great sermon, his lesson on humility and love. Alone of all his sermons it was never written down. Later it was darkened and distorted even in the memory of those who had first heard it, even in the memory of those whose lives it changed. Later on, the memory of the master's words were twisted into just another reason to believe a lie, but at the time, many of the people in that stifling room felt they caught a glimpse of some new country through an open door, and everything that here is dark and strange and terrifying, there is clean and plain. Or that they had been taken up onto some clean mountaintop, and they were standing where the air is bright and hard to breathe, and they were looking down on where they used to live and all the people that they used to know. To them suddenly the small streets of the village were laid out in a pattern, and they could see the pattern of the reeds upon the river, and even the minute pattern of the stones upon the bank. And some felt they could see for the first time the subtlest and smallest pattern of all these, the pattern in their own suffering and joy, the proof they had not lived in vain.

This lesson, which was the single clearest distillation of the master's thought, exists only as the memory of an ideal. Later theologians have speculated that the master had intended it that way, that he had intentionally sent from the room his faithful, perfect secretary upon some minor errand. For by the time Palam Bey returned leading the old novice, followed by Mr. Sarnath and the child, the master again had closed his eyes.

And he was roused only by the sound of Honest Toil's snuffling tears, and the sound of movement in the crowd. Finally the old man flopped down in the inner circle with the tears wet on his cheeks. For though his memory for facts was more than perfect, and though he could more accurately than anybody in the room have recited the history and prognosis of the master's illness, still his memory for the importance of events was flawed. In that hot room where the master lay dying and his students sat in concentric circles fanning themselves with pieces of banana leaf, it was as if the old novice was confronted for the first time with the significance of what he knew. He burst into tears, demonstrating once again for anyone who cared the truth of the master's apothegm that passionate emotion comes from a deficiency of understanding.

"Stop that," the master said. Honest Toil knelt down and held his breath, puffing out his cheeks and wiping his eyes with the backs of his hands. In this way he dutifully suppressed his grief, though all that day from time to time his sobs would burst out suddenly redoubled, venting as if under pressure; then he would gulp and swallow and control himself.

But even in that first flush of emotion, with the tears still running down his cheeks, he smiled suddenly, as if remembering some secret joy. And when his breath was quiet enough for speech, he leaned forward. "Sir," he said, "I would like you to meet my friend Sarnath Bey."

The master smiled in his turn. "But there's no need," he said. And he raised his eyes to where Mr. Sarnath stood with Cassia by the screen, and indicated with a gesture of his head that they should come forward. Again the senior students had to budge themselves, and it was not until Mr. Sarnath was sitting near him, cross-legged, with Cassia on his lap, that the master spoke again. At this time his face was sometimes touched with quick spasms of pain.

"What have you brought for me?" he asked.

Mr. Sarnath bowed his head, unsure of what to say, how to behave after so long. He stared at the back of his own hand, meditating in silence. And it was not until the master had repeated his question that Mr. Sarnath pulled his knapsack from his shoulder. It was almost empty: just a few worn shirts and T-shirts, and a ragged quilt. Then from the bottom he produced a bundle, wrapped in a tangle of worn paper and bound up with strips of linen.

He untied the skull and held it up. The master reached out his hand, and with his forefinger he traced the inside of the skull's left eye socket. Then he let his finger run along the cranium, which was carved with scenes from his own life:

how his parents sealed him in the bell of a bass horn when he was ten days old; how they smuggled him away out of the siege of Caladon; how they were set upon and killed by members of the Desecration League; how a drunkard, finding the horn abandoned in the grass, was astonished by its mournful voice.

"What did you see?" asked the master, taking the skull into his hands.

Mr. Sarnath said: "The night when I decided to start home—it was a Friday. I saw the junior customs deputy at Camran Head. He gave me gifts, too much for me to carry. But I kept this—he carved it as a gift for you."

The master shook his head. "Tell me about what you saw."

"I saw the moon reflected in a bowl of water. A moth was sticking to a piece of flypaper. It fell into the bowl and drowned, spreading water on important documents."

"And?"

"I wanted to come home. You told me when I went into the world—you told us we would be hated and condemned. You told us we would find new masters. You told us we would be rejected for our differences—all that was true. You told us to wait patiently. Seven months, and I had other postings before that."

The master settled back upon his pillows. His eyes had a new milky cast to them, and his voice was soft and weak. "A moth drowned in a bowl," he said.

"Sir," said Canan Bey. "Perhaps it would be better—"

"No," persisted the old man. "You listen to this. It is important." He was holding the skull loosely in his hands.

His voice had sunk to a harsh whisper, audible only to the first circle of spectators. Many of the others had grown restless. Many of the children, especially, had become irritable in the heat and the bad smell. Infants had begun to cry; their mothers took them out on the veranda and then down into the town. The master appeared to have dozed off. And as noon approached, more and more of the adults got up to go.

Carpenters who had left their hammers balanced on the lad-
dertops, farmers who had planned to dig a certain acreage
before the worst heat of the day, housewives who had left a
pot of water on the fire—they bowed their heads respectfully
and slipped away.

Cassia sat motionless on Sarnath's lap, her head upon his
thigh. He might have thought she was asleep, only sometimes
he saw her nose wrinkle slightly as some new waft of putre-
faction reached her from the master's bed. Honest Toil was
kneeling with the tears running down his face. Around them
the room had emptied out. Only a scattering of villagers
remained. Now a few more bowed their heads and rose to
leave, responding to a small gesture from the hand of Canan
Bey, dismissing them to do their work.

The master's eyes were closed, and he had sunk down deep
into his pillows, so that he was almost prone. "My head is
full of shadows," he complained. But then he roused himself.
"Stupider," he said. "Stupider and stupider. You carried this
dead piece of bone from Camran Head? If we all carried on
our backs the burden of our errors, just to remind ourselves . . ." His voice sank into nothing.

Canan Bey leaned forward. "Leave him now," he whispered. "All of you."

He was leaning forward across the master's body, making
a small gesture with his fingers. Then he bent down to wipe
some spittle from the master's lips, but at that moment the
old man started awake. His eyes started open and he reached
up to grab the student by the ear. "What are you doing?"
he demanded.

"Sir," said Canan Bey. "I thought you should rest. Perhaps
you should rest, and I could change the dressing on your
leg." He tried to pull his head away, but the old man grabbed
him tighter. "Please, sir, you're hurting me."

"No!" shouted the old man. Then he let go. He turned
instead to Mr. Sarnath, who had begun to rise. "Talk to me!"
shouted the master. "Talk to me—you understand. How

long were you a prisoner of your own thoughts? You know what it means to wait and wait. Tell me—what did that moth mean to you?"

"Sir," murmured Mr. Sarnath. "I took it as a sign."

"It was a sign. And this"—here he lifted the skull up in his two hands, so that they could see its strange dead grinning face. "Is this also a sign? A sign for me? My God, my God, my God, my God, my God," and these words were peculiar, for never before in his whole life had he called upon a deity, or even mentioned the possibility that one existed.

"No," he said. "But take this and destroy it. Burn these papers." Then he muttered something incoherent. Then he died.

3

BROTHER
AND SISTER

"The day the master died," said Langur Bey, "he was attended at the end by Canan, Mayadonna, Palam, and myself. This was on the ninety-second of November of the fourteenth phase, near one o'clock in the afternoon. We had feared that he would die during the night—his pulse was very weak. But in the morning he revived somewhat. He even took a little bread. And he was resting comfortably. He did not appear to be in pain. We were discussing, as we often did, some point of natural philosophy—it was a favorite topic for him, the relation between natural philosophy and ethics. As I remember, he was making the point that in human intercourse, just as in science, it is important to select the simpler explanation: that it is always the simpler explanation that has a tendency toward truth.

"Toward noon he grew a little weaker. I remember he had fallen into a light doze, and we students were still carrying on the conversation, though in a distracted way, of course. It is what he would have wished; in any case he woke up.

He was staring at the ceiling, and we could see his eyes were unfocused. And it was then that he called for all the towns-people to come in. He knew his time was growing short. He was too impatient even to listen to their questions, though some were bothering him with trivialities and emotional dis-plays. He cut them off—there was no time for such things anymore. He cut them off so that he could pronounce his final discourse—you have it in your copybooks—on the na-ture of obedience and the suppression of the will, which I would like you to memorize by next Friday.

"And that was very near the end. He spoke a few words to Sarnath Bey, part of our mission to the Port of Caladon, who as luck would have it had arrived that morning. Cassia, you remember that—he was asking many careful ques-tions, though his voice was weak, and then finally he paused. His face seemed to relax into a smile that was also grave and dignified; he lay there for some little time. He was lying near the window, and he asked for the screen to be removed. I remember it had just begun to rain. He asked Canan Bey to help him turn onto his side, and he looked out of the window toward a patch of bamboo trees, which at that time grew beside his house. And he said, and these were his last words, 'There is another village in the forest, identical to this. The houses are laid out on the same plan. It sits, like this one, in a grove of almonds. Yet in those trees the fruits are made of gold, the leaves are made of silver. And in the center house there sits a teacher. He is waiting for me, and he has made a place for me among the last circle of novices.'"

Langur Bey, dressed in a white robe, sat cross-legged on a dais in the schoolroom. His left hand in his lap was pressed into a fist. Next to it, he had joined the fourth finger and thumb of his right hand over his palm. His hands were thin and long, his gestures graceful and precise. Now he took his hands out of his lap. He held his left hand spread out above his knee, and with the smallest finger of his right hand he wiped away a tear, a small accretion of white dust in the outside corner of his eye.

"For tomorrow," he said, "please meditate upon these words, and ask yourselves especially whether in any way they can be taken literally, or if their meaning is purely metaphorical. Please ask yourselves also . . ."

Rael lay on his stomach with his hand stretched out along the matting of the floor. He was staring at the back of Cassia's head; she sat ten feet in front of him with her back perfectly straight, and she had tied up the mass of her black hair, exposing her neck and the rims of her ears. Even at that distance if he stared hard enough, he could see the circle of small hairs between her shoulder blades, over the line of her white dress. Even at that distance he could catch the smell of her skin; he breathed deeply, and tried to separate that one small disappearing scent out of the stench of the Treganu all around him. Even at that distance he could make her sense his presence. He imagined the pressure of his stare reaching out like a long stick, touching her gently on that dark circle of hair until she shuddered without understanding why.

Or he could make her turn her head. He could make her turn her head and look at him. He could make her smile, just by releasing one small sound into the air, some breath or gasp or whistling tune, something to remind her that in this schoolroom full of alien creatures there was one who was like her, whose heart struck the same beat. Rael was lying stretched out on the mat. He raised his cheek up from the floor, and he was humming the first note of a small tune, very carefully and low, molding it and aiming it so that it would reach her ear and no one else's.

"Sir," said Langur Bey. "If there is anything that you would like to say to me, either on this subject, or on any other, I would be glad to listen and respond. As you can see if you consult your schedule, our session for today includes a period for questions, which however does not begin for fifteen minutes. Until then, I beg you to refrain from disturbing us with these noises, the meaning of which, if in fact they have a meaning, can only be clouded and obscure."

Rael raised himself up off the floor. All around the little classroom the students had turned to look at him, all but one. His sister still sat with her back to him; all the rest had turned their strange, sad, thoughtful faces toward him. Strange and not strange—these were boys and girls he had grown up with. He knew them. Yet as always at times like this he found that he could barely tell one from another. Their separate individuality seemed to recede into their faces. Looking around, all he could see were the small characteristics that kept him isolated and apart: their frail, bony faces, their eyes too close together, their weak chins.

"Please, sir," he said. "I beg to be excused." It was a phrase that he had carefully rehearsed.

The teacher bowed his head.

Outside, the sun was sinking down the western sky. Rael paused on the veranda, rubbing his forearms, rotating his wrists. Then he tramped loudly down the wooden steps, and for emphasis he pounded loudly on the bamboo banister, making a racket that no one else in the entire village could have made, for of all of them he was the strongest and most powerful. A woman was squatting in the wet dirt near the pump; she glanced up to look at him, then she smiled and waved. She was washing out a piece of red cloth in a bucket.

Clouds of midges danced around her head. Rael squatted down next to her to wash his face. He washed under his armpits, and rubbed handfuls of water through his hair while the woman pumped the pump. "Lesson over?" she asked.

He shrugged. "Thinking in my thoughts is idiot fool."

She clicked her tongue against the ridges of her teeth. "We are not all gifted in all ways," she said, quoting a bromide of the master's.

A leechfly, drawn by the scent of human blood, had landed

on the lip of the bucket—a repulsive creature with a snout almost an inch long. Rael flapped his fingers and it drifted away. Anywhere outside the village, he would have crushed it gladly.

The woman said: "In six months Langur Bey will let you go to work. You'll like that better, won't you?"

Rael felt the water trickle down his ribs. He brought his wet hands to his face and inhaled deeply, then he shrugged. In front of them, the neatly swept dirt street curled down into the forest.

She said: "It will feel good to use your strength."

He doubted it. To the right and to the left, the street was lined with wooden houses upon stilts. He lowered his knee down into the mud, and lowered his head so that he could peer under the veranda of the nearest house. There was some movement in the dark, the scurrying of some animal or bug.

The woman didn't hear. She was smiling at him. He smiled back.

Down at the bottom of the hill, the path wound round the edges of the paddy field. Rael stepped up onto the embankment. In the far corner of the field a group of men in wicker hats stood up to their ankles in water, and they were coaxing the village's lone bullock into position with soft pats upon its rump. They were building something on the far bank, and the bullock was pulling a sledge loaded with sand: a stupid plan, thought Rael, because the bullock was crushing the young shoots of rice under its hooves. A few strokes with a split bamboo would have brought the beast onto the ramp, thought Rael, but instead it was wandering contemptuously through the field, losing sand with every turn, ignoring the melodious expostulations of the men.

A tall boy moved ahead of the beast to frighten away any minnows that might drift beneath its hooves. Standing on the embankment, Rael shook his head, seeing in the boy a premonition of his own future. The boy had been in school ten months before, but he had graduated last in his class.

Rael stretched his arms over his head, taking pleasure in the long, heavy muscles of his shoulders and his arms. Then he was gone, jumping down off the embankment and running east along the almond path. He was itching to get away; at moments like this it seemed to him as if there were a boundary around the village, a mental boundary beyond the barricade of thorns, a moment when the incoherent burden of his mind was finally lifted and he was free, leaping away between two trees appreciated only by himself, leaving the path and running up the dense and crowded slope, his bare feet leaving no mark and missing as if by a succession of small miracles all the sharp roots and thorns and edges of the forest—slipping through the undergrowth, protected from each clawing branch by an integument of sweat that covered his whole body. And even if he did from time to time feel a thorn rip across his skin, or if he gashed the instep of his foot against a stone, no matter, no matter, it made no difference; he had all the blood in all the world and he could run forever in that forest without drawing breath.

He ran up the bed of a small stream, and the slope was steep on either side. There were savak bushes and disgusting joberoot, each plant a nest of writhing leaves. Monkeys hurtled overhead among the limpus trees, their hairless bodies smashing clumsily among the upper branches, shaking loose a patter of small leaves and sticks, and disturbing a whole colony of anvil birds—he didn't know these names, he didn't care. But where the slope curled back upon itself, reaching toward the perpendicular, and the stream turned into a small rain above him, he stood up to his shins in a slough of mud and knocked the sweat out of his eyes.

Nearby, the remnants of an ancient bicycle protruded from the earth, a metal, twisting plant. Creepers stretched down through the rocks, and he reached out to steady himself with his left hand, while with his right he pulled a stick out of his yellow hair. He stood as if in a pit of wet black earth; near him a tree had tumbled down the cliff, clearing a gap in the forest canopy, and he could see the sun there burning like a blowtorch, that whole swath of sky a molten blue. And in the gap the anvil birds staggered unsteadily into the air, five feet long with little stubby wings, their heads encased with helmets of bright bone which made a whistling, whirring noise as they rose up.

It was a java tree, its fat trunk covered with a scarlet tar. Half its roots thrust up into the air; the other half was still embedded in the earth. Rael squatted down and pulled himself into the triangular cavity under the tree. When it fell, the trunk had cracked apart, and there was a fissure in the wood above his head. Rael pounded the heel of his hand against the bark, hoping to frighten away any biting lizard or constrictor that had made its home inside. Then he reached in and pulled out his equipment, which he had secreted there on previous visits: one long perfect spear of heartwood and a steel spike.

The heartwood he had cut himself. During the long march to the village when Rael was still a child, Mr. Sarnath had from time to time explained the properties of certain plants. Cassia had learned them all; he none of them but this, for he had tripped upon the heartwood root and gashed himself so deeply that he had remembered when he chanced to find it in the forest. He had stripped away its leaves, its branches, and the soggy, fibrous flesh of its long stalk until the heartwood was laid bare. Yet it was so tough that even then he had not contrived to break it from its root.

So he had left it there, naked, pointed to the sky, half a day's peripatetic journey from the village, and he had returned only when he found the spike. That he had scavenged from the wreckage of an old factory—one of the ruins in the jungle hills. Most of the metal had already found a second life—put to more productive uses in the village, but this spike he had found himself when there was no one else around. He had worn it sharp between two stones, and brought it to the heartwood tree. Then he had smashed the tree down to the ground and scraped clean his long spear.

Now he pulled it from his hole in the cracked trunk.

At that time, fifteen hundred days after the master's death, Mr. Sarnath was living in a one-room cabin, which the novices had constructed for him at the top of the hill. As he got older he had drawn into himself, and he preferred to spend his time in solitary meditation. Cassia came up every day after school to care for him and cook his food.

The cabin was constructed on a frame of dry bamboo. Its walls were plaited palm. In the heat of the day, the dark interior was pierced with beams of light. One, stretching unbroken between a spot on the floorboards and a small hole in the roof, gave him particular pleasure, and often when the sun was bright he would spend an entire day seated on a comfortable cushion, watching that taut beam of light change color subtly in front of him, and change its angle by methodical degrees. Whatever countryside his mind was traveling, he found in that bright wire a small connection to the world, for without thinking he could see the turning of the earth, and see also with immense precision just what kind of day it was, by examining at any moment the metallic content of the wire—how much silver, how much gold, how much copper, how much brass.

He was never taken by surprise, for example, when the sun passed behind a cloud. He would close his eyes the instant before the beam of light was broken, and open them an instant after it had reappeared. Or when evening fell and the sun sank at last behind the teakwood trees, already he'd have turned his face away.

As evening fell he would get up. He would put on his dressing gown and he would sit out on his small veranda with a glass of water. He would watch for Cassia to come along the rutted track. At the crest of the hill there was a bald place in the trees with the cabin in the middle of it, built on thin and rocky soil. Mr. Sarnath could see from the veranda a hundred yards along the track, to where it emerged from the wood beside a banyan tree. And though in those days his mind was never concentrated on one thing, still part of him would watch for her, and he would wait for the sight of her in her white dress. Below the banyan tree the path fell steeply to the village; climbing up, she always paused to catch her breath beside the tree, just at the moment she came into sight.

Near sunset on the same evening that Rael drew his spear out of the hollow log, Mr. Sarnath was sitting out on his veranda at his desk, a small wooden table with a top of lacquered ebony. It supported an oil lamp, an inkwell, and six hundred sheets of paper scattered over a palm-leaf blotter. Among them in its nest of parchment lay the dull brown ancient, strange, distorted skull, covered with carvings, which he had taken from the customs deputy at Camran Head and carried on his back a thousand miles, all the time that Cassia and Rael were growing up.

Now he picked it up in his thin hands. With the sleeve of his dressing gown he polished it behind the jaw, where the deputy's carving was most exquisite. Then he held it up to stare at it, looking deep into its eyeholes. They were rimmed with silver, and there was silver too behind its grinning teeth.

After the master died his senior students had tried to burn the parchment, as he had commanded. But it was treated with some chemical that rendered it impervious to fire. And so they had buried it too, buried it and the skull together in the same hole, obeying the master as completely as they could. Mr. Sarnath had been with them. But at about the same time that he moved out of the village and up into his cabin on the hilltop, he went out to dig it up, carrying a lantern and a mattock in the black of night. That night too he had stood polishing it, wiping the dirt out of its face, surprised to see that it was no different, that the paper which surrounded it was still intact, for the earth was full of vermin. Vermin crept out of the hole that he had made.

Much later, after Mr. Sarnath's death, scholars from the University of Charn would hold an inquest, and with the superstition of born atheists would suggest that he had trafficked at this period with Magdol Starbridge, a loathsome succubus with naked breasts. It was not true. Sarnath was simply curious. And if there was a sin involved, it was at most the sin of arrogance. Sitting by himself day after day, meditating on the master's lessons, he felt that he had reached a wall he could not cross. The master was pragmatic in all things: his goal had been to found a village and then help the villagers to live in it, at peace with others and themselves. His maxims had been practical, his metaphors concrete, accessible to everyone.

But Mr. Sarnath, ever since the night when he had seen the moth drown in the bowl, had felt himself blessed with the potentiality of understanding. As he thought more and more about them, the simplicity of the master's lessons became frustrating. He was no longer interested in what to do, how to behave. Especially as he saw the village go astray, and the power in the village gathered into hands he did not trust, he was no longer content to obey. He wanted to follow the master into a rarefied and better world, where all phenomena were understood.

Five months—five hundred days—after the master's death, he disinterred the skull and took it to his house. He felt it was a clue, because he had seen the reaction of the master, how in the moment of his death he had been shocked out of his thoughts. At that instant he had found out something that had stunned him, opened his eyes, perhaps, the way Mr. Sarnath's had been opened on that night at his desk in Caladon. It was as if the master had mounted on a ladder through the door of death, and if he had turned around at last and ordered that the ladder be torn down and burnt and buried in a hole, perhaps it was because he did not trust the villagers to use new knowledge wisely, when he was not there to guide them.

In the village Mr. Sarnath had kept his thinking to himself. But on the veranda of his cabin on the hilltop, he laid the skull out on his table, where he could see it every day. That evening as he sat watching, he held it up between his hands and rubbed it, moving his dry fingertips over the parietal bone, following with his fingertips the complicated sequence of small figures: the master gathering his scattered people and striking out into the wilderness to form a new community. He picked a cloth up from the table. Wrapping it around his thumb, he rubbed at an imagined blemish on the zygomatic.

In fact, long contemplation of the skull had told him nothing. But after ten months, his translation of the manuscript was already half complete. It lay around him on the desk, almost a thousand verses, or, as he called them, "paradigms." He searched for the first page. There it was: "Oh my beloved, let me pleasure you and kiss you, for you are like a God to me, that I may worship with my body, and your kisses help me, and heal me, and give me comfort, and illuminate my life. In your presence my heart is full of a new sensation, which is partly joy. . . ."

His was a race that was gifted with languages. Always they had lived as foreigners in other people's countries. Whatever place had been their home was lost, its location forgotten in the cryptic past. Myths and stories that referred to it tended to lack interior logic; anyway the myths had changed over the generations, so that they no longer represented clues to a real place, a real culture, a real past. Instead the stories had been cast forward to a future where their inconsistencies would matter less: a vision of some ideal future in their own country, and they would be welcome like lost friends.

But in the meantime they had lived in other people's cities, and they had adopted other people's habits. And most of what distinguished them, beyond the physical differences of their bodies, had been in some way forced upon them—their limited employment opportunities, their long gauze robes and masks, the bells that in some southern cities they had been obliged to wear, sewn into their sleeves. They had taken these restrictions and made a culture out of them. They had spoken a dozen dialects of other people's languages.

When the master had come out from Caladon, and with a handful of refugees he had founded in the deepest woods his little town, and he had said, "This is the place; the time is now," it had been part of his dream that they should form one people, speak one tongue. Nevertheless, Sarnath had learned snatches of many languages when he was growing up. And in the world he had learned more, when he was teaching the precepts of the master to his clients at the Caladon frontier. He had taught them humility, and detachment, and the futility of all human enterprise, the counterproductive nature of desire. In return he had learned patience, and thoughtfulness, and wisdom, and obscenities and supplications in another fifty tongues, all of which were useful when, in solitude on his veranda in the evening of his life, he bent his mind to his translation of the Song of Angkhdt, from the original Bekata manuscript—an unknown alphabet but not completely unfamiliar—into his own Treganu dialect.

During the day he meditated in his room. In the evening he worked on his translation. In the endless litany of love that makes up the first part of the Holy Song, he had searched in vain for clues to what the master meant. "Burn these papers!"—why on earth? What was the harm? Now, waiting for Cassia, holding up the skull in his starved hands, he thought he understood. For only in the past day had he finally recognized what he was doing. It is not until the 940th verse that the prophet's name is actually mentioned in the text; at ten o'clock the night before, when he had sounded out for the first time that crabbed, mysterious syllable, he had sat back with a strange lurching in his heart.

All winter and long into spring, the citizens of Charn and Caladon had been obliged by law to memorize large portions of the Holy Song. But by midsummer, so thoroughly had the questioners performed their work, all that learning was forgotten, broken, rooted out, persisting only among covens of witches, Starbridge renegades, and followers of the Cult of Loving Kindness. It was possible for an educated man like Mr. Sarnath, a man whose work had actually involved from time to time the persecution and exposure of the Cult, never to have known any of the old words. It was not until he had deciphered the 940th verse, working close to midnight by the light of his oil lamp, that he understood.

> *I will bring a bag of pearls,*
> *Enough to spell my name out on the ground.*
> *And you will spell my name out on the ground,*
> *And you will spell it "ANGKHDT."*

He had written "Onket." He had stared at the unfamiliar word, testing it in his mouth for the first time. Then he had sat back. His hand and pen had fallen slackly to his side.

That day, almost for the first time, his meditation had seemed bitter and unprofitable to him, and he had risen from his cushion prematurely, with aching knees. Now the sun was going down. Long shadows slunk across the floor of the veranda. With his thumb he rubbed along the maxillary bone, along a sleeping image of the master. Then he paused, remembering the statue of St. Abu Starbridge, which he had kept upon his desk that last night at his post in Caladon. He remembered the golden star inlaid upon the saint's copper palm, glinting in the moonlight. Perhaps that too had been a sign. A moth was drowning in a bowl of light—one tiny circumstance had led him on a long and weary path. But perhaps also it had been the image of the saint that had led him to the place where he now sat, a mental journey just as long and complicated as the physical had been, through swamps and forests just as thick.

He raised his eyes. There at the clearing's edge, Cassia stood beside the banyan tree, her skirt rucked up around her hips. She was standing with her hand outstretched, her fingers buried in an enormous tassel of roots which hung down near her, searching for the ground. She was carrying a basket of fruit upon her back—jackfruit, selamat, and durian.

There was a place for him to lie invisible above the pool. He lay crouched behind a boulder in the mouth of an old culvert, which had fed the dye pit of some ancient factory. Near his hand crept one of the fat rael bugs that had given him his name, its carapace clicking in the dirt. When he was a child he had been able to imitate the sound.

The silver pool was a round concrete cistern, perhaps fifty feet from edge to edge. Opposite where he lay hidden, a narrow waterfall coursed down a slope of bricks, pure water from the stream above. But whether there was still some residue in the bottom of the cistern, or whether some of the numerous pipes which hung out over it still dripped some ancient effluent, the pool itself retained a milky color, a distinctive smell.

Birds circled overhead. Near Rael's hand, lizards crept among the mossy pipes. On an overhanging ledge a monkey and a dinko grimaced at each other; one threw a stone. Apart from that it was a peaceful place. The waterfall provided a soft, comfortable clamor; it ran down into a steep-sided basin at one end of the pool. But at the other end the slope was gentler. Shyer larger animals came down to drink at a beach of concrete rubble intermixed with pebbles of worn glass—small forest antelopes, and tapirs, and wild dogs. At sunset it seemed as if they had a pact among themselves. Once Rael had seen a tiger squat down by the bank to clean his paws, while nearby slept a fat potbellied pig, dug up to her nostrils in the silver mud.

But there was another beast, one whose malevolence and hunger never rested. This pool was its stalking ground. When it was hunting, the temperature around the pool subsided, and there was milky scum upon the surface of the water. When it was hunting, Rael could feel a prickling on his skin, an ache in his back teeth. It exuded a small sound, an intimate small whispering that seemed to touch Rael in his inner ear. Then he would crouch down out of sight and wait until he saw a movement on the other bank.

He had waited at the pool a dozen times, and felt the change in temperature, and smelt the scum upon the pool; he had watched the creature make a dozen kills before he knew what he was seeing. Only when it was finished he had gone down to the little beach, and he had looked at the creature's track in the wet sand. And he had looked at the wet bones of a dozen animals half buried in the sand, each one sucked clean, and perhaps a few rags of tattered flesh or feathers.

Now if he concentrated, he could see exactly where the creature was. But its shape and form were still indefinite. Appearing always in the twilight, it seemed covered in a skin of shadow. Sometimes he could see it better from the corner of his eye.

Once, after it had made its kill, he had seen it creep down to the pool to drink. Then he had climbed down to the opposite bank. He had hoped to catch a glimpse of its reflection. But the surface of the pool was too disturbed. He had gone down on his belly, not twenty feet away from it, and he had stared at it across the pool, and listened to the gentle sucking sound it made. Then it had raised its head. For the first time he had seen the glint of its sour eyes and felt a whispering in his mind. "Who are you?" it had asked. "Who are you, that you see so clearly?"

The next day he had waited for it and had watched it feed. Seven small peccaries had come down to the water. And as the strange, amorphous darkness formed in back of one of them, coming down from the jungle on its track of slime, none of the others seemed to notice. None of the others seemed to notice the drop in temperature, the new cold wind. They grunted cheerfully upon the beach. And even the intended victim, turning at last to face its attacker, never made a sound. It stood fascinated, with its head low to the earth. Even when Rael threw a stone to panic all the other animals, still that one stood.

Once Rael had accompanied a novice from the village, who had come up looking for an intact sheet of glass. When the moment came, Rael had seized him by the arm and pointed out across the pool, but the man saw nothing. Only he was concerned that Rael had touched him; with a wry smile on his bony alien face, he had pulled his arm away.

In the weeks that followed, Rael had gathered weapons, a spear of heartwood and a steel spike. On the evening of the day that Mr. Sarnath had spent meditating on the Song of Angkhdt, at the moment when Cassia stood by the banyan tree, her skirt pulled up around her hips, Rael raised his head off of the boulder. The sun had sunk below the hilltops, and the basin of the pool had filled with shadow. A scarlet ibis and its somber mate were wading near the beach.

Cassia untucked her skirt and it fell down around her legs. She squatted to pick up the gourd of water, which she had carried in her arms up the steep slope. She worked her bare feet down into the dirt. Squeezing the fat gourd between her palms, she lifted it in one clean rush and settled it upon a ring of wicker on her head. Then, supporting it with one hand, she rose up slowly, the other arm outstretched for balance, her tongue protruding from the middle of her lips.

Mr. Sarnath watched her make her way across the clearing toward his house. He had been the master's favorite pupil when he was a boy, and the master had taught him to be careful always, even in the midst of speculation, to appreciate the offerings of his senses. Mr. Sarnath, though his mind was at that moment full of blank misgivings, allowed his heart to be lifted when he saw her. He moved the dry pads of his fingers over the incisions in the skull. A fly was buzzing on the steps. The garbage pile behind the house exuded a sweet smell. Cassia's hair was black, her lips were wide. As she got closer he examined her more closely—the sweat around her mouth, the spot upon her chin—with a minute appreciation that included not the slightest spark of sensuality.

She stood beside the steps that led to the veranda. Curling the fingers of her left hand under the lip of the gourd, she twisted herself out from underneath it, so that it fell straight down to earth. It made a glug, and slopped some water on her hand.

Mr. Sarnath had risen from his chair. He stood on the top step. Cassia stripped the wicker basket from her back and held it up for him. When he had taken it, she wiped the hair out of her mouth. Bending down, she took a double handful of water from the gourd and rinsed her face with it. "Come," she said. "Leave that and come down into the sun. I bet you've been inside all day."

Mr. Sarnath shook his head. He stared out at the shadows on the grass. Then he turned. The brown skull watched him from the center of the desk.

"Come down," cried Cassia. And there was something in her voice that changed his mind and helped him to decide. Carrying the basket, he disappeared indoors, and then returned almost immediately holding an old cloth bag. It had once been yellow.

"Vanity," said Mr. Sarnath. "Vanity is still the hardest."

"What?" Cassia had come up to stand behind him. Surprised, she watched him wrap the skull in parchment and stuff it down into the bag. The bag had a long throat. He twisted it, then tied it in a knot.

"When you light the fire tonight, use that paper."

He motioned toward the tabletop, where the six hundred sheets of his own handwriting lay scattered. Then he turned around to face her.

"But you worked on it so long," she said.

"I was deluded."

He slung the bag over his shoulder and walked down the steps. The heat of the day was now abated, and the sun was shining through the long trunks of the trees. He scuffed his sandals in the dust—an area of crushed stone near the steps. Then when his toes had settled in their thongs, he set off toward the wood, the strips of alternating sun and shadow causing minute fluctuations in the temperature of his long cheeks.

His people did not sweat, not like the humans, whose skins were always damp. He could tell that she was close behind him by her smell, for she was quiet as a cat, and in the movement of her greasy limbs he could hear none of the incidental noises that he made when he walked. None of the small creaking, the whisper of the flesh rubbing the bone, just the silence of a wild animal, her and her brother. Then he paused, and turned to her and smiled, aware that his own disappointment had turned outward, as it sometimes did. Hundreds of nights of wasted labor hung suspended in his yellow bag.

She smiled back at him, and then they walked companionably into the wood, following a path that ran in back of the cabin, past the garbage dump, and left the crest of the hill at right angles to the way that she had come. "Where are we going?" she asked once, but he shrugged his narrow shoulders. He had decided, and in fact the path led only to one place. They pushed through a dark undergrowth of spiderbushes, rhododendron, jacaranda. Stepping carefully downhill, Cassia had to raise her forearms to protect her face against the branches whipping back. In a few minutes she came out at the lip of the ravine, a cleft between one hill and the next. Mr. Sarnath was standing in the sunlight on a bare place on the rock.

The ravine followed a break in the forest canopy, and the yellow sun was shining, its strength not yet used up. It was cooler here than on the hilltop, and the air was fresh and smelled of water. Deep below them at the bottom of the hill where it was already dark with shadow, she could hear the gurgle of a stream.

"This will do," said Mr. Sarnath. He was standing on the edge, his arm outstretched, the long bag dangling from his hand. He opened up his fingers and the bag dropped down, bouncing off the incline and then rolling in a scatter of black dirt until it disappeared into a crevice in the rock.

He turned around. "The sun leaves here last. It's perfectly safe." In fact the rock seemed free of beetles and corrosive slugs; it was a wide flat piece of limestone. Mr. Sarnath sat down suddenly, collapsing on his creaking knees. Perched cross-legged, he looked like a gaunt bird atop its nest. Cassia took a seat more gingerly. She was very thirsty.

"Now," said Mr. Sarnath, leaning toward her. "What did you learn in school today?"

He had asked her the same question many times and never listened to the answer. When he was irritated or distressed he would take refuge in a few stiff, formal questions, designed to take him out of his own thoughts. He would set his face into a mask of concentration, which never fooled her, for she knew him well. But this time, as she started to recite the circumstances of the master's death, she could tell that he was listening. His body started to relax and sag, and he slipped toward her down the rock.

" 'In the center house there is a teacher,' " Cassia recited. " 'He is waiting for me there, and he has made a place for me among the last circle of novices.' "

Around them, the first peepers of the evening had come out, scarlet tree frogs, and when they sang their throats swelled up as big as they. Mr. Sarnath turned his head. There was one sitting on a rhododendron tree ten feet away.

"Interesting," he said at last. He furrowed up his brow and then turned back. "What did you say to that?"

"No one said anything. It was the last lesson."

"But you remember."

"Of course," said Cassia. "It was just this afternoon."

"No—you remember when the master died. You were there."

Cassia frowned. "I was just a child."

"No. Is that what Langur Bey told you? You sat there between my legs. Don't you remember what the master said?"

She would have answered, but he raised his hand. He pointed toward the lowest branch of a tall tree, which hung out over the edge of the ravine. Just for an instant she could see a flicker of movement there, a flash of iridescent feathers.

"Interesting," Mr. Sarnath said again. "That you can tell a lie to a whole group of people who were witness to the truth."

"Oh, Papa, it was school. That's all."

"I am not your father," he said automatically. Then he smiled. Around them, the world was settling down, the shadows spreading, the colors mutating in the last of the sun. The sweat was dry on Cassia's skin. "Shouldn't we go in?" she asked. "It'll be dark."

But Mr. Sarnath put his finger to his lips. On the other side of the ravine, in the cleft of a bloatwood tree, a man-of-the-forest stood erect. His studious little face was turned to them, and he was nuzzling shyly at a piece of branch, the trunk of a long sapling that he had pulled down from above, revealing a crown of flowers on its leafy head. Slowly, tentatively, he stretched out his naked leg, shifting his weight until he hung suspended between the sapling and the tree, spread out against a silver patch of sky. There he was at rest; in a little while he let loose a stream of urine out of his fat paunch, which arched over the lip of the ravine, spattering the darkness down below.

There was scum on the water and a dry, cold wind. Rael saw the bird explode in a flurry of bright feathers. He swung himself out of the culvert, dropping thirteen feet onto the bricks, which were confused near there, and so he came down on the side of his right foot and sprawled down to the water, falling on his hands and knees. He staggered up, and already he could barely keep his weight on his right ankle. Already it was swelling; he gathered up his spear to lean on it and looked across at the opposite beach, fifty feet away, where the female ibis strutted unconcerned, and for a moment Rael was sure the beast was gone. He was crying out with anger, kicking at the water with his injured foot, but then he stopped and stood watching the dark, long-legged bird, for she was searching the surface of the water for insects. Untroubled, she was wading through a wreck of scarlet feathers, untroubled also by the raving figure with the useless foot, and then Rael knew her mind was still held captive, as his was. There was a shadow that he couldn't see with eyes made careless by his injury, a shadow that was waiting for him on the beach under the trees, a creature that was slow and weak, whose only power was a mental one, as he discovered when he took tentative, damaged steps around the pool and found his mind assaulted with a riot of strange shapes and an insinuating noise that seemed to grow inside his skull by slow degrees until it blotted out the beach, the bird, the sinking sun, and he was limping slowly through another, darker place, a darker landscape of the mind which nevertheless had one great burning dot in it, a dot pulsing with light, and he was limping slowly toward that dot until the shattered bricks beneath his feet gave out onto another surface. And though with all his force he was tending toward that dot as if against a pressure that was almost irresistible, still part of his mind was firmly concentrated elsewhere, because he guessed that when his mind was elsewhere he might move faster against an animal whose strength lay in its powers of misdirection; so he was concentrating on the darkness all around him, as if the pure force of his concentration could just puncture through. And all the while he was tending toward the dot, limping and shaking his sharp stick, and raging now with a noise that rivaled the cacophony inside his skull, convinced that if he could just touch that dot with the end of his sharp spear, then he would find the moment that resolves all doubts, the moment also when the beast appears out of the mists of illusion and spews its life out in a cold, choking rush—convinced also (and this was why he was shouting and raging with a maniac desperation) that if the skin of darkness which surrounded him could be punctured, then he would find himself inside another landscape utterly, a landscape that would have nothing to do with the hot wet fecund jungle and the greasy pool, a landscape he had never visited, yet it was achingly familiar: a high harsh grassy upland held in a fist of snow-capped mountains, where he could run and run after the rats, the does, the rabbits, and the silver wolves, and when he found them he could stab and stab and stab.

He killed the creature in the water near the bank and dragged its body to the shore. Now he could see it clearly; it was smaller than he'd thought. Dead, it looked like any other kind of beast. It had short, powerful arms and legs, a pale belly that was punctured now, and its back and head was covered with dark hair. Its yellow eyes had been an illusion. Poking with his spear, Rael could not judge where on the beast's head they might have been. A small, feature-less triangle, a red soft mouth—the beast appeared to have no natural defenses. It had no claws, no spines, no teeth.

Squatting in the shallow water, Rael ran his hands over his body, searching for wounds. His skin was covered with a dirty slime, and it was mixed with his own blood. He knew it, knew that he was bleeding still, and yet he could not find the source, even after he had washed himself clean. The sun was setting. The entire pool was tinged with red.

In time he pulled himself up on the sand and lay upon his back, watching the sky change color. Tiny beads of blood were forming on his chest, gathering like sweat, dripping down his ribs.

Staring up at the dark trees, his mind chased dazzling afterimages among the leaves—a flock of radiant birds. For a few minutes he lost consciousness. When he awoke, the body of the beast was gone. He turned over in the sand, propping himself up onto his elbows. A wet track led away into the bushes—too dark now to follow.

In the cabin on the hillside, Cassia stirred the fire with a stick. It had sunk down to almost nothing, a glow of yellow embers, the only light in that small room. Outside, the wood was full of noises, now that night was come.

Behind her in the darkness Mr. Sarnath lay asleep, his face turned to the wall. As was his intermittent custom, he had drunk a glass of laudanum with dinner, then wrapped himself from head to toe in a white sheet. Now he lay immobile in his narrow bunk under a row of moldy paperbacks upon a shelf.

Sometimes in the evenings he would lie down for a while with a book, some gentle comedy of manners, set in a more sophisticated region of the continent, or else even overseas. He would read until he fell asleep. That night Cassia had made him peanut curry and pressed rice, but he had been uncommunicative, had gone to bed earlier than usual, had left her with the pot.

Now she sat stirring the fire, waiting for her brother's whistle, and from a wicker basket by the hearth she took out handfuls of paper—Mr. Sarnath's manuscript—and she was burning it. At first she had taken each sheet and crumpled it up separately, but that took time, and she was anxious to return to her dormitory in the village before it got too late.

And there was something else: For reasons that she couldn't specify this labor made her anxious. Once, a month before, she had carried in her hands the brown, carved skull that Mr. Sarnath had kept out upon his table on the porch, and it had given her a queasy feeling just to touch it. She had been glad when he had dropped it down the cliff. But now this paper gave her some of the same feeling; she picked up a big clump of it, all that remained, and loaded it upon the fire. The room went dark. The fire was struggling underneath the mass of paper. With her stick she tried to spread it out, to make it burn more easily, but every time she poked at it she felt light-headed, feverish, worse. Tongues of fire curled over the dark mass of the manuscript, and she could read it:

> *Nutmeg from the orient,*
> *Candied ginger I will bring you.*
> *Topaz, diamonds, and quartz,*
> *From the mines of RANAKPORE,*
> *From the turbaned NEGRO's toil,*
> *From the fabled mountainside,*
> *From the bottom of the sea,*
> *Pearls as big as PLOVER's eggs.*
> *I will bring a bag of pearls,*
> *Enough to spell my name out on the ground.*
> *And you will spell my name . . .*

She knew the rest. She knew the song. She knew the errors Sarnath had made in the translation. When the page was too charred to decipher, she sat back on her heels, her hand locked around the small copper medallion he had once given her, and which she wore on a string around her throat. Sometimes in the evening it seemed to burn under her fingers, as if the engraved image of the sun possessed some warmth.

She stared into the flame, afraid to raise her head, afraid to meet the eyes that she felt suddenly were watching her from across the fire, from the dark corner where the brooms were propped.

She raised her head and there was nothing. The fire had guttered down to nothing.

And yet there was a lingering smell that reached her through the black smell of the fire and the rank smell of her sweat. It was the smell of incense and of perfumed oil; once she had had a dream, a dream that had been like a journey. Awake, she could remember its beginning, middle, and its end. Awake, she had been terrified, but in the dream she'd felt no fear, and everything she saw had seemed familiar: an altar that was like a stage, and at the back of it a four-armed statue of cast bronze, thirty feet high, sitting cross-legged with a fat, gleaming belly, and in the shadows above her— for she had been a dancer on this stage, dressed in silk clothing with a candle in her hand—an enormous, vague, distorted head with a sharp muzzle like a dog's. And there had been incense on the altar, and her tattooed hands were glistening with a perfumed oil.

There was nothing in the corner of the cabin. But she had no desire to stay longer. She would wait no longer. So she rose unsteadily to her feet, rubbing her legs, and she took the lantern from a nail near the door.

Outside, the sky shone silver-grey. Above the small roof of the cabin, a triangle of stars burned brighter than the rest. She looked up; she was standing on the middle step. In her left hand burned a stick which she had taken from the fire, the small blue flame untroubled in the quiet air. Her lantern was a candle in an ancient mason jar held in a net of wicker braid.

She lit it and then tossed the stick out onto the wet grass. Then she stepped down. Around her, lantern bugs were rising through the weeds, each one carrying its intermittent glow. She took a few steps down the path. To Rael, watching sore and weary from the trees, it looked as if she were surrounded by a cloud of light.

He called to her, whistling like a curlew, three low notes and one high. It was his signal, and she was happy to hear it, for the walk to the village was uncomfortable in the dark. Her night vision was poor. She often stumbled on the rocks, and around her she could always hear the crashing of the beasts.

But that night her brother's whistle sounded different. He missed the note. The pure curlew's trill was harsh and garbled. Then she saw him; he was sitting by the banyan tree, his head bowed low.

She stood above him with the candle, then she went down on her knees. "What happened?" she said. "What happened?" but he shook his head. His skin was covered with a crust of blood, his hair was stiff with it. To her bad eyes, it looked like dirt. "What's wrong with you?" she asked. She put her arms around him and helped him to his feet; he was wearing a ripped pair of shorts and nothing else. Beside him was a long, sharp, broken wooden stick—he picked it up and leaned on it, and that was good because she never could have supported his whole weight, not with the lantern too.

He didn't say a word. He was limping through the darkness, slipping on the path, and she was holding him up with her left hand under his armpit all the way to the new barricade of thorns. There he seemed to revive somewhat, for he made it over the gate, and above the village he picked up his stick, and pointed down the slope off to the right. It was the way to the bathing pool, a track used only by themselves, for the Treganu disliked getting wet. A spring of water ran down through some rocks, forming a narrow pool two hundred yards above the village. They could see the lights.

They turned toward it, and Rael slumped down between the rocks. Cassia put the lantern down onto the rock. She pulled up her skirt and knotted it around her hips, then she stepped into the icy stream. She splashed water over his shoulders while he groaned and shook his head. She rubbed the water through his hair, washing him clean while he sat with his cheek against her leg.

Then she stood up. She stepped out of the pool and moved up the stream. Standing on the hump of a wet rock, she unbuttoned the bodice of her dress, for there was a smell on her skin now that she found intolerable, a smell of perfumed oil mixed with blood. She knelt, and brought up handfuls of water which she poured over her neck and breasts, turning away from Rael so that he couldn't see her, confident he couldn't because to her eyes he was just a shadow in the stream, unaware that as he looked up with his eyes of a night animal he could see her clearly, see the reaction of her skin to the cold water. He dropped his head, turning his back a little also, so that in the light of the lantern near his hand she could not tell what was so evident to him, even in his pants.

4

DECCAN
BLENDISH

By September of the sixteenth phase of summer, 00016, the city of Charn was once again the primary conduit for trade in that whole northern country. Ships from the gulf would anchor at the big container port below the town, and stevedores would then transfer their cargo, depending on its nature, either to the flatbeds of the railway or else to barges that were floated upstream, thirty miles up the river and up into the city itself, through the uninhabited swamps at the eastern end of Lake Nineteenth of May. Here the barges off-loaded onto smaller craft that motored over the flat waters of the lake, past the old Mountain of Redemption. This edifice, a gigantic prison in prerevolutionary days, was now the cultural museum in Charn, a showplace for the horrors of the old Starbridge regime. Its enormous bulk still dominated that whole section of the valley, dominated also smaller domes and towers that still rose up through the water. From time to time these smaller buildings would collapse, causing sudden hazards for the boatmen passing through them toward the city; occasionally also the surface of the water would be troubled as the lake flowed into some new subterranean chamber.

Boatmen in straw hats with colored ribbons navigated their flat craft through a series of shallow but massive locks, which ran under the power plant and let them out into the river marketplace of Charn. On all days except national holidays the water there was crowded with a vast array of boats, selling printed fabrics, batteries, and a myriad of foreign gadgets, as well as produce that for whatever reasons could not be grown locally. And they were joined there by other, smaller boats that had come down through the city on the radial canal, selling grains and oils and nuts and spices and a hundred different kinds of fruits and vegetables at dementedly low prices, for in those days there was no shortage of food in Charn, in Caladon, or anywhere in that whole region. Even the humblest, poorest rooftop garden could provide food for an entire extended family, and the terraced hills beyond the city were so fertile that—the old joke ran—you could drop a handkerchief at dawn and harvest an entire suit of clothes by noon. At the end of the sixteenth phase of summer, orchards and rice fields extended hundreds of miles outside the city—more and more each day, for they were cutting down the forests of teakwood, limewood, and the scented ebony, and shipping the timber overseas.

In those days, in Charn, from noon to five the streets were almost empty, and the temperature would rise above a hundred. From three-fourteen to five o'clock the rains would come; those were the hours of the afternoon siesta, for sometimes the rain was hot enough to hurt the skin, and sometimes in the streets the water rose up to midcalf, despite the excellent new drains. But at five o'clock precisely every afternoon the rains would stop, the clouds would wash away and disappear, and the provost of Sabian College would fire off a signal from the tower of the University of Charn. Then as the water receded underfoot, every afternoon a new fresh breeze would waft up from the gulf, and the shops that had been closed since morning would reopen, and a steady throng of people would flow from the houses down into the streets, and they would pack the tree-lined boulevards, the bars and the cafés, and especially the parks and public squares. In those days Charn was full of children, and there were thousands upon thousands of children everywhere, almost six for every adult. In a crowd the heads of the adults would protrude above the mass, and they seemed isolated and self-conscious like a race of freakish giants.

At six o'clock the streets were cleared of traffic, except for the bicycle rickshaws and the occasional private cars. And the kids would play stickball and kick-the-can until it got too dark to see, and then the streetlights would go on among the canopies of leaves, and they would shine among the leaves and turn them a peculiar, livid shade of green. At the same time the restaurants would have opened up their doors, and the rotten garbage and tar smells of the streets would be infiltrated slowly with the odor of hot oil, ginger, and cayenne. Then at nine o'clock the youngest children would go off to bed and many of their mothers and fathers would go with them; from then on until far into the night all these commercial, downtown sections of the city would be relinquished to the artificial intrigues of unmarried boys and girls—artificial because in that weather only one outcome was ever possible. Nevertheless in some cases the ritual could last for hours, and would include much bold hot staring and much cold indifference, the boys dressed in imported sneakers, pants cut slippery and tight around the crotch, and rayon shirts; the girls in high heels, stockings, black denim shorts, and halter tops that left their midriffs bare. In those days also it was the style for girls to wear long, embroidered shawls and orchids in their hair—these shawls were part of numerous dances of the period, when at midnight in the public bandshells, groups of music students from the university would unpack their instruments, and the asphalt esplanades would fill with lithe, expectant couples. In September of the sixteenth phase of summer, one band especially was popular in Charn, and it included a trumpet man who was, or had been, or seemed to be, an antinomial. He was both blind and mentally deranged, for he couldn't dress himself or talk; he had to be dragged out to the stage but once there he would play for hours, blowing till he burst, the trumpet like a toy in his huge hands, for he was almost eight feet tall and his enormous yellow hair made him look taller still.

On the evening of September ninth, a pockmarked graduate student named Deccan Blendish stood in a crowd in Durbar Square to watch the first public interrogations of that season, a victory, if it can be called that, for a certain extreme faction in the school of law. Seven men and women sat on a metal scaffold at one end of the square, while tape recordings of their confessions were broadcast over loudspeakers. The seven had been dismissed in student papers as an "assortment of reactionaries and assassins." But the *Free Word,* still at that time the most prominent independent daily, had been more thoughtful, and had pointed out in an editorial that all but two of the prisoners had been accused of spiritual offenses: divination, sodomy, transmigration, consubstantiation, sorcery, etc. To see them indicted on charges of this kind (the paper claimed) was reminiscent of the ancient Starbridge days. To which the *Law Review* had retorted in a special article that it was to prevent the reoccurrence of the Starbridge tyranny that these measures had been adopted, and that several of the prisoners had pleaded guilty to the crime of "Starbridge revenantism."

A gang of first-year law students had broken into the offices of the *Free Word,* but had been arrested before they could do much damage. And on the ninth of September the interrogation proceeded as scheduled. Deccan Blendish left before the end. It was enough to see the prisoners, bruised and dazed and drugged, being strapped into their chairs above the crowd. It had been enough to hear, from loudspeakers set on poles throughout the city, the broadcast of the self-evaluation sessions—jumbled and inaudible for the most part, except for one, which followed Deccan Blendish as he turned and pushed his way through the gaping mob of children, out of the square, up through the streets to his own lodgings. In front of his own building he fumbled for his key, and listened once again to the proud voice that spread out from the loudspeaker on the corner, reciting its litany of absurd crimes. The prisoner had pleaded guilty to nine counts of anal intercourse with the devil Angkhdt, guilty to having seen a vision of the devil Abu Starbridge in a dream, guilty to having attended thirteen secret subterranean meetings of the Cult of Loving Kindness, guilty to having caused through sorcery an outbreak of cholera in the river ward, guilty to having poisoned several important wells. His strong voice held no remorse; in his study on the third floor Deccan Blendish could still hear it.

He was a student of primatology. Books and articles were spread out in piles upon his desk. He sat down in front of his old typewriter and switched on his desktop lamp. But the small buzzing of the loudspeaker reached him even here; he put his hands over his ears. Then to distract himself, he reached out to the center of the desk and picked up the book that was lying on the largest pile of papers. It was one of the foci of his research, a rare volume of the aphorisms of the "master," an anonymous and obscure sage.

This book had appeared mysteriously in Charn twenty months earlier, when a certain kind of careful humanism had been in vogue. It had enjoyed a tiny popularity, and at that time the author was supposed to be a prominent Caladonian essayist and lecturer, who had died the same month that the book appeared. Lucius Piltdown (formerly with the UC Department of Philosophy, now also deceased) had written the definitive paper on the subject, in which he had cited stylistic and internal evidence.

Deccan Blendish had another idea. The book had been a favorite of his mother's. The volume in his hand had been her gift to him. She had told him not to believe the professor's paper, which had been reprinted in the introduction to the book. In him also, something had rebelled against the fat, self-satisfied visage of the essayist, whose photograph had appeared as a frontispiece. Halfway through his first reading he was able to formulate his first objection: The essayist had lived in Caladon for his entire life. But in the master's book, every metaphor was drawn from nature or from simple agriculture. It was not the product of a city mind. It could not be the product of a city intellectual, even one who had possessed (as Professor Piltdown dutifully claimed) a lifelong interest in botany.

Later, after reading it again, Deccan Blendish had acquired other clues. By the time he had started on his thesis, they had achieved a certain force: Some of the varieties of plants and animals that the master mentioned had a limited territorial range. And one especially, described in the section that he was leafing through the book to find, to see if it could distract him, or at the very least could offer him some consolation for what he had witnessed in the square. Here it was:

"No, my friend," said the master gravely. "What you have said is neither true nor just nor wise nor sensitive, nor even kind. In this matter you are like the monkey in the sand, our predecessor, which can disguise itself with lies. You have tried to fill our minds with rainbows. But do not be downhearted. Never be downhearted. For the truth is like . . ."

He let the book sag to his lap. Surely he was right. Surely this passage was a reference to the so-called "hypnogogic" ape, that elusive and quasi-mythical creature that had figured so prominently in the folk legends and scientific speculations of the past.

Surely he could not be wrong. On the wall above his desk he had thumbtacked a square piece of ikat fabric, and next to it, one of the most recent survey maps. He had drawn a circle on the map eight hundred miles northwest of Charn, a circle with a radius of fifty miles. Now he cast the book upon the desk. He stood up. He had an appointment with his thesis adviser at seven o'clock the following morning, and as he paced to the window and then back, he marshaled his arguments in his mind. But soon his enthusiasm led his mind away, off on the same tangent—the hypnogogic ape! Which Parthian Starbridge (Spring–Summer, 00011) had claimed, perhaps erroneously since he had never seen one, was of all primates the most anatomically similar to man. Which had been reported at intervals during every summer except this one since the beginning of contemporary records, and never outside a certain fifty-mile radius. Which no one had ever succeeded in capturing or dissecting. Which nevertheless had been accepted in some circles as the "missing link" in man's evolutionary chain. Which had the apparent ability, unique among animals, to alter the perceptions of both predators and prey. Which may, in fact, now be extinct. Which more than likely never had existed. The reference to which, in the master's manuscript, was probably proof of Piltdown's theory—the damned joke of the damned essayist from Caladon.

Outside his window the loudspeaker buzzed and twittered, a wordless, static sound. He stood immobile, listening, and then opened the window, for the heat inside his room had grown oppressive.

Standing with his nose pressed against the gauze mosquito screen, he looked down into the narrow street toward the corner. The streetlight had come on. Behind him on the map above his desk, in the middle of the fifty-mile circle, a colored push-pin marked a tiny dot, the site of a small village.

*   *   *

In the sixteenth phase of summer, Mr. Sarnath was living by himself at the top of the hill above the village in the trees. This was the expression that he gave to his sorrow and frustration; during his exile in Caladon and during his long journey home, he had gotten used to thinking that the master's theories were self-evident, and that their application also was self-evident. While the old man was still alive it had seemed easy to believe. Now, not yet two thousand days after his death, there were changes in the village that sickened Mr. Sarnath and made it impossible for him to live there.

This was the first change: After the master's death, no one ever left the village to take up a mission in Caladon or Charn. It no longer was the custom for the brightest students, male and female, to go out into the world to spread the teachings of the master. In the opinion of Canan Bey this custom had always been unfortunate—since the founding of the village twenty-seven people had gone out, and of them only Mr. Sarnath had ever returned. The size of the village had been diminished. Families had been disrupted, lives had been lost, and for no reason.

Until he died (said Canan Bey) the master had been under the illusion that the young people of the village had formed a school somewhere along the coast, were teaching dozens, hundreds of human children how to live peacefully, how to achieve happiness, how to destroy selfishness. And (continued Canan Bey) it had been the shattering of this illusion which had killed the master in the end, when he heard Sarnath confess that he had spent his exile as a customs officer in Caladon.

This suggestion was painful to Mr. Sarnath, for reasons that he did not share. Aloud, he pointed out that the master's own father had been a postal inspector in Caladon City. Sarnath's family had worked in customs houses long before the master was born. The tradition of their race was in the civil services—he was not ashamed of this tradition. Nor was it useful to pretend that wisdom could be attained and shared only in ideal conditions. The master had once said: "Anyone at all, at any time . . ." Nevertheless, after his death, no new students took the almond path out of the village. None seemed to want to go.

The second change was one that had immediate and tragic consequences, because it was as a result of it that the first outsiders visited the village—the first traders and travelers, the first agronomists. Mayadonna Bey, the oldest of the five members of the council, remarked one evening that it was against nature and against efficiency for everyone to labor at all tasks, that people were not gifted equally, and that they naturally enjoyed what they did best. He held up a square of fabric—dyed ikat in a complicated pattern—which had come from the loom of a woman in the village. He suggested that this woman and her family, because of the beauty of her work, should be exempted from all other village tasks, and that she should train others in her new technique.

Mayadonna was supported in this opinion by Canan and Langur Bey, opposed by the two others. Mr. Palam argued that most villagers had several hours of free time each day in order to pursue their inclinations or their gifts, but that nothing was more central to the master's vision than that the work of the village be shared communally, as all else was shared. " 'In every task,' " he quoted, " 'no matter how minute, we find a small piece of ourselves. How then, in doing one thing only, can we hope to become whole . . . ?' " Nevertheless as time went on, more and more villagers seemed to spend all their time outdoors, while others labored in their houses. The flax field was expanded after a time, and it seemed that half of all households were engaged in the production of cloth, more than anyone could wear. After a time also, the first peddlers appeared, trading copper kettles, steel implements, and books.

That first square of fabric, which Mayadonna Bey had displayed before the council, was the one that Deccan Blendish had thumbtacked to his wall. He had bought it in a shop of curios and handicrafts, and he carried it with him on the train from Charn. He left the city on the morning of September twelfth, one of the first passengers on the new rail link to Cochinoor.

How quickly, once the process started, the forest was being opened up! His journey, over much of the same country that Mr. Sarnath had traveled so laboriously, took him twenty days. But even that was a long time for someone who had never been anywhere, and it included many hours of worry. He had no idea what he would find. His research on the Treganu unravelers had uncovered many contradictions. He had found portraits from the Caladonian civil service, from midwinter of the year 00015, which were horrible—revealing alien, grotesque, inhuman features. Yet forty thousand days later, by midsummer of the same year, the faces which stared out of the pages of official documents and travelers' sketches were mournful, softened, regularized, not far out of the range of normal human variation.

The drawings of the Treganu themselves, while tending toward the abstract, did not suggest anything monstrous. Nevertheless, it was hard not to feel anxious, and some of the most frequent reports—for example that they had no blood, but only a white powder sifting through their veins— were certainly bizarre. And yet the skeletal record did not preclude (to say the least) a common proto-human ancestor.

From Mayalung he had to walk three days over a new road, under an old rain, worrying all the way. Yet gradually all feeling subsided in the wet mud; on his arrival, if he hadn't been so sick, he might have felt relieved. He might have been proud of his most optimistic predictions, proud of the preliminary sketches he had made of thin, frail, hairless, tailless men and women, with flat, impassive faces. But instead he felt a vague kind of regret, which time only made worse. By the middle of September he felt nothing but remorse that he

had come. Though perhaps, rather than any presage of ca-
tastrophe, he was just disappointed not to be the first.

One evening, sick and disoriented, he stood on the veranda
of the house of elders and watched the rain fall down upon
the village in the trees. The veranda ran the circuit of the
house, which was built on stilts above the level of the neigh-
boring roofs. From where he stood he could see the whole
village spread out in a circle around him: the small, simple
houses of bamboo and palm, the different colors of the patch-
work fields, the black shadow of the forest. Even under the
grey sky the largest paddy was an intense shade of green,
and in the middle of it, Deccan Blendish could see the leader
of the team of agricultural consultants whose arrival in the
village had preceded his. The man was standing under an
umbrella, arms akimbo, legs spread wide. He was surrounded
by a group of slighter figures, farmers from the village, huddled disconsolately in their wicker capes.

In back of Deccan Blendish, in the room that had once
been the master's and that now contained his statue and his
altar, he could hear a murmured conversation. "It is because
we work to separate the web of truth into its component
strands," said Langur Bey. "That is why they call us that.
'Unravelers.' It is not a word we use ourselves."

The elders of the village sat cross-legged on a single mat
in the middle of the floor, five old men in a line. Kurt Sofar,
the youngest member of the team, squatted in front of them.
As Blendish turned to watch him, he rolled down onto his
rear. A black plastic notebook was open by his side.

"You understand what we are doing," he said after a
pause. "You understand the implication. I realize it must
seem intrusive. Threatening. But I tried to explain. . . ."

"We were expecting it," the old unraveler said gently. "It
was inevitable—you want more than you have."

"Again," said Kurt Sofar. "That's not the point. It is not
a question of our own production, which is ample. We are

thinking of the future. We anticipate enormous climactic changes in your children's lifetime. What will you eat, when winter comes?"

The old man smiled. "We will be dead."

Kurt Sofar scratched his leg. Dr. Cathartes, seated in his armchair, had a different response. Blendish watched him turn his head toward Langur Bey, an inquiring expression on his thick red lips. Always watchful for the devil's mark, he was interested in the old man's smile. "According to your religious faith," he said. "In some circumstances is death considered beneficial?"

The old men sat in a line: Langur Bey, Canan Bey, Mayadonna, Palam, Sarnath. Their alien, chinless faces were so hard to read, yet Deccan Blendish sensed a terrible sadness there, a terrible sadness in their delicate, weak smiles.

"We have no religious faith," said Langur Bey.

In the paddy field, in the rain, the agronomist was smoking a cigar. Turning to the rail again, Blendish watched him take it from his mouth, stare at the end of it, cast it away. "We're straying from the point," said Kurt Sofar. "As I told you— we're trying to build up a big supply of food, to prepare for the cold weather here and elsewhere. We're planning big repositories of grain that will be available to the entire region. The logistic problem is enormous and requires sacrifices. That's a larger consideration which does not concern you. The fact is, by adopting the measures we have suggested, you'll be able to triple your output of essential foods. That's good for us and good for you."

Canan Bey smiled. "We will be dead. Now I see—it is inevitable."

Exasperated, Sofar slapped his knee. "It's true—you may not live to see this program in effect. It may not benefit you directly. But maybe, just maybe, a decision you make now might make it easier for your children, when this land is under snow."

Deccan Blendish turned away from the veranda, and

stepped inside the open screen. "You don't understand," he said to Kurt Sofar. "He's saying the changes you've suggested will require the destruction of the village. They know what you've been doing in this area."

Sofar stretched his legs out on the floor. He was stretching out his hamstrings. "You shut up," he said. "That's not true and you know it. Besides, this is our project. You're here as an observer."

There was silence in the room, and Deccan Blendish could hear the scattering of rain upon the roof. Then Palam Bey spoke for the first time. "'It does not benefit the rat, when three dogs fight over its carcass.'"

Blendish recognized a quotation from the master's book of aphorisms. Dr. Cathartes recognized it too. "'Therefore work to reconcile your enemies,'" he said. He leaned forward in his chair and touched his hands together. "Let me make it clear to you," he said to Palam Bey. "My colleague is with the department of agronomy, and his only concern is with the grain augmentation program. Mr. Blendish is here by chance. I am with the department of theology, of the University of Charn, and my interest is different. In a sense I am the senior member of this team. So you will pay special attention to my questions, and do not answer flippantly."

His voice was strong, mellifluous, and reassuring. It seemed to Deccan Blendish an extension of the rest of him, a tool perfectly suited to his hand. Cathartes was a handsome man, tall, with thick brown hair.

It stopped raining as suddenly as it had started. As soon as he could, Deccan Blendish left the house, partly in disgust, and partly for more pressing, private reasons. Ever since he had come out from Charn he had been sick. His first days in the village he had spent in bed. It was the change of diet; in distress, he groped his way toward the latrine, situated on the outskirts of the village in a grove of thick japonica. Once there, perched on the high seat of the first cubicle, he stayed a long time. He listened to the villagers come and go.

The wall to his left was almost covered by the web of an enormous spider—fat-bellied, yellow, red, immobile, suspended near his hand. Above him, a sprig of japonica had forced its way through a crack in the palm roof.

He was beginning to distrust these overburdened forest blossoms, beautiful as they were. All through his journey, especially since he had left the farms behind and come into the forest, he had been made miserable by growths and itches and rots and funguses which seemed to sprout over his body. This outhouse when he had first visited it had seemed to stink of alien creatures; now as if by silent agreement the Treganu had abandoned it to him, and he was conscious of a new smell that was all his own, sickeningly sweet, as if his stomach and intestines were packed full of flowers.

For consolation during the long wait he pulled out of his shoulder bag the master's book of aphorisms, wrapped in the square of ikat fabric that had led him to this place—remote, exotic, the lair of the hypnogogic ape, perhaps. Since his arrival in the village he had not spoken to one person who had seen the beast. Langur Bey, to whom he had quoted the master's reference, had given him a metaphorical interpretation.

He spread the piece of cloth out on his knees. Each thread was dyed separatedly in a different pattern. Woven together, they made the picture of a butterfly. Around the edge a row of multicolored triangles in cross-stitched embroidery. He remembered the triumph when he had solved the clue, when he had stood in the peddler's shop in Charn and heard him say, "It's a language, sir. Those triangles. Each one has a special meaning."

"What does it say?"

The peddler had frowned, and pointed with his dirty finger. "Bird," he had said. "Arrow. Sky."

Sitting in the outhouse, Deccan Blendish leafed forward toward the beginning of the book, although he knew the quote from memory: "The hawk falls like an arrow from the sky. What are the reasons for its fierceness. There are three reasons at least . . ." Then, his mind had been full of triumph. Now, he remembered the peddler's doubtful frown, the way he'd scratched his chin and said, "Might be. It just might be. They're all unravelers up there."

He laid the book and the cloth aside. Turning slightly on the seat, he checked the wall behind him for corrosive slugs. Then he fell into a waking daze, which gradually subsided into sleep; he settled back against the outhouse wall. And when he opened his eyes, his dream was still inside his mind. It was a noise that had disturbed him, a faint intake of breath, and he sat staring at a girl, a woman dressed in white, framed by the outhouse door. She looked in on him and then she disappeared. And through the afterimage of his dream he saw her different than she was. For an instant she became the hypnogogic ape, the shape-changer come to mock at him, so unexpected was the sight of her in her white dress.

BY MOONLIGHT | 5

In fact, on the night of his arrival at the village, Blendish had been so sick that he was actually relieved to hear that someone from the university had preceded him. Dr. Cathartes had arrived the month before, and was staying in a house near the south barricade. It was a house apportioned for his use. He gave directions that Deccan Blendish be guided there and put to bed.

That first evening he had taken Blendish's temperature himself, and had sat up with him during the worst hours. He had sat beside him on the bed, touching him often. At the time, Blendish wondered if it was a symptom of his fever that made his impression of the man so intense. Cathartes seemed to be sitting very close to him, his face loomed very close, and even at his moments of greatest discomfort Blendish was aware of the man's personal beauty. A kerosene lantern burned on a chair beside the bed. It cast a roseate glow, which seemed to coat one half of the man's face, and when he turned his head the outline of his profile seemed unnaturally distinct.

When Blendish was well enough, he moved out of the professor's house. He rented a room in the house of a Treganu family. After an argument over the destruction of forest habitats, he ignored the other members of the professor's team—agriculturalists from Caladon and Charn. But Cathartes was different from them. Cathartes at least seemed interested in the unravelers—he was putting in a grant proposal to study them, their culture, their history, their religion. Cathartes always had remained friendly, and on the morning after he had seen the girl dressed in white, framed in the outhouse door, Blendish went to the professor's house to search him out.

He found Cathartes shaving in his room. "There is a human woman here," said Blendish.

"How do you know?"

"I saw her."

Cathartes had nailed his traveling mirror to the wall. He stood in front of it, washing a long, straight razor in a bowl of water. Already in the early morning, the weather was intolerably hot; the steaming water on its stand had filled the air to saturation, so that instantly on entering, Blendish's skin was covered with a flush of sweat. His shirt was soaked under his arms. By contrast, the professor's shirt was clean and freshly ironed.

He rubbed his fine jaw not with soap, but with a scented grease. Holding the razor at a prudent angle, he stroked his face with brisk, energetic strokes.

"She's pretty, isn't she?" he said presently.

"Who is she?"

"Sarnath kidnaped her from Caladon. Her and a boy. That's the story I've pieced together from the others."

The morning sunlight spilled over the windowsill into the room. It spattered through the screen. In spite of the heat, Blendish shuddered.

"Ah," he said, concentrating on the razor's stroke. Then he turned away and looked instead around the room, noticing without admiring the perfect luxury of the professor's personal belongings: the expensive luggage, the gilt-edged books, the silver combs and brushes on the palm-leaf chest.

"What do you think?" Cathartes asked. He turned toward Blendish with the razor in his hand.

When Blendish said nothing, he continued: "What would it be like? To be stolen away from home at birth and raised by alien primitives."

The pout of his red lips seemed both mesmerizing and repellent, and again Deccan Blendish turned away. "Is that what they are?"

"In a manner of speaking. Who knows what they are, or where they come from, really? A man in my department claims they are of extrasolar origin. He has the proof, he claims. They are fundamentally unlike ourselves, and for this reason they disgust us. Have you read Thanakar Starbridge's autobiography?"

The house that the council had given to Cathartes and the others was at the outskirts of the village. Separate from the other buildings, it was separate also from the forest, unalleviated by any shade, a squat block of palm-leaf thatch, crushed by the pressure of the insistent sun. Inside, Blendish listened to the buzzing of the flies upon the windowsill. He found himself nodding and smiling.

"It's a peculiar book," continued the professor. "Peculiar and instructive. For a while the author was held captive on the Caladonian frontier—Thanakar Starbridge was definitely a liberal, by prerevolutionary standards. An atheist, even. But I don't think I've ever read anything more full of loathing than his descriptions of these people. Part of it is just aristocratic prejudice, an instinctive hatred for all civil servants. But that's not all. There's more to it than that."

He had replaced his razor on the stand. Now he was standing by his bed, a towel around his neck. He had taken a book from his bedside table and was holding it out; for an instant Deccan Blendish felt a spasm of dumb fear. For an instant he was afraid that the professor would require him to read the whole fat, boring book right there, right then, in that stupefying heat. Smiling, he shook his head and put his palms up in appeal.

Cathartes shrugged. "It's interesting. For my survey I am reading all the references that I can find. In every one, the tone's the same—the same unmitigated loathing. Most of them are from a time when the unravelers were far more common in the cities than they are now. Canan Bey tells me that Sarnath was a customs officer in Caladon. If that's true, he must have been one of the last."

The buzzing of the flies seemed very loud. Blendish put his hand up to his face. "What could it be, I wonder," said Dr. Cathartes, replacing the book upon his table. He was buttoning up his shirtfront, fingering as he did so the emblem of the university upon his collar. "Why such hatred? It is not their physical peculiarities. If anything, it is their similarity to us that makes them seem grotesque. It's certainly not their manners—they're an inoffensive lot. And there is nothing in the teachings of the master that explains it—superficially."

Perhaps the flies were attracted to the sweetness of his voice, the smell of his minted breath. In his mind's eye, Blendish saw an image of the house, circled by a swarm of flies. The teachings of the master . . . he thought. In this matter you are like the monkey in the sand, our predecessor, which can disguise itself with lies . . .

He cleared his throat. "There are others who think differently," he said aloud. "There is another theory of their evolution."

Cathartes didn't seem to hear. "These woods are crowded with reactionaries," he said. "I'll be relieved when they are all cleared out. Listen: not sixty miles from here there is a village near a lake. Old men and women, mostly—honey gatherers, harmless, peaceful. But they had priests—I found them hiding in a cave. I was doing my dissertation, and it was my coup—they had carved a wooden statue of the devil Angkhdt, and they had lined their palms with colored berry juice." He gave an elaborate shudder. "I'll be glad when this whole forest is clear-cut."

Back in his own room, Deccan Blendish lay down on his mat, and in a little while his nausea had subsided. He selected a tetraqualamine tablet out of his bag of pills and sat up with a glass of water to swallow it. Langur Bey had given him an herbal remedy for diarrhea, a powder of ground roots; he took a pinch of it and chewed it dry. In his own room the air was cooler. The buzzing in his ears had stopped. Yet still he felt a certain grim presentiment, and to distract himself he took his fieldbook out of his knapsack, together with some mimeographs of source material. For almost the first time since his arrival he thought about his project—about the animal he hoped to find.

He was a sixth-semester student only, inexperienced, and because of that, he had not yet learned to put a distance between himself and his ideas. They seemed part of him, part of the structure of his brain. His theory of the hypno-gogic ape was too instinctive to express, even though the desire to express it had made him light-headed and confused. "Are you familiar with the principles of evolution?" he might have said. But Cathartes was probably a creationist of some kind, or a derivationist. Cathartes would have laughed at him—the man was an associate professor of theology, a ter-rifying accomplishment for one so young.

The old woman brought him rice and laid it on the table. Sitting on the side of his bed, he pulled his notebook from his bag, comparing for the hundredth time the diagrams that he had made from the skulls of various primates: views from the front, the back, the side, the top of human skulls and monkey skulls. On another page, tables of measurements and notations in his indecipherable handwriting. And then a series of engravings: skulls of the Treganu, identified by their long cranial ridge. More human skulls. And last of all: a collection of sketches of the hypnogogic ape.

After he had eaten, he put on his student's cap and set out for the forest. He had seen monkeys in the trees along the almond path the first day he had come.

There was no method to his theory, nor had he an idea of how to prove it. It depended from the master's chance remark. "Our predecessor," he had said. "Which can disguise itself with lies." The master had not been, to say the least, a trained professional in the field. Nevertheless, that day Blendish went in search of evidence. He was carrying a daypack and a small pair of binoculars. Beyond the mangrove swamp he turned off of the path, and climbed laboriously down the slope.

As he did so, he became aware for the first time of a new ailment, or, rather, an aggravation of an old one. So when he reached the stream he rolled his pant leg above his knee, revealing a discoloration of the skin along his outer thigh, and a swelling there. By that time he was familiar with most spider sores and slug bites, but this was different. He had first noticed it two days before. An area upon his right thigh as big as the ball of his thumb had turned dark red, and it was itching terribly. The swelling seemed hard, as if there were something solid underneath his skin.

Standing by the water, he shrugged his shoulders with a new resignation. He pulled out a plastic tarpaulin from the daypack, which he laid over a tussock of black grass. Then he sat down on it, arranging his body so that he could see the outside of his knee, touch the offending sore—it seemed to have grown in the past day, even in the past few hours.

Suddenly he felt light-headed. He looked up at the trees. The pool before him was a tiny thing, just a thickening of the stream, the water slow and orange and full of algae. On the far bank a clump of marshgrass stirred in the soft wind, and beyond that the forest undergrowth began again. He was sitting in the shade. The track behind him led uphill toward the almond path, and he was surrounded on all sides by tulip trees—their thin, feeble trunks overburdened by their heavy heads, so that damp masses of foliage hung almost to the ground. In one place the sun was shining on the water.

"Don't touch it," said a voice.

He had been scratching at the sore place on his leg. Now he pulled his hand away, embarrassed. He balled his fingers up into a fist and then released them. He looked around the pond and back uphill.

There was silence for about a minute, and then the reeds on the far bank split apart. Not twenty feet away the girl stood in a clump of grass. The reeds grew up tall around her, and she was holding them apart. Her feet and legs were bare; she had pulled her white dress up and knotted it around her waist to keep it dry. Now she stepped into the slow water, and in a moment it had risen past her shins.

Deccan Blendish was conscious of a sudden sick feeling as he watched her cross the stream, a familiar sensation when he was near a woman. This time it was given a new intensity by the weakness of his stomach. She stepped across the stream and climbed out on the bank, then checked her legs for leeches. She was looking down at him with an expression on her face—what was it? Pity, shyness, curiosity, indifference? It was impossible to tell.

Her unkempt black hair was pulled back from her face; her brows were thick and dark. There was something inescapably romantic about her presence at the stream, alone with him. He was conscious of a small feeling of pleasure that was swiftly overcome by nausea.

She was looking at his leg. Now she stepped onto his plastic tarpaulin and squatted down, taking his fat knee easily between her hands. She worked the joint. She touched the sore place on his knee with a light forefinger; now it had grown even larger, but he didn't notice it. He was conscious only of her smell as she bent over him, the smell of something edible and good to eat, some sweet kind of dessert, a spice cake or a custard caramel—her skin was dark.

"Have you brought your first-aid kit?" she asked.

She spoke the dialect of Charn better than anybody he had talked to from the village, except for Langur Bey. Just a few inches away from him, she raised her head to look into his face, and he was overpowered by the smell of her. The sickness in his stomach was more urgent now; he nodded his head weakly, and without a word she turned and rummaged in his daypack, pulling out a soft white case.

"What did you expect?" she said. "I was born up on the Caladon frontier."

There was a pack of one-edged razor blades. She unwrapped one, sliding it out of its cardboard sheath. Then, from someplace at her waist, she produced a battered metal cigarette lighter, in whose weak flame she sterilized the blade. She gave him an inquiring look; he nodded and lay backward, supported on his elbows, and turned his face to the sky. He was concentrating on his stomach, hoping to suppress it by an extreme effort of will and by swallowing repeatedly. He didn't even watch her when she slit the skin over the bulge upon his leg, didn't even feel it. "There," she said. "It's simple. But it hurts like anything when they burst out."

There was an insect on his thigh, perhaps two inches long. His leg was stretched out on the ground, his knee locked straight, and she was holding his leg still. He shuddered and breathed deep, but her hands upon his leg seemed to calm him, to keep him from moving. He looked down again—the insect, dark, wet, and bedraggled, seemed to be moving too, according to the rhythm of his breath. He watched one of its wings start to unfold; it was a butterfly.

Behind him on the slope, Rael was peering through the trees. He watched his sister bending down over the stranger's leg. He watched her work the stranger's knee. In his hand he gripped his broken stick of wood. He reached out and thumped it lightly on the ground. Not loud enough for them to hear; he turned and climbed back silently up to the path, perfectly silent in the complicated woods. Perfectly silent, he walked back to the village, his head cocked at an uncertain angle.

For several months he had been working with the bullock in the lower terraces. It was work he liked, and he was better at it than the others. By humming songs, he found he could influence the bulk's meager thoughts, and with his hand upon its hump he found that he could guide it, for it responded to his strength.

That morning he had been working in one of the new rice fields below the village, which the new strangers had designed. That morning he had fastened chains around a teakwood log, but then he had gone away, down to the stream below the almond path, obeying an impulse that he didn't understand. He'd left a boy working the bullock, but he'd made a mess of it. When Rael returned, the boy was gone. The log was stuck inside a hill of mud, invisible except for the chain that led to the beast's yoke.

In the middle of the flooded field, the hot mud reached above his ankles. Opposite him, its front legs splayed apart, its big head lowered almost to the surface of the mud, the bullock stood its ground. Its heavy features were cast in an expression of distrust, of disappointment and intolerable stupidity; Rael found his broken stick was twitching in his hand, his mind full of the image of his sister Cassia, bending over the flabby stranger.

Ah, he thought. Is broke now wrongness in this town is touching all is breaking now apart.

As he bent down behind the animal to unhook the chain, the mud was slippery and disgusting around his feet, around his legs also. It gave off a hot, fermented smell; the chain was slick with it. He was humming a small sad wordless song to calm the beast, but he must have hit a bitter note, for suddenly, without warning, the bullock lurched forward with a grunt. Rael, his fingers in the chain, was pulled off-balance and slipped down into the mud; then he was up, his stick gripped in his fist. He seized the bullock by its nearer horn and yanked its head around until he was staring down into its dim-witted, bloated face. Then he was slashing at its face with all his strength, slashing at its hairless cheeks, trying to find its eyes. Tormented, it yanked free, but it was held fast by the anchored chain, and Rael was leaping around it, slashing at its eyes until it screamed.

Honest Toil was standing on the dike. Honest Toil was there. He came splashing down across the mud. "Oh, no, no, no," he said, just as Rael took one last swipe at the beast's head.

After she had cut the insect from his leg, the girl retreated to the far edge of the tarpaulin where she sat hugging her knees. He thought she was embarrassed to have touched him, embarrassed to have come so close—now she was shy. She hugged her knees, watching Blendish as he cleaned out his leg with hydrogen peroxide. Living here with only her brother to keep her company, perhaps—he thought—she did not understand his pockmarked ugliness. He carefully repacked his box of medications. He took off his spectacles and wiped them, and then returned them to his sweaty nose.

"I was born on the frontier," she said. "Is that where you're from?"

"I'm from the city."

"Ah."

She raised her head up from her knees. "I can remember Cochinoor," she said. "That is the city, isn't it? Sarnath took a job there in the post office, when my brother and I were children. I remember the main street. We were living in a room."

Blendish also remembered Cochinoor, a stinking lumber

town where he had drunk some of the water that had made him sick. "I am from Charn," he said.

"Ah."

In this syllable he thought he could detect a tone of longing and regret. "Ah," she said, "why did you come?"

Suddenly, he didn't know. Suddenly, his mind was back in Charn, and he was loitering there on the riverfront, and he imagined it as she might see it. He imagined standing on the waterfront, watching the lights come on across the river, listening to the street musicians underneath the trees, drinking beer and eating peanuts with the smell of all the foodstands in his nostrils; here in the forest, he had eaten practically nothing but lentils for a month. Lentils and pounded yam.

The girl was staring at him, hugging her knees, and it occurred to him with a sick nervous rush that he could use her interest. There was something in her face, and it occurred to him that if he chose the right sequence of words and acts, then he could touch her there upon that plastic tarpaulin, she would let him and be glad. If he could make her taste some of that beer, smell some of that ginger sambal—it was possible; he looked at her and then he dropped his eyes.

"I'm studying a kind of ape," he said unhappily. "I wonder, have you ever seen any large apes down here?" An idiotic question, and he felt her gaze slide past him momentarily toward the marshgrass. Then she looked back.

"Apes," she said.

Her head was small, her neck was long and brown. There was a string around the bottom of her throat, a medallion on a string. "What's that?" he asked, at random. She put her hand up to her throat.

"It's my lucky coin."

It was a small copper medallion. "Let me see."

She looked at him. Then she shifted her position and moved toward him, leaning forward so that once again he could smell the sweetness of her skin. Her skin was smooth and sweet like custard, and the top of her dress had slipped open an inch or so. Again, Blendish felt a sudden rush of nausea. He told himself: This is the moment. This is the moment, and it will not come again. Panicked, he reached out his hand. But instead of touching, as he meant to do, her cheek under her ear, instead of brushing back a strand of hair out of her eyes, instead of reaching out to stroke her shoulder, instead of stroking, as he meant to do, the heart-breaking distension of her breast, he allowed himself to be deflected at the final instant, and at the final instant he grabbed at the medallion as if at an amulet—something to save him from irrevocable shame. He wanted to preserve the moment when she had not yet rejected him, even if by doing so he risked and ruined everything. And he was risking it and ruining it, he could tell. Already by the time his fingers touched the metal, something had changed. He was chafing the copper medallion between his fingers, thinking something had changed—what was it? She still sat as before, still inside the circle of his reach. Her face still kept its serious look, as if she still took him seriously. Something had changed, and perhaps it was just wishful thinking; he clutched at the medallion, feeling in his heart and in his belly a mixture of relief, nausea, and regret, while his mind repeated dumbly: Abu Starbridge, Abu Starbridge. The reverse side of the medallion was engraved with a mark he recognized: the shining sun in splendor, the mark of Abu Starbridge.

"Where did you get this?"

She smiled and shook her head. She pulled back her neck so that he could feel some tension in the string, but he did not let go. The moment had passed, and now he was aware of something else in her, some new kind of concern.

"Give it to me," he said.

She smiled and shook her head, but now he was aware of a new look in her eye, a sudden closure in her eye. It did not alter her expression in the slightest, yet somehow she had changed. A small window had closed, and he grasped the medallion, using his strength for the first time, clutching it with a new kind of desperation, as if he could drag her back just a few inches, just thirty seconds or so back through their conversation, back to the instant before that window shut.

"You can't wear this," he said. "Not with Cathartes here."

He closed his hand upon the devil's mark, the shining sun of Abu Starbridge. "Give it to me," he said. "I've got a steel dollar in my pocket."

She shook her head. The smile was gone, and he had not seen it go, although he had been studying her face. She pulled back, and Blendish could see the pressure of the string upon her neck; it made a thin pink line and he thought for the first time: I could force her. It was an idea he suppressed as soon as it had taken shape—suppressed it with a feeling of self-loathing, replacing it instead with a desire to protect. He was right. Doubtless she had picked the medal up somewhere, found it in the woods, got it from some traveling cultist; no one who understood its meaning would dare to wear it openly as decoration. Not with Cathartes here. He tightened his grip on it and then he yanked back with all the force of his frustration. The pink line turned red, and then it disappeared, and he was holding the medallion in his fist.

She was standing above him, her hand upon her neck. What was the expression on her face? Who knew—who ever understood what anyone was feeling? She was standing above him, and then she stepped back off the tarpaulin onto the grass.

"You want too much," she said.

Her gaze—frank, serious, untroubled—filled him with shame. He bowed his head. When he looked up, she was gone.

He sat by the stream until the late afternoon. Toward four o'clock, the butterfly upon the tarpaulin separated its wings for the first time. They split apart suddenly, easily, like the halves of a rock, revealing a seam of turquoise that was completely unexpected, for the underside of the insect's wings had been dirty and uninteresting. Blendish sat watching, waiting for the butterfly to take its first brave leap into the air. Its wings were dry and fully extended. There was nothing to be gained by the delay. Yet for an hour it barely moved; suddenly disgusted, Blendish brushed it off into the grass. He rose to his feet and packed his things into his bag. Then he climbed back up onto the almond path, sweaty, bad-tempered, out of breath.

A hundred yards below the barricade he saw Dr. Cathartes striding toward him. He was frowning and smiling at the same time, and the language in his body seemed to speak of tension, purpose, and excitement. "I was looking for you," he said, not loudly. Yet Blendish heard him from a dozen yards away, and there was something in his tone that seemed to pierce the pressure of the dull, hot, humid afternoon, pierce it and drain it away. His face was radiant, triumphant.

He was dressed in tailored jungle fatigues, made of pleated cotton, and on the collar Blendish recognized the logo of a fashionable department store in Charn. Weary and dispirited, he stopped in the middle of the path, feeling his gorge rise and his bowels sink as the professor strode up close to him—too close. He stood inches away, and his breath was scented with some kind of mint. He was a handsome man, his skin perfumed and smooth, his lips voluptuous and red—Blendish stood sweating, pimpled, miserable, his mouth slowly filling with saliva.

He had kept the copper medallion in the pocket of his jeans. With his right hand he reached down to touch it, to chafe it in his fingers. "I've been looking for you," Cathartes said. Then he smiled. "Did you find your ape?"

Blendish shook his head. "I've got to work farther afield. Today was a dry run. I'm too sick to work properly." In his pocket, his hand squeezed the medallion tight between his index finger and his thumb.

"You should take a guide. For safety's sake." Still smiling, the professor shook his head. "It's not safe here by yourself—listen, do you remember what I said this morning?"

Blendish did not reply. He was conscious of a subtle ringing in his ears, and his mouth was full of spit.

"I said there was something strange about this place. Now I found a clue."

He was standing very close. Blendish could barely understand what he was saying, so conscious was he of the professor's presence—"Listen. An hour ago I went by the new field. Kurt Sofar asked me to come down. There is a retarded man who lives here. An old man. Have you seen him?"

Blendish nodded.

"He was standing in the middle of the field. He had a club in his hand, and with it he had just finished beating a cow almost to death. The animal will have to be destroyed, I think. It was blinded in one eye."

Blendish nodded. He tried to swallow.

"Can you imagine it? It's against nature. Wanton cruelty to animals—I wish you could have heard it shriek. The old man just stood there. Sofar was incensed. He needed the animal for his project. This is an act of sabotage to him. He wants to have the fellow whipped."

The ringing in Blendish's ears seemed to increase. He brought his hand up to his mouth. "He is retarded," he ventured.

"Not like that. I had spoken to him before. He was a gentle old man—no, there's more to it than that. I've read about this countless times. I've seen photographs. Cruelty to animals—that's often the first sign. And destruction of property; that creature was important to the village."

"And so?"

"It's like poisoning a well. I told the grant committee that there might be some form of devil worship here, some alien offshoot of the Cult of Loving Kindness. I based my proposal on a similarity between some of the sayings of the master and a quotation from the Starbridge catechism. At the time, I thought it was a long shot. But this community was formed after the revolution, when all the devil worshipers had been expelled from Charn."

Blendish held the medallion in his fist, making a bulge in the pocket of his jeans. He was squeezing it tightly, and as he increased the pressure the ringing in his ears seemed to increase also. He wiped his mouth with his left hand.

Cathartes smiled. "It's flimsy still, I know. But I'm making progress. And I could make something from this. That man Sarnath is the key. Canan Bey told me that he kept some bones up at his shack, which he was using for some private ritual. And it's terrible what he did—to kidnap a young human girl and take her from her family. I can't believe it doesn't serve some purpose."

Blendish felt some vomit in his throat. He put his left hand on his mouth. Inches away, Cathartes watched him curiously. "Are you all right?" he asked, his face full of a quick, intolerable solicitude.

Blendish squatted down. With amazement, he watched himself take his right hand out of his pocket. He was squeezing the medallion as hard as he could; then suddenly he stopped, relaxed his fist. And when he opened it to reveal the medallion on his palm, the buzzing in his ears suddenly stopped.

In the evening, Mr. Sarnath sat by the old peepul tree below the village. In the middle of a rapidly expanding glade, that one ancient tree stood isolated from the rest. The soil was particularly good there, in the bottomland between two hills. The new agronomists wanted to flood the stream and dam an area eleven acres in extent, where they hoped to experiment with a new type of ochoa shoot, a hybrid developed at the University of Charn.

Their plans called for the eradication of the tree, whose roots spread under the entire field. It was a subject that had been debated in the council of elders, debated with a gentle melancholy, for the tree had been among the master's favorite places. Every morning while he was still strong he had meditated for an hour beneath its branches, and every evening he had slept there for an hour upon a bamboo mat. Remembering this, still Langur Bey had argued for the tree's destruction. Hesitantly, almost in tears, he had reminded the others that the symbol of a thing is different from the thing itself. Under that very tree, he said, the master had once warned him to be cautious of corporeal attachments.

The council had not yet reached a conclusion. But in anticipation, the agronomists had already marked the trunk—a red X painted on its shaggy bark. In the darkness the mark appeared to glow. Sarnath sat under it, cross-legged, straight-backed, his heart full of a despair too rich for words.

Through this excess of feeling, in his careful, controlled way, Sarnath had approached a kind of peace. The heavy branches stirred softly above him in the tiny wind. So he had often seen it, separate from all the stagnant forest, its massive leaves sensitive to breezes that no other tree could feel. Around him a soft glow from the sky fell upon the silent grass, fell upon the excavations and the fallen trunks that littered the edges of the glade, gilding them, making them perfect, reminding him of the transitory nature of all beauty, reminding him also that no change is wholly bad. His heart felt drunk on poison. Why is it? he asked himself. How is it we have failed? We are not evil men. Our hands were greedy for the grasp of truth, yet it has slipped away.

Nor could he blame the rest of the council and not himself. Yes, he had argued against the production of the ikat trading cloth. But he had taken joy in questioning those first travelers, when the location of the village became known. He had advised the council what to trade for—medicine, laudanum, utensils, books, all of which he had used and enjoyed. Yet he could remember seven separate times when the master had told him to value self-containment above all.

And on that other night of meditation, when he had seen the moth drown in the bowl and his ability to concentrate had reached a keenness it had never approached since—on that same night he had taken the copper medallion from his desk at Camran Head. The guard he'd hoped to bribe had been asleep, yet even so, he had slipped the coin into his pocket instead of throwing it away. He had kept it in the bottom of his pocket, even though he knew how dangerous it was. Who knew better? A dozen times he had chastised the owners of similar medallions—he knew what it had come to mean. Yet he had given it to Cassia to play with. He had threaded it upon a string, so that she could wear it round her neck.

With the pads of his fingers, he tapped himself three times upon his high, flat forehead. Aloud, he repeated a quotation of the master's: "'When it is no longer possible to live correctly, then it is time to think of further options.'"

That night he was waiting for the moon, which was rising in those latitudes for the first time since the month that Cassia and Rael were born. A silver glow was shining to the east. The clouds were full of light and darkness, and they were combed in strips across the sky. Sarnath imagined the clear pure airless void above them, where perhaps the soul mounted after death. Then the moon rose out of a low bank of clouds.

Once, when he was a child, he had sat out with the master underneath the peepul tree, one night when the moon was visible from earth. Then the master had told him of the Starbridge myth, of how the souls of men and women had descended from the moon, had been reborn on earth. And after death, perhaps, they might reascend, either to their lunar paradise, or else farther still to planets less hospitable even than this one.

When he was a child, the moon had been remote. The master, raising his hand toward it, had been able to occlude it with his thumb. Then, the legend had seemed ludicrous to him, and he had not understood how something so absurd could have enslaved whole generations. Now he could understand it better, now that the moon was truly Paradise again, fully one quarter larger even than the last time he had seen it, when Cassia and Rael were born. Now it rose out of the clouds, luminescent, pale, wonderful, the bright sister of the dark and troubled earth, and on its sweet, miraculous surface he could see contours that he could imagine might be mountains, ranges of mountains, shores of glistening seas. And if he looked closer he could see patches of light and darkness, a rolling stippled plain, and on the verge of it what looked like the refractions from a million mirrored roofs— perhaps a town.

He sat staring till the clouds came in again. And when Paradise was covered up he rose to go, pulling himself slowly to his feet, for his knees and back were aching. He put his hand out to the tree trunk for support. Erect, he stood rubbing the bark fondly, sadly, giving a loose strip of it a final farewell tug, and then bringing his fingers to his nose to smell them. Then he was off along the path, climbing through the almond trees up toward the village, his head bent low.

On the way, he passed the new logging camp, and the boundaries of the new plantation. The lights from several long barracks glimmered through the trees. Inside: new men from Cochinoor; he could hear their voices. Underfoot, moonlight glinted on a litter of tin cans. He stepped around them delicately and then stepped over the bridge; there he felt better. And as he came up through the houses of the village, people greeted him, for many were sitting out on their verandas, where they had been watching for the moon. Their soft voices, their soft gestures followed him as he climbed the main street, up to the house of elders, where a light was burning. He put his hand out to the railing at the bottom of the steps, and then gathering his forces, he mounted quietly, allowing not a single creak to escape out of the split bamboo. And when he reached the porch, he stood still next to the bamboo post.

As luck would have it, the screen was drawn along his side, shielding him from the council chamber. He could see the light shining through the carved palm slats. The council was in session. Sarnath could see a row of four black, bulging shadows, projected along the bottom of the screen.

He could hear the drone of voices from within. Or rather one single voice, mellifluous and soft. Sarnath listened with appreciation to the sound, not bothering to wonder if he could distinguish words. That wasn't the important part. The important part was just to look, to understand, to see her once; and so, after standing still for several minutes, he moved forward noiselessly across the porch, until he stood behind the screen.

Just below eye level, a tracery of geometric patterns was cut into the slats. Sarnath bent down carefully, applied his eye to a triangular hole.

They had placed a lantern in the middle of the floor. On the nearer side, the four elders sat upon a mat, and Sarnath could see the outline of their backs, and see the light reflected off their polished heads. Beyond them on the other side, next to the master's statue with its garland of fresh flowers, Cathartes sat upon a bamboo armchair. He had had it constructed in the village for his use. Occasional pain in his lower vertebrae made it impossible to sit upon the floor.

His knees were splayed apart. The light was on his face. His mouth was open; he was smiling. He wore a milk-colored shirt, brown trousers and high boots, and he was holding in his hand next to his ear, pinched between his thumb and finger, Cassia's lucky coin.

A bug had settled on his shoulder near his neck. He made

a small spasmodic motion, and it walked a few inches down his arm.

Only Sarnath had not been required at this gathering. The three members of the agronomic team were there, sitting near Cathartes on the floor, whispering among themselves. And the young student was there also, the syncretist, the evolutionist. Watching him, Mr. Sarnath felt a mix of pity and revulsion which was like his feeling for himself, for it was as if the two of them had conspired to bring the others to this place, conspired and then regretted it, for the student's face was pale and unwholesome. Doubtless he knew, as Sarnath did, that what was happening was in a larger sense inevitable and their stupidity had not caused it, nor could their cleverness have avoided it. If so, he took, as Sarnath also took, no consolation in the fact.

Honest Toil was there, sitting with a simple smile upon his face. Yet he was moving his lips a little as he listened to Cathartes, perhaps repeating certain phrases. Perhaps he was happy about two good things—he was not blamed for the bullock's death, and Rael had run away.

Only Cassia was to blame, thought Sarnath: Cassia and himself. Though they would all be punished for it, only Cassia was to blame—Sarnath had looked at everyone except for her, studied all of them in turn, as if trying to make a context for her in his mind, as if trying also to prolong the moment when he still had not yet seen her for the last time. But then he moved his eye into the middle of the triangular hole, and she was there, seated on a woven mat next to Cathartes's hand.

Her legs were bent beneath her and her knees were pressed together. The weight of her body was supported on her left arm, while her right arm lay across her lap. She had been looking at the floor but now she raised her head. Her hair fell away from her face, revealing an expression that was full of . . . something: pride, contempt, fury, sorrow—what was it? Human beings were so hard to read, their crowded faces.

And at first he didn't know whether it was just by chance, but she was staring at him, focusing her eyes upon that little hole, though surely he could not be seen. He flinched and pulled away. But then he bent back down again and took a long look, studied her for a long moment. Soon she turned her head. But she had splayed the fingers of her right hand in her lap; now she raised them toward him, and they were trembling a little.

Paradise had risen through the clouds now, and was shining at the apex of the sky. Or it was as if the roiling clouds had been vanquished by its power, and had been pushed back from around it in a perfect circle, whose edges were still touched with light. Mr. Sarnath felt the pressure of it on his head as he came up the path toward his cabin at the top of the hill. Out of breath, he rested by the banyan tree. And then he moved forward into the clearing, the moonlight like a hand on his bald head, pushing him down into the earth, for his pace was faltering and old as he crept forward toward his house and shambled up the steps onto his porch. There again he waited until his eyes got used to the new darkness, then he moved across the threshold into his small room and sat down on his cushion near the fireplace. The light made bulky silver boxes on the floor, protruding from the doorway and the single window.

He sat there for perhaps an hour, contemplating each detail of the little room. He sat until he could read the titles of the books above his bed, see the pattern of the weave of the dry matting on the wall. Then he got up, his knees whispering and complaining, and gathered six or seven of the books, and tore down several strips of the dry palm. He arranged the books and matting on the hearth, and then, turning again, uncorked a bottle of imported fuel water and drenched the pile he had made. The water puddled between the hearthstones; sitting down again upon his cushion Mr. Sarnath pulled two of these stones aside, so that the liquid spread across the floor, until it was absorbed into the dry bamboo.

Then he sat still again, breathing the aroma of the water fumes. They attacked his nose and made him feel light-headed, and he breathed deeply until he felt habituated, and the effect of the fumes had subsided. Then he took up the box of matches from its place by the hearth, and with careful, studied gestures he removed one matchstick. He struck it; it flared up, burning fiercely in the saturated air. The flame illuminated the whole room, and it was roaring softly in his ears, and by its light he could see a small fragment of charred paper, which had been uncovered when he moved the rocks. It was a part of his translation from the Song of Angkhdt, which Cassia had burned there months before, and by the light of the match, in the moment before he dropped it on the hearth, he could read a few charred words:

It is our ability to deceive, which makes us men.

That same night, Rael sat by the silver pool. He stretched his feet out in the shallow water. His foot was sore. He had bruised it on his run through the forest, away from the village, away from the hurt beast.

He was sitting on an outcropping of brick, soaking his legs in the water, letting the mud soak away, and it wasn't until almost midnight that he raised his head. Around him, the water seemed to glow. The moon had risen up above the clouds, and he could see it groping through the forest canopy until a single finger of it stretched down through the leaves into his crevice in the jungle, stroking the rim of the pool near where he sat, rendering the water suddenly opaque, shining like a coin.

Toward midnight also a pale scum of foam rose to the surface of the water. When Rael finally raised his head, it was to see the hypnogogic ape standing erect upon the opposite beach.

For the first time, he could see it clearly. Or rather, its face was still in shadow, but the moon had laid its hand upon the creature's head and neck, giving an illusion of bright hair.

The ape stood about four feet tall. It bore no trace upon its body of their previous struggle. Unlike that time also it seemed naked, devoid of hair below its shoulders; the moonlight fell across its wide hips, its flat sunken dugs. In the crook of its small arm the shadow had accumulated, but it was holding something there, a tiny precious bundle, perhaps a child.

FLIGHT | 6

In summertime, the woods stretch north and west into the mountains, twelve hundred miles from the sea. They are the home of hairless foxes, capybara, and a hundred thousand kinds of birds. They are the home of ground sloths, lizards, gibbons, as well as larger and less manageable beasts: leopards, anacondas, tapirs, men.

In summer of the year 00016, the woods provided shelter for all the refugees who had ever fled or been expelled from Charn. A dozen cults and sects persisted in small, secret, isolated, ingrown groups. Cadres of the Desecration League were there, still mouthing the precepts of their martyred speaker. Adventists were there, inhabiting the sparser, drier uplands near Mt. Bromo, calculating on the bark of trees the date and hour of God's thunderbolt, arguing and struggling over their results. Rebel Angels were there, as well as many subsects of the Cult of Loving Kindness. In an area of deep ravines and shallow limestone caves, doddering Starbridge priests still administered the sacrament to furtive congregations of the faithful, and offered prayers to Angkhdt, the god of love. And in the deepest fastness of the forest, scattered families of antinomials wandered north into the hills, hunting tigers, eating meat.

During the sixteenth phase of summer, 00016, there was new pressure on all these groups, as the University of Charn mounted new gigantic projects in all sectors of the forest. This process was accelerated by the completion, with the help of foreign capital, of the new system of trains and roads, which opened up much of the area as if for the first time. By September of the sixteenth phase, the school of forestry had inaugurated twelve new "campuses" in various locations, the largest of which employed a population of twenty thousand laborers. They lived in barracks built of black mahogany, and they had already cleared a tract of hardwood seventy miles by twenty-five, from Kivu to Mt. May. There Professor Marchpane, acting in collaboration with the school of mines, had reopened the glass factory at Crystal Lip, and had rebuilt the old blast furnaces at Carbontown.

Closer in around the city, some of the student food cooperatives covered as many as one hundred thousand acres. Every week the Board of Overseers issued new statistics to the team leaders, along with new and dismal charts and graphs. Always there were fierce debates over their accuracy, but in those days it was possible to measure that the productivity of the soil was already past its peak, that the earth had made its turn, that the climate was already changing by infinitesimal degrees, while at the same time the population multiplied unchecked. And since the new imported swath machines, the threshers, and the twenty-four-man combines all had to be paid for in hard currency, or else in millet, rice, and maize, the storage silos in the city were barely one-third full. Though almost thirty thousand days remained until the first frost, still the work was behind schedule.

*　*　*

But in those days, fragments of the forest still remained untouched, beyond the village in the trees. The back side of Mr. Sarnath's hill descended steeply through black undergrowth and the coarse black trickling rocks—a path known only to Rael and to one pregnant tapir, which he had seen climb down that way.

Late at night, after the fire at Mr. Sarnath's cabin was almost out, Cassia had crept from her bedroom and crept up the hill. There was no one to watch her. Cathartes's inquest had broken up in confusion at the first alarm. Now a guard was posted in the clearing, one of the three agronomists, but he was already asleep, wrapped in a cocoon of mosquito cloth. So she had stayed on the fringes near the trees, sitting with her arms around her shins in the sharp grass, watching the red embers glimmer out one by one, watching the white muffled shape of the agronomist, waiting for her brother's whistle: the three notes of the curlew.

And when it came, finally, it was in the blackest part of the black night, when her eyes were so weak he had to hold her by the hand and guide her back into the trees. The sky was overcast; the moon was hidden, and Cassia's own dark tangled thoughts were taken over by the forest. She was putting out her hand to take hold of a root and she was slipping down along the steep wet muddy track, and she was aware of nothing but the slow exertions of her body. She was thinking nothing but bare simple thoughts from which the covering of what was past, the covering of what might be to come had both been stripped away. Only she was holding her brother by the hand, letting him support her weight, letting him think and see and feel for her, closing down her circle of sensation until the only things that penetrated it were sudden roots and branches, sudden stones. Once she was aware that they were walking through a stream.

They rested and went on, rested again. Inside of her there was an ember of red fire, a hot red burning place, but it was suffocated by the darkness. And when she sat to rest, she curled herself around it, turning her attention inward until her body had become an inmost layer of darkness. Only she was aware of small sensations: a drop of sweat along her ribs, the ache of some cut on her big toe—a small throb, but it hurt when she moved it, and when she tried to move her mind it felt the same. It was by keeping her thoughts motionless that she could tolerate them. And in the meantime her body had become part of the darkness, and the darkness was clenched around that coal of fire like some suffocating hand, hurting itself, allowing neither light nor heat nor memory to escape.

They rested and went on, rested and went on. Once Rael carried her for a few steps across the channel of a swamp— she turned her face into his neck and smelled his skin, and the odor was mixing with the slow miasma from the mud. She could feel the vapors beading in her hair. And she was aware also of the sulphur smell of phosphorescence, and when she turned her head she could see it flickering and scattering in the grass, a weak white flame that burnt itself out as soon as it was lit. Rael was standing up to his shins in the black swamp. He had lifted her into his arms and she could feel his arms begin to slip.

Twenty feet away, a broken concrete bank protruded down into the water. It was overgrown with moss, crumbling with age, a broken boatslip from another season. From the top of it a chimera stood looking down on them, a jungle cat almost three feet long. Phosphorescence played along its flanks. Lit by that ghostly radiance, it seemed to rise up from the darkness, a sentinel upon the threshold of another life. Later she would look back to that vision as the start of a long journey back through time, for it combined with the shock of the night to open up a part of her that could never be resealed. Later she was to enter into it as if into the storage chambers of a long-dead soul, peering at portraits, sorting through the alien memories. And the first memory was the flash of lightning, and a golden cat.

Behind them, all around them, the world was covered up in darkness. Rael, with his cleaner eyes, could see much more—the single horizontal stripe upon the brow of the chimera, the cage of rotting reinforcement rods upon the concrete pedestal. Above his head rose up a bloatwood tree with its suspended veil of moss. On the bank—the white walls of a ruined bungalow, where he had hoped to stay for a few hours.

Something was splashing in the water to his left.

He could feel his sister's body sag, her muscles loosen. Her cheek was on his shoulder. He looked down to find his footing, and when he looked up the cat was gone.

He crossed over to the bank and laid Cassia down in the high grass. A mosquito, disturbed by the pressure of her body, rose up whining but he batted it away. Cassia appeared to be sleeping; he shook her shoulder and she responded groggily. So he watched her for a moment and then gathered her again into his arms, and lifted her up into the bungalow.

Inside there was a raised platform built of cinder blocks. On an earlier occasion he had cleared away a pile of fallen plaster and had made a bed of bamboo leaves and branches. He had slept there many times since he had first discovered it by chance, when he was still a child.

Around the bungalow stood others farther back, away from the water. This was the only one that had retained its roof of corrugated tin. The forest had taken back the rest, and there persisted only an odd pattern of broken walls, covering several acres. It was all that remained of the infamous slave-labor camp of Seven Saints, which had chewed up lives by the thousand at the time of the last autumn harvests, when all that land was under cultivation. The swamp which Rael and Cassia had crossed was all that still remained of Sorrow Lake, whose waters in the old days had been fouled and silted with crushed bones. The gigantic holding pens upon the far shore had disappeared; conditions there had been so miserable that even the bishop had come to hear of them, the twenty-ninth bishop of Charn. He had ordered the camp closed, surprising many, for he himself was a hard man.

Rael sat by Cassia with his hand upon her arm. Her breath had settled down. The platform of cinder blocks had once supported the desk of Father Labial Starbridge, the last commander of the camp. He had shot himself where she now slept.

She was dreaming. But in the dream she imagined herself awake, reliving the events of the past night. And because it was a dream she felt no emotion—no emotion when from the porch of the council house she saw a fire glowing in the belly of the clouds above Mr. Sarnath's hill. She felt no emotion, and her heart wasn't hammering and her breath wasn't choking her, and she couldn't hear the cries of the men around her, the cries of people in the village. All was silent.

And then the dream transported her up to the hilltop, and it was as if she herself were standing in the clearing on the hilltop when the flames went up. Suddenly all sensation came back to her, and in her dream she could smell the smoke and hear the crackle of the flames. Above her the smoke spread like a black veil, covering the moonlight, while flecks of burning ash made constellations of new stars.

And there were others, also, near her in her dream, so that she didn't have to look into the burning building, and didn't have to imagine a dark, seated shadow there. But when she turned around, she could see the light on the men's faces as they spread out to watch the cabin burn. She admired their different expressions: Cathartes red with anger, pacing back and forth. The student with his pimpled, livid cheeks, the fire burning in the lenses of his spectacles. Then she was moving through the council of elders, and Canan Bey was grimacing; his lips formed silent words. And Palam Bey was shielding his eyes, and Langur Bey was crying out, his face transfigured, wet with tears. Mayadonna Bey had fallen to the ground.

She turned back toward the fire. And in her dream she understood that she had reached the dividing point. Rael, sitting beside her as she slept, understood it too. Before she had been turning and twitching in her sleep. But now she fell back into another layer of slumber, and the dream was using memories that were no longer her own. The fire was still burning, but now it was burning in the middle of a walled enclosure, and she was watching it from a high window. From the window she could see also towers and domes and battlements above the streets of a strange city, and a fire burning under the starless, moonless, black night sky. The courtyard below her was full of strangers in red robes, and they were laughing, crying, shouting with amazement at the sight of a tree growing up out of the flames, taking shape as they watched, an enormous chestnut tree with silver blossoms and red fruit, spreading its limbs out over the courtyard. And Cassia understood also that this tree was hers, that it was responding to her power as she stood watching at her prison window. Rael was there also, and he was sitting near her with the golden cat upon his lap, stroking it along its spine again, again, again, and he was not her brother in that world.

When she woke up he was gone. But he had left a rusted hubcap on the platform where she slept, filled with clean water. Her head was singing, her face felt puffy, stung. She could see the morning through a fissure in the wall, and it was saturated, overcast.

For a moment all the fragments of her dream were plain to her, and all the fragments of the night before uncovered, bare. But then the conscious day was seeping into her again, covering them up. She lay on her side, watching some termites struggle with some eggs among the plaster shards. She watched them. Sarnath had often told her to let the present moment fill her like a cup.

Outside, the sun hung low over the trees. A fallen log protruded from the bank into the swamp, and it defined an eddy that was cleaner than the rest, the water black instead of green. She stripped off her dress and soaked it in the water, and balancing upon the log she washed her head, her armpits, and her crotch. Then she pulled on the dress again, grateful for the slap of the wet cloth against her skin. She ran her fingers through her thick wet hair.

Then in a little while she heard her brother's whistle, coming from the trees beyond the bungalow. He was smiling when he appeared, and he was holding in his hands a rolled-up blanket, which he had secreted in a hollow tree upon some earlier occasion. Bees were buzzing lazily around his head.

Also he was carrying a single, massive durian. And his pockets were full of a small fruit, which Mr. Sarnath, long before, had shown them how to eat. The hide covered a poisonous wet pulp, which covered in its turn a nut just barely edible, for it was mottled, sour, dry. Nevertheless, with water and wild durian they made a kind of breakfast, sitting on the concrete bank beside the log. Inside the blanket Rael had stored a sharpened metal spike, and with it he managed to puncture the durian's armored plates, levering them back to reveal the pungent fruit, so nauseating, yet so sweet. He reached in his hand and pulled out a slick gobbet of the flesh; it was sliding down between his fingers, and she was sucking it from off his fingers until Rael started to laugh. He rolled onto his back. He rubbed his sticky fingers on his stomach and then fell asleep for a half hour or so. It wasn't until midmorning that they were ready to depart.

But then he led them swiftly, following a path he had discovered months before, part of the old trail of tears at Seven Saints, up through the rotted concrete bunkers, climbing up away from the old lake, up to the low place in a ring of hills, where they rested underneath the portals of a church.

Wide stone steps led to a brass door. Rael had no interest in the place. But Cassia was listening to an echo in her mind; she brought him up the steps. "I want to see," she told him, and he shook his head. But he was smiling, unresisting, his gut still full of fruit; she brought him to the door.

Its surface, originally carved with scenes from the life of Beloved Angkhdt, had been broken with a hammer and defaced with blue spray polymer—slogans from the revolution now illegible with age. The door was two feet thick. The staples which held it to its stone frame had subsided, yet there remained a crack. Cassia squeezed through it into the nave of the church, while Rael waited outside.

It was a narrow, roofless building. Again, the carvings which once decorated it had all been smashed, except for one single frieze above the level of the windows, which was still partly intact. A procession of stone letters made the circuit of the walls, verses, Cassia knew, from the same document that Mr. Sarnath had translated. "Fill me with your sperm," it said, but most of the rest was hidden by the leaves of saplings which had grown up through the flagstones. They were smaller and more stunted than the trees outside, as if they still felt the effects of an old power. At the transept of the church there was still an open place around the pedestal where the statue of Beloved Angkhdt had stood.

The pedestal was split in half. Of the statue, nothing remained. Yet Cassia, walking through the piles of broken masonry remembering her dream, found her mind possessed by an image of how it might have been, scowling down at her with its dog's head, and its brass penis pointed toward the sky.

That was on the first day. It wasn't until the fourth day after the fire that they passed outside the limit of Rael's knowledge. They had been climbing steadily while the land changed around them. At night the wind was cool, the air was dry, and on the fourth day they came into a forest of rhododendron, all in bloom. They walked through glades of white and pinkish flowers, following a path that was well maintained, though they saw no one.

During this time, also, the way they knew each other underwent a change, and the long silences between them became galling, frustrating to each of them, for different reasons. When they were children, they had lived together almost without speaking, and it had always been comfortable to them, during the time that they were traveling with Mr. Sarnath, and then later in the village in the trees. This was partly because Rael had learned to talk so late, long after they had come to know each other well, partly also because among the Treganu there had been no competition for their sympathy. It had always seemed to Cassia that they shared a closeness that was subtle, fluid, fully formed, and yet separate from language. In fanciful and in exasperated moments it seemed to her that they were part of each other in some new organic way, that together they formed one organism, she the mental, conscious part, he the physical, unconscious. It was not that they always understood each other, still less that they always agreed. Two halves of the same mind, she thought, may be hidden from each other even though they touch at every point.

The village had been an insulating, alien cocoon for them, providing an outside pressure that had kept them close. Mr. Sarnath too had formed a link between them. But in the days following their flight, it became clear to Cassia that they needed some new thing to replace that link, that pressure, which was now dispersed. Now also, for almost the first time, they had plans and subjects to discuss. Now especially because after the fourth day Rael could no longer guide them—the rhododendron forest was as strange to him as it was to her.

She thought it was not possible for them to wander on forever, eating wild fruit. Yet always it was difficult to talk to him precisely, and difficult to understand him when he talked. Pronouns for him were interchangeable; the distinctions between "I" and "she" and "you" were always jumbled in his mind. Adjectives and adverbs he disdained, or else he had incorporated them into his small store of nouns—he would talk about "a bitter," for example, or "a quick." Verbs made up the bulk of his vocabulary and included many he'd invented, or adopted from other parts of speech. Yet he used them in peculiar ways. To imply another tense beside the present, he would put a verb into the negative—"not eat," for example, could mean "will eat," "want to eat," or "ate." It was as if everything that was not actually happening was equally unreal.

"Not burn is a Sarnath not not not dead burn black dead," he once asked her. There were no interrogatives in his language.

Often, during those first few days, Cassia would ask herself whether he even remembered the village, remembered Mr. Sarnath. For there was nothing in the way he behaved to suggest he had regrets, or that he found anything unusual with their present way of life. Only he was surly and distracted, and she guessed it was because he was feeling something of what she was feeling. It was not jealousy alone that had made him kill the bullock. But he too had sensed that their exclusive closeness had depended on their isolation, and that their isolation was now coming to an end.

On the fourth night, miserably hungry, they stayed in an abandoned building near a stream. Perhaps a granary or a garage in the old days, it was a vast, dark, airless place, built of naked cinder blocks, and unrelieved by any windows. They slept on a floor of blank concrete, wrapped in the old blanket that Rael had taken from the hollow tree. Cassia had been afraid that animals might come—perhaps a tapir or a waterlion—she pulled close to Rael during the night. She was lonely, hungry, and more than ever she hated the way he turned his back and turned his head and stretched down flat upon his stomach. Yet that was his way; terrified and lonely, she put her head upon his shoulder, and all night she dreamt of men with lion faces, tapir faces—a variation on erotic dreams that she had had since childhood—until she shuddered and woke up.

Then for an instant she was still more terrified. Her hands ranged over her body, and she could smell her own sweat and her own moisture—her breasts ached, and for an awful moment she had no memory of where she was. She thought perhaps she was safe in her dormitory, yet why was she sleeping on the floor? And who was that beside her? Then the whole sickening finality of Mr. Sarnath's death came back to her, the insecurity of the past days, and she put her hand out to Rael's shoulder for comfort. But it was too much to ask, though he was not asleep. Those nights he never seemed to sleep, and she could feel his wakefulness and feel the tension in his body, and feel the way he drew away from her.

Always they had slept apart in the village, in different houses. But often when they were together she could feel his physical excitement. When she reached the age when she was curious about such things, and the first of her dreams started to bother her, she would embrace him sometimes, and she would wonder why he'd always pull away. In part she understood his reticence; in part she felt it too. They had needed nothing in the village in the trees. But now when she lay sweating in the night—alone with her fears, alone with dreams that left her empty and abused—she felt he owed her something, some small comfort or at least some part of his self-possession. She had lost everything, and she resented knowing that he held something back. She wanted something real, to give something and receive something in return that would replace their inadequate attempts at communication, would replace the lost enclosure of the village. And she was half asleep.

She shook his shoulder. "Rael," she whispered. "Rael." He didn't move, but she could feel the tension in his flesh. She raised her head, and rubbed her fingers down the muscles of his back, pushing along the groove of his spine until she reached his tailbone underneath the drawstring of his pants. She stroked his tailbone for a long time, and yet he didn't move. Then she undid the bodice of her dress and rubbed her naked breasts along his back—he too was sweating, and the night was hot, and there was no air in that windowless black building by the stream. The blanket was already damp with their sweat; earlier in the night they had been bothered by insects, but now she stripped it off. And with her left hand she was rubbing his tailbone, and working the drawstring of his pants loose with her wrist.

She raised her head. She could hear the muffled roaring of the stream, ominous to her, because of all the subtle stirrings of the animals that could be hidden by the sound; her head was roaring also. She bent down to kiss Rael on the shoulder. Still he hadn't moved. He hadn't turned his head. But now he shifted his legs slightly, and she slid her hand over his tailbone. She slid her hand underneath him to hold his stiff unwieldy sex. She rubbed her breasts along his back. She squeezed with all her strength, showing no mercy until finally he yielded and turned over. Then she moved over his body. She put her hands upon his shoulders, sliding down on him, possessing him, grunting in pain at first, because he was bigger than the dreams that had prepared his way.

But she had not even finished that first grunting descent when she regretted it. The pain seemed to clear her head. She supported herself upright, her elbows locked, her hands splayed on his chest, her knees suffering on the bare concrete on either side of his hips. Her head fell forward and her hair tumbled in her face; still, except to turn over, he had not moved and she sat there for a long moment, feeling not much of anything where he had penetrated her, feeling also with a kind of horror the muscles of his arms and neck and chest start to relax, to gather strength.

His legs stirred under her legs. Almost she wanted to jump up away from him, so insecure she felt, so meager in her control. Then it was too late, and he had reached up to touch her breasts with his heavy hands, gently, softly, but she felt as if he'd broken the breath out of her. Gasping, she fell down onto his chest. His arms closed around her and she felt his body come alive. She couldn't see his face.

In time, he turned her over onto her back, so that he lay above her. In time also, he experimented in different ways, though she was scarcely aware of it. It was as if she had retreated deep inside herself, and even her sensations had pulled back from the surface of her skin. Her thoughts chased each other in a tumbled mental landscape, appearing and reappearing, sometimes dim, sometimes with fleeting starkness, like figures in a fog. Yet all the time, and as it seemed, far away, she was conscious of the movement of her body, conscious of Rael, conscious of the odor of his skin, his intermittent weight, even her own groaning, her own muted feelings of pleasure and pain, all against the background of a slow, rhythmic grinding, an unstoppable and distant engine. Because he rested for a while, and then entered her again, and again in the early morning when the first haze of light was gathering by the ruptured metal door.

In the morning he rolled away from her onto his back, his head turned away. She lay stupefied for a time, "Rael?" she said. And he answered nothing, even though she knew he was awake; she could feel the presence of his brooding consciousness beside her. Quietly she lay, listening to him breathe, until she could no longer tolerate the thought that his feelings might be as ambiguous, as resentful as her own. Then she stumbled to her feet.

Outside, as it happened, the morning was fresh and clear. A breeze had come up during the night. The sun was visible through the treetops. Because of their change in altitude, it seemed softer than she was used to, and the quality of light was different too. A bird sang as she stumbled to the stream, down through a copse of mimosa trees. The sound she had heard during the night was from a waterfall, a narrow chute of water perhaps ten feet high, splattering into a shallow pool.

"Look around you," the master had often said, and Mr. Sarnath often had repeated. Cassia was close to tears, yet still she took a breath. She stood on the bank of the pool and put her hand out to a flowered twig. She stripped off her dress and threw it on the bank, and then she stepped down into the cold water.

The stones on the bottom of the pool were sharp, and she moved carefully across them, until the water was around her shins. Dark, syrupy, fragrant water trickled down over a lip of moss and she stood underneath it, rinsing her hair, washing her arms and legs. Then, sputtering, she stepped away from it and, bending down, examined the insides of her thighs, combed her fingers through her pubic hair, poked gingerly at the lips of her vagina, for all that area felt bruised. As she did so, she heard a woman's voice, a snort of laughter from the shore.

"You've got a pretty one, don't you? I was listening to it all night, and it was music to my ears. Oh, yes, I remember that old music, though it's been too long."

BROTHER
LONGO

7

Some of this vocabulary was strange to Cassia. But she understood the gist. She stood with one hand on her genitals and she crossed her other arm over her breasts, provoking more laughter from the woman on the bank.

She was small, wrinkled, and extremely thin, an albino specimen of a dark-skinned race, perhaps. She was sitting on some rocks under a mimosa bush, on the opposite side of the pool. Her pose suggested she'd been there a long while, though in fact the rocks had been unoccupied when Cassia had first come. Her skin was mottled, orange-colored mixed with white, her hair orange too, plaited in coarse, irregular braids which stuck out all over her head. She was not old; her teeth, few and widely spaced, were white and strong.

She wore a ragged but capacious red smock, unbuttoned down her chest, so that Cassia could see her wrinkled stomach and her ribs. Her eyes were bright and penetrating and blue.

Cassia had been so shocked to see her that she took all

this in, staring evenly, her hand clasped over her sex. Cassia's upbringing among the Treganu had been so sheltered that her instinct for modesty was not well developed. The posture was a reflex, and since it only seemed to invite ridicule, she soon abandoned it. Instead she turned her back. Splashing clumsily over the sharp rocks, she retrieved her dress and slipped it on.

"Ooh, and a pretty tail too! Lift it up and let me see what's underneath. Sore this morning, aren't you? I can see from here!"

Cassia was not modest. But she felt vulnerable as she splashed toward shore. Something in the events of the past night had scraped the inside of her heart, and it required the words of this strange, ugly woman to make her understand how raw she felt. And even though the morning was still fresh, and a red-throated, long-beaked bird still perched upon a twig above her head, Cassia broke into tears as she clambered from the pool and clambered up the bank.

But because she could hear the woman stir behind her, and because her cheeks were stinging and her eyes were full of tears, she mistook the way back to the garage, though it was only a few yards. Its roof was hidden in the trees. Confused, she continued past it, knowing she had gone too far, and yet not wanting to retrace her steps. She could hear the woman coming up behind her, scrabbling through the brush. And she had no wish to see Rael either at that moment; she just wanted to be alone among the rhododendrons and the frangipani bushes, someplace quiet where she could clean her face and sit down and recite a few choice precepts of the master. "Wanting is the thief of love," perhaps.

Instead she stumbled up into a clearing near the path. There, a woman and two men sat by a fire. Cassia had smelled the smoke as she came up the last few feet, and heard also the sound of the guitar that one man was strumming. And yet the smell, the sound, had not suggested any thoughts to her; she smashed through the leaves into the clearing, and she was shocked to find it occupied.

But because emotion had so hampered her capacity for judgment, again, as they had been by the pool, her perceptions were unnaturally clear, unnaturally complete. It was as if her usual scrim of thinking and assessment had been torn— the drab, semitransparent curtain that is caught between ourselves and the bright world, and for a moment she was able to step through the rent. She looked around. Two men and a woman. She saw, before the note of the guitar had died away, the circle of bare earth ringed with smoldering logs to keep the bugs away. And in the middle a wide mat of palm next to the smoky fire, supporting several bundles of old rags and a row of playing cards. On the far side of the fire, stirring a tin bucket, crouched a squat muscular young woman with a wide face and enormous naked breasts, also big buttocks that were covered with black bark cloth from the pontu tree. Her skin glistened as if it had been oiled, and she was pregnant.

She was pouring a cup of broth into the bucket and stirring manioc greens with a charred stick. A man stood next to her, dressed in a long yellow robe that was embroidered with white thread. His hair was knotted at the back of his neck. Each of his cheeks was decorated with a spiral of white paint. He held a small mirror in the palm of his left hand, and at the moment when Cassia burst through into the clearing, he was retouching one of them with a sharp splinter of wood.

And finally the guitarist, propped up against a Y-shaped stump. He had a gigantic chest, gigantic arms and shoulders, and his hands were callused, massive. The neck of the guitar was wide, the strings were far apart, so that he could curl his mighty fingers onto them.

By contrast, his legs were thin as reeds. He sat cross-legged, his ankles locked above his knees.

In that moment of clarity, all was still. The charred stick

was quiet in the pot. The splinter of wood was immobile in the air. The note of the guitar, hovering above them, seemed to emphasize, rather than diminish, Cassia's perception of silence. But then the strange, chaotic world rushed in again; Cassia could hear the orange woman in the red smock crashing up behind her, and she half turned. A bird was in the tree above her head, a big, featherless, carrion bird, stretching its leather wings.

The cripple laid his instrument aside. Cassia's tears were drying on her cheeks, and even though the woman in the red smock now stood behind her at the clearing's edge, she couldn't give her more than part of her attention. This was because the pregnant woman by the fire had taken from a pouch at her waist six silver pods—hot sweet peppers which were Cassia's favorite food in all the world. In four days she had eaten nothing but cold nuts and a few durian, and the smell of the hot food was making her weak, was filling her mouth with a sweet liquid, so that she wasn't even aware of the woman coming up behind her until she smelled her breath. Cassia was hungry and she barely noticed even when the woman put her hand out to touch her.

"There, sister," she said. "I didn't mean to scare you. I've got a dirty mouth. Everyone tells me so, but I don't mean no harm."

She spoke the traders' lingua franca of the forest. Cassia moved forward out of reach, so that the woman's hand fell awkwardly on nothing. "I told her she's a pretty piece of tail," she explained to the assembled group. "Though naturally the worse for wear—wasn't I right?"

The pregnant woman grunted and then turned her head aside. The cripple was smiling; he had a fine strong face, with black brows and a short beard. The other man was holding one long-fingered hand out in fastidious disgust, which provoked more laughter from the woman in the red smock. "Don't worry about him," she said, as if to Cassia alone. "Or her either," she continued, nodding toward the fire. "She's as stupid as a lump. But the Prince told us to be kind to strangers, and besides, the food is hers."

If the pregnant woman heard this, she gave no sign. With careful fingers she stripped the silver peppers and dropped them into the pot. And all the while she was looking to the clearing's edge, where a stand of tall ferns filled up the space between the trees. Cassia could detect some movement there, and the heads of the ferns were twitching underneath the trees. Then closer, until the frontmost ferns were pushed aside, and two children trundled out. It was a little boy, carrying on his back his infant brother.

They were dark-skinned, like their mother. The younger child was naked, while the older one wore only a ripped T-shirt, which showed signs of having once been green. He had a fat little belly and a deeply serious face; he trudged along like an old man carrying a sack to market until he stood next to the fire. There he tried to loosen his brother's choke hold on his neck, without success until the woman intervened. The baby started squalling; she took him onto her capacious lap.

In the meantime, with her other hand, she had lifted the stick out of the pot. The cripple, moving adroitly on his knuckles, had picked a wooden bowl up off the mat. Holding it in his teeth, he swung himself over to the woman's other side. Balancing upon his withered knees, he tried to thrust the bowl into the pot of food. The woman poked her stick at him, and for a while she succeeded in keeping him away. But at a certain moment her attention was diverted by the baby on her lap; he was kicking at his mother's mountainous breasts, and the cripple, seizing the instant, raising himself up upon one hand, dug the bowl down into the hot manioc greens. Then he was away, avoiding once again the poking stick; with the bowl clamped in his teeth he swung himself over the bare ground toward Cassia until he was beneath her, balancing again upon his knees. Then with a smile upon his handsome face, he held the bowl up toward her.

* * *

The woman in the red smock was Mama Jobe, he explained. Efe was the cook. The man with the painted cheeks was Karan Mang.

The cripple spoke in a careful, cultured, city accent, lying on his back on the palm mat, staring up at the sky while Cassia sat by him and ate. For a little while she was so hungry she could think of nothing but the food, and then it was all gone. "Thank you," she said, wiping her mouth.

The baby was quiet now. The little boy stood by his mother, his hands clasped around a cup of greens. Karan Mang had retreated to the border of the trees, where he sat upon a fallen log. He had a metal basin between his feet, and he was washing his hands carefully, finger by finger. "He came last night," explained the cripple. "This is a resting place along the path. I don't think he'll stay with us. He's carrying a message from an important personage."

Cassia glanced at him, and she collected in return a brief disdainful look, a flutter of long eyelashes. She turned back to the cripple. "What's your name?" she asked.

He smiled. "At this moment I have none. 'Servant of God,' I call myself. But in two days' time my oath will be fulfilled. Then I will stand up, and pick up my old name again."

Mama Jobe flopped down on Cassia's other side, a radish root clutched in her hand. "All things are possible with God," she said, shaking her head.

"Or I will not," continued the cripple softly. "In any case, the oath will be fulfilled."

"What oath?" asked Cassia.

"He made an oath at the midsummer festival," said Mama Jobe. "Under risen Paradise. To sit that way, the way the Prince sat on his final ride."

The position of his withered legs—his knees turned out, his ankles crossed on top of them—had once been popular among mystics and teachers. Mr. Sarnath, when he meditated, had often sat in the same way, sometimes for half an hour at a time. "I was the strongest runner in my zone," the cripple said. "It was the gift I made to God."

He was lying on his back, his face turned to the sky. One hand was folded underneath his head; the other chafed the beads of an amber necklace, which hung down on his chest.

Mama Jobe had split the radish with her thumbnail. But she was looking anxiously toward Karan Mang, who was unwrapping a small package of silver foil. "Baklava," she muttered. "The Prince tells us to share everything we have."

"And to avoid covetousness," the cripple reminded her. "Remember when he was in prison, and he told the people not to envy him, for he would soon be dead."

They were both smiling, and Cassia smiled too. "Who are you talking about?" she asked politely. But Mama Jobe just stared at her, and the cripple raised his head up from the mat.

"Well, if you don't know, I'm not the one to tell you," said Mama Jobe after a pause. She had levered out the pink meat of the radish. Now she was scraping her thumbnail along the worthless husk, suddenly industrious, and she was avoiding Cassia's eyes.

But the cripple was looking at her calmly. "Where are you going, child?" he asked.

Putting one massive palm flat on the ground, he pushed himself upright, aided by a deft movement of his spine. Then he balanced himself on his frail hams and leaned forward toward her, his finger in the air. "Where are you traveling, along the path?" he asked.

"I don't know," said Cassia. "I was with Rael." Just saying his name brought back all the misery of the long night. Where was he now? She could not imagine he had stayed in the garage; she raised her head and looked around the clearing. Perhaps he was standing in the woods somewhere invisible. Perhaps he was standing in the rhododendron trees beyond the clearing's edge. He would not come to find her, not with these people here.

"I was following Rael," she said.

And in a little while, she went on. "They built a train from Cochinoor. The university reorganized our town."

Next to her on the palm mat lay a row of playing cards. She examined the one nearest her hand, a nine of stones, painted in bright colors. She put her hand out to touch it, aware also that the Servant of God was studying her too, just as intently. "Where are you traveling," he said again, "along this path?"

"This is the road to Brother Longo's house," added Karan Mang. "Brother Longo Starbridge."

He had finished his pastry, and now again was washing off his hands. He skimmed his fingers over the water in the basin. His voice was harsh and full of aspirated consonants. It did not suit his face, and Cassia found his accent difficult to understand. She had barely finished puzzling over the last words when Mama Jobe spat out a clot of insults and invective in some foreign language. Even when she relapsed into common speech, she was using words that Cassia didn't know. "Eunuch!" she said. "Stupid catamite!"

Not understanding, Cassia concentrated on the tone, which was composed in equal parts of anger and of fear. Unconcerned, Karan Mang had drawn a symbol with the heel of his slipper in the dirt, and then obliterated it by pouring out his basin over it. Now he sat polishing his fingernails, a prim expression on his mouth.

But the Servant of God sat next to her, studying her face. Cassia glanced at him nervously, then bit her lips. She was aware that he was still assessing her, and that his decision, when it came, would be final and irrevocable. "Let me see your hands," he said. She held them out. Supported by one massive forearm, he leaned toward her.

His own hand, as he raised it from the ground to enclose the two of hers, was the more remarkable—callused and strong, and covered with smudged lines of symbols in black ink, which ran from the base of his palm up to his fingertips.

They were meaningless to Cassia, yet seemed somehow portentous, especially when combined with the careful way he studied her own naked hands. Cassia also was aware that Mama Jobe was leaning in to look. Even Karan Mang seemed interested, though Efe, seated on a stump with one child between her knees, the other at her breast, had closed her eyes to blissful slits.

"Have you always had this mark?" asked the Servant of God. He was chafing the middle of her right palm between her finger and thumb.

In fact she had not seen it before. It was a rough, mottled octagon between her headline and her heartline, lighter than the ordinary color of her skin.

"I was born in December of the tenth phase," she said. "My father was named Sarnath."

Mama Jobe's gaze was sharp and piercing. The cripple didn't look up right away; he sat forward on his ruined legs, chafing the mark upon her hand. "That I doubt," he said, and when he raised his eyes they seemed unnaturally large, unnaturally liquid. "Where is the other one?" he said. "Is he also here, upon the path?"

She thought he meant Rael, perhaps. She looked around, trying to sense Rael's presence underneath the trees. There was a hibiscus bush not yet in bloom, a hundred yards beyond the cripple's shoulder. Perhaps he was there, waiting for her among the tight new buds. She shook her head.

The cripple chafed her hand. "These are the days of grace," he said. "With Paradise above us—until tomorrow night we can be free and open with each other. Nothing happens now by chance, and nothing now can harm us, till my oath is at an end. Will you come with us? Efe has brought food."

Distracted, Cassia shrugged her shoulders. Or perhaps Rael was there beyond the ferns, standing in the open, only motionless and silent, hidden in plain view. Often when they were children she had marveled at the way that he could disappear into a patch of woods, merging with the dappled shadows like a leopard or a faun.

She knew he would not show himself. Angry, frustrated, she forced herself to listen to the cripple's voice: "For these two days, until the festival, the path is free to all. Open to all. Tonight we sleep at Brother Longo's mission. Will you join us? I would like him to see what I have seen." Between his finger and his thumb, he squeezed the mark upon her hand.

While he was speaking, Efe had gotten to her feet, and she was breaking camp. She emptied the uneaten manioc onto a big waxy leaf, and with a piece of twine she made a package out of it. This she accomplished with the infant clasped to her hip, while the child took the bucket and trudged off with it. He returned a moment later dragging it along the ground; it was full of water, which his mother used to wash the bowls. That chore finished, she retreated to the far side of the clearing and, still in plain sight, squatted down upon the ground. The urine descended from her body in a noisy, smoking stream; it scented the air, and she was squatting down and holding the infant out in front of her at arm's length, and she was making faces as it clucked and fretted, its big head lolling in a circle. Then she moved a few steps away, and sitting down with her legs stretched out in front of her, she perched the infant upon her thighs and encouraged him also to relieve himself. After a few minutes she was rewarded with a few ambiguous drips, which fell down into the crack between her legs. In the meantime, the child had dragged out from the ferns a conical woven basket, almost as tall as he, with a tumpline around the open end. This he balanced against the Y-shaped stump and commenced to load with blankets and bundles; he would lift a bundle up above his chest to drop it over the basket's lip, and then he would climb up onto the stump to tamp it down with the charred stick.

In this way he loaded everything, except for the emptied

water bucket and a single blanket, which he kept for last. Then he sat down to wait for his mother, a dour expression on his tiny face. At the same time, Mama Jobe had gathered together her own bundle, and Karan Mang had already packed up and departed. His own equipment had fitted easily into a shoulder bag, and Cassia had watched with interest how he had folded together his imported mylar blanket and his sleeping pad; she had never seen such things. He had walked away into the trees without a word, without a backward glance, and all the while Cassia was sitting on the palm mat. And the Servant of God was sitting with her, studying her face, holding her hand.

That day, all day she was aware of him, although she never saw him. But sometimes she could sense him moving along one side of the trail, perhaps a hundred yards into the bush. Sometimes on the other side, sometimes behind them, and once they passed a place where the fallen blossoms made a pattern that she found significant. Once she raised her eyes to a tall tree, the crossing of two branches, and one of them was trembling in a way that seemed unnatural, as if Rael, perhaps, had just leapt down.

Sore and peevish, she walked slowly, carrying Servant of God's guitar and rolled-up mat. He swung along beside her on his heavy hands, balancing occasionally also on his knees. He rested often and she rested with him, until all the others had disappeared in front—Karen Mang, Mama Jobe, who was carrying with sudden poise her bundle on her head.

Finally even Efe and her children had disappeared. With a great deal of grunting and spitting she had loaded her basket onto her back, the conical end of it caught in the cleft where her spine met her buttocks, the tumpline round her brow. At the final instant she had sunk the pail into the top of her basket; wrapped in his blanket, the infant perched inside like a sailor at the masthead of a wide-bottomed boat, and he peered at Cassia over the edge of the pail while his mother labored underneath, his little face jerking up and down with every step she took. Just behind, his brother trudged along with his eyes upon the trail, similarly loaded with a fat small pack.

Eventually they labored out of sight among the trees. Eventually Cassia could no longer hear them, and she was left alone with the Servant of God. But only for an hour or so, because as the day wore on the path became more crowded, and they were often overtaken by other groups of pilgrims. From time to time, also, other smaller paths joined theirs, and at the junctions there were often resting places where the ground was beaten flat, and where families of pilgrims sat and talked. No one was in a hurry—these folk were in a holiday mood. They wore brightly colored clothes and chattered together in loud voices. And although among them there was a complicated mixture of races and languages, still they seemed to be in good humor, and they were smiling and greeting each other, and making conversations out of gestures and repeated phrases. In time this made Cassia restless, because everyone seemed to know Servant of God, and with enormous smiles they would stop him on the path; they would bend down to embrace him and kiss him on both cheeks, and talk to him in unknown languages, while all the time peering at her curiously. Especially on these occasions she would be aware of Rael watching her perhaps, and with hot cheeks she would stand restless in these little glades while Servant of God conversed with Rais and Gurungs and Tamangs—tall spindly folk from Banaree and short squat westerners—specimens, in fact, of all the races Cassia had ever seen when she was on the road with Mr. Sarnath. Despite her natural self-possession, she was awkward and unquiet, because she had never seen so many human beings all together since she was a little girl, and she was not used to their loud voices, their abrasive laughs, the way they never cared how close to you they stood. Awkward also because Servant of God would never introduce her or even look at her during these moments of greeting, though she imagined many of his words and gestures must refer to her; for this reason people glanced at her with smiles on their faces.

Often he would sit down to rest while he was speaking, and he would reach up to take her right hand in one of his, and he would caress her palm in a way that as time went on she felt to be more and more presumptuous. But to let go of him at such an instant would be to let him fall. So she resisted the impulse, and at the same time she reinforced her patience by imagining Rael's frustration and jealousy to see her standing in what surely would appear to him to be the center of attention, hand in hand with this strange cripple. How jealous he would be! How he would curse his timidity and whatever else it was that kept him lonely and apart—if he were watching her at all, she thought, and were not someplace miles away, running through the forest by himself.

In the afternoon she found herself moving in a long line of people. The path had widened by this time, and in places several travelers could walk abreast. From scattered snatches of conversation, Cassia understood that many had been on the path for weeks or even months, and in these especially she could feel an intense and growing excitement, above all in the children, who were everywhere. They formed the majority of every group—long-legged, wraithlike girls skipped by her, with shaved heads and luminous fair skins, and they were chattering and talking with their hands. "Tomorrow night," one called, and made a song out of the words, for there was singing everywhere along that ragged and unruly line which trailed on behind Cassia out of sight. Carrying the guitar she did not feel out of place, for many others carried pipes, fiddles, concertinas, xylophones, and drums. At gathering places on the trail, children would sit in circles around lone musicians, and the line of pilgrims, passing, would pick up the song, and it would run along them like a wave until it clashed with something else, coming down the opposite direction. In time Cassia found herself smiling and humming too, not from her own happiness, but because the festival atmosphere was difficult to resist.

Every hour there were more people, and now the path was wide. The pilgrims rushed along it in a stream, dividing behind Cassia and Servant of God, jostling them on either side, re-forming in front of them. Children looked back with curious impatient faces. "*Koori, koori sana*," they called, words unknown to Cassia, although she found herself repeating them. These newest pilgrims were a dirty bunch, with clothes and faces thick with grime and skins that smelled like smoke. They were barefoot, and the rips in their T-shirts showed tight bellies and thin shanks. But they were happy too, laughing and singing, their eyes bright with expectation, and when they opened their mouths their teeth were stained with kaya gum. They were carrying bundles of bark, bundles of roots, bundles of rags.

Or else others, more sophisticated but not especially cleaner, would limp along in broken plastic shoes, or would be carrying plastic shoulder bags emblazoned with bright foreign trademarks. Some of these were students, holding books and notebooks and ballpoint pens; some wore thick, unwieldy, battered spectacles. "Good morning," they would call, though in fact it was near evening and the sky was dark and overcast. And they also were singing, and they clapped their hands and snapped their fingers to sophisticated, trendy rhythms; one even carried a radio, blaring static, and under it a tiny song.

Toward nightfall the line stopped for twenty minutes. The way forward was obstructed for some reason. People ranted and complained, and yet in the end they waited patiently. Cassia and Servant of God sat hand in hand without speaking. His eyes were closed. He was in pain, and he winced when she roused him to move forward again. The line was moving, and only a few minutes later it debouched into a clearing. First there was a barricade of broken trees and then they moved into an open space of trampled earth. And there they found Efe again; inside a circle of smoky torches, she and several others had set up a kind of kitchen. Six women had lit fires, and they were cooking manioc greens and lentils in big rusted barrels. And all around them people sat wrapped in dirty blankets, for the wind had come up again and it was cold, now that the shelter of the trees was gone.

The path had wound uphill all day, so gradually that Cassia had noticed only the change in vegetation, the rhododendron trees giving way finally to stunted pines. In the clearing, people squatted around fires of pinecones and pine needles, and the air was full of the smell of burning pitch.

And the soil was thinner too, a dry sand mixed with pine needles, which covered ridges of sharp rocks. It was as if, during the days of Cassia's journey, the rock foundations of the land had slowly risen up through layers of sediment until finally it had punctured through. In the clearing it was uncomfortable underfoot, for the volcanic rock was as sharp as glass.

But some people had spread out canvas tarpaulins, and many others had scrounged in the forest for branches and dead leaves, which they had arranged in rough untidy piles for the children. More than five hundred people were camped in the glade; already a circle of canvas shelters had sprung up, and as the lamps were lit and Cassia came in, she passed a man with a mattock digging trenches for latrines, splintering the rock with heavy strokes.

Servant of God led her forward toward Mama Efe's fire. Twenty feet from it she laid out his mat and he flopped down onto it. His knees were cut up from the rocks and he was tired, and yet his great liquid eyes were full of peace. He was lying on his back, staring up at the sky, while all around him milled a circle of admirers. To Cassia, sitting next to him with his guitar on her lap, it seemed that he, or more particularly his upturned face, had become the still center of that entire rustling mass of people. As it grew darker, she could see less, and all the activity around her seemed slowly to subside, and she could see patterns in the circles of the torches and the shadows of the shelters, and hear patterns in the cries and bangings and the laughter of the children. Again, there was music everywhere, but as the evening wore on it seemed less strident, less combative, and all the different songs around her seemed to resolve into a dreamy hum. She was tired, yet wakeful too, and she was always trying to pay attention as another person knelt down by Servant of God to mutter a few words. She would nod and listen to the cripple's soft sweet voice as he greeted everyone by name, a tranquil expression on his upturned face. In time, Paradise rose behind a mask of heavy clouds; the sky assumed a silver sheen like another layer of light over the flickering torches, something permanent and luminous and thick. Then especially the noise and music around Cassia settled down, as if muted by the thickness of the air. All around there was an expectant sense of gladness. Cassia found herself happy, not knowing why, and in the new light the cripple's face gleamed like a silver mask.

Mama Jobe sat down next to them, and she had brought them wooden plates of food—hot masses of lentils over sticky rice. Servant of God took nothing. He appeared to have entered a soft trance—"Ah, ah, ah," he muttered. "Abu, ah, ah." But the firelight was shining on Mama Jobe's teeth, and together she and Cassia ate mountains of the wet, hot food, and it was loaded with peppers so that their mouths burned and their eyes watered. Mama Jobe had also an old orange cola bottle, full of a homemade liquor that was the first alcohol that Cassia had ever tasted. "Tonight's the Prince's night," said Mama Jobe. "Tonight we're drinking like he used to drink."

Which seemed to mean to excess—all around them people were uncorking bottles. Cassia's head was ringing after seven sips, and she concentrated with difficulty on the sound of the nearby radio. A young man had perched upon a rock outcropping behind her; he had a studious and bulbous face, and he was dressed in a clean white button-down shirt, with two pens in his pocket. He held the radio against his ear, and even though he never turned the knob, still the signal seemed to fluctuate between stations: sometimes music, sometimes static, and just once a loud clear voice, for the antenna of the labor camp at Danamora was just ninety miles away. "Tigers versus Wolverines," it said, "one-nineteen to twenty-five," words which made no sense to Cassia, even though they brought an image to her mind.

"Where's your man?" asked Mama Jobe. Cassia smiled and Mama Jobe smiled too. But she was looking at Cassia out of the corner of her eye, and when Cassia said nothing she clicked her tongue against her teeth. She took another swig of liquor and then wiped her mouth. "I'd a doubt this morning," she said. "And I told you so. Because you know we must be careful. But when they sent the Prince to jail, they put him in a common cell with six hundred prisoners. Which means to say, everyone is welcome. Here around us you've got folk from everyplace. They'll be sneaking from their families, their husbands, and their wives. Whole villages of outlaws. But tonight we are protected. All stupidity forgiven. Because you know, he was not a perfect man."

"Who?" asked Cassia.

Again the woman clicked her tongue. "Abu Starbridge, child! The Prince! Why do you think you're here?"

All around them, the night was settling down. With the alcohol, the world was starting to contract, and Cassia no longer felt the presence of the folk outside a certain small contracting circle. A woman in a greasy blanket, puffing on a pipe. A family of children in a pile of leaves. A row of men along a rock, passing a bottle back and forth. The student's radio had quieted down to static only, though he still pored over it. And Cassia was most aware of smells, which seemed to take on a new power as all the sights and sounds diminished. A sea of smells was rising up around her, and it was made of smoke and unwashed bodies, lentils and frangipani, and hot powdered milk. From time to time also, a fluctuation in the wind would bring a smell of excrement and urine from the trench, and as time went on the smell of undigested liquor, regurgitated food. A child retched softly, rhythmically, over to her right.

"He was not a perfect man," repeated Mama Jobe. "For this reason all frailties are forgiven in advance. To become pure like him requires neither willpower nor strength. But only say the word."

These sentences were different from her normal speech, and it seemed clear that she was reciting something. "What word?" asked Cassia. Again Mama Jobe looked at her out of the corner of her eye, and again she took a drink.

"You're with us now," she said at last. "The Servant chose you. Maybe he chose you for your helplessness, so that we could show you loving kindness. Maybe he chose you for your ignorance, and that when we told you these things, we'd find ourselves repeating them and knowing them. For Abu Starbridge was a teacher. Once when Paradise was full, he went down to the dock in Charn among the poorest people of the town. They were the antinomes—they too were ignorant. But they knew music and the dance of death, and they were antinomes and they were living in the holes of the earth, and they crept out of them to sing and dance for him. So today we honor singing and dancing, which is the gift of the stupid to the wise. And in return he taught to them their history, and taught to them the story of the world, and taught to them the force of loving kindness, when he was living in their caves with them for two nights and two days. And when Lord Chrism Demiurge was king in Charn, he sent the soldiers to destroy them. But Prince Abu stood against them on the dock below the Harbor Bridge, and he raised his hand and scattered all of them with the power of loving kindness, and he had no other weapon, for he was the protector of the weak, the broken, and the miserable against the powers of the world. He raised the laundress to her feet and kissed her on the lips. For this reason we raise up our hands to him and on our palms we mark the shining sun, which is the symbol of the heat of love, which is our mark."

These words were spoken in a halting singsong. And they seemed to come not only from the lips of Mama Jobe, but also from the darkness all around her—a muttering of voices not always in unison. When she reached the end she raised her hand; others nearby raised theirs also, and they spread out their fingers to mimic the sun's rays, and then with the thumb of his other hand each one marked a symbol on his forehead or his tongue. The old woman laid her pipe aside, the student put away his radio, the children raised their heads up from the leaves. Servant of God also was moving his lips, and he unbuttoned his ripped shirt to show the sun drawn on his chest in silver ink. Even in the darkness Cassia could see the crude thick lines.

Now all around her the music seemed quieter, and all the sounds of talking settled down. People lumbered from the darkness to sit down beside her, and they were sitting with their children in their laps, wrapped in blankets against the freshening wind, leaning in to listen when the cripple said:

"Drunk with the whiskey, drunk with wine, drunk with compassion for the poor folk of the world, he abandoned his high tower and his life of luxury; he abandoned his family and his friends. In the secret hour of the night he came into the streets of Charn, wearing just the clothes upon his back. In this way he showed us that all men are equal, and they do not shine by their own light, but it is the touch of God that makes them shine. And if we strip ourselves of pride, and arrogance, and the weight of our belongings, then we can forget false differences. We are naked and helpless, and we have nothing to give. Yet everything will be provided if we only say the word."

Cassia, stupefied by alcohol and ignorant of the legends of St. Abu Starbridge, sat back with her hands around her knees. The story, indeterminate and vague, nevertheless lulled her to a kind of peace, for it seemed to speak about the triumph of goodness and simplicity over a large and complex evil. Above her, Paradise was climbing toward its zenith, its rays diffused behind thick layers of clouds. Yet its power every moment seemed intensified, a fine mist that filtered down upon her head. Its light was in the air she breathed.

She closed her eyes. She seemed to feel its heat upon her face. She felt its heat upon her lips, as she listened to the words rise up around her:

"Though he was not subject to our laws, still he came down to live among us, and to die. 'Kindness is the only thing,' he said. 'How can our hearts be dirty, if our hands are clean?' he asked. So he dispelled the myth, and showed us all the way to Paradise, which is not reserved for one or two, but for all men and women. When he went into the church at Beggars Medicine, he broke the chains of those condemned to death. In their place he offered himself up, and he was put in prison in their place. He was put into a cell with seven hundred others, in that dark black Mountain of Redemption, and even though they had no right to hold him, still he stayed there of his own goodwill, and he put his sacred hands upon them, and he gave them candy and good things to eat, and especially the children. And he taught them hopscotch and the jumping rope. In the place of judgment when they offered him his freedom he refused it. And a third time he refused it in his cell before his execution when Lord Chrism Demiurge had gone down on his knees. For he knew the chain, once broken, could never be reforged. For he knew the rope, once broken, could never be retied. For he knew when Starbridge blood was smoking on the altar, only then the oath could be renewed."

Cassia felt the heat upon her cheeks. And she saw fluctuations in the light: She opened her eyes. Nearby, the cooking fire had burned up bright, and people were dragging limbs of trees into the circle and building up a bonfire. As her senses came back to her, she could smell the smoke and hear the snapping of the twigs. She could see the flare of the pine needles and the pitch-soaked pinecones.

Also nearby she could see a man who passed among the ranks of seated pilgrims—a tall, broad, bearded man, dressed in a red shirt. He too seemed to know everyone; a swell of murmured voices followed him around the glade, and he would often stop and squat down next to some dark huddled form. As he came closer she could see him clearly in the firelight, his thick black hair and heavy hands, his trousers and black boots. But especially his hands, for his palms were covered with some kind of luminescent paint, which caught the firelight and reflected it back. As he spoke to the people he made wide, expansive gestures with his hands, and Cassia could see the circles of light that his hands left in the air, a golden afterimage of his golden palms.

Now he was kneeling between Mama Jobe and Servant of God. Both of them were still repeating the catechisms of Prince Abu Starbridge, but their voices dwindled slowly until only their lips moved. The man had put his hand upon the cripple's shoulder, and he had bent to whisper in his ear, but his eyes were on Cassia, and he stared at Cassia from under bloated eye ridges and black brows. He had a brutal, crushed, repulsive face, until he smiled. When he smiled, and it was as if his face had cracked open to reveal some soft interior, soft fruit inside an ugly bark. He reached out one-gleaming forefinger to touch her hand.

"I am Brother Longo," he said.

And that was all. But something was about to happen. Servant of God sat up suddenly, and Mama Jobe raised her head to the sky. The bonfire was burning brighter, and Cassia put up her arm to shield her face from the glare. The smoke made her eyes water, but Brother Longo was smiling at her, and then the expression of his mouth and eyes took on a quality of vagueness as his gaze slipped over her head into the crowd. His knees creaked as he got to his feet.

Behind Servant of God a sharp pinnacle of rock protruded

from the soil, not more than three feet high. Brother Longo stepped up to the top of it, and such was the power of his presence, and such was the sense of expectation in the crowd, that the whole chaotic mass of people seemed to reorient itself subtly, until it seemed that almost without moving they reorganized themselves around him in concentric rings. The fire burned at his back, and in a moment the area around it and on the far side to the clearing's edge was bare, except for a few tents, as people rearranged themselves in front of him to listen. Cassia, at his feet, squinted up into the light.

Perhaps there was a special clarity in the air. Or perhaps his words were amplified somehow by the attention of the crowd, so that they achieved a special resonance. Whatever the reason, Longo Starbridge didn't raise his voice. His words were just a heavy rumble in his chest, at least at first. He stared down at his feet, so that it appeared to Cassia, who sat beneath him, that he was speaking for her only—his beard against his neck, his eyes almost closed. But she imagined that to every person in the crowd he appeared in the same way, and to each person his voice seemed intimate and low.

"Brothers and sisters," he said. "Tonight we celebrate the memory of Prince Abu Starbridge, who was martyred in a great fire on the forty-sixth of October, in the eighth phase of spring, in the city of Charn. He was burned alive by that old devil Chrism Demiurge. That same night he came back from the dead. He was seen drinking in the Regis bar, according to the signed testimony of many witnesses. That night also he was retaken by the soldiers. He did not resist them, though he could have freed himself by raising up his hand. He was imprisoned, and questioned, and tortured, and tormented, until he had beaten that old devil in the silent struggle, and the revolution came. Nor was he freed, but he was questioned again under the new government, and again he was condemned to die, so that it could be said of him, according to the retroactive prophecies of Freedom Love, 'Every hand was raised against him, whether of the right or of the left.' On the seventy-second of November he was buried alive with two others, a princess and an antinomial, so that it could be said of him, 'He was a comfort to the king in his high place, and also to the garbage of the earth.'"

As he spoke, Longo Starbridge put his arms straight out to either side of him, and his phosphorescent palms were shining, silhouetted by the darker firelight. Also he raised his face up to the sky, and in his new position his voice flowed louder, unimpeded.

"In the blackness underneath the ground, he met and talked with our great teacher Freedom Love, who was the founder of our New Society of Loving Kindness. This was in a dream of darkness, which is described in Retroactive Prophecies, and written down when Freedom Love was living in a cave beneath the streets of Charn, when he too was an outlaw in the revolution time. In his dream he spoke to Abu Starbridge, and took him on a journey through the underworld, and showed him all the wonders of the darkness which existed in those days. He showed him the Morquar Dam, which held back good from evil. He showed him the King's Walk. He showed him the Snake of Relativity. He showed him that old Satan of the ancient days, who was called the White-Faced Woman, and who held the chain of winter in her hands. Then for five days in the darkness Abu Starbridge fought with her, and pulled her to her knees, and broke the chain under the earth, so that the rain came down, so that the world turned toward the sun, so that the babies climbed down from their mothers' wombs, so that grass and flowers, leaves and trees, and all the comforts of the earth broke free out of that bondage."

Now Longo Starbridge changed the position of his arms again. Keeping his left arm stretched out to his side, he raised his right arm straight above his head, and pointed to the zenith with his shining forefinger.

"This is part of the vision of our great teacher Freedom Love, and like all truth it has two parts. For Freedom Love did take refuge in the crypts of Charn during this period of turmoil. In secret chambers underneath the city, most of which are now submerged under the waters of Lake nineteenth of May, he lived with the first converts of the New Society. And it is true—he rescued condemned prisoners from the burial pits. It is true—there seems to have been also a female spirit who lived at that same time, the ruler of a black tribe of the underworld. For there were catacombs in Charn that stretched for miles. There were villages and towns that never saw the light—all gone now, all submerged.

"But do not think, because of these facts, that the importance of Abu Starbridge lies only in the symbolical part. It is true—spring came to Charn, but it comes every year. The lying tyrants, Chrism Demiurge and his false Starbridge followers, were overthrown, but that required no act of God. It was the season of rebellion. And I have heard others say of Abu Starbridge that he opened up the gates of Paradise to the poor and weak, to anyone who loves him. They talk about the laundry girl who seized him by the legs when he was going to his place of execution: how he raised her up and kissed her, and said, 'Among a hundred thousand I will know you.'

"This is part of the story. But it misses the point. The importance of Prince Abu Starbridge is not only in the realm of myth, or in the supernatural. These stories and these legends—who can be sure? But this I know: Abu Starbridge showed us a new way to dedicate our lives. At the time of the worst decadence, when Starbridge offices were being bought and sold, when the false doctrines of predetermination and the inheritance of grace had sucked the heart out of our ancient faith—this is the importance of Abu Starbridge. He showed us men and women can perfect themselves through their own efforts. He was not a brilliant man. He was not a gifted man. We have no great store of wisdom from his lips. But from the example of his life and death we can see how every one of us, even the most humble, can rededicate himself to the old Starbridge values—that contract from the earliest days which made men into gods. For at the moment when the Starbridge race was sunk in luxury and violence and sin and empty privilege, this simple man rose up to change all that. Tonight I exhort every one of you to take that vow to sanctify yourself, to swear the same oath that our ancestors swore upon the altar of Beloved Angkhdt, on the day when time stood still in the beginning of the world."

By the end of this address, Cassia had been lulled almost to sleep. These events had taken place long before her birth. There seemed scarcely a connection between that time and now. So she was surprised to see men and women rising around her in response to Brother Longo's words; Cassia's head fell back and she was wide awake. She was awake enough to understand immediately that the scene had been rehearsed, for all the men and women who were getting to their feet—perhaps twenty out of all that crowd—were dressed in the same clothes, in rough white tunics and white pants. Their heads were shaved. All carried unlit tapers. They stepped through the seated audience and gathered in a group beside the bonfire.

There, a place had been prepared for them around a strange metal contrivance perhaps four feet tall, which Cassia now noticed for the first time. At the summit of it perched a book, which was held open to a certain page by a pair of metal pincers. Below it, three short metal arms stuck out from a central shaft. One supported a small lantern, and one supported a small pail which hung from a wire handle. The third arm ended in a clamp, and at that moment some young women from the mission fussed with it. They were dressed in yellow shirts, printed with the symbol of the mission hospital—two stick figures holding hands.

One of these young women knelt beside the bonfire, and she was poking at something in the coals. Two others were spreading out strips of white cloth on a tray, and they were rubbing them with unguent from a plastic tube. Another mixed a beaker full of a shining liquid; she held it up and Cassia could see a flash of light from it, transferred or reflected from the bonfire. Then the women poured it in a glowing stream into the bucket hanging from the metal stand.

"Come to me," said Longo Starbridge. He had turned around on his small pinnacle of rock, so that his back was to Cassia. The group of supplicants gathered beneath him, between him and the fire. They had dazed and frightened faces. Brother Longo raised his right hand to them and they stared at it like rabbits at a snake; staring with them, Cassia could see that there were lines on Brother Longo's shining palm, deep lines of red and black beneath the phosphorescent sheen. The pattern was unclear to her. Her own hands itched and sweated.

One of the orderlies approached him, and gave him a glass bottle. He held it up in his right hand.

"One night," he said, "Abu Starbridge and his cousin came down from their tower, and they passed among the shanteytowns and slums, distributing food and money, chocolates and medical supplies, which at that time were forbidden to the poor. In return the people told them stories, and they sang and danced. That night Prince Abu's eyes were opened, and he saw in a new way. He raised up his hand to help them. He raised up his hand below the Harbor Bridge, and there was never any going back. That night the people gave him wine to drink, and he drank the wine which opened up his eyes. Therefore tonight we give you wine, to numb the pain that comes from holding a new life, for there is always pain."

The woman who had been kneeling by the fire now rose. She held a glowing metal bulb in a pair of glowing tongs, and with some clumsiness she affixed it to the clamp upon the stand. Now everything appeared to be in place: the book, the lantern, the ointment, and the brand. On its surface, Cassia could see raised orange lines against a deeper red.

One of the supplicants stood forward now, a tall, gaunt, beak-faced woman. She lit her taper from the lantern on the stand. Then, turning, she took the bottle out of Brother Longo's hand. She swallowed a gulp of it and wiped her lips. The effect seemed instantaneous—her eyes rolled back in her head, and on stiff knees she tottered back and forth. And in a garbled, intermittent voice, she repeated after Brother Longo the words of the first Starbridge catechism:

"To be more than human, that is my vow.
To suffer without speaking, that is my vow.
To help the weak,
To speak the truth,
To live in chastity,
In loving kindness with all men and women,
That is my vow."

There was more, which Cassia never heard. Up until that point she had watched with a sense of curious detachment. She also had drunk some of the wine, and though it was doubtless of a lower grade, it had been enough to relax her and confuse her. It had been enough to allow her to study each small event as it happened, without joining it to others in the past or in the future. But at a certain point, what was going to happen became clear. The gaunt woman was reaching her hand out toward the brand, nerving herself to grasp hold, while around her orderlies from the mission were preparing bandages for her, and stirring up the shining ointment in the pail.

The wine rolled uneasily in Cassia's stomach. She looked around at the people near her, at Mama Jobe, at Servant of God, and saw how they were hunched forward, entranced by what was happening; they knew what to expect. They had known it all along. But Cassia jumped up. She pushed her way over the seated ranks, disturbing many. Then she wandered down away into the woods, not turning when the silence in the crowd was broken, and the shouting rose up from five hundred mouths.

That morning after Cassia had left to go down to the stream, Rael had lain down by himself upon the concrete floor. She did not return, and for a long time he had lain upon his stomach with his head in his hands, thinking of nothing. Except he was expecting her, and when she did not come he was possessed by an intolerable, increasing restlessness that seemed to flow in waves, and made his whole body shake until finally he jumped up to pace the length of the tin warehouse, knocking his hands together. An hour passed, then two. Then he ran out of the door and to the stream, following marks in the accumulated blossoms on the path.

But he was confused by other traces; in the morning as he lay awake he had sensed the presence of other travelers nearby, and when Cassia was gone he had let his hearing dwell on certain sounds: the crack of a stick, the banging of a spoon against a pot, a shred of laughter. These sounds suggested motion. People moved nearby, and yet as Rael lay on his stomach he felt none of his usual shyness, none of his usual caution, for everything he heard seemed separate from his world and Cassia's—the residue of actions performed by ghosts, while he and she were the only real human creatures in the forest. He thought that nothing possibly could interfere with them. So that it was with disbelief that he saw the print of Cassia's foot mix with someone else's, with disbelief that he climbed up to the deserted glade where she had met Mama Jobe and the rest.

He searched for signs upon the trampled earth. The fire had been covered up, yet it was smoking. Cassia was gone. In a panic, he paced in circles around the glade, for it was as if Cassia had stepped away from him into a world of ghosts, of strangers, deeds, and motives. In desperation he ran a little way along the path until it reached a wider way. And there were people. He crouched behind a bush and watched the people walking past, and some were carrying knapsacks and bundles on their heads. He felt that she was gone among the people, and she was disappearing like a drop of water on the surface of a pool.

A man with a long beard stalked past, carrying a basket full of wood. Rael let him go by, and then he leapt to his feet and rushed back to the tin warehouse, back to the floor where he and Cassia had lain. Already someone else was there—some woman was holding up his blanket. He pushed her down and ripped it from her hands; then he was gone, running to the stream away from the path, running up the slope upon the other side, striking out across the woods, moving close to the ground through the small branches, the rolled-up blanket clasped to his chest.

And in a little while his mind was clear. Or it was full of forest problems—detours and thorns and biting nettles, insects, swamps, unsteady branches, submerged logs. Cassia was lost beyond these things. He was following an animal trail, perhaps a deer run or even an okapi, for he was picking through a thorn bush that held tufts of striped black fur.

The sky was overcast. Toward afternoon, he descended down the side of a steep dark and tangled dell. The undergrowth was thicker, and he stopped to rest. The dell was full of laurel trees. Branches hung down over the trail, and he was pushing through suspended clusters of the sharp leaves, each one as thick and stiff as pottery, and they clanked against one another as he disturbed them.

There was no wind.

He saw the tracks of another animal.

There was a patch of bare ground near where a rivulet had spread over the trail. He bent down to examine two large paw prints. They had filled with water, yet even so they were still fresh, the mark of each claw still articulate.

Rael knelt down at the rivulet to drink. He wiped the sweat out of his eyes. He felt a presentiment of danger. He felt a strange, airless constriction in his chest, which was fear, although he didn't recognize it. Around him from time to time, the laurel leaves banged randomly together.

He sat back on his heels and pushed the hair out of his face. A man stood erect in the shelter of some saplings. Rael's eyes traveled up his long dense golden legs, almost hairless, knotted with muscle, bleeding from six parallel cuts along his outer thigh.

He was wearing the skin of an animal, tied around his hips and again around his heavy shoulders. Rael stared at the black and white striped fur, the cruel paws hanging down. The man was wearing the skin of a dead tiger. Also, the surface of his arms and throat were striped with lines of shadow, for the sun had burned down to the bottom of a layer of clouds, and the trees were full of a new color and a new dappled light.

For a moment Rael stared at the man's curled ear, the hairless jaw, the coarse yellow hair that was like his own. And then he bent back down so that his face was in the mud. He turned his cheek to one side and laid it in the dirt. So that when the music came he couldn't tell whether the stranger had produced it with his mouth and with his voice, or else from some small instrument. It was nothing: over in a moment, a small scattering of notes, an interrogatory tune, or perhaps a puzzled warning. But Rael was staring at the stranger's toe. He closed his eyes, and when he opened them again the toe was gone. The sun also had receded back, and there was nothing around him but the muffled banging of the leaves.

Soon he picked up his blanket roll, and wandered back the way he'd come. By the time he had retraced his steps, it was already dark.

In the darkness, Cassia paced back and forth under the trees, beyond the trench for the latrines at Brother Longo's mission. She crossed her arms over her chest. From where she was, she could still see the lights in the clearing, and she could still hear the crowd: the gravid silence first, and then the roar of voices, not always loud enough to cover a shrill scream.

The air was cold away from the fire, and Cassia was rubbing her bare arms. A thin, harsh stink of urine was rising from the trench, mixing with the sickness in her stomach and the liquor in the back of her throat, which she was swallowing again and again to keep down. And she was thinking of Mr. Sarnath, his gestures, his inflections, his dry voice. She was thinking of the way that he would hold up his forefinger when he quoted from the master. Once when she was a little girl, just after she had moved into the girls' dormitory, she had refused food for three straight nights. The keeper had told Mr. Sarnath, and he had come to see her in her room, and he had stood in the doorway with his forefinger raised. She had ignored him; she was lying in her cot with her face to the wall, studying a crack in the palm matting. Some light was seeping through. It was in the morning.

The master had not approved of self-mortification. Nor had Mr. Sarnath—he called it the easy path. In time he came to sit beside her, though he did not touch her. In his left hand he was carrying a ripe persimmon, and as she listened to him talk, her mouth had filled with a sweet anticipation.

She found herself walking among pine trees. And it was not quite dark. Paradise still glowed behind its layer of mist, and the entire sky glowed silver. Somewhere nearby she heard water dripping, and then she was aware of someone in the woods with her, among the pines, and she could hear his footsteps, and the crack of a dry branch. She crossed her arms over her chest and turned to go back toward the fire, but then there was a shadow in between two trees and it was he, it was Rael; she knew him by his height and strength and shoulders as he took her in his arms; she knew him by his smell, his roughness as he crushed her without speaking, and ran his hands over her breasts, her buttocks, and her thighs.

There was some sickness in her belly, but it was lighter now, and she was conscious of another yearning, also, as he pushed her up against the rough bark of a tree and made a kind of love to her there, lifting her up until she clasped her legs around his waist, all soreness and all nausea forgotten.

Then they lay together on the pine needles. Rael lay on his stomach, and she curled up beside him. His skin seemed hot, and it was hot enough to keep her warm. "Just pay attention," she said into his ear. "Just be careful." But she could feel his tension and his wakefulness; once she woke up in the middle of the night to see him standing over her. Later, he was gone again. She woke feeling empty as a broken bottle. But he had left the blanket, and she wrapped herself in it and sat up until the dawn.

MT. NYANGONGO

8

At the end of the sixteenth phase of summer, the citizens of Charn elected a new mayor, who went on to surprise them with his energy and daring. Inheriting a massive public debt, nevertheless he managed to negotiate new loans with the city's foreign creditors, while at the same time expanding his commitments to education, nutrition, health care, rural literacy, and rehydration. These priorities differed from those of previous governments, which had tended, with the encouragement of foreign banks, to favor large public works. By September of the sixteenth phase of summer, most of these projects had been curtailed or abandoned, so that the countryside beyond the city was full of half-built bridges, and stadiums, and dams.

The mayor was a man named Marcus Gentian, and he was squat and stout and stupid-looking, with an elaborately wrinkled face and a permanent expression of befuddlement. But he brought great force of character to his job. Almost single-handedly he managed to coax various austerity measures through the council, including taxes of 500 percent on luxury and imported goods. In this way he hoped to encourage domestic manufacturing and reduce the hemorrhage of raw materials abroad.

Also at this time he was working on a universal employers' code, specifying new levels of minimum pay, and including new provisions for overtime, vacations, and sick leave. This code was already in effect in the city and in all government-owned businesses, but in the rural areas it was ignored. Most of the large agricultural and mining projects were still owned and managed from abroad; since they had involved major investments in land reclamation and technology, most had been started and maintained with foreign money, foreign expertise. The major's new survey on abuses, which so far had been blocked from publication, had mentioned seven industries in particular, and had even suggested criminal proceedings against the owners of the mine at Carbontown.

On September fifty-third of the sixteenth phase of summer, 00016, the mayor of Charn inaugurated a week-long celebration of civic harmony. This was to coincide with the dates of the old Paradise festival—the moon was visible that week, and made a strange, disquieting addition to the summer sky. The mayor hoped that this ceremony, this demonstration of public pride, would help to salve a new dissatisfaction among the middle classes, caused by the sudden disappearance of tape recorders, portable cameras, dishwashers, cassette players, and motorbikes from the city's shops. He sought to evoke a spirit of solidarity, and at the same time to counteract a new insidious phenomenon—the secret worship of Immortal Angkhdt, which after the hiatus of a lifetime was beginning to resurface even within the city limits of Charn itself.

On the night of the sixty-third, for the first time since the days of Raksha Starbridge, the temples of the old regime were opened to the public. The mayor hoped that he could preempt their old significance by using them for his new ceremony—the interiors had all been renovated and redone.

During the revolution, the thousand temples of the city had been used as barracks, stables, shooting ranges, public restrooms; they had been gutted and vandalized by semiofficial partisans, and many had been subsequently torn down. But the stonework of the great old churches was still intact: St. Dimity's, St. Soldan's, the Cathedral of a Thousand Tears.

All reference to the old religion had been expunged. The space inside the Church of Morquar the Unkempt was empty. The frescoes on the sanctuary walls—portraits of the thirty-two bishops of Charn—had been painted over. The mosaic of the dome had been redone. With infinite and patient labor, tile by tile, the figures of the saints had been transmogrified, their faces and their gestures changed, their bright halos eradicated. Of course the new work was cruder, easy to distinguish from the old, but that night among the crowds who packed inside, there was not one who could have possibly remembered what the dome had once been like. They gazed up dully, yet even so, many thought it was peculiar in a way they could not quite identify, to see above their heads on the great central panel a representation of the first national assembly of the revolution. There, standing in their seats, were figures who to the people had already taken on the attributes of myth, glimpsed only through official statements and the foggy reminiscences of their parents and grandparents. There—Valium Samosir, dressed in white, representative of the seventh ward and later president of the Board of Health. There—Earnest Darkheart, leader of the Rebel Angels. There—Martin Sabian, ugly, tiny, crippled. And there, an enormous black gaunt figure on the central throne—Colonel Aspe, the Liberator, Lord Protector of the city until his death from cancer in the ninth phase of spring.

No one could have guessed by looking at it what the mosaic had once represented. No one could see the glorious convocation of the first Starbridges around the throne of Immortal Angkhdt. Yet even so in the packed crowd some seemed to understand, and even there were some who mumbled secretly a part of an old prayer, or made tiny secret gestures with their hands.

The mayor had rededicated each of the five largest churches in the city, and had declared each one a monument to a distinct aspect of civic progress. That night, at nine o'clock precisely, the spotlights were turned on around the new palaces of Hydroelectricity, Justice, Agriculture, and Nonviolence. In preparation for the celebration, new streetlights had been erected all over the city, in an attempt to rob some splendor from the risen moon.

Yet even so the ceremony was less than a complete success. Even with the new mosaic, the interior of St. Morquar's— the new Palace of Industry—had an empty, purposeless look. Alcoholic beverages, in short supply since the embargo on imported hops, were distributed free from a long table in the nave. There was an enormous crowd, yet somehow their reaction to the spectacle which formed the heart of the evening was unsatisfactory. People shuffled their feet, yawned, sweated, smiled inopportunely, scratched their heads.

The drama was performed on a square dais underneath the dome, and the people stood around three sides of it. The sets were gigantic, the costumes pleasingly expensive. Several celebrities—members of the city council, the postmaster general, the dean of the school of law—had taken roles. Some of the speeches, including several in praise of the inventor of a new process of smelting, had been written by the mayor himself.

In the final scene, seven young women represented the seven liberal arts, and they danced provocatively with an equal number of young men, whose hats suggested different industrial procedures. The men were prominent sports figures, the women the seven runners-up of a pageant that had been held the previous day. Yet even so, some energy was lacking, some vital spark. And in this it contrasted with other, smaller, private celebrations which were taking place all over Charn that same night. Illegal, punishable in some cases by long prison sentences, they persisted especially in the slums, where in hot broken rotten houses, not yet reconditioned into workers' flats, fervent gatherings of the faithful squatted around single candles in the dark. They were rubbing worn crude homemade fetishes, and chanting stories from the life of Abu Starbridge, stories from the life of Angkhdt. In those days the two mythologies had come together, to form a potent new religion of the disenfranchised and the miserable.

It was a religion made of stories. This is a story that they told in those days: Abu Starbridge was carried in a cage through the streets of Charn, on the way to his place of execution. And he was stinking drunk. And they had loaded him with chains, and covered up his face with the dog-headed mask. In the back of an old truck, he was driving through the streets of Charn, while the people yelled curses and threw stones. When he was passing up the avenue of Seven Sins, a laundress from the lowest caste jumped up onto the tailgate. She asked him for his blessing and bent down to touch his feet. But then he reached out through the bars of his cage. He raised her up. He said, "Do not fear. Among a hundred thousand I will know you. And when I see you in the land of Paradise, I will kiss you on the lips."

Or this—Beloved Angkhdt went traveling, marked with the tattoos of a gardener. It was the starving time, the dark part of the year. Wherever he passed, grass grew under his feet. It poked up through the snow along his footprints.

When he got to a town, the men and women brought their children, for he had the healer's touch. He would touch them in the secret places of their bodies. Sometimes the women came out while their husbands slept. They lay with him inside the cowsheds, among the cows.

He came to the city. The primate heard that he had come, and then the primate gave him money. But Angkhdt had seen the primate's daughter. He said he would plant a garden in her stomach, and then he went away. But she lost flesh, and she was almost dead, and she was the only fruit upon her father's tree. Then the primate took his bow, and hunted Angkhdt through all the hills and the high pastures. He saw him on the hill, a black shadow standing up, and he shot him with an arrow through the thigh. He chased him through the wood. Beloved Angkhdt, he left a trail. And his blood was falling on the snow. There was a flower which sprang up, and a scarlet berry. Then the primate found his clothes discarded in the snow. He was following the track—human footprints, then they changed.

On the morning of the sixty-third of September, Cassia waited in the pine grove for Rael to return. A cold mist was hanging in the trees, beading in her hair. At the end of an hour she was too cold to keep on sitting as she had been, wrapped in Rael's blanket with her bare feet dug into the pine needles. So she got up and walked back to the clearing.

There the bonfire was still smoking, and she stepped among the rows of sleeping pilgrims to reach it. She pushed her toes down into the warm ashes, and bent to rub the stiffness out of her legs. Near her the branding tree had fallen to its side. The book, the lantern, and the pail were gone.

The pilgrims had lain down to sleep where they had sat the night before, and most still lay inert, crushed in together for warmth, their arms around each other. Many snored. The ground was scattered with discarded bottles.

But the children were awake, huddled up among their parents. Some had gotten up, and were laughing and playing among the trees, throwing pinecones at a marmot in a tree.

Servant of God was still asleep. So was Mama Jobe, her hand still clasped around her bottle. But Efe was awake— she was returning from the edge of the clearing with a burden of firewood. Her face was puffy and streaked with charcoal, and she was grunting to herself. Her baby was tied to her back in a red strip of fabric, which only left its feet and head uncovered. And behind her, also with his bundle of sticks, trudged her little boy in his old man's cap.

Mama Efe squatted down near Cassia, poking with a stick into the ashes, searching for embers from the bonfire. In the cold morning she was wearing a black cotton jacket, which nevertheless she had not buttoned; it did not close over her breasts. She laid her cooking fire with efficient movements, while in the meantime her little boy filled up a bucket from a standing tap near the latrine. It weighed almost as much as he did himself, and he was spilling most of it as he dragged it toward the fire.

Cassia went to help him. But he would not relinquish the bucket; he glared at her with dull hostility, his fingers tugging at the handle when she tried to lift it. Water splashed onto the neck of an old man who was stretched out nearby snoring. He slapped at his neck as if trying to kill a bug, then woke and cursed. Mama Efe cursed too, and whispered something Cassia didn't understand. She let go of the bucket's handle and stepped back.

Brother Longo was there, standing by Cassia's elbow. "You're up early," he said. But she was startled to see him, and disgusted by her memories of the previous night. As she turned, her face must have betrayed it, for Brother Longo's expression also changed.

She moved away from him, away also from the cursing old man, and stepped instead into a more open place, leaving Efe's son to drag away the bucket by himself. Brother Longo followed her, and hearing his step, she felt a sadness and a panic in her that she couldn't identify. But part of it came out of a new feeling of aloneness—Rael had not returned, and she was guessing for the first time how alone she was in the big world. This feeling had been ebbing and flowing since she woke, but at that moment it was at its height. She turned again.

Brother Longo was holding out his hand to her, a smile upon his face. In the light of day there was nothing impressive about him. His skin was covered with red spots, red hair, and she could smell the odor of his armpits. Her mind was full of regret, full of Mr. Sarnath, full of Rael, and she had no patience for it.

She could see the mark of the brand upon his palm, upon his fingers. In the misty morning light, the effect of the phosphorescent paint could not be seen—his hands looked dirty, that was all. And his smile, which was widening, included a broken canine. Next to it, one of his incisors appeared to have been filed down.

His voice seemed thin and vicious, now that he was no longer speaking for the crowd: "You didn't enjoy our demonstration," he said, still holding out his hand. "I saw you leave just at the moment of surrender."

She interrupted him. "There were priests in Charn—my father told us stories about the old days there. Starbridge priests—they worshiped idols. They blinded themselves upon their altars, cut off their own fingers. My father told me once when I refused to eat. Out of a sense of privilege, he said. Of privilege through pain. He said that we must guard against these marks of privilege."

Brother Longo shrugged. "Maybe," he said. "But look at your own hand."

She opened up her palm. The birthmark, which she had noticed for the first time the day before, seemed to have grown larger, and to have acquired an alarming color—purple, yellow, blue—as if she had been bleeding underneath the skin. But her palm was not sore or swollen.

Later that morning they continued on—Cassia, Servant of God, Mama Jobe, together with the mass of pilgrims. The track continued uphill. Past the outbuildings of Brother Longo's mission, past a crumbling concrete ramp which rose up to the level of the treetops and then ended, past a field where nothing grew, in which stood the rusted hulks of boilers, engines, generators, turbines, and where the soil was still slimy from some grease or oil or tar that bubbled up out of the polluted earth—four miles from the clearing the track widened and there were remnants of tarmac for a while, remnants of stone gutters. Other smaller ways came snaking through the trees. By eight o'clock, when the sun rose, the track was many yards across.

Always they progressed uphill. Servant of God swung himself over the sharp volcanic rocks, his enormous hands wrapped in strips of cotton. Often he would move aside to rest, and then Cassia would look back to see the line of pilgrims coming through the trees, visible a long way, many thousands now, all with their knapsacks and bundles and children and bright ragged clothes. Weather-beaten, grimy, battered, happy, they jabbered to each other up and down the line, and they sang hymns and songs. Now, after weeks of weary traveling, they were close to their goal; it was the last day of the Paradise Festival, and the weather was beautiful once the sun had burned away the mist. The sky was a hard, sweet, cold metallic blue, visible now through the thinning trees, and occasionally the sun shone in their faces.

Servant of God was sweating, panting, and his knees and hands were bleeding. Yet even he was smiling as they climbed up slowly toward the open sun. At times now through a bare place in the foliage they could see the jungle far below them, its black canopy punctured here and there by giant tulip trees, each with its yellow crown, each with its surrounding cloud of birds. And in those same bare places Cassia now caught glimpses of the slope in front of her, rising out of sight, a shoulder of Mt. Nyangongo, whose enormous bulk appeared so gradually. As they climbed, sulphur fumes pinched at their nostrils, and sometimes a hot sulphur mist would rise up around them through a crack in the rock, turning the grass yellow, brittle, dry.

Sometimes they would cross a lava flow. Here especially Servant of God would grunt in pain as he labored over fields of pumice and obsidian. Even Mama Jobe, whose thin shoulders were bent that day under the burden of a crushing hangover, protested when they reached a place among the thinning laurels where the path disappeared among dunes of powdered glass. "Stupid," she said, "you'll hurt yourself," and she grabbed him by the hair to yank him back out of the press of pilgrims. In fact many had turned aside to tie bandannas round their mouths and to lift their children up onto their shoulders, and to drink a few swigs of water before they continued on. From up ahead there came a squeak, squeak, squeak—the shuffle of their plastic boots upon the glass.

Servant of God had hurt himself. The cuts upon his knees and hands were coated with black powder, and his tongue also was black with it. But still he struggled grimly forward: "No," he said, "I'm almost there." They had to pull him back out of the dust; then he relented and let them care for him and wash him clean while he lay gasping on his back. They wasted water from Mama Jobe's canteen, and he was sputtering and complaining. But whenever he relaxed his face, it returned to the smile that was now his natural expression.

Cassia had been walking in a daze of self-absorption. Intent on the confusion in her heart, entranced by the power of her own senses, she had barely noticed the cripple's pain until they stopped. Now she chided herself, and with acute and careful fingers she picked the glass out of his wounds.

"No," he said. "This is nothing; let me go." But his struggles were halfhearted and in a little while he lay still. While Cassia washed him from the water bottle, Mama Jobe unwrapped from a rag six stiff narrow leaves. She crushed them on her palm and then she retched up from her throat a glob of phlegm, discolored from tobacco juice, and mixed it all into a paste. Then she was rubbing it into the torn flesh along the cripple's shins and knees. Cassia put her finger out to touch some of the goo. She took some on the end, and soon the sensitivity of her skin was less, her hand felt alien, apart.

"What's the matter now?" grumbled Mama Jobe, for there were tears in Cassia's eyes.

"What are we doing here?" she asked.

Once Mr. Sarnath had come upon her in the woods, where she was sitting by a pool. So intent was she upon a water spider that she had not heard his footsteps. "Do not be misled by your sensations," he had said. "Intensity is not the same as understanding. Surely I am part of this as well as you."

She was sitting on a dusty tuft of grass, over a soil of sharp stones. Stunted, spindly trees hung over them. The sun was hot. Ten yards away, the stream of pilgrims passed unchecked, raising a mist of powdered glass out over the lava flow. Thin men, pregnant women, children, and none of them was Rael.

"What am I doing here?" she asked.

Mama Jobe rolled her eyes. She had ripped part of the hem of her dress to make a fresh bandage for the cripple's hands, and she was smearing it with her anesthetizing paste. She was in no mood for foolish questions; her particolored face was full of wry disgust. Servant of God was lying on his back, quiescent now, his body daubed with grit, dappled with sunlight. His arm was over his face and he was smiling.

"Go and find someone," said Mama Jobe. "He's right—it's not far now."

Cassia wiped her hand across her cheek, and where her finger passed it made a long cold line. She turned her face aside. Now the woods were full of an ominous banging, a scattered roll of drumbeats. Perhaps a hundred men were marching in step along the path, fat men in crimson robes, with shaved heads and puffy faces that were covered with white greasepaint. Their eyes were lined with black and violet, and they had huge, grotesque false eyelashes, and they banged on heavy wooden drums with sticks wrapped in cotton batting. They were carrying flags too, awkwardly because of the overhanging branches. Cassia recognized the golden sun, the fat face of Abu Starbridge, the great dog's head of Angkhdt.

Once more the tears rose to her eyes. She turned back to

Mama Jobe, whose expression was kinder now, more humorous. "What's wrong with you, girl?" she asked. "Is it your friend?

"Here," she said. "There's cakes in the knapsack." That morning Efe had given them little flour biscuits baked in ashes. Now Cassia unwrapped one from its sheath of leaves and nibbled on it tentatively. "Not for me," said Mama Jobe. "I'd puke." She was sucking on a big plug of tobacco, which she held in the pouch of her jaw. "God, my aching head," she grumbled, spattering the dusty bushes with brown juice.

Cassia's ears were ringing too, with the drumbeats and the gongs. Now a new crowd of pilgrims were filing through the woods. They wore masks of stiff red cloth over their eyes. Again, their heads were shaved, in imitation of the saint. But each one had kept a single lock of hair, which was clubbed and oiled, and which protruded sharply from the nape of his neck.

These ones carried long brass horns that twisted round their bodies, though mercifully they did not blow them. Cassia had her hands over her ears. When they paused before entering the lava flow, she got up and went among them, for they were fat, strong men.

With one crashing beat, the drums stopped. Some of the men sat down to rest, and others turned to look expectantly down the path. Soon Cassia could see more coming, dressed in black and carrying guns. Some had other burdens. A man beside her, a ragged, toothless pilgrim different from this new array, was muttering, "The fleas! They've brought the fleas."

Four pairs of men were coming up the path, each pair carrying a metal cage between them on a hand sledge. And Cassia was amazed to see in each cage an insect as big as a dog, with a hard, heavy carapace and a bulbous abdomen. The cages were not large enough to let them move; their jointed legs protruded through the bars. Yet Cassia could see they were alive. The small claw on the end of each sharp foot was opening and closing.

She went up to one of the trumpeters who had paused to rest among the trees. "Please, sir," she said, "my friend is sick." But she was doubtful of his uniform and mask, the automatic pistol in his belt, and she was easily interrupted when he raised his forefinger to point back down the path.

There, four masked men were carrying a larger hand sledge, a kind of stiff wooden litter. Perched on it was a woman. The sunlight shone on her black dress and tattered shawl. Her hair was tied back in a dusty scarf.

Behind her and ahead of her, men carried banners blazoned with the dog's head of Beloved Angkhdt. She clapped her hands and her bearers came to a quick halt. They stood unmoving, unblinking in the sun, their naked chests coursing with sweat.

She was looking at Cassia with a peculiar expression on her face. Yet it was not unfriendly; Cassia gathered up her courage and approached.

The woman was immensely old. Her face was covered with a web of wrinkles, so numerous and fine that from a few yards away they were invisible. From a few yards away she could preserve the illusion of a kind of youth, but once Cassia stood in front of her, her nose was assaulted with a smell of ancient dust. The woman's skin looked thin as paper over her sharp bones, and her black eyes were speckled with white motes. Nevertheless, she appeared to see Cassia clearly. Though Cassia was tempted to believe that it was not her face but another's that the old woman saw. She was looking at Cassia with a bemused expression which suggested recognition.

"Please, ma'am," said Cassia, and then she stopped, embarrassed. But Mama Jobe was there to help her. She was standing by the hand sledge, and before she spoke she hawked up her entire plug of tobacco, and dribbled it out into the grass.

"For the love of God," she said, wiping her grey lips. And then she put her fist against her forehead and mumbled: " 'Every man and every woman I desire equally, with equal appetite.' "

It was the beginning of a verse from the Song of Angkhdt. But then she too broke off, and allowed her natural impudence to overwhelm this small attempt at piety. She reached out to seize hold of the sledge's rim. "Get off of this," she said, wiping her lips again. "Please. My friend needs this more than you."

Without moving, without changing their expressions, the men in red masks seemed to acquire bulk, seemed to swell up, so that Cassia was aware of them again. But then the old woman got up from her cushion and hopped to the ground. She paid no attention to Mama Jobe. She was staring at Cassia's face. When she smiled she showed a perfect set of tiny teeth.

"Well, so what about it?" demanded Mama Jobe, glaring around at all of them. "Abu Starbridge told us to share everything we had. He kissed the laundress on the lips. We are the poor folk, and we love him best." But she was protesting for no reason, because the old woman wasn't listening. But she was staring at Cassia's face and smiling with an odd vague hazy smile, showing teeth that looked too fragile for use. "Where is the cannibal?" she asked. "Where is the skull?"—words that made no sense to Cassia.

Ancient as dust, yet still spry, the woman caught Cassia by the arm as she stepped backward. Her voice was clear and high, and yet remote, as if it reached them from a long distance away. "How could you know?" she asked. "How could you know anything? Not yet—but I will show you."

The old woman was called Azimuth; she had no other name. She was the last person still alive in what had been the diocese of Charn to have been born into the old tradition. A consecrated priest of Angkhdt, a curate from the Temple of Kindness and Repair, had escaped out of the city after the revolution, hidden in a wine jar. He had disdained to flee the country with the others, and until his death he lived in Caladon, disguised, nocturnal, hunted, hidden from the police in safehouses and caves. He had held celebrations of the mass among small covens of believers, and before his martyrdom he had managed to baptise a few infants according to the old rite. Azimuth was one, the only daughter of a wealthy wholesaler of cocaine. The priest had listened to her wailing, as in the words of the newborn she had told him of her life in Paradise, and of the sins that had compelled her down into the world, to be reborn in the harsh world. He had marked her penance on her body. "Look at my hands," she said to Cassia. And in fact there was a great deal to look at. Cassia was accustomed to the way the pilgrims would adorn their palms with ink or chalk or charcoal patterns. She had seen a man cut a crude symbol into his hand with his own pocketknife, and then rub ink into the wound. She had seen the gleaming hands of Longo Starbridge. The old woman's hands were not like his.

Her hands informed her how to act. "You're right," she said, turning to Mama Jobe, raising at the same time her emaciated index finger, which was wrapped in the scarlet double helix of generosity and loving kindness. "You're right," she said, squinting toward the rocks where Servant of God lay propped, chafing the tiny black nutcracker upon the ball of her thumb, the mark of empathy for the unfortunate. She took a few steps toward him, her head cocked at the end of her brittle neck. Then she turned: "Stop here for lunch," she said to her red-masked captain, who was standing by the trail with an automatic rifle in his hands. "Carry these people to the altar," she said, touching the rooster's purple silhouette upon her wrist, the symbol of random and arbitrary authority in small matters. "Follow us there and keep the others back. Keep the people back for half an hour," she said in her remote high voice. "We'll go alone," she continued, turning back to Cassia. "Ah!—it will be time to talk."

She smelled like dust, and Cassia hated her. But her fragility made her hard to resist. She took Cassia by the elbow and led her up the trail. The men in red masks held their rifles to their chests, and turned aside to let them pass.

And so they stepped out from under the shadow of the trees, under the blank sun. They came out on the lava flow and climbed over the first hills of powdered glass.

They had left the others where the trees gave out. Miss Azimuth was nimble, but her bones seemed dry and weak. Cassia was afraid that if she fell down among the complicated rocks, the shards of glass, then she would break them. She allowed the old woman to take her by the elbow. With her other hand, Miss Azimuth was making elaborate gestures while she talked. "Look at my hands," she said.

Underfoot, the path was full of crushed obsidian, and it rose over a dune of black rough powdered glass, glinting with an intolerable and shifting brightness in a thousand parts. Cassia hesitated, closed her eyes, and for the first time she could feel the effect of the new altitude, a throbbing in her ears, a buzzing in her blood, and her breath was small and shallow in her chest. Far ahead the path wound down into the trees again, and above her rose the wooded slope of Mt. Nyangongo, up to the rim of the first caldera. She felt as naked as a fly among the harsh sharp shards of glass, as if her body had been reduced to some elemental smallness; she raised up her hand against the sun. On the lava, all color had been leached away, and there were dusty blacks and whites and greys, a long dry river which had flowed down from a crack in the caldera rim, shattering the trees for a span of half a mile.

In that place, all color seemed to come out of the hands of the old woman. Her hands were covered with tattoos, a myriad of letters, words, and symbols. She was working her hands ceaselessly, and they were talking as she talked. Each phrase out of her brittle lips seemed to require a different and specific gesture that would bring a different and specific image into prominence. Out on the lava flow, they would pause often to rest. There she would let go of Cassia's arm and let her hands talk together.

"Don't worry about them; you'll see them soon," she said, for Cassia was looking backward at the trees where they had left the others so abruptly. The soldiers had spread out among the broken trees that marked the edge of the flow, and Cassia could see them with their rifles in their hands, keeping the people back. "The cripple is a holy man," said Mistress Azimuth. "I've heard of him. Under risen Paradise he will walk again. But he must save his strength. I have medicine for him, a special dose."

She was of the caste of scholars and apothecaries. The image of a row of old glass bottles ran up the inside of her middle finger, and her clothes smelled like the laudanum that Mr. Sarnath had taken sometimes with his tea.

On the mound under the old woman's fourth finger, floating in a sea of indigo, shone Paradise. Her skin was dry as paper, like painted paper stretched over a cage of dry bones, and on it shone the silver orb of Paradise, covered with its strange and regular patterns of lines—the cities, the towers, the castles of the blessed. Beneath it, the deep night indigo had lightened to a molten rose; looking closely at the central panel of the old woman's palm, Cassia could see the unmistakable flank of Mt. Nyangongo, rising in full eruption, spattering the sky with light, its black slopes streaked with rivers of fire. "This is the mixing point," said the old woman. "This is the crisis of my life."

Her voice was little and remote as they struggled up the hills of glass. Her legs were thin as sticks; she tottered over the uncertain ground, and if she fell, Cassia knew that she would break them. "It is the crisis of my life," said the old woman. "This is the crisis of my life," she repeated, staring up into the sky. The pupils of her eyes were closed to steely dots. And she kept on mumbling these words and others in a small drugged singsong as they came down over the flow and into a black dell. There was a puddle of black water at the bottom where the footprints of a thousand pilgrims had turned the trail into a gritty swamp. Cassia's bare feet, toughened to leather from a lifetime out of doors, nevertheless were now abraded and sore. She stepped carefully from rock to glinting rock, but at the bottom of the dell she slipped and gashed the high arch of her foot against a shard of glass. When the yellow blood came bubbling out, the old woman bent to examine it. She bent down from the waist until she was touching Cassia's foot. She kept her legs straight, her knees locked, her back straight too, and her jerky sudden movement was so exactly like a puppet's or a wooden doll's that Cassia felt her stomach and her temper rise. She forgot about the pain. The old woman was mumbling to herself and rubbing a drop of blood between her thumb and index finger, over a tattoo of a wicked blue face. Gradually a stain of green seemed to spread out over her fingers as the blood mixed with the pigment underneath; she stared at it, mumbling and clucking.

Disgusted, Cassia stood up. Her feet were sore. But now she could see the far side of the flow, a line of stunted dry-leafed trees. A sudden gust of wind, and she could hear the leaves rattling among the dusty branches. Doubtless there was some dirt under them, and at least some honest rock, and perhaps something to drink; people were there. She could see four children sitting on a boulder.

She dragged the old woman upright and then dragged her forward. She was not gentle. She dragged the woman by her creaking elbow until they stood under the trees. Even then she would not stop to rest, though now the path turned sharply uphill. Her feet were sore and she continued onward with a long loping stride, eager now to get wherever they were going; the path led straight up to the caldera's rim. Her mind was full of inconsequent images of Rael standing, Rael sitting, Rael's shoulder, Rael's naked waist; she barely looked where she was going. And she was dragging the old woman after her—a useless bulky burden like a large battered empty suitcase with something rattling inside, because the faster they went, the more the old woman was mumbling and chattering, not in anger, not even in distress.

As they continued, the woods filled up with pilgrims once more. Cassia was concentrating on a few small things: the scratches on her feet, the heat of her breath and thump of her heart as the path grew steep. She was anxious to know what lay ahead, anxious to find someplace to dispose of the old woman. But even so she had to notice how the pilgrims reacted to the sight of Miss Azimuth, how they cleared the way for her, how they stepped aside out of the trail and put their knuckles to their foreheads. The old woman was a personage, a figure of authority. Dry as she was, useless, empty, still the children knelt down reverently among the rocks, while the men and women hid their eyes. Cassia felt a gush of anger in her belly—anger and contempt for the deluded crowd. She remembered the brutality of the hot brand the night before, the stink rising up, the pilgrims crying out in drunken ecstasy. She thought about the coarseness of Mama Jobe, the futility of the Servant's sacrifice, and above all her strange loneliness amid this mass of souls, and where was Rael? Where was Rael now? She felt amputated from him, isolated, as if she were the only creature on the mountainside. In an open space between the trees where the path suddenly leveled out, she let go of the old woman's arm.

Miss Azimuth collapsed onto the rocks. Her dry hair protruded out from the left side of her head. Her scarf had slipped over her right eye. Her legs were splayed apart under her dress, and her face retained for several minutes an expression of remote astonishment. Cassia's blood was beating in her head, her breath was ragged in her throat, and there were tears in her eyes, tears that could not manage to drip down her cheeks the whole time that she stood there. Inside she was a swamp of anger, a fountain of contempt; still after a moment the water dried out of her eyes and she could see more clearly. Her breathing settled, and the grunting at the back of it resolved itself into a few small words, a saying of the master's, which Mr. Sarnath had taught her when she was a little girl. " 'There's nothing sweeter than your love,' " she said aloud. " 'There's nothing sweeter than your love.' "

This was a portion of a longer verse that Mr. Sarnath had taught her as a calming exercise, a way to vanquish feelings of self-righteousness, a way to climb back down into a comfortable humility. But now she could remember only the last line, and now the sick sensation of anger in her belly was driving her up out of herself, into a new high place inside her head. Her contempt came back redoubled as the pilgrims crept out from behind the rocks, behind the twisted trees, and they were kneeling down. Now from that high mountain in her head, it was easy for her to realize that they were bowing to her, that they had stepped aside for her. For her they had made the gestures of respect, her with her gashed foot and the golden blood painting her instep.

An old man came out toward her, creeping along the ground, his hand outstretched, his eyes averted. She turned away from him and hurried up the last remaining slopes until the trees gave way completely. She clambered up over the bleached rocks until she stood atop the rim of the caldera. Still above her, the bulk of Nyangongo loomed up to the sky, surmounted by its column of smoke, its cloud of mist. Below her the path descended a few dozen yards into a shallow flat circular expanse of sand and rock. It was the old collapsed caldera of an earlier and now extinct volcano. It formed a natural amphitheater more than a mile across, and it was full of people, perhaps ten thousand people with their baggage and their children. At the center of it stood an altar, a scaffold of wood and steel.

*　*　*

Rael hunted in the forest all day. He found a rubber wheel. He could not guess its age—whether it had lain there through the generations, preserved by chance or else some ancient process, or whether it had been discarded recently. There was no sign of any metal carcass, any truck or motorcar. The wheel was imbedded in the moss. Yet why would anybody carry it this far and no farther?

The tread was worn and cracked. He took the steel spike out of his belt and levered the edge of the tire up over the wheel's rim, exposing the inner tube. Yet still his mind was full of questions; he sat back in the moss and shook his head, a sadness inside of him. Questions in his mind—they were like bats in a cave. And each one had a sentence printed on its wing, and each was talking words out of its mouth. Thoughts and feelings, thoughts and feelings bending to caress his face and then fleeing away.

He pulled the spike in a circle around the rim. And then he reached into the cavity and pulled out the old tube, its white corroded surface covered with small cracks. Yet there was still some suppleness left. He took out from his pocket the brass jackknife that Mr. Sarnath had once given him— a feeble tool. But he had kept the blade battered to sharpness, and now he cut a strip of rubber from the tube, a yard long, six inches wide.

He made a slingshot out of a small Y-shaped stick, and then he sat back on his heels in the moss, and sat there most of the whole day. With deliberate care he emptied out his mind, concentrating on sensation only: the ache in his feet and knees, the sweat upon his body, the smell of old rubber on his hands. After an hour or so of stillness he was conscious of a new spectrum of forest noises—the leaves, the insects, the stir of branches in the tiny wind. Animals too—after an hour and a half a family of swamp martens clambered up onto the long branch of a cypress tree. They were happy creatures with brown pelts and fluffy tails, and they were chattering to each other, and arguing, and playing. From time to time one of them would stop, reacting to some tiny noise which Rael too had heard with his new ears—the turning of a leaf, the click of a beetle's foot against a stone. Then one of the martens would crouch down upon its branch, and Rael could see how in its stillness it had found a new intensity of action, straining, pregnant, and implied, where all its heart and fear and hope were concentrated to a single point.

A mother and two daughters, perhaps. And in time another one, an older male upon a stump. This was one was slow, missing one foot, and with some naked cancerous growth upon its head. In its moments of immobility it seemed to achieve an even purer essence of awareness. When Rael lifted up his sling, it turned to face him. And when he pulled the strip of rubber, loaded with its shard of glass, against his ear, it assumed a stillness that seemed preternatural. Rael could hear the rubber creak, begin to break apart, yet still he did not release the stone. He kept it to his ear until the final moment. Then he let fly. The stone sailed harmlessly into the trees. The family of martens disappeared.

SOLDIERS OF PARADISE

9

The summit of Mt. Nyangongo, in the days before its most recent eruptions, rose eleven thousand feet out of the valley floor. The main cone of it was rarely climbable, because of the constant fog of poisonous gases at the top; even halfway up a change of wind could always bring a trace of some debilitating odor. Toward the top the angle of ascent exceeded sixty degrees, and the vitrescent rock was sharp and smooth and sheer. In those days the mountain was still growing, and new lava seeped out regularly from a split in the narrow crater. At night the summit of the mountain glowed through a cloud of mist, its contour described by a small tracery of fire.

Halfway down the western slope, the old crater bulged out of the mountain's side. Long collapsed, long extinct, impressive, isolated, easily defended, it had become over the months of summer a place of refuge for the faithful, a meeting place, a gathering place. Thousands of people from all over the old diocese of Charn had made the trip up through the woods for Paradise Festival, and they had brought liquor and marijuana and coffee and imported goods to swap or sell.

In winter, the festival had been a bitter ceremony, a celebration of the hundred kinds of slavery. The rites had been imposed, determined by the Starbridge hierarchy—the bishops and the princes and the priests. Now, in summer, the impulse for the festival had come up from below, and it was still a joyful, mirthful, hopeful thing. When at sunset on the sixty-third, Rael arrived upon the rim of the caldera, he stood for half an hour listening to his breath, summoning his courage to descend. For it seemed to him that the old volcano still showed signs of life—the whole round plain below him was ablaze with shifting light, speckled with ten thousand fires that were dwindling and growing as he watched, winking out and reappearing. There were cookfires, bonfires, lanterns, flashlights, fireworks, and acetylene torches. To Rael, who had lived all his life in the forest and had rarely seen an unimpeded sunset, it was as if the mass of fire in the bowl in front of him had torched the sky. And though it was cold on the mountain and he could feel a cold wind along his spine, his face was glowing from the heat that was rising from the crater. The separate sounds of cherry bombs and shouts and music and ten thousand conversations had combined into a roar. The smell of gunpowder and food and smoke and unwashed bodies was rising like a steam—an acrid steam that hurt his eyes.

He turned around for a moment so that the heat was at his back, and looked down the way he'd come. He felt giddy in the new altitude, giddy and unsure. The valley where he had seen the martens was opaque with shadow, and it was as if a flood of shadow was mounting toward him up the slope, obliterating every rock and tree. Soon he was standing on an island in the middle of a sea of shadow, an atoll of red rock, with only the red mountain and the red sky still above him. In front of him, at the level of his eye, five thousand feet above the valley floor, a bird turned swiftly, the last of the sunlight in its wings.

When he was a little boy, before he could even speak, he had cut twenty-four lengths of dry bamboo and arranged them on a frame of strings. Mr. Sarnath had helped him. Alone in the woods, he had beat on it for several days. Then he had stopped.

Now, on the mountainside, an image from his childhood appeared to him. A young boy with an angry face, half-naked in the woods—it was himself, his sticks upraised above his xylophone. Six notes occurred to him. Whether it was a song from those old days, whether it was something put into his mind by the hunter he had seen among the laurel trees, whether it was something new—he couldn't tell. Even there, standing with the hot roar of the crowd behind him, he thought he sensed somewhere in the cold high air the whisper of a song, a few notes of a melody that was meant for him alone. Six notes only, yet they seemed significant. He turned around.

A quarter of a mile away there was a crack in the rim of the caldera. A path ran down from it among the rocks into the shadow, back the way he had climbed up, and Rael could hear the voices of late-coming pilgrims. Their lanterns mimicked the flow of lava from the crack of Mt. Nyangongo high above—a tiny stream of fire that trickled down into the dark. Climbing from the valley, Rael had tried to stay just out of earshot from it, just out of sight. Now, above timber, the path seemed close, and Rael could see the scurrying black figures underneath the torches, and he could hear their anxious voices.

Then he turned back again. Or perhaps the stream of fire was like a cable which brought power up from down below. Taking a few steps down into the heat of the caldera, Rael could hear the thump thump thump of a gas generator, which someone had lugged up all that way.

It stood amid some boulders, surrounded by canisters of fuel. Some men stood near it, drinking and shouting above the noise. One, stripped to his waist, was lying on his stomach with an expansion wrench in his left hand. He was making some adjustment among the whirring belts and wheels around the generator's underside. His face, twisted with effort, was illuminated by a spray of sparks. As Rael approached, for an instant the thumping sound quit suddenly, and a whole wide area of the caldera floor went dark. Curses and whistles rose up all around, turning to cheers when the generator started up again. The lights came up. Near Rael's foot, the thick and knotted wire jerked suddenly as the electricity rushed through.

It was not two dozen yards from the rim of the caldera to its floor. With every step downward Rael had felt an increase in the heat, the noise, the light. When he stepped out onto the sandy floor, he turned his face up to the sky. But it was gone—the wind, the quiet, the color, the solitary bird, all replaced by a harsh artificial glow, the sound of drunken shouting. People were all around him. It was as if he had stepped into the streets of a city. A long erratic spiral of tin, cardboard, and canvas shelters curved away from him.

He was dressed in his old tattered cotton shorts which Mr. Sarnath had made for him, and which he had scarcely taken off since he left the village in the trees. His upper body was wrapped in his blanket, which he had pulled up around his neck and shoulders. It hid most of his face; summoning courage, he stepped out along the first turn of the spiral. Almost for the first time in his life he was conscious of how he must appear to other people: a brooding, ominous figure. These folk were as alien to him as the Treganu. For the festival they had put on bright, gay clothes. They had painted their bodies with bright colors, and most of them wore masks. It was a hot night, and many of the young women had stripped down to almost nothing—just a pair of red spandex knickers, for example, or, as in one spectacular case, white legwarmers, white gloves to the shoulder, a white mask, and a wide white plastic belt. Their bodies were slick with oil, pungent with sweat. They walked arm in arm between the tents, talking and laughing. Many had painted their teeth and mouths and throats with silver Day-Glo, which was particularly effective under the electric lights. When they threw their heads back to laugh, their breath seemed to share some of the silver glow, appearing for a moment in a glinting cloud.

Rael was hungry. In front of almost every shelter the occupants had lit a cookfire or a primus stove. It was the hour for eating, and whole families squatted around them now. Rael was assaulted as he passed between them by the smell of vegetables in oil, of puffbread fried in bell-shaped pans, of spattering hot grease. His nose was assaulted by a hundred thousand cries and groans and shouts and yells, rising everywhere above the murmured conversation. To his right and to his left, old men sat on blankets spread out on the sand, and they were smoking sinsemillian cigars, and playing dominoes and chess. They were shouting at the children, who scattered sand in their faces as they chased each other down the curving path, and hid from each other among the tents. There were children everywhere, laughing, screaming, fighting, playing games. In front of Rael five little boys were setting off bottle rockets and flying saucers under the supervision of an older sister. Behind him, boys lit strings of squibs and threw them at each other. They were the only ones who paid any attention to Rael; they threw firecrackers and ran after him, pulling on his blanket, taunting him with questions that he didn't understand. When he turned on them they backed away.

The first curve of the spiral path ran close against the wall of the caldera. Halfway along it, Rael came out into an open space, where the tents and shelters gave way temporarily and the path ran through an assortment of ramshackle structures made of wood and steel and glass, twice and three times as tall as men. Another generator hummed nearby. Black cables ran over the sand, for these structures were electric and alive. From time to time, in sequence, each one would shudder into life, its red and green and silver neon tubes would light up from its base to its crown, its wheels would move, its arms and head would move, its lights would flash on and off, and for ten seconds or so it would describe in jerky and repetitive pantomime one of the episodes of the immortal life of Angkhdt—stories unknown to Rael, who wandered between them with his mouth open in amazement, but serious as death to the assembled pilgrims, especially the older ones. Old men and women knelt before each one, and some had worn grooves in the sand from the pressure of their foreheads. The children didn't care as much, and they were running through the thicket of mechanical statues, intent on their own missions. Occasionally one or two would stop as Rael did, wide-eyed before some spectacular tableau—the defenestration of the yellow gypsy, for example. Angkhdt appeared first, his silver neon dog's head barbarous and impressive. His cobalt eyes glowed. His scarlet lips grinned. Then his arms, which had been hanging by his sides, disappeared as the lights that described them were extinguished. New arms flickered on, these ones holding in their massive clasp the foreign whore, naked with red hair, her breasts perfect circles of yellow neon, her nipples dots of red. Angkhdt turned his head to show his profile, and then the entire structure moved several feet along a greased and creaking rail toward the window, which had suddenly appeared, outlined with glowing ruffled curtains.

A voice said: "Aren't you hot?"

Rael turned. Beside him stood a girl his own age. She had silver glitter in her hair. The inside of her mouth was rinsed with silver.

She said: "Great Angkhdt tells us to be kind to strangers. My grandmother said you looked lonely when you passed our tent. She sent me to give you this."

In her right hand she was carrying a paper bowl of dahl

baht, garnished with two sprigs of broccoli. In her left hand she held a yellow pear. She was smiling as she raised them up, but then her expression faltered, for Rael had not moved. She looked away and then looked back. *"Kamesh nidiri,"* she said. And then in a third language, *"Ku'un sabh,"* she said, even more timidly. Then she switched back to the first. "You understand me when I speak?"

Rael nodded. In fact he did feel hot, his blanket scratchy and uncomfortable. He pulled it down from around his face and loosened it around his neck.

The girl smiled. "That's better. Grandmother asked me to invite you back. She said no one should be alone tonight. She sent me to invite you."

Rael loosened the blanket from his shoulder until his hands were free. His fingers were shaking as he put his hands around the paper bowl; it was still hot. He raised it to his lips. "Thank . . ." he said, and then stopped, interrupted in his thinking by a single mental image of Mr. Sarnath in the woods, his hand upraised for silence, trying to teach him how to use the thanking word. "You," he concluded, after a long pause.

His mouth was burning, for the dahl baht was full of chili peppers. As he chewed, he could feel a tingling flush overtake his cheeks, could feel the sweat bead on his forehead. In front of him Great Angkhdt and the yellow gypsy shuddered to new life, after several minutes of darkness.

"Let's get away from here," said the girl. "I hate this one." She took a few steps into the dark and Rael followed her.

She was dressed in a grey leotard and denim shorts. Her arms were bare. Rael followed her, chewing the fiery rice, his face covered with sweat. Then she turned back toward him, holding out the yellow pear. He took it gratefully and gave her back the empty bowl, which she crushed together in her hand. "Thank you," he said again.

The pear was so cool in his mouth, so fresh. The taste of

it seemed to spread through his body. His blanket had fallen open to reveal his chest, covered with dirt and streaked with sweat. There were four cuts on his stomach, scabbed over but still oozing blood.

"Look at you," she said. "You're shaking. How long since you last ate?" He didn't answer, because he didn't know, couldn't remember, couldn't bring back any image from the recent past. Only the six notes that had occurred to him upon the mountain—seven, eight notes now, and she was right. He felt tired.

"Look at you," she said again.

She had followed him along the outer circle so as not to miss him. But going back they took the short, straight way, which led them through another section of the fair. Merchants and peddlers had set up booths. Some were merely lamp-lit tents, or stools supporting wooden boxes, their small shelves lined with toothpaste, incense, aspirin, biscuits, razor blades, and bags of stale bread. Others were more elaborate: permanent wooden booths on wheels, with windows cut into one side and lined with neon or electric bulbs. People sold kaya gum and hashish oil, comic books, icons, syringes, antibiotic capsules, fireworks, and, donated by a foreign government, strings of condom prophylactics in bright foil packages. People sold imported rhinestone jewelry, and calculators, and transistor radios—these booths especially were packed with customers, for it was all untaxed contraband, and the prices were low. People sold ice cream, curried sweet potatoes, and fried dough from little stalls. Rael found his mouth still chewing as he followed his companion through the crush, even though his pear was long gone, and he had swallowed even the stem and the seeds. The girl turned back to him. And she only hesitated for a moment before she took his hand and led him past rows of blackjack booths and wheels of chance. He allowed himself to be led, for his eyes were overwhelmed by the cascade of lights. People touched him with their greasy skins, touched him everywhere. His blanket was gone, lost, snatched away, and his ears were deafened by the shouts and yells, the scratchy carnival music from the loudspeakers.

His companion bought some cotton candy from a stall. "I promised my sister," she said. Then she stepped into a dark place between two tents, and instantly the noise was less. The lights scarcely penetrated ten feet from the thoroughfare; she led him down a corridor in back of a row of tents, and it was dark there, and they were alone except for someone urinating in a ditch. Again Rael looked up at the sky. He could see the stars, and again that small song occurred to him—ten, a dozen notes now, just a small flicker of music in his mind and it was gone.

"Come on," said the girl. "We're almost there." She pulled his hand. She turned between two rows of cardboard shacks, stepping daintily over the entwined legs of a man and woman copulating in the sand. Tied together in a sheet, their pulsing bodies blocked the way. Rael followed the girl past them a few yards, and then he stopped. "Look," he said.

She frowned. Rael could see a small crease in her brow. "Don't bother about them. It's true—they don't quite understand. Not yet, says Grandmama. But they're closer than some others."

Rael shook his head and tried again. "Looking now," he said. "Not find her is finding. A sweet now," he added, turning his face toward the sky.

"What did you say?"

"Yes," interrupted Rael. "But not seeing."

They had reached a thoroughfare, quieter than the one they'd left. People sat outside their tents, smoking cigarettes.

The girl walked out into the middle of the road and peered along it. "What did you . . . ?" she started, but questions always irritated Rael.

"Many," he said, raising his hands to the sky. "Many many

many." He felt a slow uncertain nausea, deep in his guts. "Lost her," he said.

The girl pushed out her lips. "Who?" she asked, but Rael did not reply.

"A friend of yours?" she asked.

"We'll help you if you want," she said after a pause. "Me and my sister. Not now—most people are inside. You'll never find her. But when Paradise comes up, they'll all go down into the middle. You'll have a better chance down there."

"You'll never find her" was what Rael understood, because it was so close to his own thoughts. He let his arms drop to his sides. "Don't worry," said the girl. "You'll feel better once you've had some food."

A smaller girl was running toward them up the street. "Oh, Enid," she called. "You got him." But then she stopped. "Oops," she said. "I know we're not supposed to use our names."

She was younger, perhaps half Enid's age. She wore a red satin dress and red shoes. She wore a scarlet mask over her eyes, glitter in her hair, and a hibiscus blossom pinned over one ear. The yellow tongue of its stamen protruded out at Rael. Behind him, the couple in the sand were generating soft wet slapping noises as they made love.

Almost he turned to go away, but Enid had grasped hold of his thumb. Her other hand was on her hip. "Jane," she said, "I told you, Jane, what Grandmother told me." And then to Rael: "My sister's name is Jane."

"Oh, well, it's stupid anyway," protested the younger girl. "We're all friends now." She took Rael's hand upon the other side. "Come on. They're waiting to see if you came back."

She pulled him forward a few steps and then she stopped. "I almost forgot. Grandma gave me this to give to you," she said, pulling the hibiscus flower from her hair and holding it up. "She said to tell you that God loves you."

The blossom felt fragile and tired in his hand. It had no

scent. "Humph," said Enid. "He knows that already. Everyone knows that." She was angry. She pulled him along by his thumb and he went with her. She pulled him along a row of cardboard crates, each one with a little cookfire outside. Men and women sat on blankets and they called out greetings. They raised up their right hands, their fingers spread apart, to show the mark of the shining sun, crudely drawn in charcoal on their palms. This was a quiet section of the spiral, with no fireworks or loud commotion, though Rael as he looked upward sometimes saw a rocket speeding off into the night.

But as they came around the turn, they saw some people grouped in front of them. "It's the apothecaries," cried Jane. She pulled down Rael's hand so that she could see his naked palm. "Did you get some? No. Come on."

A steel cage lay in the middle of the road, and at each of its four corners stood a man in a red robe with an automatic rifle strapped across his back. Inside the cage was the largest insect Rael had ever seen, a fat six-legged cockroach or a flea, more than two feet long from its blind head to the end of its abdomen. Its snout protruded through the bars; its mandibles and claws made a spasmodic clicking noise.

Beside it, another cage lay upended in the sand. Three old men, also dressed in red, were sitting on a spread-out sheet. In front of them lay the gutted husk of another insect. They had pulled off part of its carapace, and on a glass mortar stone they were crushing it to a powder. They were mixing it with other powders from a row of bottles.

Men and women from the tents and shelters stood in a circle around them. "It's the fleas of Angkhdt," whispered Enid as she pulled Rael forward. "It's for the festival." Never letting go of his thumb, she slithered to the front. Jane was there already, kneeling before one of the old men, holding out her hands.

He was a small, fat-bellied man. He lifted up a fragment of the insect's leg, and with it he made portentous passes over the head of a brass statue of Immortal Angkhdt, also cross-legged, also fat-bellied. "You're too young," he said to Jane. "Besides, weren't you here already?"

"It's not for me. It's for him," she protested, motioning back toward Rael.

"Then let him come."

The apothecary's voice was hollow and empty. His words meant nothing to Rael. But Enid pulled him down until he too was squatting in the sand, and she tugged on his thumb until his palm lay open. People made way for him; smiling and friendly, they helped him down onto his knees. They held him by the shoulders as the apothecary passed a smoking stick of incense over his hand, and then marked it in charcoal with the mark of Abu Starbridge.

The apothecary seized him by the wrist. Rael could see the man's bare arm up to his shoulder, and it was flabby and unmuscled and relaxed. Nevertheless, Rael felt his own arm pulled forward, and he was staring into the apothecary's cold grey eyes. At the same time, another man with equally strong hands scratched him on the inside of his forearm with an iron stylus. He sealed off the vein in Rael's elbow with his thumb, and then massaged the scratch that he had made until a line of tiny beads of blood appeared amid the smudges from his dirty fingers.

And that was all. Suddenly released out of the old man's grasp, Rael staggered to his feet. He staggered backward out of the circle of onlookers into cooler, less obstructed air. Already as he did so, a peculiar sensation was spreading up his arm. He caressed the inside of his elbow, and rubbed his fingertips together. "Don't worry," said Enid, reaching for his thumb, pulling his hand away. "It's for the festival."

Already he felt giddy. Her words seemed distorted and remote. But it was only a few more steps to her grandmother's tent. When he reached it, he sat down on a blanket, staring straight in front of him. Someone brought him food from a pot by the fire, and he just managed to finish his sixth bowl of cauliflower curry before he fell asleep. His head sank down upon his chest, and it required the help of several neighbors to move his body inside the tent, and stretch him out upon a cotton mat. He was not aware of them. His sleep was smooth and black and still.

Cassia, though, was rolling and tossing in her bed. She was mumbling, and shaking her head back and forth. Her hands were clenched, her breath ragged and hoarse, for she was drowning in a pool of dreams.

But after the first hour she stopped struggling and slid down to a darker level. Then she was quiet: her body stiff, her spine taut. For forty minutes the only movement which her observers detected was the trembling of her fingers, the trembling of her eyelids.

In the middle of the second hour she relaxed somewhat, and rolled onto her back. Her breathing now was slow and deep. The fist of her right hand unclenched, and her fingers lolled open on the coverlet. Miss Azimuth, waiting for the change, chose that moment to pull back the lid of her left eye. Miss Azimuth held the lantern up, to demonstrate to Karan Mang and to the priest how Cassia's pupil was expanding and contracting, expanding and contracting. The old woman had observed the process, but she had no way of understanding what it meant: how at that moment Cassia's dreams were changing. Images appeared to her. A series of images appeared to her. On the surface of the pool where she was drowning, there appeared a knotted rope. It was the story of a life. She seized it; she grasped hold of it, and moved along it knot by knot, and the first knot was the image of a cat, scratching at the outside of a windowpane.

"I do not understand," said Karan Mang in his accented, careful voice. He had come late, after the end of the first hour. Yet of the four observers he was the most restless, often getting up and moving to the entrance of the big silk tent and looking out over the festival grounds. Now he pulled back the white silk flap so that the others could see the workmen at the altar, a hundred yards away. With a block and tackle they were hoisting up onto the stage the enormous wicker statue of dog-headed Angkhdt. Under the klieg lights the God's twisting shadow reached almost to the tent.

Cassia was dreaming: First there was a noise at the window, an animal scratching at the pane. Precipitation had coated the outside of the glass with sugar scum, and the animal's claws cleaned out a circle. Through it she could see a circle of black night and glimpses of a furry face. And then the casement gave way, the window swung open, and a cat jumped down into the room.

"I do not understand," said Karan Mang. "What are we waiting for?"

Miss Azimuth was in an armchair, the lantern by her side. The others were still sitting on the floor beside the bed. One of the priests was dozing and the other was running his big thumb along the inside of a silver bowl, hunting an elusive shred of okra. During their wait they had been served dinner, and the remnants of it lay around them. Miss Azimuth had eaten nothing.

"Ah," she said, "don't you remember? When I was a child I watched a chrysalis change to a butterfly. I watched it for two days."

Cassia dreamed that she was standing by the window of her own room in her own high tower. The room was small and spare, with walls of quilted silk. Part of it was a private temple lit with candles. There was an altar lined with brass bowls full of water. The wind from the open window roughened the light. It disturbed the surface of the water in the bowls. Outside, she could see the lights of the city, far below. Beyond, lightning caressed the hills, soft and thunderless.

"I do not understand," persisted Karan Mang. "It is the effects of a narcotic, is it not? Where I am from we do not have this drug."

"Ah," continued Miss Azimuth in her faint, clear voice.

"I must have had some of the powder on my skin. I touched the blood upon her foot—she is susceptible. It will be hard for her. Harder for her than for the rest of us, you see, who have a single nature."

"What do you mean? What is this drug?"

"Ah," said the old woman. "Even in my childhood the fleas of Angkhdt were tiny." She held up her finger and thumb an eighth of an inch apart. " 'Mutations,' said my father. I don't know. I have read the treatise on the subject, by Dr. Thanakar Starbridge. Cousin of our saint. It was a case study, but not reliable. An overdose, you see, and not reliable. The effects speak for themselves."

Cassia could hear these voices at the outermost limit of her consciousness. They were like the lightning on the hills outside her window.

She stood with the cat in her arms. Its golden fur was caked with sugar rain. Though she was a stranger, it was docile, not stirring when she bent to take a strip of fabric from the altar—a strip of ikat once used by the God Himself after a bath. Not stirring when she rubbed its fur clean with the ikat, and tried to pull out some of the hunks of sugar crystal from its fur. And then she stopped. She stood holding up the cat against her cheek, as a naked arm reached up over the sill. She said nothing, only muttered one of the fifteen anthems against fear. She was reassured, because the cat was purring now, as the boy dragged himself up over the sill.

The statue of Angkhdt now hung suspended in the air, twenty feet above the stage. It spun first clockwise and then counterclockwise, as its cable twisted and untwisted. It was built of painted paper on a wicker frame.

Karan Mang let go of the tent flap, obscuring it from sight. He turned around into the silken room, breathing as he did so a barely audible sigh. He came back to his stool beside the bed and sat back down, crossing his legs fastidiously. He was inspecting some of the embroidery upon the sleeve of his gown, the silver image of a bird. He said: "What effect?"

Miss Azimuth had dozed off between sentences. But now she woke. Her thin neck jerked her head upright; her thin lips smiled sweetly, and she started speaking again where she'd left off. "It gives you images from your past life, you see, and from your life in Paradise. It gives you images from Paradise, you see. Not me, of course. But I've seen other places. I've seen eleven moons in a red sky, which must be Proxima Vermeil. And I've felt sensations, horrible sensations of heat and pressure. Intolerable sensations, but only for a moment. Sometimes an image of a fiery lake, a wind of fire, which must be Chandra Sere. The fiery planet, but it never lasts for long."

"Paradise," said Karan Mang, examining his painted nails.

The priest had found some candied apricots on a cut-glass dish. "Paradise," he agreed, sucking his finger. "I have seen it. I and my friend. We saw a vision of an empty desert, and the grains of sand were made of gold."

"That sounds very nice," murmured Karan Mang.

The priest's black eyes were rimmed with red, and then another circle of black. He was thin, but his flesh had that unhealthy looseness that suggests dangerous fluctuations of weight. He said: "We saw a vision of a garden, and the grass was made of emeralds. A tree grew in the garden, and its bark was made of agate strips. Its boughs were made of chalcedony, and its leaves were malachite and chrysoprase. A bird stood on a branch. It was made from steel clockwork, and its wings from silver mail. Every hour on the half hour it would open its jeweled beak."

As he spoke, a slow wash of color spread across the walls of Cassia's small tower room. In her dream, she was standing by the altar with the cat in her arms. The front of her grey velvet dress was stained with sugar efflorescence. It stank in her nostrils—an acrid odor that rose also from the boy's naked back as he dragged himself up over the sill.

He crawled toward her on his hands and knees. Rain from the window spread a phosphorescent sheen across the cotton mats. Purring, the cat jumped down. The boy, gathering strength, sat back on his heels and then rose trembling to his feet. He was trembling with fatigue. His massive arms, his massive hands, were trembling. He raised his head for the first time, and his face was Rael's face.

Or rather, not completely. Even in her dream, Cassia was aware that Rael's face was not as strong, not as beautiful. Nevertheless, it was him; it was him in some more perfect world. She felt no fear, just a small mix of joy and trepidation and uncertainty, and she went to him as naturally as she would if she had seen him in his flesh. She had the cloth of ikat in her hand, and she touched his face with it and wiped some of the rain out of his face. "Why did you leave me?" she said. "Why did you leave me in the wood?" In her dream his tongue was loosened, so that he could answer her.

Someone pulled open the flap of the silk tent, and a draft fell across her as she lay upon her bed. In her dream, a wind came through the open window in her tower room. Time had moved, and she was lying on her bed with Rael in her arms. To her observers at that moment her body was perfectly still, but a mile and a half away across the festival Rael stirred upon his mat and cried out, even though his sleep contained no dream, but only empty blackness. Enid and Jane's grandmother had undressed him, and were scraping the dust from his body with a mixture of ground pumice and ginger oil; when she saw his penis stiffen, she rolled him over onto his stomach, to hide him from the girls.

But in her dream Cassia was making love to him, and the sensation in her body this time was one of pure fulfillment. Gently, tenderly he entered her and searched her body for their happiness. And he was talking to her also, saying, "Is this right? Is this right?"

Brother Longo Starbridge was standing at the entrance to the tent, and now he took a few big steps inside. He looked over toward Cassia on the bed, and then turned to the bulimic priest. "You!" he said. "Why can't you give me a straight answer? Everything is ready." He pulled his sleeve away to show his wristwatch. "Half an hour ago. Why can't you ever get it right? You've had a hundred generations to work out the math."

His voice woke up the sleeping priest: a bearded pardoner in scarlet robes. He raised his head from his fat breast, and opened his lids to disclose white blind eyes. The bulimic, meanwhile, had found a piece of sugared ginger and was rubbing it beneath his nose.

"It is one of the enduring mysteries of Paradise," he said at last, "that we can never predict exactly when it rises. Try as we might. I told you that. 'Between seven and nine o'clock,' I said."

"You said seven o'clock, you stupid piece of shit." Brother Longo rubbed his face and rubbed his broken nose, then ran his fingers back through his red hair. "I haven't slept," he muttered, sitting down on the side of the bed where Cassia lay dreaming. Then he caught sight of Karan Mang. "Your guns have started to arrive," he said. "At least that's one thing going right."

The eunuch shrugged. "I am gratified to hear it. But you do not surprise me. A caravan of seventy men, is it not? They were never more than twenty hours behind me."

He was examining the back of his hand, an arch expression on his face. Longo Starbridge sat forward with his elbows on his knees and studied him with nude contempt. Then he shook his head. "I'm glad you can afford the time," he said, and the gesture of his hand encompassed all the dirty plates and dishes, the hashish pipe in its crystal ashtray. "God," he said, turning to Miss Azimuth. "I feel like I'm running this entire show myself. Shouldn't you be doing something?"

All the time that he was speaking, Cassia and Rael were making love in Cassia's dream. Brother Longo's voice was like a thunder in the hills—threatening, but meaning nothing. "I have missed you," Rael said. "I have missed you so."

But she sat up and put her finger to his lips. She had heard a step upon the stair.

"Testing," said a voice outside the tent. A hand stagehand blew into a mike. "Testing one," he said, heavily amplified. Then came a thumping sound, followed by a whine of feedback. The klieg lights on the stage moved back and forth. They cast patterns of blue shadows even in the tent, for they burned brighter now. Even at a hundred yards they penetrated the thick silk.

"Ah," said the old woman. "Ah, my dear, don't scold me. If you knew how we've been blessed. Look here."

She gathered herself up out of her chair, gathered together her thin arms and legs and stepped carefully among the dishes to stand by Brother Longo's side. "We are blessed," she repeated in her highest, faintest voice, for it was full of suppressed laughter. She had smoked a lot of hashish, which had helped to calm her; she put her hand on Brother Longo's wrist. "Only believe," she said.

Behind her, Cassia had rolled onto her side. Her face was hidden in her hair. But now Miss Azimuth sat down on the coverlet, and she drew Longo Starbridge by his wrist so that he turned around. "Look at her face," said the old woman. "Look." She leaned over Cassia's shoulder, and slid her hand into her thick black curls, and brushed them from her cheek.

"I've seen her before," grunted Brother Longo.

"Yes, yes, yes, but do you know?"

Cassia was responding to the old woman's touch. She pushed her face against the old woman's hand, nuzzling her dry palm. In her dream she put her cheek against Rael's cheek, and put her finger to his lips. "Hush," she said "Be quiet—we are not alone."

On the pillow beside her head was an album of old photographs in a gilded vinyl binding. Miss Azimuth held it open with her free hand. The klieg lights made a pattern of blue shadows on the page. Nevertheless it was still possible for

Brother Longo to make out rows of snapshots, postcards, newspaper clippings: the record of a vanished world. They were photographs from wintertime and early spring in Charn, before the revolution. Each was marked in the old woman's spidery small hand; the bulimic priest had gotten up now and was standing by the bedside with the lantern in his hand, so that Brother Longo could read the captions—Prince Mortimer Starbridge and his sister. The Amethyst Pavilion (East View, Center). Officers of the Bishop's Purge. Monks at Drepung Monastery. Men of the 11th Cavalry. Skaters in the Snow.

Miss Azimuth had taken her fingers from Cassia's hair, and she used both hands to turn over the stiff page. There on the other side, a menu from Old Peter's restaurant, the golden letters barely faded. Recipes that were lost forever, and underneath the date: September 92, Spring 8, 00016. Less than a month later, the mob had sacked the temple.

On the facing page a watercolor portrait of Lord Mara Starbridge, the high constable of Charn. The artist had captured an expression of the purest vacuity upon his handsome face.

Again Miss Azimuth turned the page, using both hands. Brother Longo put out his forefinger to touch a photograph: Princess Charity Starbridge, age eleven months. Still a child, she smiled gleefully out of the picture, hands on her hips. For the sake of the portrait she was dressed in the clothes of child laborer, a glass miner, perhaps. Artfully ripped, yet they were all of silk and velvet. She was carrying a pair of goggles and a white asbestos mask.

Brother Longo ran his thumb across the print. The phosphorescent paint upon his hand was barely lit now. Yet still it mocked him. These were the real Starbridges, not like him. He raised his eyes. "So what?" he said.

Miss Azimuth was crooning faintly in her throat. "Patience," she murmured. "Patience." More rapidly now she pushed back the big pages, until she reached the final three.

A single photographic print was mounted on each one. The first: Chrism Demiurge, secretary of the Bishop's Council. After the bishop's death, Lord Regent of Charn until the revolution. He was sitting on his obsidian throne, his ancient emaciated face, his blind eyes raised toward the camera. And underneath, a reproduction of the tattoos of his right hand, showing the silver skeleton.

The next: Prince Abu Starbridge, photographed upon the day of his execution. His bald forehead, his jowly and unshaven face, his panicked drunkard's eyes. He stood on the steps of Wanhope hospital in the white robes of a martyr, his hands locked together in a pair of silver handcuffs. Underneath, in pen and ink, a reproduction of his golden sun tattoo.

The last: Cosima Starbridge, thirty-second bishop of Charn. Also dressed in white, the photograph also taken on her execution day. An expression on her face of angry sadness, which only added to the poignancy of her doomed youth, her black-eyed, black-curled, black-browed beauty. Underneath, a photograph of her right palm, showing the bishop's silver crown. Caught in its six points, the silver cratered face of Paradise.

Longo Starbridge chewed his lip. "So what?" he said at last.

The bulimic priest held up his lantern. "Her own council condemned her. She was burnt by Chrism Demiurge before the first uprising. The people—it was for her sake. That's why they attacked the post office—the general strike of October fourty-eighth, all that. And so forth—because the people loved her. To kill her was an act of mania."

"What was her crime?" asked Karan Mang from the other side of the tent. "It was sexual imperfection, was it not?"

The priest's voice was guttural and dry. "Chrism Demiurge had her sequestered in the Temple of Kindness and Repair. But there was a boy from one of the persecuted sects. An antinomial. He found his way to her tower. He climbed up by the drainpipe. He tried to kill her, but of course he couldn't. She seduced him. She kept him hidden in her room. Chrism Demiurge—he had them burnt for witchcraft."

The priest talked in odd breathy gasps, swallowing air after each phrase. Now he swallowed a small belch. "That was his excuse. He had them burned in Kindness and Repair. My great-uncle saw it done."

As he was speaking, Miss Azimuth had put her hand to Cassia's head again, to stroke the hair out of her face. She stirred; she cried out softly and rolled onto her back. Miss Azimuth stroked the girl's hair away and Longo Starbridge chewed his lip. Cassia's face was the same as the face in the photograph.

She still had some silicon dust from the road stuck to her cheek, and she still lay in the torn dress that she had taken from the village in the trees. Her hair was dirty, and in her posture there was no Starbridge grace—her skirt had pulled up above her knees. But in a sense that too increased the similarity, because the photograph was taken on the day when the bishop had left all of her wealth, all of her power behind for the last time. Perhaps it was just an imperfection in the print, but she too had a black stain under her eye, and for her execution she was dressed in a simple white shift. Her legs and feet were bare.

"Look," said Miss Azimuth. She brought Cassia's hand up from her side and stroked back the fingers. The birthmark on her palm, which had been gathering shape all through that week, seemed to be clearer now. It was as if during that time it had been rising to the surface of her skin, and now it was obscured by just a few thin layers. The six points of the bishop's crown were clear now. The face of Paradise was clear.

"But she didn't go, you see," said the old woman, and her high voice was barely audible. Yet it was all around them, diffused and filtered, like the light from the klieg lanterns which was making a blue pattern on the bed. "She didn't go to Paradise. When she stepped onto the pyre, she disappeared. Instead there was a tree, a tangerine tree, flowering and bearing fruit. Though of course it was not the season," she said, and the bulimic priest was nodding. His arm was tired. He had let the lantern slip, so that it was darker now. Most of the light came from the klieg light through the wall

"Chrism Demiurge made a show of burying her bones," Miss Azimuth continued. "But when the place was dug up, there was nothing there. And the graverobbers, they found a message. 'Look for me,' it said. 'Look for me among the days to come.' "

"I know the story," murmured Brother Longo.

"And I knew it too!" exulted the old woman. "I knew it when I saw her. It is the lily on the stump—it is the sign, which Freedom Love predicted. This is our hour, you see. This is our hour of need."

"The resemblance is certainly extraordinary," said Karan Mang, examining his painted nails.

On the bed, Cassia was stirring. She moved her head back to one side, and rubbed her cheek upon the counterpane. "She's waking up," said the blind priest, who up to that moment had not spoken.

Now she could distinguish what they said to her. "She's waking up"—she heard it clearly. In her dream she was sitting by the altar in her prison cell, and she was praying to the image of Beloved Angkhdt. She was moving incense underneath the brass nose of his statue. And she could hear the spirits close to her, conversing in low tones—the old woman, she was death. And then the men: the loud voice, the foreign voice, the rasping guttural voice. These must be the different aspects of Immortal Angkhdt, indicated by the four faces of the statue. Two human faces peeked out of the dog's ears, and another was peering through the fur at the back of his head. Now these faces were conversing to decide her fate; they were arguing with death and with each other. "She's waking up," said the face behind the fur—the first time it had spoken. All-seeing, yet its eyes were blind, at least in this world. It looked into her heart to see that she was waking to a world of spirits and a world of miracles. It was telling her that her prayers were answered.

Rael called to her from the window of their prison cell. He was sitting on the windowsill with his cat in his lap, and he was looking out through the bars. "Come look," he said, but she could see it all from where she sat by staring into the dog's head of Angkhdt. She could see it reflected in his eye. She could see the courtyard below the prison tower. She could see the funeral pyre and the assembled monks. She could see the image she had put in all their minds: The great tree spread its boughs above the courtyard. The fire licked its leaves.

The blind priest clapped his hands. In her dream, Cassia heard a crack come from behind her in the dark. It was the breaking of the lock upon her prison door, the breaking of the lock that held her to this world and to this time. Beside her lay the bag that she had packed for their journey—no warm clothes, for it was hot where they were going. Just a little fruit from her garden, just a cotton blanket, and wrapped inside of it, the earliest codex of the Holy Song, together with the holy skull of Angkhdt.

"The locks are broken," she said. In the silk tent, Miss Azimuth bent as low as her dry bones would permit, to try to decipher Cassia's sleepy mumbling. She could not. But Rael heard her and Rael understood her; he was lying on his stomach in another tent a half a mile away, and when Cassia spoke he was instantly awake, his eyes open, his mind clear.

An oil lamp was burning a few inches from his face. He lifted his cheek up from the mat and then turned to the other side, away from the light. Now in front of him he saw a low, narrow table, and it had a statue on it, and several brimming bowls of water.

He heard a woman's voice. "It is Angkhdt," she said. He squinted in the uncertain light and saw a small, potbellied, animal-headed figure with seven hands. It sat surrounded by plastic and wooden models of machines. Rael recognized a few—a bicycle, a gun.

He raised himself up onto his elbows. The woman spoke out of the shadow behind the lamp. From his raised position he could see her sitting there. He could see something of her face.

"It is Angkhdt," she repeated, responding to his baffled expression and mistaking its cause. He cared nothing for the statue. He was trying to remember where he was.

"It is an incarnation you might not have seen. But an important one. Especially now. He is surrounded by the gifts he brought to humankind. To all of us, although the rich have stolen them away. There you see—a motorcar, a camera, a radio, a freezer, an electric range."

Rael was lying in a canvas tent. It had a peaked ceiling, supported by two poles. The woman sat next to the zippered entrance, the ceiling only a few feet above her head. It was too low for her to stand upright.

"Angkhdt teaches us to share ourselves," she continued. "If the poor don't help each other, who will help us? Not the factory owners and the bureaucrats." In a sweet low voice she quoted:

> *"I was lost; you found me.*
> *I was hungry, so you fed me.*
> *I was empty and you filled me.*
> *Then you kissed me on the lips."*

To Rael she looked both old and young. Her body was supple, her face was smooth and unlined. But her eyes were ancient, and her hair, which hung in a long braid over her shoulder, was coarse and white. Her hands upon her knees were wrinkled, and the veins on them were thick and knotted.

"I saw you wandering in the crowd," she said. "This is the festival of loving kindness—no one should look like you. No one should have a face like yours. You have lost a precious thing. Is it not so?"

Now he remembered. A string of firecrackers exploded outside the tent, and he remembered. Somewhere he could hear Enid's laughter, and his world, which had seemed so dark and cramped when he awoke, now expanded to include the entire unseen festival outside. "Yes," he said.

Smells and noises filtered through the canvas walls. And part of it was the smell of his own body. He lay naked on the mat, and his skin was sensitive and fresh, as if several unnecessary layers of skin had been scraped away. He raised himself to his knees, searching for his shorts.

"Take these," said the woman. She put her hand upon a pile of clothing by her knee. "They belong to my husband, yet he will share them. Great Angkhdt tells us to share everything we have."

A pair of baggy trousers and a grey cotton shirt—Rael fumbled the shirt over his head. The woman sat watching him. He struggled with the trousers in the tight space, saved from embarrassment by the gravity of her expression, which nevertheless could not conceal a certain soft amusement. "My husband is a smaller man," she said. "Smaller than you. But these are large for him."

Outside, Enid shrieked with laughter. "You've been asleep two hours," the woman said. "Now it is time. Paradise is rising now. I can feel it rising in my heart."

"Something gone," said Rael carefully. "Now lost." He was on his knees, with his head close to the mildewed ceiling. He too could feel something in his heart; he raised his fingers to his breast and tested the flesh there experimentally. He looked into the woman's face and he saw something. Her eyes were brimming over with tears.

"Hush," she said. "Hush."

She was dressed in a loose tunic made of the same fabric

as the clothing she had given him. Her sleeve fell away from her arm as she raised her hand to her cheek. "Ah," she said—her face was full of pain, and then she smiled. And at that moment there was a noise outside the tent, a shouting and a whistling and a banging of pots and bells and fireworks—a sound so full of layers, so full of different tones and loudnesses that Rael wondered whether everyone on the entire mountain had found a noise to make, except for him and the old woman.

But then the zipper near her hand was torn open from the bottom to the top, and the quiet darkness in the tent was severed by an edge of light. First a single straight line, and then a triangle, and Enid's face was in the burning gap; she had a sparkler in her hand. "Come out," she cried, "it's happening."

She yanked back the flap to show them, and even from inside the tent they could see how the horizon above the eastern wall of the caldera was ablaze. There were strange patterns in the sky, shifting waves of iridescent light, streaks of orange that opened up the sky in the same way that their tent had been ripped open, to reveal some impossibly bright firmament.

The old woman was already scrambling out, and Rael followed her. "Grandma! Grandma!" shouted Enid and Jane, dancing up and down with sparklers in their hands. A whole group of men and women were with them—neighbors from other tents, perhaps, and they were laughing and embracing one another, and pointing at the sky. From all around came the noise of firecrackers, of shouts and screams that mingled with the smell of gunpowder and hashish. People were cheering and clapping, because at that moment, as Rael and the old woman stood side by side, the silver rim of Paradise showed above the eastern wall.

There was a cooking fire outside the tent, and a few men still squatted by it with bottles in their hands. One held a metal spatula, and he was covering over the embers with dirt. When he was finished, he came and shook Rael by the hand. "Welcome," he said. "I'm glad to see they fit okay." He reached out to brush some sand from Rael's sleeve. "How was your trip?" he asked, indicating the scratch on Rael's forearm. "Did you learn anything?"—words that were scarcely audible in the blare of the crowd. Rael smiled and nodded, not understanding, not listening, for he was staring toward the east, where Paradise was rising. "All of us are looking and not finding it," the man continued. "I just want you to know, you're among friends."

He was a dense and compact man, with a strong handshake. His head was shaved on top, to commemorate the baldness of St. Abu Starbridge. "It is traditional tonight not to share names." He smiled. "But you've met the girls. They told you—we're from Cochinoor."

"Thank you," said Rael, shouting above the din, which every moment had grown louder.

"I've asked the girls to take you to the stage tonight. But remember, you're free to come back here afterward to sleep."

"Thank you," repeated Rael. "Eating, sleeping in the darkness, and that sweet silver, that bright golden, and that orange light."

For the first time the man's frank gaze was complicated with a small trace of uncertainty. Then he smiled—"Exactly right," he said. In his left hand he still held his spatula, while with the other he caressed Rael's forearm. Now he let go to turn and face the sky.

Above them, the mists on the summit of Mt. Nyangongo had blown away, revealing red streams of lava dripping through the rocks. Now Paradise was rising, impossibly huge, almost too bright to tolerate. Rael lifted up his hand. He turned back to the mountain, where the silver light of Paradise was chasing its steep flanks. Now the darkness was cracked open, and Rael put his hand to his head.

"Snow," he said, a word which Cassia had taught him,

when she had told him about the north part of the world.
"Snow," he said again. For he saw the high mountain in the
snow under the moon. The snow thick as the silver light of
Paradise, and the light was catching at the mist upon Mt.
Nyangongo, so that the sky was full of silver flecks.

Around him, the crowd, the clamor, and the bustling din
fell silent. He took a few steps forward and almost fell. And
with one part of his mind he was aware of the man's hand
upon his arm, and the old woman's voice saying, "It's the
drug, don't worry—it's the drug." In the other part he was
alone in the bright snow, in that far northern land.

But not for long. Paradise was rising. The sound of the
crowd rose up around him, and now another sound too, the
stuttering of gunfire.

Slowly, laboriously, a helicopter struggled over the caldera's rim. Painted silver, shining with the light of Paradise,
it wobbled like a wounded insect in the sky. Something was
wrong with its steering mechanism, and its tail was revolving
slowly around its head. It was flying low. And it was firing
rockets and flares out of its belly. They were hitting something; Rael could see the flames rise up nearby. Yet in the
crowd around him no one seemed to be afraid. The helicopter
was a magical and, for most of them, unprecedented sight—
only a few had ever been imported.

Built for a different climate and a different atmosphere,
it seemed fragile and unwieldy in the air. For that reason,
perhaps, it was unthreatening. Its thumping rotors and its
blinking lights made it seem part of the festival. Some children clapped their hands as it turned slowly overhead. Enid
was trying to make out some of the writing on its side.

"'Property of the University of Charn,'" she said. "'Rural
Initiative #2: Donation. Inter-Cooperation Friendship
Group. Carbontown.'"

But then a klaxon was sounding over the loudspeakers,
and in time the gunfire was returned. Soldiers moved along
the street dressed in black uniforms and carrying automatic

rifles. Their captain carried a megaphone, and he was warning the people to stay calm.

This was almost the first deployment of Longo Starbridge's militia, the so-called "soldiers of Paradise." Unkempt, barefoot, young, they gave no indication of the expert ferocity that later would distinguish them. Except as they came past, the harsh mist of their perspiration rose around them, and Rael turned his head aside.

A rocket had exploded, and two cardboard shelters were in flames. The soldiers moved around them. Some were firing guns into the air, although the helicopter was already out of range. It had drifted away, off to the east.

But suddenly Jane and Enid were tugging on Rael's hands. "Come farther in," they shouted. "This is the children's part." And in fact children were making up most of the crowd now that the soldiers had passed. They were crawling from the tents; they were leaving their parents behind. They were clapping their hands and shouting. Their faces were painted in strange bright colors, or they were wearing masks. They had capguns and sparklers and noisemakers and squibs, and they were moving in a slow mass down the spiral toward the center of the caldera, toward the altar of Beloved Angkhdt. Rael could only see the top part of it where it rose above the arcades and the booths, the shelters and the tents—two towers of scaffolding, hung with spotlights and crowded with people with their legs hanging free over the edges or poking through the struts. They were pointing up at the face of Paradise, and some had turned their spotlights from the stage between the towers, so that beams of multicolored light shone upward.

But now Paradise was rising like a silver sun, overwhelming all but the brightest lights, bleaching the faces of the children in the crowd, bleaching the faces of Enid and Jane as they pulled Rael inward through the spiral. He looked behind him to see the old man and the old woman with their arms around

each other, and the woman waved. Then they were gone,
and they had disappeared around the bend. Enid and Jane
were chattering to each other, pulling Rael until he lurched
into a run. He felt confused and shy but somehow happy,
and the silver light of Paradise was beating down upon his
head, flattening his thoughts. There was no movement in his
mind, just the mirrorlike reflection of image after image.
"Look," said Enid. "Look at the servant. Look at the Servant
of God."

   In the middle of the arcade a space had been kept clear,
where the booths were arranged in a ring. The crowd was
parting around a white circle of sand, where all night there
had been fire eaters and trick cyclists and jugglers. Now a
woman with piebald hair and piebald skin had spread a sheet
out on the ground. Two men in robes held torches, while
between them, a black squat pregnant woman was dancing.
She had a rope of bells tied around each wrist and each knee,
but apart from that and a cloth over her sex she was naked,
and the torchlight was shining on her buttocks and her belly
and her fat bare breasts. She was raising her wrists to the
sky and knocking them together until the bells clashed; she
was whirling round and round with her head flung back. Her
eyes were rolled back and her tongue was thrust out past her
teeth. Her skin was slick with vegetable grease, and the sweat
ran down her breasts. Rael could smell her. In all that mass
of people Rael caught a wisp of an odor that could be her
alone, something raw, something alive, something so hungry
that he found himself attracted, drawn forward by a force
that was greater than the two girls tugging on his hands. "Let
me see!" they shouted. "Let me see!" And he gathered Jane
up, and put his arm around Enid's shoulder, and then he
pushed his way through the people, not understanding their
curses as he trod on their feet. He pushed them aside until
he stood in the front rank of the ever-thickening crowd, with
the girls beside him.

Between two men with torches, the woman was whirling in a circle. She was describing a circle perhaps twenty feet across.

The piebald woman was spreading out the sheet in the middle of it. On the sheet lay a cripple with massive arms and shoulders and thin, withered legs. He was also naked. He was lying on his back under risen Paradise, with a frightened expression on his face. He was looking toward the edge of the crowd to where another man was drawing figures in the sand—long strings of numbers. He squatted over them and rubbed his jaw, often consulting his wristwatch and a pocket astrolabe.

A copper lantern stood before him on the sand. It was fashioned in the shape of a man with an animal's head and a long penis, which he held out in front of him between his hands. Now the man in red took out a butane lighter, and he lit the lamps so that a small jet of flame protruded from the statue's foreskin. This was a signal, for at that moment some people in the crowd started to sing, and many others started clapping to the rhythm that the dancing woman made. She was whirling in a circle, shaking the bells upon her wrists, but now she stopped. She knelt down beside the piebald woman.

The cripple lay on his back, his long legs crossed, each ankle locked over the opposite knee. The two women were kneeling on either side of him. The piebald woman had unscrewed the top from a jar of ointment, and she was rubbing this ointment on the cripple's legs. Still the crowd was singing and clapping to the rhythm that the pregnant woman had abandoned; she was out of breath. Her naked breasts were heaving as she bent down low and took some of the ointment on her palms.

Now the man from the edge of the circle joined them. He squatted down by the cripple's right knee, which he took between his hands. There was a bandage on it, which he removed. Then he was pushing his thumb into the joint, while with his other hand he kneaded the pitiful flesh. Then he seized hold of the cripple's right ankle, where it lay crossed above his other knee. Bracing himself, he yanked the leg straight; there was a crack as the frozen joint unlocked, and the cripple's back arched off the sheet where he was lying. Around Rael, the clapping and the singing wavered and then recommenced. The cripple's face was twisted up with pain and fright, but then he relaxed somewhat. He was staring up at risen Paradise while the pregnant woman rubbed his thigh.

Now his right leg lay straight. It seemed to flop around under the woman's hands as though it had no bones. But his left leg was still bent. The priest moved to it, and again Rael heard the sharp crack of the joint. Again he saw the cripple's back lift from the sheet.

The noise from the crowd was more urgent now. The priest got up to retrieve his lantern from the circle's edge. It had gone out, and he stood fiddling with it while the two women massaged the cripple's knees. His legs were so frail that they could easily join their hands around them, even at the thick part of the thigh. His penis seemed as big around as either of his legs. It was swelling and distending underneath the women's hands.

The two men with the torches stood as still as rocks. The priest had lit the lamp again, and now he walked between the cripple's outstretched legs. He was saying something that Rael couldn't hear, and he was making gestures with his hand.

Rael turned his head toward Enid, who was standing beside him holding his hand, her face soft and composed. And then toward Jane, who had climbed up upon the crook of his arm. She had her right arm around his neck. She had pushed back the red mask from her face, and she was sucking her thumb. Her eyes were open wide. Rael could see the glare of the torches in her pupil, and in the contractions of her iris he could see the scene; he didn't have to look. In the minute adjustments of her iris he could see pity and

anxiety and disgust and fascination all succeeding one another, across that tiny circle. He could see the pain in the
cripple's face. And in the waxing, waning noise of the crowd
he could hear how the priest was trying to raise him to his
feet—trying and failing, trying and failing until finally, with
the women's hands under his armpits, the cripple took a few
false steps.

Jane closed her eyes for several seconds and then opened
them. Her pupils now contracted to hard dots, and she hid
her face in Rael's shoulder. He could smell the henna in her
hair.

"Come," he said. They went. Jane climbed down to the
ground, and then she was off, her slight figure fading through
the crowd. Rael and Enid followed more slowly; they turned
again into the spiral path, which was widening as they approached the center of the caldera. Soon it led out into an
open space around the altar of Beloved Angkhdt. The crowd
was thicker there, but it was mostly made of children. Rael
moved through it easily, not stopping until he stood between
the towers of scaffolding. Then he looked up. A wide stage
rose in front of him, ten feet off the ground, and it was
surrounded by soldiers dressed in black.

He raised his eyes. A painted wicker figure dangled from a
chain above the stage, just grazing it, swaying slightly to and
fro. Beside it, a man stood with a microphone. Rael examined his face and saw that he was saying something. Then
Rael heard his voice, coming from the loudspeakers on either
side of the stage. What had been a loose rattling in Rael's ears
now became words, and he realized that he had been hearing
this noise for a long time. It had been meaningless for a long
time, growing louder as he approached it through the spiral.
But now, when he saw the movement of the emcee's lips, he
could distinguish for the first time the shape of the words, and
he could even understand some of them, although many were
still beyond his comprehension: ". . . yes sir ladies and gentle-
men, a gift of seventy-five thousand dollars in cash, as well as

twenty-five hundred fully automatic assault rifles, and you have only just seen demonstrated tonight how necessary that kind of firepower is to us and to our cause—though I'm happy to say that the injuries to Mr. Myron Callisher and his wife are not as serious as were first reported. But even so, that airship, now luckily repulsed by our brave freedom fighters, just goes on to demonstrate how we can never be safe from these attacks. Our basic freedoms have been consistently denied us. Well I say it's time to stand up and be counted. I say it's time to say that we won't tolerate it. I say it's time to stand up for our rights, time to say no to torture and death. So I know you'll join me in giving a very warm round of applause for his high excellency Karan Mang, who arranged for the delivery of this gift. Also a very, very warm round of applause for his sponsor Prince Cotillion Starbridge, foreign minister of the royal episcopal government-in-exile of Charn, who naturally could not be here tonight, but who has sent this inspirational message from his palace near Lake Baladur, which I will read to you . . ."

The emcee was a short, bald man, with a white satin shirtfront and a white mask over his eyes. Rael looked away from his mouth, and instantly the words from the loudspeakers turned back into random noise and static. But Rael had something new to look at, although again it took a while for him to decipher. Behind the emcee, a big white curtain formed the backdrop for the stage. A portrait of a woman had been projected onto the surface of this backdrop. Rael could see the beam of light from the projector, full of motes. And he could see the image of the woman drifting in and out of focus as the curtain stirred.

Rael bent down to the girls on either side of him. "Finding thanks," he said. "She and I and joining. Now go back." He shook each of them gravely by the hand. Then he stood. He turned toward the stage, toward the row of soldiers, and walked forward with his hands open in front of him, because the woman's face upon the curtain was Cassia's face.

THE SKULL | 10

Two generations before these events, in the eighth phase of spring, 00016, a revolution had come to Charn. Following the executions of two popular figures, Prince Abu Starbridge and the beautiful young bishop of the city, there were demonstrations in the streets. The loyalty of the army was split apart. Even some priests joined in the rebellion, which culminated in the siege of the Temple of Kindness and Repair. There Lord Chrism Demiurge had sat with his council, but on the fiftieth of October in the eighth phase of spring, the temple's gate was broken. The thirty thousand shrines of the Beloved Angkhdt were looted and ransacked, the idols smashed or smeared with excrement. All over the city the Starbridges were hunted down, dragged from their palaces and offices and barracks rooms and sacristies. Four thousand men, women, and children were executed during the month of November alone, though many more were able to escape abroad.

In that purge the power of the Starbridge caste was broken,

as it had been in many other springs. The bishop's council was overthrown. The pass laws, the transit laws, the birth laws, the laughter laws, were all repealed during a single triumphant session of the new National Assembly. In the following weeks, all the thousands of lesser statutes by which the priests had regulated people's lives—whom they married, where they worked, what they wore, where they lived, what they named their children—were abolished one by one. And most important, the system of belief was banned, the cult of Angkhdt, the Paradise cult. For it was at the heart of the old slavery—those found practicing its rites were jailed or flogged.

But despite the best endeavors of the police, these beliefs persisted underground, mutating and transforming as the season changed, and spring changed into summer. It acquired new prophets and new saints—Abu Starbridge, the martyred bishop, Freedom Love.

This last was a defrocked priest. During the revolution he had lived with a few followers in the catacombs of Charn. He had celebrated secret masses in the lower crypts, and on Fridays people had climbed down from the streets of Charn to listen to him speak. "The word of God is like a creeping vine," he said. "It has its seasons underground."

These gatherings in the dark formed the small root of a great movement, called at that time the New Society of Loving Kindness. The name itself Freedom Love borrowed from an extinct heresy. He borrowed also the precepts of human brotherhood and spiritual equality, which he combined with new interpretations of the Song of Angkhdt. He rewrote certain portions, claiming that the Starbridge priests had mistranslated them. He rejected the old vision of a social hierarchy of grace, described in Angkhdt 113–117, which the winter priests had used to sanctify an entire caste.

In place of the dead oligarchy, he envisioned something new. He envisoned a new kind of society, governed by a new class of saints. Accidents of birth would be discounted; these saints would choose themselves.

In the days following the Paradise festival, Miss Azimuth explained these things to Cassia as they sat together in the silken tent. "They take the Starbridge vow," she said in her faint voice. "You saw it in the mission hospital. Anyone can do it, who has the strength to live the perfect life, you see. They are the soldiers of Paradise—bound for Paradise, yes, well. They live the pure life; it is not for everybody. I would hate it." The old woman smiled, and looked down at her bright tattoos. "Five hours a day for spiritual meditation. Five hours a day for bodily exertion. They eat only water, and the holy grain that Angkhdt brought down. They do not ... procreate."

Here she gave a little giggle. She sat in an armchair, almost overwhelmed by its tall back and sides. On her narrow knees she balanced a book. Its bulky title—*The Posthumous Epigrams of Freedom Love Dictated from Beyond the Grave to His Disciple X*—was printed in gold letters at the top of every page.

"You see how he foretells all things," she said. She put her finger on the open page. " 'The word of God is like a living thing. It has its season underground. In winter it recedes. Hard it is then. Tough and dry and crude. But in spring the sap is stirring, and the root inside the earth. In the summertime a flower will grow. Flame of the forest, and its colors will be white and silver and bloodred. Ten days it will lie open on the stump. Then it will fall.' "

Cassia sat shivering on her bed, her arms around her knees. Two days after the end of the festival, it was unseasonably cold, and a wet, cold wind blew over the caldera of Mt. Nyangongo. The door flap to the tent slapped open miserably from time to time. Now it curled back upon itself, and through it Cassia could see some of the deserted stalls.

"What does it mean?" she asked.

"You. You, my dear." The old woman smiled. "A lily flower upon a stump. White and silver and bloodred—the colors of your father's family, you see. They are the colors of the bishops of Charn."

Cassia closed her eyes. "Ah," she said.

"That's what they're claiming now. When the bishop's grave was opened, there was nothing in it. No body. No bones. The urn for her ashes was sealed with Lord Chrism's seal, but it was empty."

"Yes. You told me."

"Yes. When they reached the cell where Chrism Demiurge had held her, they found a map under the bed. 'Look for me among the days to come,' it said. There was a date."

"What date?"

The top part of the old woman's body was wrapped in a black shawl. Nevertheless, the cold did not seem to bother her much. Her legs, too short to reach the floor, were bare. Her sticklike ankles were uncovered, and her feet kicked rhythmically against the wicker leg of the chair. "No one knows," she said. "The map is lost. Stolen by the Desecration League during the revolution."

She put her hand upon the open book. "This man saw it in a dream. But even then the numbers were obscure. The pattern of the continents—he says we must have faith to keep ourselves prepared. To recognize the moment when it comes."

"And have you . . . recognized it?"

"Yes. We are all agreed. The map was of Mt. Nyangongo. The date was the sixty-third of September in the sixteenth phase of summer."

"And from that day," said Cassia, "the flower is open on the stump—how long?"

"Yes," sighed the old woman. "Ten days and the woodman comes. The gathering man. He cuts the flower on the stump. But where the axe hits, there the blood runs down. Blood from the flower runs down through the bark. It runs down into the root. Ah yes, that is the freedom day. Eight days from now.''

"But I will die," said Cassia.

"Ah yes—you will not feel it. You have not come to live in this world, but to redeem it. Your life was over more than twenty thousand days ago. Lord Chrism burned you at the stake.''

"Ah," said Cassia.

"Life and death, they are not real to you," crooned the old woman. "Nothing is real, except the love of Angkhdt." She was intoxicated. The backs of her fingers were stained with hashish oil. She had dipped six tobacco cigarettes in a cup of hashish oil, and already that day she had smoked three, though it was not yet noon.

"Why was she condemned?" asked Cassia.

"Witchcraft. That was his excuse—she was a sorceress. Lord Chrism had her burned because the people loved her, yes. But he had a pretext when he found her coupled with the antinomial. The meat-eater. It was an impurity, he said.''

That morning, the antinomial lay in a corner of the tent, lashed down to the naked springs of a steel bed frame. His face was still puffed up from the beating the soldiers of Paradise had given him. One eye was still swelled shut. On the night of the festival he had tried to push through them as if they weren't there, for he was searching for Cassia among the tents. They had struck him with their rifle butts and perhaps they would have killed him. But the old woman had come running. "It is the meat-eater," she had cried. "It is the cannibal," she had shouted, before falling into a narcotic swoon.

Now he lay quiet on the bed, tied down with canvas cords, which he tested from time to time with his crushed hands. From time to time the bedsprings sang as he moved his weight. His left eye was swollen shut, but his right eye was open, staring up at the roof of the tent as it billowed and shuddered in the wind.

And now Cassia asked her: "What do you mean, a cannibal?"

Miss Azimuth giggled. "Oh, not literally. That's what they used to call them. You know, like an animal. A carnivore. Oh, they were a wild lot. North of the River Rang—they had lived there in the snow. Vagrants, you see, no property. No families, no language even. Nothing but the music. My mother told me about it when I was a little girl."

"Music," repeated Cassia.

"Yes—she said you used to hear them sometimes, singing in the abandoned buildings. They used music as a kind of language. In Charn, that was, before the revolution. They were big and yellow-eyed, like him."

Cassia got up and walked over to the steel bed frame. She stood above it. She said: "I looked for you—where did you go?"

Behind her the old woman was still talking. "He came to kill her in the temple, because her soldiers had attacked his people. She lay down with him—as you must know."

The tent flap curled open to reveal the grey day. A grey mist was gathering. Still visible on the altar, the wicker statue of Immortal Angkhdt was lying on its side. Only its charred skeleton was left. It had been lit on fire at the crisis of the festival.

"I looked for you," said Cassia. "Two times I looked for you. Why did you leave me with these people? Now it is too late."

Rael moved his hands in the canvas straps. The bed frame sang a little song. He opened his bruised lips. "Free me," he said.

She shook her head. "I am not that person anymore."

It was true. There had been a surface in her mind like the surface of a pool, and everything that she had known about herself had floated on it. Now some new creature whose shape she had sometimes seen moving in the darkest water had lurched to the surface, scattering it into a thousand tiny flecks. How to put back together that broken mosaic of light? How to retrieve what she had thought, what she had felt, with that creature flailing in the pool? Deformed, inhuman it had seemed, and yet not strange.

Behind her the old woman had sunk into a drugged perusal of the book. Cassia, standing in the draft from the open doorway, shivered and looked down. A tear had formed in Rael's eye, the first one she had ever seen there, and she watched it with a kind of fascination as it grew and grew until it leaked out past his eyelash and down his cheek.

Many of the pilgrims had already dispersed. Most of their tents were gone. The cold wind picked through a debris of newspapers, balloons, and plastic cups.

The last night of the festival, Brother Longo had stood upon the stage under risen Paradise. He had shown Cassia to the people, and he had asked them to share this piece of destiny, for it was of limited duration. Ten days, and it was done.

The people had cheered. They had shouted themselves hoarse, but by morning some had already decamped. More left the next day, especially parents with their children. Many had taken their small vacations to coincide with the festival. Others were content just to have seen the bishop's face.

By the morning of the second day, Brother Longo had begun to understand a bitter fact. The miracle had happened, and he was unprepared. How many times had he exhorted his followers? We do not know the hour, nor the minute, nor the second when these truths will come. Therefore be prepared, he had said. Therefore be prepared to seize the moment as it comes. Yet he had eight days left before the woodman came to cut the lily from the stump, and he was stuck upon the slope of Mt. Nyangongo—a site that he and Azimuth and Mang and Porphyry had chosen for its isolation. Furthermore, he had no food. The pilgrims had carried what they needed for the week. Those who had stayed—he thought as he stood in the doorway to his tent, looking out over the caldera—must already be reckoning what they had left.

Behind him the bulimic Reverend Porphyry sat in a canvas chair. He was examining a newspaper. "Did you see this?" he asked, folding the page back to reveal a long column.

"Somebody's read it. They marked it with a pencil. 'Egghead Professor Discovers Skull of God.'"

In the doorway, Brother Longo turned to stare at him.

"'Carbontown,'" continued the priest. "'September sixty-first. Professor Benjamin Cathartes, working at the new plantation eighty miles east of here, has claimed to have discovered an old relic, which disappeared from Charn in revolutionary times. Using a combination of photographic and textual evidence, he has identified the so-called "Skull of Angkhdt," which until its disappearance had been on public display in the old Temple of Kindness and Repair—now the metropolitan campus of the University of Charn.'"

"I looked for you, but you were gone," repeated Cassia.

To Rael she looked beautiful standing above him. And it was the first time that he had ever been conscious of her beauty. Always she and he had been too close for that. They had been together every day since they were born. Even in the village in the trees when he had gone away from time to time, still she had been with him. When he turned around, when he stood steaming, out of breath, often he could feel her vanished presence, as if just that moment she had passed behind a tree. Sometimes miles from the village he had heard her talking in his ear.

She was as close to him as his own body, and for that reason he had never stopped to think: She is this way, she is that way. He had never, during all the times that he had seen her, thought to himself—she is so beautiful, the way she pushed her hair behind her ear.

But now he felt it, and he felt also the single tear roll from his eye, because he knew something had changed. Not just because she said so, but he could feel it in her new beauty, her new distance. He could feel it in the futility of his bruised hands as he strove against the straps. She had changed, and yet she was the same. Only she was wearing new white clothes of some soft, smooth material. She wore stockings on her legs. The corners of her eyes were painted with a purple powder, and her hair was clean and fastened up in a new way.

"Not understand," he said, but he did understand. For it was true: For two mornings in the forest he had thought to leave her, to go away and not come back. He had gone away and let these changes come.

"Don't know," he said. "Free me." She sat down beside him on the bed frame, and the springs made a soft groaning noise. She bent over him to untie his hands, and the smell of her skin was so bewildering, the soft skin over her jawbone was so close to him, that he closed his eyes and turned away his face. But he could feel her fingers on his wrist. And in a little while he felt them on his cheek, pushing tentatively at the swollen place. His hands were free; he rose up from the bed and took her into his arms, but she was cold and awkward there.

Reverend Porphyry was reading from the paper. " ' "There have been objections to the nature of my project here," says Professor Cathartes. "My discovery must answer those objections. It shows that this small village was the center of a complex net of witchcraft, devil worship, and reaction. It is not a neutral act to romanticize such things." ' "

"Where does he mean?" asked Longo Starbridge.

"It's the Treganu site—the new plantation. Manioc and lumber. That's what the plans are. Forty miles southeast of here."

"I never heard of anything that way."

"Nor I. They kept to themselves."

He read for a while in silence. Then he said: "That was on page four. But look at this. 'Graduate Student Claims That Bone May Be of Extraterrestial Origin.'"

Miss Azimuth had fallen into sleep. Her head had fallen back on her thin neck, and the hinge of her jaw had fallen open. A creaky whistling emerged from her dry mouth. Rael turned his head to listen.

After a moment he turned back, and pushed his face into Cassia's hair. "Bitter gone," he said. "Sweet gone and disappear. Now door."

The door to the tent curled open. Mist lingered there along the flap as if awaiting permission to come in.

Outside the tent a torch was stuck into the sand: burlap soaked in oil and set alight at the top of a long pole. The fog clung to it, blurred it, spread the weak flame into a weaker glow, an imperfection in the dark day. "No," murmured Cassia. "They won't let me."

"Secret. Dark in dark. Soft in soft."

"No," repeated Cassia. "They won't let me go."

Rael nodded. "Let," he said. "Let—not let." He raised his fist up to the doorway. Then he spread open his fingers, quickly, suddenly, so that they made a little noise.

Cassia shook her head. "They have guns," she said. "They will hunt for me."

Rael nodded. "Hunt. Then fast."

Outside, the fog was thicker, condensing on the flap. Cassia shivered, and Rael picked up a blanket which had lain at the bottom of the bed frame. He wrapped it around her shoulders. Again the frame made a small music.

"You don't understand," she said. "Maybe I have a mission to the truth. Sarnath would say . . . I don't know. He wasn't afraid to die. These people need me—they will not abandon me."

She brought her hand up to her face, to look at the tattoo upon her palm. "And even if they did, what difference would it make? I have no place, except for here."

She put her hand out to touch him on the forehead. "What are you thinking?" she asked. "I've known you all my life and you're a stranger."

Rael frowned. "You know what they told me?" she went on. "They said your mind was empty. They said you had no word for love. They said you climbed up to my tower window to kill me. That much I remember too."

Rael turned his face away. "Not no," he said.

Again Cassia reached out to touch his forehead. "Or part of you," she said. "Part of you and part of me, when we were together on the night before they burned us."

Rael felt an anger in him that was building, building. With his clenched fist he touched her on the lips. "Burned," he said, "not burned. Is a bitter, is a black soft hard, is a sad. Is a dead thing dying now and counting—one, two, and nothing gone. Now far away I know now is a something. Somewhere is a something. Now your heart is some, your heart, and this will die. Me, and killing you."

Cassia shivered, and pulled herself against him. "Yes," she said. "Eight days. That's all. But what else is there?"

Rael stared out through the open doorway. "Don't you understand?" she said. "There's nothing there. Here at least there's something." She looked around the tent, empty except for the old woman snoring in the corner. "These people listen to me. I can teach them something. They have a ritual—that's all. This dog's head that they worship, what does it say to them? Does it teach them how to live? Does it teach them how to free themselves and live in peace, according to the thirteen honorable precepts of the master? No, the body is in place, but it can't move. It lacks the power of truth."

Reverend Porphyry was reading from his paper. " ' "It is less solid, and less dense. The ratio of animal to mineral material has been reversed. In its makeup, almost it is like a child's skull—plastic and cartilaginous, even after so many full years. Yet you can see how large it is...." ' "

The priest raised his eyes. "That's a quote from the graduate student. There's a sketch."

Longo Starbridge had squatted down behind him, to read over his shoulder. "What a prize," he said.

"Yes."

"Where is it?"

"At Carbontown. Dr. Cathartes has removed it to the aerodrome, to wait for transport. Both these stories come from there."

Longo Starbridge said nothing. He was staring at the diagram of the skull, his eyes narrowed down to slits.

CARBONTOWN ‖

In those late summer days, the mines at Carbontown were just beginning to approach their peak efficiency. They were located in mountainous country about sixty miles southwest of Nyangongo, which formed part of the same massif. At Carbontown the mountains were arranged in a close circle around the pit—an enormous open quarry whose lease had been renegotiated in summertime of each of the past six years. The miners lived perched above it on a ledge of rock in forty-six loose rows of barracks. This was the town of Crystal Lip, with a population in that season of almost seven thousand men and women.

The blast furnaces at Carbontown, the company offices, and the processing plant were all located on the low point of the ridge above the town, near the terminus of the new road. There the ingots of polished glass were loaded onto trucks to begin the first stage of their journey all over the district and abroad. The road descended sharply from the plant, down through the gate, out into the forest.

On the inside of the circle, away from the forest and the road, the ridge was piled thick with the accumulated slag. A mountain of garbage, refuse, loose rock, and smashed glass loomed above the town, always in danger of collapsing. Occasionally a flow of slag would rumble down into the streets; it was a source of friction between the miners and the company. Earlier in the summer, the miners had initiated a series of slowdowns and strikes, and had even succeeded in extorting some promises from the university provost. That had changed by the sixteenth phase of summer, when the pressures of production had required a new kind of management. Charn and the new quality-of-life laws were far away. The mine was more than half owned by a foreign holding company.

By the last months of the sixteenth phase of summer, 00016, the mine was functioning around the clock. By night the miners' headlamps made moving skeins of light over the glass faces of the pit as lines of men trudged upward, trudged downward, carrying baskets of raw shards.

By night the pit was illuminated by torches, and dozens of small fires. By day a cloud of smoke hung low over the town, and everything down there was covered with a film of soot. The tarmac streets were slippery with soot.

Tuesdays was the obligatory washing day. On Tuesday afternoon, the sixty-seventh of September, Dr. Benjamin Cathartes stood at the window of the company weight room, looking down on the maidan. Some of the miners' wives were boiling their grey laundry in communal outdoor vats, poking at it with long sticks.

He found it a dispiriting sight. Also dispiriting was the constant roar from the blast furnaces behind them, the pounding and clanking from the cog railway. Every effort had been made to keep the company offices pleasant. They were situated on a crag of rock next to the heliport, and were surrounded on three sides by gardens. Yet because they were high up, they commanded a more complete view. That was

enough, Cathartes thought, to make them the most depress-
ing section of the whole.

The athletic facility was well appointed, though, with thick
carpets and new equipment. Since his arrival at the mine five
days before, Cathartes had spent much of his time here. Hot
mineral water was pumped up by some mechanism into a
whirlpool bath, which occupied a cabinet in one corner of
the room. Cathartes had just come from there; he stood by
the window in his spandex exercise shorts, a towel around
his neck. His arms and chest were naked. He rubbed them
with the towel, liberating the smell of the mineral water—a
by-product of an industrial process, he knew, yet pleasant
nevertheless. It gave his skin a chalky feel.

He examined his body in a row of wood-framed mirrors
along the far wall. Each one presented a different view. He
frowned, and rubbed some water from his neck. Then he
walked over to the side wall and put both hands upon the
vinyl seatcover of the new universal exerciser—a complicated
pile of brass wheels and weights and pulleys, set in a wooden
frame.

For several minutes he stood chafing the seat between his
palms, frowning at his reflection, feeling a new and uncus-
tomary inertia. The sight of his own body, normally so sat-
isfying, touched him not at all.

Behind him came a knock at the door. "Enter," he said
without turning round.

Still looking in the mirror, he watched them march the
fellow in until he stood next to the trainer's desk, a guard
on either side of him. His eyes were bloodshot, his lips dry.
His face was slack and vacant, mere flesh over the bone, and
his student's uniform hung off of him, as if it had been made
for a much larger man. To Cathartes there was something
contemptible about how close he was to dissolution. How
long had it been since he had first stumbled into the Treganu
site, sick then already, but still plump? Not forty days. Since
then three weeks of dysentery, one week of confinement,

and the poison that had crept into his blood from his infected leg had stripped him down to almost nothing. Had affected his brain also, or else they would not be in this predicament.

"Give him his spectacles," Cathartes said. One of the company guards pulled them from the pocket of his shirt. They at least were still unchanged—the bows repaired with tape, the lenses still as fat as ever. The guard thrust them at Blendish and he took them, and balanced them upon his pock-marked nose.

The spectacles were the key to his face, which opened up his thoughts and his expressions. They were the detail that gave sense to the rest of him. Turning to look, Cathartes now conceded that the amiable but foolish student, whom he had taken in that first night in the village and nursed until his fever broke, was not completely gone. At least his eyes were there; his eyes remained, stubborn and futile in his new thin face.

"Leave us," he said. The company guards, stolid men in brown uniforms with truncheons on their belts, saluted smartly, turned crisply, and marched out. It was a display of efficiency diluted only by the bovine boredom on their faces. As he watched them go, Cathartes found himself wondering whether in the coming crisis they could be depended on, whether they were capable of more than the routine punishment of strikers and trade unionists.

Again he wandered over to the bank of windows. Below and to the left, the helicopter stood on a circle of grey concrete, a lone mechanic working on its tail section. If it had been functional, if it had been capable of the long flight, he would have commandeered it to return to Charn. Already he would have returned in triumph to the university, the skull of Angkhdt locked in his pouch. But in this wilderness of zealots and fanatics even his safety was in jeopardy, since the damned student had made his idiotic claim in print.

The effect of his bath was dissipating, and the sweat felt cool upon his chest. Cathartes flicked the towel from around his neck and dropped it into the laundry can. An attendant had laid his bathrobe over the trainer's chair; he strode over to the desk and slipped it on. As he did so, his eyes fell once more upon the issue of the *Carbontown Gazette*, now almost a week old. He picked it up from the linoleum surface, scanning the headline for the hundredth time, feeling once again a rush of heat suffuse his face—it was unbelievable. "Idiot," he said. "You idiot."

Blendish flinched. A shudder passed over his face. But then he seemed to relax somewhat, to pull himself together. His voice, when it came, managed to achieve some sickly dignity.

"Sir," he said. "I want to know why you are treating me like this. You have taken me from my researches and locked me up as if I were a criminal. I have not been allowed access to a lawyer, nor have I yet been told what I'm accused of."

This was a speech that he'd rehearsed. As he completed it, his relaxation left him, and when Cathartes struck the side of the desk with the folded newspaper, he flinched again.

"Lawyer—are you crazy? I am an associate professor of theology." Cathartes wiped his forehead with his sleeve, and when he spoke again his voice was lower and more soothing: "It is for your own protection. I have felt myself responsible for you and for your welfare. Where you were, you could not be given the correct medical supervision. You're sick—you understand that."

"Yes, I know."

"Do you? I'm glad. Because your sickness seems to have infected your mind. It's true—I had to bring you here. I meant to bring you back to Charn with me. I think you should be grateful for my abuse of university funds, instead of trying to destroy my work."

"It was my work," said Deccan Blendish. He squinted and then looked down at his feet. "I found it," he said. "It was part of my research."

"Your research! You lunatic!" Again Cathartes let his

anger rise, and the student took one step backward away
from him.

Cathartes threw the newspaper back down upon the desk.
"I was responsible for the project. Naturally I claimed responsibility. Besides, I knew immediately what it was, and
you had no idea. You thought it was some ape. Some ape
from outer space."

"I stick to my conclusions," muttered Deccan Blendish.
He gave his head a sudden shake, as if an insect were caught
inside his ear.

"Your conclusions have destroyed my reputation. Your
conclusions have robbed me of my greatest triumph. What
were you thinking of, to say such things to a reporter?"

"You could issue a retraction."

"Thank you. Thank you for your advice." Cathartes
moved a little way into the center of the room and then turned
round again. He crossed his arms upon his chest and stood
with his legs spread wide, his pelvis straining forward. "Success in academia," he said, "is a long, slow, humble process.
For every step you climb, a dozen people are trying to pull
you back down. So you have to be careful. Now, I made a
claim—a modest claim in some ways, but it would have been
enough. Because I had the facts behind it—I had documents,
I had photographs, I had witnesses' reports. A valuable ar-
tifact disappeared from the Temple of Kindness and Repair
during the revolution. I have found it—it's as simple as that.
I make no claims about what it is. I make no claims about
how it got to where I found it, except to say what everyone
already knows—that there was more to the Treganu cult than
just asceticism and nonviolence."

"But you didn't find it," said Deccan Blendish. "I found
it. I found it in a bag with those old manuscripts—you still
don't know. It was my discovery, and I don't understand why
you stole it. You didn't need it. But they might have given
me some funding, some grant money, I'm sure. Perhaps even
a lectureship."

His voice sank to a murmur, and he was staring at his feet, staring at a pattern in the heavy carpet that might have been a water stain. As always he was confused by the professor's presence, his red lips. His white terry-cloth bathrobe was open down the front, and Blendish could see the fur on his muscular chest, his hard, flat stomach. Lower down, the outline of his sex was visible against the sheer blue spandex.

Also, Blendish found it hard to think. There was a roaring and a buzzing in his ears, and his vision was tormented by small flecks of color in the periphery. They darted back and forth, making geometric patterns which vanished when he moved his eyes.

Cathartes took a few steps closer, and as he did so, he seemed to penetrate some barrier of intimacy. "Ah," said Deccan Blendish. "What's wrong with me?" he said, his nose attacked by a strong male odor, made softer, sharper by the hint of some cologne.

Deccan Blendish found it hard to think. Cathartes's words sounded distorted: "The doctor here says you have developed quite a combination of exotic illnesses. Hepatitis, of course—you must have known that. From the food. But that infection on your leg—do you know what that is?"

"I don't know," said Deccan Blendish. Over the past week, his thigh had swelled up so that he had had to cut his pants along the seam. And he could see there was an infection in his blood, for the veins and arteries of his leg had swollen and changed color, and his thigh was crisscrossed with angry purple lines.

"It is the guinea moth," Cathartes said. "It breaks out of the skin. The doctor says you dug it out yourself—without sterilization, without antibiotics. You didn't get it all. The eggs have spread into your blood."

"She did it," mumbled Deccan Blendish.

He raised his head. Cathartes was staring at him, his face intolerably close, his dark eyes radiant. "What did you say?"

"She did it for me. The girl who ran away."

Cathartes let his breath out in a slow, even rush, and Blendish caught the odor of some mint. "She poisoned you," Cathartes said.

"I don't think so. . . ."

"Yes. The sorcerer is dead. He buried his relic of the devil Angkhdt and burned himself to death rather than give up his secret. But the girl escaped—you must have heard."

"Heard what?" Deccan Blendish stood up straight. He took a step backward so that he could press his leg into the desk, and he was blinking and squinting, for his eyes had trouble coming into focus. "Heard what?" he repeated. "I've been in the hospital."

"The girl's come back. She's claimed to be the new bishop of Charn. She's raised some kind of armed rebellion. The Cult of Loving Kindness—they attacked a town. Four days ago she was at Nyangongo. Now she's coming here."

Cathartes had moved behind the desk. There were some papers spread across it; he lifted one to reveal an envelope full of photographs. "These were taken from the airship the night of the full moon."

He shuffled through them. "As you see, there were some technical difficulties. But some are better. We had an agent in the crowd."

Several showed the stage at Nyangongo, at the moment when Longo Starbridge had lit the statue of Beloved Angkhdt on fire. Off to the side stood a woman, hidden by the raised hand of someone in the crowd. But in the last photograph, the man's fingers had spread apart somewhat, and Cassia's face was clearly visible, dazed and bleached under the spot-lights.

But Deccan Blendish paid no attention to that one. He reached out and plucked another from the envelope: a smear of yellow in the sky. It was a view of Paradise, taken from the crippled helicopter.

"That night I saw it from the window of my room," he said.

* * *

The guards took him away, leaving Cathartes alone inside the weight room. And as soon as the door closed, his posture changed. He slumped a little bit as he pulled in his chest and tied his bathrobe closed. He was smiling to himself in a soft way, and shaking his head as he walked toward the bathing cubicle where he had left his clothes. Water had condensed on the glass screen. He pulled it open, releasing a small mist of steam. Then he stepped inside and closed it behind him, just at the moment when the center mirror on the wall opposite the windows levered outward on its frame to reveal a listening booth. An old man stood behind it, his hand upon the one-way glass.

He peered into the room and then climbed down. He closed the mirror carefully behind him. Then he stepped across the carpet toward the desk.

He was a small man, robust, vigorous, and barrel-chested. His dominant feature was his sharp bony nose, so big that when his face was in profile, all his other features seemed to recede from it—his brow, his skull extending backward from the ridge while his chin sloped away under his nostrils. His grey hair was combed backward.

This was Professor Marchpane, the inventor and metallurgist. He was dressed in an old uniform that gave no hint of his prominence in the company or in the university. In this way he contrasted with Cathartes, who always wore his dissertation ribbon and his various insignia. When he reappeared out of the cubicle he was wearing a starched shirt and linen pants.

"You do seem to have a hold on him," said Marchpane.

Cathartes smiled. "I'm using what I have at my disposal."

"Quite." Marchpane crossed his hands behind his back. "I appreciate your expertise in this," he said. "I appreciate your help in these . . . spiritual matters. I'm not sure I saw what I was supposed to see."

"I have an idea."

"Quite." Marchpane stepped over to the desk. He picked up the envelope of photographs. Shuffling through them, he also hesitated at the photograph of Paradise. "Why did you bring him here?" he asked.

Cathartes shook his head. "I gave my evidence to the police, and I was done. Kurt Sofar is in charge of the plantation now. I was looking for a fast way back. I never thought that I'd be stuck here while they fixed your damn machine."

"Ah yes, our helicopter. But what about him?"

"I was doing him a favor. After all, he had made the actual find."

"Ah yes, the find," said Marchpane. "You never told me what his theory was."

Cathartes shrugged. "It's not even that original. It's just another hope that science will conform in some way to mythology. You've heard the story of a monkey called the hypnogogic ape?"

Professor Marchpane raised his eyebrows. He often answered questions in this way.

"Yes," Cathartes said after a pause. "He became convinced of the existence of this creature. It was part of his research—all from secondary sources, but he came to the Treganu site to look for it. Unsuccessfully. And he was sick too—he was already sick. As he got weaker, he got more obsessed, especially as the site was changing; his failure to find traces of the creature seemed one more proof of its powers of illusion."

"So?"

"So he has a theory. His theory is that this creature is earth's only true indigenous primate. He thinks we're all descended from it. He thinks it's the source of our capacity for deception, which, according to him, distinguishes us from other mammals."

Marchpane looked up from the photographs. He had rearranged them in a careful block; now he laid them down upon the desk. "Interesting," he said. "And what about the skull?"

"He believes the skull to be the relic of some godlike creature, which in prehistoric times was able to mate successfully with this ape. Who knows how, but anyway, he's quite a gifted draftsman. He's made all kinds of diagrams from what he claims to be the fossil record. You know the sort of thing. Just a piece of jawbone an inch long, and he's reconstructed an entire skeleton."

"Interesting," repeated Marchpane. "And am I right in thinking that this creature . . . ?"

"Came from the moon," Cathartes interrupted. "Of course it came from the moon. It came down from Paradise in a chariot of gold. Can you see why this is dangerous and reactionary? How it's just another version of the same reactionary nonsense?"

Marchpane pressed his lips into a line. "I would like to see the diagrams," he said.

Cathartes shrugged. He produced a key from his pocket and then walked around the desk. Sitting in the trainer's chair, he reached down to unlock the left-hand bottom drawer, and then he pulled it open. He lifted out a metal box, which he placed on the desk.

"I'll show you the whole thing," he said. There was a combination lock above the box's hasp; he entered three numbers and flipped open the top.

"Here," he said, taking out a sheaf of drawings.

Marchpane pushed aside the photographs and newspapers, and made a space for them upon the surface of the desk. Then he laid them out with his long, pale hands. He ran his forefinger down the paragraph or so of text that explained each one, his lips moving as he read.

Each drawing showed a skeleton, and then beside it a naked figure, sometimes in profile. Each one was labeled at the top: TREGANU, STARBRIDGE, CAUCASIAN, ANTINOMIAL, DUAURVEDIC, and a few more.

Notations along the right-hand margin described differences in bone structure, hair growth, pigmentation, average size, brain capacity, dentition. Occasionally these differences were illustrated. Three or four circles decorated the bottom of each page, containing close details of fingers, tailbones, teeth.

The last two pages were unlabeled. One showed the ape— a small squat-legged primate with an anxious furry face. The other showed a human body, heroically muscled. Its head was disproportionate, deformed, with a protruding jaw.

"I see," murmured Professor Marchpane. He raised his eyebrows. "And the model?"

Cathartes lifted it out of the box, still in its nest of paper. "Here," he said, raising the skull. Marchpane placed an interrogatory finger on the manuscript.

"It is the Bekata Codex of the Song of Angkhdt," explained Cathartes. "It disappeared from the temple at the same time."

"Ah," murmured Professor Marchpane. He took the skull into his hands, and then lifted it up to stare at it face-to-face.

"It's interesting," he said, "what a seductive explanation this could be. It explains, for example, the sexual character of the text, as well as the sexual emphasis in the iconography."

"Of course," answered Cathartes, a hint of impatience in his voice. The professor was turning the skull in his thin hands, examining the minute carvings.

"What are these?" he asked.

Cathartes shrugged.

"Ah." Marchpane lowered the skull again, and his face took on a soft expression. "My grandfather once told me how Paradise was a new arrival in our system. He didn't explain. But he told me stories of a perfect world. There were no men yet, just smaller animals. He used to make up stories about them."

"It is an ancient myth," said Cathartes coldly.

"No doubt. But that's the point, you see. Now I'm an engineer, but I know enough astronomy to understand what a peculiar science it is. Peculiar in this way—there seems to be a separate explanation for everything that has to do with Paradise, a separate category of natural law. All of the nine planets describe simple, regular orbits, or at least they would, except for the gravitational effect of this one rogue. But Paradise—I once saw my teacher compute on the blackboard the time and date of the next apparition—this was a long time ago, when I was just a student. It was inconceivably complicated—he posited literally hundreds of small epicycles, as well as many strange fluctuations in speed and gravitation. And even then his calculations were off by a few hours."

As he spoke, he patted the top of the distorted skull, and then replaced it on the desk. "Who can explain it? Who can explain the strange lack of consensus in our history from season to season, year to year? The reports of even trained observers differ wildly, and I have read some which swear the moon has phases like the other planets; others which claim that it itself is a source of light, and that it moves around us like another sun. Now the other night it appeared clear to me that I was witnessing a reflective effect only. So what am I to make of that? Can I dismiss for that reason the statements of so many other observers . . . ?"

"And why not?" demanded Cathartes. He leaned forward in his chair. "Why can't you conclude that eyes diseased by superstition and religion cannot observe properly? For example, people from the period tell many stories about the sugar rain, which falls here at the end of spring. They describe how it is like snow or glass or fire or ice or stone or acid falling from the sky. They analyze its chemical composition. They fill book after book with speculations. Yet we know for a fact that it is only rain. Its force and its duration make men lose their objectivity."

"I see," said Marchpane. "Still it was not so very long ago." With a small sigh, he replaced the skull upon the desk.

But Cathartes was angry. He leaned forward, and his handsome face was flushed. "What do you mean?" he demanded. "Explain yourself—what do you mean to say about it?"

"Nothing at all. Only that cleverer men than I have speculated whether Paradise was quite a . . . natural phenomenon."

He was staring out past Cathartes's shoulder. Outside the window, the sky had gotten dark. The exercise room was provided with electric lights set into the ceiling. At seven o'clock they had turned on—automatically, unobtrusively. As the day had darkened they had grown brighter, maintaining always the same level of illumination in the room. It was a steady, yellow, shadowless, pervasive light.

A lamp stood on a corner of the desk. Now Professor Marchpane turned away from it. He stepped over to the bank of windows and stared out into the night. He spread his delicate thin fingers out against the glass.

"You told your spy I wanted to see him," said Cathartes after a little while.

"Yes. He's off in fifty minutes. We're going to meet him."

"After dark?" Cathartes frowned.

Marchpane stared out past his own reflection, out into the night. "He's in the pit. It's never dark."

"But is it safe? What kind of man is he?"

"He's a spy."

The glass under his hand was vibrating—a steady rhythm from the mine. Marchpane stared out past the reflection of his eye.

"Shall we go?" he said after a little while.

Outside the window Carbontown was burning in the darkness. Below and to the left, five conical smokestacks rose beside a long, low building—the top level of a nine-tiered gallery. Long streams of fire blew out of each stack, twenty, thirty feet into the air, alternating with putrid clouds of ash.

The gallery spilled down over the steep slope toward the mine. A yellow glare was pushing through its nine rows of slitted windows. It was a livid, constant glow. But over the course of a few minutes the color shifted somewhat, became deeper, blacker, redder, according to the cycle of the March-pane convection. The building housed the famous blast furnaces of Carbontown, rebuilt and improved, now operating around the clock, through all the twenty hours of the day.

Light streamed also from the cars of the cog railway, which climbed up toward the gallery from the mine. At the terminus the ten-acre off-loading pit was full of fire, because here also was collected the raw slag from the furnaces. From above Marchpane could see the tenders in their helmets and their insulated suits, standing in a line upon the concrete rim of the containment reservoir, raking off the distilled brandy-glass.

As always, he was astounded by the scale of it. Seven thousand men and women lived and worked in Carbontown. From where he stood he could see how all the pieces moved together—the furnaces, the railway bringing up the raw shards from the pit, the excretion unit, and the final product being loaded in the platforms—as if the mine were just a single mechanism, tended by its miniature crew.

But in another sense the view was insufficient, he thought later, when the elevator had deposited Cathartes and himself at the building's base. As the metal cage had sunk down through the scaffolding, Marchpane had felt the temperature rise. In the trembling guywires he had felt the churning of the engines. Yet even so he was surprised, as always, by the intensity of the noise and heat which closed around him and enveloped him as the doors slid open and he stepped outside into a world of harsh sensation. He had perceived only light from the window of the exercise room. Infants in a mother's womb, thought Marchpane. He felt the sweat rush to the surface of his skin.

With them walked a single overseer, armed with a rubber truncheon and a gun. Cathartes was grinning for some reason, and the light was shining off his teeth; as they moved on down the concrete maidan, past the heliport, past the security post, Marchpane felt his clothes grow limp and damp. His saturated collar curled away from his wet neck; they were walking through a fine hot drizzle, which was partially the blowoff from the stamping press and partially a genuine piece of weather. Overhead the clouds were low, and they reflected back some of the fire from the stacks. They reflected back also some of the noise from the press—a hollow booming all around them.

They took the escalator down toward the collection pit. Again, every meter of descent brought with it a corresponding rise in temperature. At the bottom, the heat was stifling, the humidity terrific. Marchpane felt it as a solid force, pressing against his body from all sides. It required all his energy and strength to cleave a passage through. Cathartes was smiling, and Marchpane was amazed to see his hair still dry, his uniform still crisply pressed. Marchpane, as they hurried past the slag pools, felt the sweat pour from his face, and he was squinting, and blotting his eyes with his wet sleeve. The overseer said something that he couldn't understand above the noise from the crushing bins. But Cathartes heard it and made some response.

Professor Marchpane was the managing chief engineer at Carbontown. He was also, as his own bad luck would have it, the only member of the Board of Directors not to have attended the September Conference of Metallurgy in Charn, whose dates had corresponded to the mayor's celebration. They had gone to protest the new production schedule, which had made conditions so unsafe.

Later, people would speculate that if a different man had been left in charge of the facility, perhaps the miners would not have dared to go on strike at such a crucial time. Perhaps the mine would not have fallen to the Cult of Loving Kindness.

Later historians, stretching taut the chain of circumstance that led up to the reconsolidation of Starbridge power in

Charn, all would remark on the beginnings of the movement: how it seemed to grow up out of nothing, how except for a few crucial successes it could have dissipated just as rapidly. Three thousand days after these events, Prince Regulum Starbridge himself seemed to acknowledge this, when he took his oath of office in Durbar Square. In his inaugural address he expressed his gratitude not to General Mechlin Starbridge, not to the Reaction Corps, who in the last days of summer had defeated the New People's Army on the tulip fields of Caladon. Instead he praised the martyrs of the Cult of Loving Kindness, which nevertheless he had by that time ruthlessly suppressed—Longo Gore (called "Starbridge"), Porphyry Demiele, Karan Mang. Then he spoke another less familiar name, and at the time it was considered lucky and conciliatory that a prince of the old blood could even put his tongue around the name of such a humble figure—Nanda Dev, a glass miner from Carbontown.

It was this miner that Marchpane was seeking on the night of the sixty-seventh of September. Another more practiced administrator would have sent for him, would have had him summoned to the company offices. But Marchpane thought it was important to show himself among the miners from time to time, so that they could understand the human face of power.

It was a bad decision. Already for the past week, since the appearance of the article in the *Gazette*, the mine had been alight with rumors of some big mythic discovery. At the same time, Marchpane had taken advantage of the absence of the Board to implement some new reforms. As he and Cathartes climbed down the concrete slope toward the terminus of the cog railway, they came in among a crowd of miners at their leisure, and some had been able to buy alcohol. They were dangerous, exhausted men, their bodies and their faces streaked with sweat and grease and wrapped in rags, their breath bloody with accumulated glass. They turned their bleared and drunken eyes to look at the two men, and then swung back to stare up at the company offices far above. The windows were all dark.

Every miner knew about the changes of the past week. The security battalion had been reassigned. They were piling sandbags by the gate, they were camping in the woods; in consequence there were fewer in the mine itself. Now the overseers walked singly, or in groups of two. And there were rumors everywhere of some new hope, a young girl who had come down from Paradise the last night of the festival to walk on earth for a short time. The keys to Paradise were in her hands.

Oblivious to this, oblivious to the speculation in the faces that surrounded them, Marchpane and Cathartes continued on. At the terminus they took the elevator, though the cage was loaded with children on the seventh shift. They squeezed in among them—shard gatherers and seekers, their bodies and their limbs wrapped in strips of muslin, their little faces covered with black grease to guard against the dust. Some wore sloppy turbans pulled down over their ears, and a few lucky ones had plastic eyeguards and nose filters—too few, thought Marchpane, for the lips and nostrils and the eyelids of the rest were caked with scabs that would not heal. He made a mental note. On the first of every month, each family was reissued the protective gear they lacked, but it was obviously not enough. There was corruption and thievery, he knew. He had read the report—how men would steal a pair of goggles and then sell it back. The children were always the losers. Now they stared up at him with red, accusing eyes—how had it come to this? Conditions had not always been this bad. Not when the plans had first been drawn. Workers had moved here voluntarily; the cottages in Crystal Lip had been written up in *Industry Today;* they had been widely copied. Children had not been allowed to work until their families insisted. There had been a school.

"It stinks in here," whispered Cathartes.

The elevator slid down straight into the stomach of the mountain. Through the bars of the cage, Marchpane saw among the layers of schist a seam of glass catch at the lamplight, and then another. They were small and few at first, glittering with pyrite and impurities. But as the cage moved down the shaft, the texture of the glass began to change. The seams were smoother, darker, richer. They mixed into one another, and from time to time Marchpane could see the fugitive reflection of his face as he pressed up against the bars.

When the overseer rang the bell at Level 29, the doors opened on a sheer blue tunnel through the glass. This was Marchpane's favorite section of the mine—the crystal heart of it, the only place where the pure schemes of the Board had not been dirtied by the needs and the desires of men. It was the access tunnel to the Ranbagh Lode: almost a thousand feet straight through into the pit, and Marchpane could hear the gas hammers of the miners as they labored on the face.

Sometimes the noise seemed sharp and piercing, sometimes dull and flat, as it caught resonances deep inside the glass.

The three men moved away from the loading dock. Twelve children had descended also; now they rushed off down the tunnel, slapping their metal lunchpails against the walls. Their laughter reverberated in the vault, glancing from the rough-cut surfaces.

The car rattled out of sight. The three men were alone. "You've never been down here?" asked Marchpane. For once Cathartes looked uncomfortable, and he was staring upward with his mouth open, toward where a cloud of glowflies buzzed around a lamp. It was very hot. The smooth blue walls were slick with condensation. Streams of moisture had worn channels in the glass.

As they moved forward, their footsteps were muffled by

the thick sand on the floor. "You've never seen the pit?" continued Marchpane, and Cathartes shook his head. The overseer followed them a few feet back.

"It's worth a look. The man we're going to meet is working on this face. I'll show you."

He turned back toward the overseer. "You know the man I mean. Nanda Dev—he's in the cutting crew. Tell him we are waiting in the guardhouse."

The overseer saluted. And when the tunnel divided he went to the left, while Marchpane and Cathartes continued straight.

Now the tunnel broadened out, the walls sloped away, and the noise from the mine was louder and more varied. They descended a few steps and then paused before an alcove that was cut into the wall. Inside, the raw glass floor was covered with candles and small oil lamps, and photographs in frames, and many personal effects—a pair of shoes, of eyeglasses, a hammer, a neatly folded pair of pants. "We've had our share of accidents," said Marchpane.

They continued on. Then finally they reached the guardhouse at the end, a small square chamber cut into the glass, near where the tunnel opened out into the pit. As they waited for the overseer to return, they looked out into the open air. The tunnel ended on a metal platform which was bolted to the rock, and which was joined by ladders and rope elevators to a mass of bamboo scaffolding over to their left. It descended out of sight below them down the sloping surface of the Ranbagh Lode. In the dark, the whole network of scaffolds and rope bridges that covered the inside of the great glass pit at Carbontown was glistening with light. It was like a web covered in dew, and each drop was an oil lantern swinging in the ropes. Elsewhere along the face the surface of the ore was lit with arc lamps and magnesium flares, and Marchpane could see the figures of the miners made gigantic and grotesque by their harsh shadows on the glass. Here the pit at Carbontown was more than half a mile across—an open gulf seething with light from many hundred sources, for every miner carried in his helmet or his turban a small carbide lamp.

They stood there for about a minute with the humid wind in their faces, listening to the crash of the pneumatic hammers and the drills. Cathartes shuddered. He pulled away when Marchpane touched his arm. "There they are," said the old engineer, pointing toward the scaffolding below them, where two lamps swayed across a long rope bridge.

They went inside. They waited in the guardroom, which was empty, except for a wooden table and some metal folding chairs. The glass that formed the outside wall was only three feet thick. A bluish underwater light pierced through it from the pit, vanishing when Marchpane lit the lantern on the table.

They sat down with the light between them. "Was it necessary to come down here?" Cathartes asked.

Marchpane rubbed his big nose. "The boy requested it."

After five minutes there was a knock at the door. It was a slab of wood on metal hinges bolted to the rock—they had not closed it. The overseer reached inside to rap it with his knuckles, though they had heard his footsteps coming down the corridor.

He didn't enter. He stayed outside to guard the door. Marchpane could see his shadow on the floor beyond the threshold, thrown by his lantern. It stretched across the doorway, thick and black. Then it was disturbed by the small young man who stepped over it and stepped inside.

He had a miner's lamp strapped to his forehead underneath his turban. It was down low: a yellow jet of flame, which seemed to obscure rather than illuminate his features. His eyes were in black wells. His mouth was hidden underneath the shadow of his nose.

His face was smeared with thick protective grease. Flecks of glass, imbedded in it, glistened in the lantern light. He was wearing shorts and sandals, and his legs were muscular and delicate. They too were greased, and speckled with the shining glass.

"This is Nanda Dev," said Professor Marchpane. "He's the boy whom I was telling you about. The boy who took those photographs at Nyangongo."

Nanda Dev bowed his head, and came a few more steps into the room. "Thank you, sir," he said. "Thank you for coming down. It's good to show you're not afraid."

Marchpane frowned. A drop of sweat was running down the ridgepole of his nose, and he stroked it away with his long fingers. "Yes. Of course." He touched his lips. "This is Dr. Cathartes, from the Department of Theology. He's helping me—he's got a lot of expertise. I have repeated to him some of the things you told me. But he wanted to talk to you directly."

As he was speaking, Cathartes took out from an inside pocket the envelope of photographs that had lain on the trainer's desk in the exercise room far above. He put them on the table. "Here," he said. "Now tell the story in your own words. I also want to clear up some details."

The young miner took another step forward. He stripped off his canvas gloves. He said: "Mr. Sebastian, from the Board. He's gone now in Charn. He gave me the camera. I did work for him."

Marchpane nodded.

"He gave me a weekend pass to Lameru. So I went up there on the last night, on the sixty-third. To Nyangongo. It's a dozen miles."

"Sit down," said Marchpane.

"I want to stand. I don't know more than I told you."

Cathartes sat forward in his chair. "How many people were there?" he asked.

The miner shrugged. "Maybe ten thousand. Maybe more."

"Tell me what they did. Was there a religious ceremony?"

"There was a stage, lit up. There was a big man with a

dog's head. Made of paper, maybe—paper and bamboo. They torched it at the end."

"What else?"

"Sir, there were speeches. A man stood up and spoke about some guns. Someone had given them a lot of guns. I saw guns everywhere."

"What was the man's name?"

"I don't know. I don't know names."

Cathartes shuffled through the photographs until he found one of Cassia. "What about her?"

"That's the bishop. They called her the bishop."

"Did she speak?"

"She didn't have to speak. She was just there."

Cathartes squinted. "What are you telling me?"

"It's not what she is, it's what she means. Just her. Without her, there's nothing there."

"Did you see any drugs?"

"Lots of drugs."

"Any sexual activity?"

"I guess so. It was a party. When the moon rose they were singing songs."

Cathartes shuffled through a few more photographs. "Sir," continued the young man. "I want you to understand, it's all anybody talks about right now. Since I got back. I say there's a lot of discontent here now. A lot of problems. They read the papers. They know you've got something. Some kind of relic in your office."

He and Cathartes stared at each other. "I've got to get back," said Nanda Dev, picking up his gloves.

"Just a minute," said Cathartes. He sat frowning in his chair, and then he spoke. "You think this is a dangerous woman."

"Yes, sir."

"A threat to the security of the mine."

The young man rolled his eyes. "Sir, I've been telling

you . . ." he said. But he stopped talking when Cathartes moved his hand.

"What could I offer you to do some work for me?" Cathartes said.

"What work?"

"Some dangerous work."

The miner made a small impatient gesture with his gloves. "Sir, I do what I do. No more—I have a wife and child. Besides, what do you want with me? Why don't you just go in there?"

He turned to Professor Marchpane. "Sir," he said. "Why can't you go there? You have the men."

Professor Marchpane cleared his throat. "They've moved now, is that true?"

"Yes, they're closer now. They moved again last night."

When he had gone, Marchpane and Cathartes sat together in the close heat and talked for a few minutes. "He's right," Cathartes said. "We have the men."

"Do we? He thinks I'm in danger just by visiting the pit without an escort. I've got five hundred men—ample for most circumstances. Not for attacking ten thousand armed fanatics.

"I'll tell you what I want," he said after a pause. "I want to get that bone of yours out of here as quickly as I can. I want you to go with it. The girl—I don't give a damn about her. I want to hold on here until the Board returns, and then after about two months I want to turn in my resignation."

Cathartes wasn't listening. "You know I had her," he said. "At the plantation—I had her in my hand. I could have avoided all of this." He shook his head. "I was soft-hearted. She was so young."

"You couldn't have known."

"Yes, I should have known. I thought it was the old Treganu, the old man. I was a fool. What was she doing out there by herself, in that village full of aberrations and monstrosities?"

"You couldn't have known."

"Ten thousand people—she's infecting this whole district. I will not forgive myself."

Cathartes was leaning forward in his chair, his face sunk in shadow. Now he raised his head and squinted out the open door. "Never," he said. "These popular delusions have long roots, which must be torn out daily." He got to his feet. "I find this place oppressive."

Again on the way back Cathartes walked with the overseer while Marchpane lagged behind. There were five miners waiting at the elevator at the end of the glass tunnel. Marchpane nodded at them while they looked at their shoes.

Suddenly he felt frightened. Yet why should he? The miners knew him. He knew hundreds by their names; he knew their families.

The cage arrived and he stepped into it. The miners followed him, shuffling their feet. They would not meet his eyes.

Why should he be afraid? Always he had fought for them— they knew that too. The disability pensions, the new hourly wage—all that was his initiative. Once he had gone alone into the prison to meet with the trade unionists.

Cathartes was talking with the overseer. The cage made several stops, and it was crowded. Someone stood on Marchpane's foot.

Then they arrived upon the ridge and they descended. There was quite a crowd. The cog railway had halted for no reason he could see. Idle men and women stood next to the boiler hole with tin cups in their hands, though it was past the hour. They stared at him with red-rimmed eyes, their faces gleaming in the firelight. One had the impudence to spit, and Marchpane was relieved to see that Cathartes took no notice.

NANDA DEV | 12

Thirty-five hours later, Nanda Dev stood in Longo Starbridge's tent. In his speech and in his posture, he showed the same proud submissiveness that he had in the crystal chamber in the mine. Here, Karan Mang took the Marchpane role. He was sitting in his canvas chair, and with his right index finger he was stroking the back of his left hand. Longo Starbridge stood behind him, his beard sunk on his chest.

It was midmorning. Sunlight was piercing through a hole in the flap. Washed, scraped free of grease, in different clothes, Nanda Dev was a handsome man with hairless skin. "Yes," he said. "It went all right. It went like I said."

"Tell us." Karan Mang's thin lips moved more than those two words justified; he seemed to be suppressing a yawn.

"He's done for. He was the last one. My man hit him with a spanner as he got out of the elevator."

"Did he kill him?"

"No. I told him not to push. But he crushed his skull behind the ear. He's in the hospital."

"And so?"

"And so there's a new man, like I said, sir. He's an associate professor of religion. But no one knows him. No one in security. No one in the hole."

"I see."

If Karan Mang had any interest in the answers to his questions, he didn't show it in his voice. With his right forefinger he stroked the back of his left thumb. Longo Starbridge stood behind him.

Nanda Dev was barefoot. The red turban on his head was carefully knotted. The tasseled end hung down over his ear. "Now's the time," he said. "You shouldn't wait more than a few days, sir. The phone is down, but there's another one in Cochinoor. One way or another, he'll get a message through."

Karan Mang shrugged his small shoulders, and rearranged the silk cuff on his wrist.

"Sir, maybe you don't get it quite," said Nanda Dev. "He's just one man. He doesn't know the mine. He doesn't know how close things are to breaking open. I told him, but he doesn't know. Marchpane knew. But Marchpane's gone."

"It's not up to us." Longo Starbridge spoke for the first time. His voice was low, deep in his beard. The hair trembled around his mouth. He shook his head. "It's four days till the woodman comes."

Nanda Dev clicked his tongue. "Who says you have to wait?"

"I do. It's the sign. The first sign is the lily on the stump. The adversary cuts the lily on the stump. The woodman, and the golden blood flows down into the root. The second sign is the flame-of-the-forest tree, and the fire burning on the mountains. The third sign is the groaning in the earth. The fourth sign is the cracking of the tower. The fifth sign is the splitting of the sky, when Angkhdt will come into his country."

"That's all right," said Nanda Dev. "But maybe we can hurry it along."

"No we can't. It's not like that. You say there are five hundred security in Carbontown. That's a lot of men. Everything must be exactly right for us, on our side and on yours."

Karan Mang pursed his lips, and then he raised his hand to hide them. Longo Starbridge took two steps backward and lifted his arm, a rhetorical gesture, out of place in that cramped tent. His fingers grazed the roof; it was streaked with sunlight.

"The first sign is the bishop's death," he said. "The second sign is the fall of Carbontown. It is the fire burning on the hilltop. It is the flame of the forest, which Freedom Love saw burning in a dream. He says, 'I was on the crack of the abyss, and I felt the flame inside my heart. And the pistons of my heart were pumping, and the furnace of my heart was bursting, and the engine of my heart was breaking. My arms, my chest, my belly, and the cavity of my brain was full of liquid fire.'"

He paused. "In fact the text retains its ambiguities," said Karan Mang, staring at his thumb. "But Brother Longo is persuasive, and at the moment the level of sophistication among our followers is low. Unfortunately the commentary on the first sign is clearer. And the schedule is specific— unfortunately, I say, because we are uncomfortable here."

"I don't understand," said Nanda Dev.

"I'm saying she's going to die," said Longo Starbridge. "She's going to die according to the prophecy. Everybody knows it—she knows it, even. Do you think these people follow us because they like us?"

There was a silence in the tent. Karan Mang broke it: "Naturally, this has to be arranged from your side. The woodman is the enemy. He is the incarnation of the enemy."

"What does he look like?" asked Nanda Dev.

"He is dressed in black. It is not complicated."

"Two hundred dollars," said Nanda Dev.

"As you like."

"I've got a family," said Nanda Dev. "I'm right, aren't I? Whoever it is will not survive. I bet the prophecy is clear on that."

"It is ambiguous," said Karan Mang.

That day, the Cult of Loving Kindness was camped along a river bottom seven miles from Carbontown, in a grove of fig trees. It was a peaceful place. Light filtered through the leaves, speckled the canvas rooftops of the rows of tents. Nanda Dev, stepping out into the open air, was hoping for a breeze. His skin was slick with sweat. In fact the air outside Brother Longo's tent was almost as wet, almost as close, almost as still as it had been inside. All was quiet in the grove, and whatever noises did penetrate—the buzz of an insect, the laugh of some small child—seemed muffled and made dull. The tents were empty. The soldiers of Paradise were in the forest, scavenging for food.

"Come," said Longo Starbridge. "She's with the children."

They walked through the trees. The flies were thick upon the leaves, thick upon the fallen unripe fruit. As they reached the fringes of the grove, Nanda Dev wrinkled his nose. The path split left for Carbontown. It ran down by the river, which ran thick and slow and noiseless in its banks. He didn't go that way. He followed Longo Starbridge through a clump of gutted bamboo huts. The meeting house, built of heavier wood, still smoldered.

They passed a shallow ditch in an open space where the ground was black and beaten flat. The dirt was looser there, turned over, and flies were crawling out of it. Nanda Dev wrinkled his nose, because a smell of carrion was rising with the burnt wood. The soldiers of Paradise had burnt the town; almost he turned aside. This is nothing, he thought. This is nothing, he thought to console himself. They'll be a pile of bodies stacked up to the moon when Carbontown goes up.

There was a murmur of voices coming from somewhere up ahead. They were in the forest now, pushing through a tangled mass of manzanita, following a tiny path which nevertheless was rutted deep with footprints. The manzanita gave out into separate clumps of tall bamboo. Here the light penetrated the foliage in sharp and dirty spears, flatter and wide-bladed and more numerous as they progressed, until they stepped out into an open glade. At the far end the bishop sat on a low bamboo bench, surrounded by children. Their mothers lay back in the shade.

Nanda Dev took out his camera from the pocket of his shorts. He had promised Cathartes some photographs. Some for his wife also, and one for the miner's shrine, cut out of the glass on Level 36. Already he had brought a wooden mask from Nyangongo, as well as a small wooden image of Beloved Angkhdt.

He made ten photographs that day, most of which were lost. One of them, however, formed the model for the portrait which later hung in a much larger shrine in the new Autumn Temple. In that dark and pungent place, full of incense and acolytes and urgent prayers, it glowed like a source of light. For the painter captured with his crusted oils the brilliance of the sunlight in that forest glade where Cassia sat in her white dress. She had raised one hand. She was talking to the children who flock around her feet.

The photograph, however, included figures missing from the painting—the figures of three adults who were with her by the bench that day. Two sat cross-legged: a grinning pie-bald woman, and an old man with his legs shrunken away to the bare bone. And one young man erect, his elbows raised, his fingers in his tangled yellow hair, his eyes mere holes in his dark face.

Nanda Dev's camera was new, imported, so small it could fit easily upon his palm. Unlike models even from a few months before, which had required that the subject pose for several minutes without moving, this one could capture minute fluctuations of expression. He folded back the plastic lid. He looked for a moment through the aperture, and then he let the lens wander over the scene. He rejected as a point of focus first the bishop's pensive face, next the young man's expression of tense hatred, of violence barely suppressed. Finally he pressed the shutter ten times at random. Looking up, he thought he could feel the tremor of a breeze floating toward him down the glade, bringing with it some sweet smell.

"God in Paradise, she's beautiful," he murmured.

At his side, Longo Starbridge grunted assent. Then he walked forward into the glade and squatted down by the side of an old woman dressed in black. She was sitting on a blanket in the shade of a litmus bush, an old, dried, withered woman, loosely put together like a bundle of dry sticks.

This was Miss Azimuth. She was busy sewing, and her brittle fingers moved over the surface of a white expanse of silk. Her joints were swollen and arthritic, yet perhaps there was some medication in the drugs she took to keep her skillful, to make it possible to sit that way upon the blanket without pain. The pupils of her eyes, when she raised them to look at Brother Longo, were shrunken down to dots.

"It's a shroud," she said.

She had thimbles on three fingers of her right hand. Her needle fluttered over the surface of the silk, making exquisite small stitches with a golden thread. Occasionally as she moved her elbow or her wrist the joint would creak. Nanda Dev, standing a dozen feet away, heard it from time to time, interrupting the rhythm of the bishop's voice.

The bishop raised her hand. "The tragedy is," she said, "how the best intentions go astray, and you can do such harm. Maybe in your own families you have seen how someone might have some idea about what to do, what game to play. Maybe your brothers or your sisters have tried to convince you to do something against your will. And even if you can admit later that their idea was good, it doesn't matter. It's too late. Sometimes I have seen such anger among the youngest children, such bitter words and fighting. It's because your ideas clash together, even with your friends, and they draw your bodies after them. A wise man taught me when I was a child. Now he is dead—he told me: 'What is it worth fighting for? Worth hurting and worth being hurt. Name it, and you will see it disappear into the air.'

"No. We must pull back our bodies from these conflicts. My father said that they will disappear, but not immediately. Maybe these ideas will fight against each other all around us for a little while. But then maybe it will be like a cradle when your mother's hand stops rocking. First it rocks for a while by itself, then less, and then it stops.

"Now this old man once told me the story of a war. And he said the tragedy of this war, which started as a fight against a terrible unfairness, was how quickly it turned into nothing, even though the people kept on fighting. Even as the forces of oppression were defeated, how quickly the men who understood ideas were replaced by men who understood ideas and power, and then by men who understood power only. So that in a few months nothing had changed, after all that death. Only the names and faces of the kings.

"It is for this reason that we must not hurt each other. It is for this reason that we must not try to hurt another living creature—not the smallest insect. It is for this reason that we must love each other and ignore our differences. It is for this reason that we must try and live in loving kindness with each other—because we have no choice. People say that these things can be disallowed sometimes, because of their ideas. But their ideas can never be fulfilled. Their goal can never be achieved, and we are left with what we do. What we do and what we are. And once we realize this, once we let go of these ideas which hurt us, then can we find peace."

In the glade, the children sat with their mouths open, staring with blank incomprehension as their mothers dozed in the shadows. But Miss Azimuth was listening as she stitched, nodding her little doll's head sometimes. Longo Starbridge was squatting on his heavy hams. Nanda Dev went to him and bent down. "Sir—does she know about all that?" he whispered, gesturing with his head back to the burnt town.

Brother Longo shrugged. "Her tent is on the far side. We have kept her separate."

"She doesn't know?"

"She doesn't want to know."

When he stood up again, Nanda Dev felt suddenly light-headed. For an instant, his vision was clouded with small shining specks. As he watched, they vanished. So beautiful she was, the last bishop of Charn, her words disappearing as she spoke them. Behind her, the big stranger with his ragged T-shirt and his angry face.

"She speaks of Paradise," said the old woman on the blanket, her voice faint and far away. "Already her thoughts are in Paradise." She had put aside her sewing, and wrapped it into an untidy ball in her black-skirted lap. Needles stuck from it at odd angles, each with its pennant of thread.

Longo Starbridge took out a stick of chewing gum. He rubbed the gum into a ball and placed it in the pouch of his lip, dropping the bright paper on the grass. "Tell him about the woodman," he said.

The old woman cocked her head. "I have prepared a map, you see. It shows the location of her tent. And here's a list of what you'll need. Though it's not you, is it? The woodman is not you."

"Not me," said Nanda Dev.

"No, he is dressed in black, you see. The gathering man. All black with a black hood. And he is carrying an axe with a single blade. And when he cuts the flower on the stump, he never needs more than one stroke—just one, you see. It's all he needs."

"The tent is isolated," said Longo Starbridge. "There will be no guard."

"No guard but the angel of our God," pursued Miss Azimuth. She held an envelope in her dry hand. "I have marked the hour on the margin. These are my calculations, which I made with Reverend Porphyry. Five-fifteen on the morning of the seventy-third. Just after dawn, you see—in the first light of day. The woodman, is he a strong man?"

"I don't know," said Nanda Dev. He was looking at Cassia, and his mouth was dry.

"He is the incarnate cruelty," sighed Miss Azimuth. "He is the evil of the world. He is the woodman, who chopped the tree of the Lord's faith, who chops the flower on the stump. But that stroke will be his last. We will rise against him. For there is something breaking in the engine of my heart—we will rise up."

"Take the envelope," said Longo Starbridge. The smile on his face was strange, illegible, and it revealed inside his lip the plug of gum.

But Nanda Dev was walking forward through the glade.

"My father had a teacher," Cassia was saying. "I saw him once, and this is what he told me: 'It is in your heart that you are free or bound, happy or unhappy. Therefore do not strive against events...'" She broke off when the miner stood before her, among the sleepy children.

He knelt down by Mama Jobe, by Servant of God. "I need your blessing for my wife and son," he said.

The emergency at Carbontown brought out the best and worst in Benjamin Cathartes. When Professor Marchpane was attacked, he had sent the overseer to run for help while he faced down the crowd. He had stood alone over the inert body of the old man. In the heat and the glare and the crashing of the railway he had seen little, he had heard little. The light reflected off a ring of ugly faces. There were shouts and curses. Someone threw a stone. And no one came to help, although the old man was bleeding from the back of his head. Cathartes had ripped part of the sleeve from his new shirt and bound it round the wet place in the old man's hair. Then he lifted him into his arms and struggled a few steps with him along the concrete curb, until one of the engineers came out from the blockhouse. He took March-pane's legs. Then a third man, a miner, had appeared out of the crowd, and all together they carried the professor by the runoff sheds, up along the maidan. There they had met the hospital security detachment.

In the days that followed, Cathartes took over the operation of the mine. This was made possible by his standing in the university hierarchy, as well as his energy and presumption. No one else among the corps of engineers and officers was eager to take responsibility during such a delicate time. But Cathartes had his baggage moved from his guest bedroom to the office of the president's executive assistant, and he commandeered the boardroom for his meetings. Unknown to the staff, ignorant of any principle of metallurgy or engineering, ignorant of any fact relating to the daily function of the company or the facility, nevertheless he was decisive. He was sure of his decisions. Professor Marchpane flickered in and out of consciousness; he languished in intensive care, and in the meantime Cathartes met with the captain of security and all the area commanders. He toured the razorwire chain-link fence that ran along the forty-mile perimeter. He sent runners out of Lameru, to Cochinoor, to Baahl—to anywhere that they might have a working telephone or an ansible. He sent a runner to the radio transmitter at Raban—a ninety-mile distance—and then another and another, in case the first was waylaid. He had technicians working round the clock upon the helicopter. Walking in a phalanx of armed overseers, he toured every section of the mine. He gave a speech. He met with the miners' grievance committee and released from prison some of the old union leaders.

On September seventeenth, the Cult of Loving Kindness blew up the access road in seven places and destroyed two bridges on the rail link to Charn. On the seventy-first, a small detachment of the soldiers of Paradise attacked the fence; they were easily repulsed.

On the seventy-second, Cathartes met with Nanda Dev for a few hours. That morning the security police, acting on a tip, had caught the man who had attacked Professor Marchpane. They had cornered him in Carbontown in his wife's cousin's house. They had dragged him out and dragged him up to the company for judgment. A rat-faced man, he had refused to talk.

"What do you think?" asked Cathartes, standing with his hands clasped behind him, looking out the window of his new office. He was dressed in his full academic uniform with the star-shaped insignia of his degree—first-class honors in comparative theology—pinned over his throat.

Behind him stood Nanda Dev, working his bare feet into the carpet. "Now is a good time to be strong," he said, his voice soft and deferential.

"I wonder." Cathartes turned into the room. He leaned back against the windowsill. "What if this was part of a conspiracy?"

Nanda Dev was silent. He waited, his eyes almost closed, while Cathartes picked at the corner of his lip—"I wonder. The man said nothing. And I asked him pointedly. I asked him repeatedly. Doesn't that suggest something to you?"

"I tell you all I know," said Nanda Dev.

"Yes. But maybe your methods of communication are not what they once were. How do you explain these conversations to your friends?"

"I say I am feeding you lies, sir."

"I see."

The office was a small rich room. The executive assistant had lined the walls with hardwood paneling, covered the floor with knotted carpets. Three framed photographs of the present governor of Charn hung above the desk. The one in the middle was dedicated and signed.

Nanda Dev contemplated the governor's glassy smile. "I don't think it matters. If there was a plan or not—you want to show your strength, sir. You want to show you don't care."

"I wonder. My security head told me to be careful. And Marchpane was conscious long enough to ask for the man's pardon."

"No," said Nanda Dev. "You have already released some prisoners. That's good. Now you can show your strength."

Cathartes touched his lips. "Perhaps," he said. "In principle."

"There is a whipping post on the maidan," suggested Nanda Dev.

On the desk, under the governor's photograph, lay Miss Azimuth's map. Beside it a black shirt, a black pair of pants, and a black hood. Weighing down the pile, a single-bladed axe, which Nanda Dev had bought at Lameru.

Cathartes stood up from the window. He moved over to the desk. "It seems cruel," he said, laying his finger on the map. "But maybe there are times when cruelty is the only language people understand."

"They are strong men," said Nanda Dev. "They respect strength in others."

"Tell me why her tent is left unguarded. You're sure they won't have moved during the night?"

"I'm sure."

"Why is she left alone?"

"Because you gave me money. So I paid the guard. Besides, there is someone in the cult who wants her dead."

"Perhaps you could have paid him to do the thing himself."

"No, sir," said Nanda Dev. "It must be like I said. Paying the guard, that's just to make sure. But they're so scared of the gathering man, they'd let him walk right through the camp."

"I wonder. Will they let him walk away again?"

"I told you. They won't lift a finger to protect her. Not if he's dressed like that. They think it's—I don't know—a spirit. Sent to punish the false prophets."

"Hunh. Is that what it's come to mean? 'He cuts the lily on the stump'—it's from the dreams of Freedom Love."

As he spoke, Cathartes moved his hand to the axe blade, and ran his finger down the edge. "All this is distasteful," he continued. "I am an intellectual."

"Just tell him to be quiet," said Nanda Dev after a pause. "Tell him to make sure to hide. They'll recognize the cut and that's enough. Tell him to leave the axe. Leave it as it lies. The clothes—that's just in case."

Soon after that, he left. And as the door closed behind him and the air expanded in his chest, he felt a sudden urge to cry out. He stood in the open air, on the steel catwalk. It was late afternoon.

There was a red glow in the dark polluted air of Carbontown. The wind, strong for that season, was hot and full of grit. As Nanda Dev ran down the metal steps, it whistled through the open girders.

He paused to pick a splinter from his eye. The catwalk led across toward the elevator cages, and it was stirring slightly in the wind. Six people waited at the elevator; unable to tolerate the sight of them, Nanda Dev turned instead toward the emergency stairs, which zigzagged out of sight. Disused, it was littered with loose newspaper and soda cans. Two hundred steel steps descended to the rock—not a huge distance, but Nanda Dev was tired. He stopped to rest at the halfway balcony, and stood looking at the lights of Carbontown through the intervening struts.

The company offices had won the governor's gold medal for design six months before. The architect, a foreigner, had since gone on to other projects, but this one was his best. The company had given him the site: a sheer rock ridge above the mine. And they had requested him to keep the building separate in its look and feel from the other squat concrete mine buildings nearby, while at the same time staying within certain budgetary constraints. The result was a cube of steel scaffolding with rooms and offices suspended in it, joined by open walkways. The architect had wanted to maintain a certain utilitarian character—the catwalks and the bridges were steel versions of the ones down in the pit, and the elevators were authentic miners' cages. He had thought the contrast with the luxurious suites of offices would provide the building with aesthetic tension.

To Nanda Dev, it represented everything he hated. It seemed to squat above the town like a huge insect on the rock, a delicate yet evil presence. Standing on the balcony, he felt unclean, contaminated, sad.

To his right and to his left, the crests of the mountains were lit with winking beacons. They described the arc of a circle high around the mine—red and green, red and green, diminishing and finally vanishing. Through the thick air he could not see the beacons on the opposite peaks, five miles away. But below him the town was glowing red, and the wind seemed to rise out of the pit, carrying fumes, which disturbed his eyes. He turned away and trudged on down the steps; as the stair turned he looked westward down the dark side of the ridge, the wooded slope that fell toward the perimeter. He could see the lights from the gate. They were shining through the trees.

The road which rose up toward him was dark now. There were no trucks on it. The mine was still producing, but in the emergency only two furnaces were lit. Since Thursday, all shifts all wages, had been cut in half. People wandered aimlessly on the maidan.

The stair came down onto the rock. Nanda Dev left the building and walked down along the ridge. He had no wish to see anyone, no wish to talk. Instead of heading toward the terminus, where the big cars rose and sank diagonally along the greased rail to Crystal Lip, he took another way. Someone waved to him; without responding, he hurried down a concrete embankment on the ridge's outer lip, until he was out of sight.

There were some storage sheds upon the outer slope, a few boys working. He didn't stop. He crossed the road behind the empty loading dock, and skirted around the far side of the furnace compound. He climbed down through the rocks and thornbushes, until he reached another service stair.

Here the ridge was narrow. The stair, which antedated the construction of the road, fell away below him, a series of concrete bastions. He stood for a moment looking down toward the gate and toward the razorwire fence, trying to find the small path that led off through the trees. There were no lights to mark it, no lights to mark the camp among the fig trees seven miles out, and he wondered if perhaps the woodman might get lost.

Then he turned around and climbed instead up to the summit of the ridge, which he reached in a few minutes. As he crossed over he could see the lights of Carbontown again. Or rather, he could see the glow, for the slope below him now was gentle, and the town itself would be out of sight for most of the hour's descent.

Again the stair was broken and cracked and clogged with refuse. He kicked down through the beer cans and plastic containers. The stair was scarcely used; it ran down parallel to the car, and occasionally Nanda Dev could hear a smooth metallic hiss over to his left behind the rocks. It was getting dark. The wind was hot and strong, stirring the refuse around him.

On the upper slope the stair ran straight. But as the angle of descent increased, it wound back and forth, searching for the gentle way.

There was a place above the town that he knew well. When he had first been shipped out from his neighborhood in Charn, often after school he had climbed up with a few friends to smoke cigarettes and drink. It was a simple turning of the concrete stair, yet almost it was the only place in the gigantic complex where it was quiet enough to talk. Out of earshot from the processing plant upon the ridge, out of earshot from the pit, the stair seemed to hang suspended between two worlds. Later, when he knew his wife, they had often met there at the three-quarter mark after his shift was over, before her shift began. In the evenings, Carbontown was spread out like a grid of fire. There was some shelter, and the wind was less.

She was waiting for him. She was waiting in the bastion. The boy was perched on the concrete parapet, kicking his bare heels. She stood with her arms around the child, staring down over the lights, her pregnant belly pressed into the wall. She was wearing her black flowered dress, and her grey hair was braided down her back.

The boy saw him first. Like so many of the children at Carbontown he was backward, not speaking yet, though he was past the age. Still he recognized his father; he clapped his little hands, and Kate turned round.

"I knew you'd come," she said. She smiled as he came down and put his arms around her. He hugged her, but there was a tension, a shyness in her body. She wanted to touch him, but there was something she wanted to say, also. She twisted away from him but kept hold of his hand. She held on to his hand and squeezed his fingers as he pushed the hair away from his son's forehead. Then she cleared her throat, showing partly a symptom of a new medical condition—a new outbreak of silicon saliva in the town—and partly something true to her own shyness. When they had first known each other, even in bed she could not meet his eyes, and often she would be clearing her throat and making small, soft, tentative noises. Now she spread his hand out on the parapet. She spread his fingers apart one at a time, not looking up except for quick glances at the boy. "I knew you'd come," she said. "Where were you?"

"Talking to the new director."

"Rasmus saw you at the offices." She glanced up at his face and turned away, squeezing his wrist hard. "Did you see the bishop?"

"Yes."

"Oh, what's she like? I got your note but I was worried. Maia stayed the night." She was running her thumbnail back and forth along his wrist. "Did she . . . say anything?"

He looked out over the grid, the red streets north and south, the blue streets east and west. Beyond, the pit gaped like a fiery jaw. Let it come down, thought Nanda Dev. Just let it come down. He pushed his hand back through his son's hair.

"I took some pictures," he said. "They're being developed."

"Did she . . . give you anything? What was she like?"

"She touched me. I was as close as I am to you. She told me everything would be all right."

"Oh, I'm so glad," said Kate. She rubbed her forehead on his shirt. "Rasmus said he saw you at the offices. I waited at the car, so then I knew you'd come this way."

Again there was something important that she wanted to tell him. She cleared her throat. "The union met last night. They're meeting now. As I came up I heard the loudspeaker."

"Tell me."

She shrugged. "Maia's husband's cousin. You know him— Enver Shaw. He's the one they said attacked Professor Marchpane. He's to be whipped. The message just came down."

Nanda Dev said nothing. He had one hand on his son's fragile head, and boy was staring at him out of black-rimmed eyes.

"Tonight," said Kate. "His wife is with the union now. Two hundred cuts—it will kill him."

When Nanda Dev spoke, he seemed to hear two voices,

and one was coming from someplace outside himself. "Marchpane banned that punishment three months ago. Now we'll have a lot to say."

As he was talking, he listened to the second voice—its tone, its inflection, its accent, and it seemed absurd to him, a cruel piece of mimicry. "Marchpane was all right," he said. "But this new man is very hard."

The wind was coming up out of the mine. Kate was rubbing her forehead against his chest. And now his son was smiling for some stupid reason, smiling and clucking.

13

THE
GATHERING
MAN

Deccan Blendish stood next to the desk in Cathartes's office. From time to time his wrists would twitch, both together.

Cathartes was looking past his shoulder. "You have an academic training," he said. "You understand the importance of these things. Not just in terms of your own interest, or because I tell you."

He was encased by his distinctive odor—sweet, oppressive, male. Deccan Blendish knew that to approach closer was to risk distress; from three feet away, the smell of the professor's breath was diffuse enough for him to tolerate. But even a few inches closer, and he could feel it in his nostrils—it was a temptation, always a temptation. He closed his eyes. Yet still he could picture the professor's red lips tensing and relaxing, puckering minutely around each word: "I trust you. These others, they have no education. They follow orders and that's all. I'm not comfortable with them. They have no loyalty to me, and I don't trust them."

"But I am sick," whispered Deccan Blendish.

"Don't you feel better?"

He felt better. For the past few days, a nurse had given him a shot of morphine every four hours. Now his joints were greasy in their sockets.

"You're getting better. Already you are stronger. Modern antibiotics—but you know that woman was the cause of this. When she's gone, you will feel better still."

Blendish had begun to sway off-balance just a little bit. Nauseated, he opened his eyes. The red lips were very close to him.

They were telling him the weakest of the three arguments. Yet the conviction never varied, the sure tone. What did this mean?

In fact all the arguments were weak, in various degrees. Over the past few days he had heard them many times in many different permutations, when Cathartes had visited him and stood beside his bed. The words never repeated and they never seemed to stop. Even alone, after his shot of morphine, sometimes he would still see the thin chain of words, glistening with saliva, drawn out link by link from that wet mouth, the red lips puckering around each link.

"I don't trust them," said Cathartes. "You, I trust. I respect your dedication as a scholar. That work you did with the Treganu, that was fine work. I was angry, perhaps slightly jealous. I know scholarship when I see it. I think this work could form the basis of a publishable dissertation."

"Under your direction," whispered Deccan Blendish.

"Partly under my direction. But I was thinking of Professors X and Y." Here he named two famous primatologists from the University Extension; in every cycle of the argument, the names were different.

"I think I could arrange a fellowship," the red lips said. "And of course if you agree to help me now, the company will sponsor you." Link by link, the chain slipped through. Yet it was a weak chain, and the flaw was that Blendish was a dead man. He could feel it in his body. Every morning, his feces in the toilet were full of wriggling shapes. Every evening when he threw up after supper, even the lightest broth had wriggling shapes in it.

"It would mean you'd have to teach a couple of undergraduate sections. You could be my TA next semester, when my leave runs out. I'd like that."

Blendish nodded. "So would I," he whispered.

He was dying. He could feel it in the dissolution of the world. It was contracting. It was coming apart. Already his vision had contracted. Though Cathartes's lips were preternaturally distinct, the rest of his face receded into wriggling shadow. That morning, staring at his wasted and unrecognizable face in the mirror of his hospital room, Blendish had noticed the parasites moving in a ring around the outside of his cornea. He had taken off his spectacles and held his face just inches from the glass. He had seen the small shapes struggling, poking through the pale membranes of his eyes.

"It is because I trust you that I offer you these things. Because you understand the importance of what we are trying to accomplish. And you understand the risk. I must tell you— the possibility of a strike in Carbontown is real. Perhaps a violent confrontation. I am expecting the return of company management anytime now, of course. A response to my appeal. But until then the security of the mine is in plain jeopardy, and it is my responsibility to defend it. Yours and mine. During Professor Marchpane's illness, I have taken over his duties, but these men are not my men. I don't trust them as I trust you."

"Thank you," whispered Deccan Blendish.

"And this woman must be stopped. You saw what she did at the plantation. What she did to you. Now she has spread her poison through the mine."

The question was: Why him? Even if Cathartes believed what he was saying, did he think Blendish was capable of doing what he asked? There was another reason.

"If you do this in the way that I've described, dressed in these clothes, no one will stop you. Her guards are on our side."

Maybe. Whatever else it was, this journey was not safe. Maybe Cathartes wanted him dead, not knowing he was dead already.

Blendish dropped his eyes down the front of the professor's uniform, over the bulge in his pants, over to the desk. The black shirt was there, the hood, the map. The axe was there. Also the skull was there, taken from its box. The circle of parasites around his eye kept all things indistinct, save for that grinning face.

"I'm asking you to do something illegal," said Cathartes. "Under ideal circumstances she would be arrested and returned to Charn for trial. There's no doubt of the outcome—for witchcraft and sedition, your testimony alone would be enough. That's what you have to remember. You and I are men of ideas, and we can make this leap of judgment. For other men it would be murder. It would be an unwise precedent."

As he spoke, he moved away from Deccan Blendish toward the window. The young man didn't see him move. He was staring at the skull. He was no judge of the passage of time. Only he was aware that the professor's smell was less intense. And he was aware of an orange glow outside the window; it threw a muted, diffuse light. Cathartes stood looking into it, looking through it, looking down through it to the world. There on the maidan, Blendish knew, a middle-aged miner was being whipped to death. No more than a hundred yards away, and yet there was no sound. No sound from the whip, and no sound from the man. Nothing from his shattered back and buttocks. The rhythmic spray of blood upon the concrete made no noise. Nothing from the crowd, which was packed all over the ridge, over the gallery roofs and everywhere that might afford a view—a thousand or five thousand children, women, men, drinking company beer from company cups.

In their tent beyond the fig grove Rael and Cassia were making love. That morning they had woken up still joined, and all day they had been making love with an urgency that had replaced words, replaced tenderness, replaced comfort. Rael wondered whether it was possible to live inside her, his sex losing and regaining stiffness in a rhythmic cycle that would become their only means to measure time.

They lay immobile, side by side. They were too sore and sensitive to tolerate even the slightest movement now. Even the slightest chafing was enough to make them cry out loud. His testicles contained an emptiness that was like hunger. Their lips were sore from kissing, even after they had oiled their mouths with oil from the lamp. His tongue had a raw place along the underside.

He was as deep inside of her as he could penetrate, yet it was not enough. It was a pitiful few inches, and even though it felt like the whole world, still it was nothing. She had secrets on every square centimeter of her skin, and he could search for them his whole life and not find them. He stared into her eye. What was at the bottom of that shaft? What thoughts were in that brain, what feelings in that heart, each so separate, so immune to touch? Joined by their one small aching link, even their bodies were like grease and water. "Ah," she said. "I can't stand it," and she pulled away.

It was evening. It was dark outside the tent. Light came from a single lamp beside the mats and pillows where they lay. A single fingernail of flame reached up to scratch the belly of a small bronze god, and scratch along the side of his big phallus. It was as big as his arm, almost.

He sat cross-legged, a pool of oil between his legs, a small wick floating in the pool. "Ah, God," said Cassia. She rolled onto her back.

A little wind was tugging at the canvas of the tent. All day it had been hot. The sheets, tangled at their feet, were damp with sweat—cool now, and their bodies too were cool and dry, crusted with salt. Without touching her, Rael ran his hand along the curve of her body, several inches from her skin. He ran his hand down over her plump throat. Without touching her, he cupped each breast along its outer side, where it had flattened down from its own weight. Her stomach had sunk down. Without touching her, he stroked it. Then he ran his hand over the soft mound of her belly, the soft mound of her sex.

He changed the direction of his body, and put his cheek down on her thigh. "Ah, God," she said, "no more." And so he raised his head, squinting in the darkness toward the flickering flame and then beyond it. Shadows moved along the outside of the tent.

A light burned out there too, perhaps a lantern. Softly, tentatively, with his dry tongue, he licked along the outside of her thigh until she stopped him. She sank her fingers into the tangles of his hair. She clasped her fingers tight around his hair and held him still. "No more," she said, her eyes shining in the lamplight.

She was cold. Under his lips her skin was tight and bumpy; she let go of him and then sat up, fumbling with the bedclothes, pulling the sheets around her, hiding her body for the first time that day.

There was a bowl of water by the statue of Beloved Angkhdt. She drank from it and offered it to him, but he paid no attention. Instead he pulled open the flap of the tent and crawled outside.

A basket of food had been left next to the entrance with a plate over the top of it to keep the bugs away. Rael stood up. Naked, he walked into the center of the glade. All was quiet. The embers were still warm upon a bald place in the grass. Men had slept there for the past few nights, guards for him and Cassia. Now they were gone.

Beyond, down past the burned-out village, he could hear voices. In the fig grove the soldiers of Paradise had set up their tents. He could see the glimmer of cookfires where they prepared whatever miserable roots they had collected from the forest.

Naked, he raised his right hand above his head, stretching the muscles of his back. He reached down to touch his aching sex. Someone was here, someone was lurking in the bamboo, squatting in the manzanita—he could feel them squatting there. Whoever they were, they had to be used to seeing his body. He understood the game he had to play before these people. He had to fuck their goddess, and the more the better. It was the only compensation they expected for their food and for their careful treatment. It was the only circumstance from his past life to have seeped through into their legend.

It was a strange sad game. It angered him to have to play it. On him and Cassia now, he always felt the touch of other people, the breath of other people. Sometimes at night he had gone down among the cult, and watched them play the tragedy of Abu Starbridge before an audience of soldiers. Now it was like that for him and Cassia, and it was robbing something from them now, even now in the most urgent time. This urge to be with her, this urge to touch her every minute—what was it? Surely he had felt it his whole life. But this physical hunger—was it because time was short? Maybe there was more to it than that.

He lumbered in a circle, to give the squatting audience a complete view.

Cassia had made him angry. "Do you remember, do you remember?" she had said. She had described her tower bedroom in old Charn. She had described her prison cell. She had described their climb up to the Temple of St. Basilon. She had described their journey to the crossroads where Mr. Sarnath found them, where they had been born into the world. And all these words had meant nothing to him, nor did they bring back a single image. Nor did it ignite a single feeling except anger when she said, "You were with me there." Her eyes would be far away, full of the reflection of that time, and as always he was like a beggar at her feast because it was all dark to him, and every single moment of it was dark. He would make love to her until she cried out, and even then part of her was rutting in her tower chamber with a stranger who had been himself.

He went back to the bucket at the entrance to the tent. It was made of silver, carved in a geometric pattern. Everything they gave her was made of silver now, and they were always given the best food, more than they could eat while the rest went hungry.

He lifted the cover and let the steam escape. They had found some rice somewhere, and cooked it with a sweet potato. He thrust his hand down into the wet, hot grains. "Food," he said. The lamp inside the tent was burning brighter, and he could see Cassia through the mosquito net, kneeling by the statue.

"In the wind now coming in the dark," he said. "Is a tree leaf flutter now." He breathed the cool and pungent air. In the distance he could hear the river, the wind stirring the trees. Bugs in the grass.

He cocked his head. Competing now with the night sounds, he could hear chanting from inside the tent, part of the song cycle of prayer that Cassia now offered daily to the little god. "Come out," he said, but he could see her sit back on her heels, her head bowed low. He pushed the net aside and crawled back into the tent, wanting to disturb her.

"Rice," he said, but she was saying words that made no sense:

> *"Nutmeg from the Orient,*
> *Candied ginger will I bring you.*
> *Topaz, diamonds, and quartz,*
> *From the mines at Ranakpore,*

From the turbaned Negro's toil,
From the fabled mountainside,
From the bottom of the sea,
Pearls as big as plover's eggs.
I will bring a bag of pearls,
Enough to spell my name out on the ground,
And I will spell it ANGKHDT,
And you will say my name,
And you will say my name out loud."

He put the bucket down beside her. He scooped out a dollop of the rice onto the plate and started eating. She had lit some incense, and she had sprinkled some powder on the lamp to make it burn up bright.

"Tonight is the last night," she said.

The food stuck in his throat. There was no moisture in it. It was dry as sand. "I don't say it to hurt you," she went on. "But it is the truth."

She sang another song while he lay back upon the pillows, chewing slowly. Then he cleared his mouth. "Go," he said. "Is going through the trees. Foot and foot and foot, in the wild run."

"No," said Cassia.

"No," repeated Rael.

"I can't be what I am not," she said.

In the bucket was a silver spoon. She took a spoonful of the rice and swallowed it. "This is drugged to make us sleep," she said.

In fact, after just a few mouthfuls a lethargy was spreading over his body. He picked up a glass ewer from the floor. It was full of water, and he drank it dry.

"Don't let us be apart tonight," she said. "I know this is hard for you."

There was a bronze crown between the statue's feet. Cassia poked the stick of incense through the tines and left it balanced, so that the column of smoke divided around the muzzle of dog-headed Angkhdt. She had the spoon in her right hand, and with her left she reached out to touch Rael's leg. "Don't let us be apart," she said.

And so he put his arms around her. He stripped away the sheet from her soft body, and after an hour they made love again, softly and sleepily as the drug took hold. At different times, each one was asleep, but the other was so gentle that it didn't matter.

Soldiers took Deccan Blendish down the road. In the guardhouse by the loading dock they gave him a nice meal, the first he'd had in a long time. He ate it all, and then he threw up on the plate.

Soldiers took him to a shower in the courtyard. He stood in it and watched the cold water bead on his body while they took his clothes away to burn them. He could tell that they were frightened. They didn't let him use a towel. They just turned off the water. He stood on a slotted wooden platform in the courtyard and let the dark air dry him. He lifted up his hand, examining it in the light of a single naked bulb, which was set into a corner of the yard.

He had kept his wallet when they took his pants. He had kept his spectacles, his mealcard, his wristwatch, and his student ID. When the shower stopped, they were arranged on the bench next to his new clothes. Even the currency was there.

He put on his spectacles and arranged his belongings in the pockets of his new pants. They were made of comfortable black cotton, loose and light; he admired the fabric as he dressed himself. The pads of his fingers seemed unnaturally sensitive as he buttoned up his shirt and put the hood around his neck. The pads of his feet seemed unnaturally sensitive as he slipped on a pair of rope-soled shoes. The axe hung from a loop in his belt.

"You in there. You finished?"

He was finished. He caught a glimpse of himself in a broken

triangle of mirrored glass, set into the stucco of the wall. He caught a glimpse of himself in the face of the guard who opened the wooden door and stood aside to let him pass. It was different; he could feel the difference just by putting on the clothes. The clothes made him understand how to walk and where to put his hands. The costume made it just a little more real—the black hood around his neck, the axe in his belt. The costume told the audience that the performance had begun. Now suddenly, the gathering man had stepped onstage—his shaved head, his pockmarked face stripped to the bone, his eyes red with broken blood vessels, his teeth too heavy for his mouth. He was the incarnation of dark death, his flesh seething with parasites, and he could see it in the guard's disgust, the way he lifted up his hand.

But this new sharpness to his senses, this was not part of the costume. It was not part of the act. They took him out and put him into a car with plastic seats and an electric motor. An intolerable hum was rising from the gearbox. Deccan Blendish put his fingers into his ears. When the soldier let the brake out, they moved slowly down the roadbed, and the metal wheels were screaming on the crushed volcanic stones. He could feel it in the inside of his ear, and it was as if the inside of his ear was a house with separate chambers, and in each chamber lived a sound, and he could move back and forth up the corridors, opening doors and closing them, mixing sounds in any combination: the squeal of the metal on the rock. The muttered questions of one soldier in the seat behind him. The responses of the other.

Those were the big rooms. But there were numerous small cubbyholes and closets; as the car headed down the roadbed toward the gate, he rushed back and forth. In one room, a row of boxes, and each contained a single insect. There to his left, an owl in the woods. The crack of a branch. He dug his fingers tight into his ears. And then he was moving backward down the corridor toward the cellar door. He leaned his cheek against it. Inside, the whisper of his lungs. The thumping of his heart upon the cellar steps. Down below, a scurrying in the blackest dark.

Or his eyes. It was true—the circle had contracted. The parasites had closed out the periphery. But in that circle everything was clear. It was as if he were inhabiting a world of darkness, a world that nevertheless contained a single spotlight. Whatever that light touched, stood out with a painful starkness.

He looked into the woods on either side of the descending road. Electric lanterns shone at intervals, hung from branches or else perched on top of poles. And when the spotlight hit them there was a reaction. The compass of his vision filled with brittle, crystalline, prismatic patterns, spreading out into the leaves.

But when they drove up to the fence he couldn't tolerate it. He put his head down on the plastic dashboard. He pulled his hood around his face. He made a space of darkness for his eyes. In it he began to see what it might mean to be the gathering man, and to be walking backward down the path toward death. In that space of darkness he could feel himself receding from the world. The strings which held him to the world were snapping one by one, and these last strings, the five strings of his senses, were stretching and aching and twisting now. He didn't have to look. Even without looking he could smell the beery sentries at their watch. He knew the brands that they were drinking. He could tell their ages.

The car scraped to a halt and he could hear through the plug of his fingertips and through his thumping heartbeat the murmured conversation. "What the fuck is this?" they asked. And a little later: "I can't believe this shit." They pulled him from his seat, stood him up straight, and stripped his hood away.

The razorwire fence, electrified and sparking gently, cast a long bright shadow of intersecting lines. At intervals concrete towers rose through the trees; he stood between the guardtowers of the gate. He looked through into the blessed darkness on the other side.

One week ago, two weeks ago—when had he last come through that gate? It had been daylight then. Coming from the village, sitting with Cathartes in the university car, he had passed by acres of sweet potato fields. He had passed through the security barracks—how different it had seemed. Now black night had come. In his hospital bed in Carbontown, he had achieved a metamorphosis. Or maybe not. Maybe it was only that he had lost so much flesh. Maybe there was an essential core of death in every man and woman, covered up by layers of life. Maybe as time went on you shed each layer like a skin, until you died. Maybe it was so gradual that you didn't notice. But with him, in one week or two weeks they had peeled away a layer many inches thick.

One said: "He's got a map. But I'm supposed to take him to the camp."

"Don't get killed."

"The prof says there's a truce tonight. This one—he's the messenger."

"Is that right? They were stealing food this afternoon."

He was the messenger. They were ejecting him into the world, hoping that whatever rag of skin he still retained would last the night. He put his fingers on the axe blade at his waist, feeling with minute clarity the imperfections in the steel.

The guard talked. Deccan Blendish stepped through the gate. The wind brought him a hundred forest smells. Off to his right, the flooded fields.

He was the messenger. Yet it was not his plan to kill a woman in an isolated tent at five-fifteen precisely. Someone who had helped him. Someone whom already he'd betrayed. Lying in his hospital bed while Cathartes talked, he had rehearsed how he would say yes. Then he would take his money and his wallet and strike out along the path toward

Cochinoor, toward Charn. He had the map. Oh, yes in Charn he had been happy, in that fellowship of scholars, and in the evenings he had walked on the embankment, eating peanuts in his waddling body, thick with layers of life. Eating peanuts through sheer loneliness and listening to the street music near the Lamont Theatre while the lights on the marquee shone green and white.

The breeze brought him a hundred dirty smells. Yet Charn was out there somewhere with its hot grease and its ginger and its peanuts, perhaps touched by a cousin of this same wind. Right now, he thought, fat lonely men were walking underneath the lights of the embankment.

And now he wanted a new plan, because he was dying. He needed a new plan, to go with his new clothes. He ran his finger up and down along the blade. "One stroke," Cathartes said. He had to smile. He would need all the painkillers in all the world to accomplish such a thing.

"You come on. You—asshole—yeah, let's get this over. It's a seven-mile walk." The guard passed him and went on down the road. Blendish followed, and in a little while a path split off into the woods.

"Asshole, this way," said the guard. Blendish followed him into the trees.

Cassia woke up. She kept an image from her dream. It was the woodman standing over her in his black robe, his bright axe was raised above his head.

She lay back on the pillows until she could no longer feel her heart. Rael was asleep, his mouth open. Breath whistled through his lips, a comforting sound. She put her hand out to his shoulder and touched the pack of muscle there.

Now she was coming to the end. She raised herself up onto her elbow and looked at the image of Beloved Angkhdt, sitting cross-legged around the burning flame. The lamp cast a wavering shadow on the side of the tent—dog-muzzled, black, ominous. How can we give these things such power?

For a moment she was Cassia again. For a moment the bishop was asleep, still sleeping in her prison cell the night before her execution. For a moment, the burden of her was gone—so beautiful, magnanimous, and full of destiny, the center of a world striving toward death, her death the spark of the new revolution. For a moment all that was like the woodman in her dream, empty, inflated with emptiness, and as she lay back on the pillow and the time ticked by, she wondered whom they had found to play the other part in the performance, to mimic the killer while she mimicked his victim. What small creature would be struggling inside the woodman's robe?

Miss Azimuth had given her a wristwatch. It lay beside her pillow, the hands at ten to four. More than enough time. She lay back. And to compose her mind, she ran it through an exercise that her father had taught her in the happy days. First with her eyes open, then with her eyes closed, she tried to reconstruct the face of a person she had known. She tried to fill her mind with it and to exclude all else, and to rebuild as if from the skull outward, layer by layer, the skin, the cheekbones, the complexion, and the eyes, nose, ears of Palam Bey, of Mayadonna Bey, of her old teacher Langur Bey. And of her father, Mr. Sarnath. The point was to allow no trace of sentiment to pollute memory—these were not images, these were not judgments of men. These were the men themselves, as close as she could come now they were dead, and she was careful to exclude any regret, any pleasure, any sadness, any sense even of recognition as she rebuilt Mr. Sarnath's long-ridged head, his long nose, his dry eyes. The point was to allow a thought to grow inside that head, a product of that brain which would be separate from her thoughts.

Her imagination faltered. She was full of warm, soft feelings of regret. She was sleepy now, drifting toward sleep again, and as her thoughts started to tumble in slow motion away from her control she felt something change, a chasm open up, because somewhere on the other side of her mind now the bishop was stirring. The image in her mind was no longer Mr. Sarnath, but some other old man with tattooed hands, a golden robe, a shrunken scavenger face—so different.

"Ah," she murmured. Cold, perhaps, she rolled away off of the pillow, and put her head on Rael's shoulder. Though it was not quite Rael anymore. Though his face and smell and body were the same, her last thought as she fell into sleep was that he had changed and the bed had changed and everything had changed, and at last it was the bishop's wild unnamed lover lying by her side.

Deccan Blendish sat beside the forest path two miles away. The guard had gone on ahead. Blendish could see his lantern shining in the trees; he had no need of it. He had stopped to rest. He sat on a log, and with his axe he chopped at the bark. He looked from side to side, because all around him creatures lurked now in the dark periphery of his cramped eyes. He thought to surprise them by quick erratic changes in his line of sight. It did no good; they were too fast. The wood was full of questing life, of seething darkness. Thick heavy branches hung above him—masses of slick leaves, their undersides gleaming with reflected starlight. Clusters of white locusts or of roaches, two or three hundred of them in a trembling ball were packed into a crack between the branches. And all he had to do was look at them to make them disappear, to make them explode into a winged flurry too fast for him to follow. A luna moth slid through the air, ghostly, transparent, swooping down toward him; it was gone. Tarsiers and bats whistled around him; he knew they were there. The undergrowth was full of larger beasts, and they were fearful and conniving too, dissolving into darkness when he turned his eyes to them. And maybe it was because they knew he was dying, and already he was living as a guest in this strange world. And maybe they knew that although one part of him was weaker by the moment, another part of him was stronger, a dangerous erratic part, the woodman, the gathering man. Now he was holding the axe in his hand, and he was chipping at the bark of the downed log.

"Asshole," came the voice of the guard, brilliant and piercing. "What the fuck do you think you're doing?"

The guard was coming back now, his lantern wandering through the trees. "Come on," he said. "I don't want to be all night."

No, thought Blendish, not all night. It was not safe. Not here—this was the lair of the hypnogogic ape, who could alter the perceptions of its predators, its prey. This was the lair of the hypnogogic ape, from whom all men and women had inherited that piece of darkness at their core. When the gods came down to mix their golden blood with the polluted earth, this was the result—this bulging net of darkness, this forest of deceit. All around him, the hypnogogic ape was chattering in the bush just out of earshot. It was grinning in the bush just out of sight. Dark shapes scurried away from the guard's approaching step.

Deccan Blendish got up, his axe in his right hand. And with his left he grabbed hold of the guard's sleeve, making the lantern waver, making long patterns of light spin around them. He peered up into the guard's face, and so great was the power of his expectation that he actually saw the mocking worried cheeks and little eyes of the hypnogogic ape, as if they had been copied from his drawing onto the guard's blank face.

"I've got you," he whispered. "Now I've got you." But he was premature. The guard dropped the lantern and stepped back.

"You goddamned lunatic," he said. And then he was moving backward up the path as Blendish came toward him. The lantern, cocked under a bush, shed only a steep angle of light, and so the guard disappeared as though he'd stepped out of the world as Deccan Blendish stumbled up the path, his axe held out, his mind empty as an open hand. It wasn't until he had gone too far, until he had reached the noiseless river, until he was standing on the riverbank that a thought began to coalesce and he grabbed hold of it. Cathartes has done this, he thought. Cathartes has destroyed me. Big-penised Cathartes, and the girl.

He was at the river, and in time he reached the camp. He walked through the camp among the fig trees, and no one challenged him. He was the gathering man; they were expecting him. The soldiers of Paradise were waiting in their tents, and they were lying sleepless. They were listening to his tread. He found the glade, and the glade's edge. Aching, tired, and in need of medication, he squatted down among the undergrowth to wait.

Rael woke up with an urge to urinate. Cassia was sleeping with her face against his arm. Her mouth was open, her cheek and lips pushed out of shape against his arm. The pillow under her was damp. A strand of hair was stuck along her teeth. And when he tried to take his arm away she grunted in her sleep and said something he couldn't understand. Then she turned her face away onto the other side.

He looked for a while at the sweet curve of her skull, her black tangle of curls, the semicircular indentations that her curls had left upon her cheek. He put his hand out, almost touching her. But her slumber barely covered her; even now she was muttering, and a crease had appeared between her eyebrows. He didn't want to wake her, and so he sat up instead, suddenly grateful that the night had passed without danger, grateful for the small grey light which seeped into the tent through the triangular opening. It had all been non-sense, and all Cassia's fear had been nonsense, part of the world of nightmares that had put that crease between her brows—almost he woke her then. But his bladder was full. He thought that if he emptied it, then he could wake her in a different way, at least if their sore bodies would allow it.

They were free now—that he knew. It was the tenth day, and the myth that had held them captive for a time was dissolving in the light. It had been her dream, and now this was his—to make love and then to go away. To take some food and go together. To travel northward to that high place in the mountains where the snow was on the crest. Where the cooling wind would bring you a stray wisp of sound.

The air was thin in that sparse landscape, and it was far away from this wet forest and these tangled thoughts, this dense articulation which had kept them separate and dark, which had hampered them and pricked them. These words to which they had surrendered such importance—in the accumulating light he could see a path through to the end of them.

How could they have thought that these words meant something? How could they have given in to them? How could they have let themselves surrender to temptation, when the earth was full of empty spaces? He crawled out of the tent. There was a white mist on the ground. The sky was white.

He walked over to the edge of the glade. Again he could sense people around him, squatting in the bushes, waiting for him. As he became aware of them, he became aware also of himself, the movements of his body. He yawned, he stretched, he rubbed his arms in the cool air, and midway through each motion it acquired a small exaggeration, a small untruth. He spread his legs and leaned into a bush to urinate, aware of people near him; he closed his eyes. The act seemed to require concentration; he could feel himself frowning, and the spray just begun when he heard a sound behind him, so gentle, not a smash or a bang but just a sudden intake of breath, as of someone suddenly awakened. With part of his mind he had been waiting for it all along.

Many things happened at once. He turned, and saw a shadow slip out of the tent and into the bamboo. A chatter of automatic rifle fire, then silence. He could feel the urine on his leg. And he was running toward the tent, again aware of every movement, every step, because there were people around him in the bushes and the mist. Brother Longo was there, suddenly, and the old puppet crow woman, and the priest. Mama Jobe was there, and then some soldiers. And they weren't doing anything except just standing there. They didn't go inside the tent. They left that for him.

The statue of Angkhdt had been kicked over, and the oil was soaking through the canvas floor. Cassia lay on her back, in a tangle of bedsheets. Her eyes were open, and a strand of hair was caught between her teeth. And she was full of life—her eyes were open and her mouth was smiling and making silent words. She reached out one arm toward him and he stumbled down across her body, and he was grabbing her and holding her as she struggled for words. Her lips were by his ear. She had one arm around his neck, but with the other she was holding a wad of cloth against her belly—at first when he saw the yellow stain spread through her fingers he thought maybe it was the spilt oil, and then maybe it was some of his own urine which he could still feel on his leg, and then maybe when there seemed so much of it he knew it was her amber-colored blood, and it was leaking out of her.

"Get something," he shouted. "Go and help." And it was as if the words were spoken by another person. They seemed so out of place in that small tent. In the outside world, people were standing, waiting, moving—he could see some legs outside the entrance, and he could see the shadows of some other people move across the side of the tent, cast by the rising sun.

"Don't worry about them," she said, close to his ear. "Be with me now."

SWEET
RANGRIVER

Early that morning, Enver Shaw died in Carbontown
hospital from the whipping he'd received. A candlelight vigil,
organized by the miners' wives, turned violent when the news
came. At seven o'clock the executive committee of the UGM
announced a four-day protest; by midmorning, the blast furnaces were silent for the first time since the mine had been
reopened. The cog railway was silent, the pit was silent, the
mountain and the town were muffled by a new cloud of
silence in which individual human voices could acquire a new
stridency. Four thousand people stood silent on the maidan
when Nanda Dev read the petition and the list of grievances.
They were still there at three o'clock when rumors of the
bishop's death began to seep in through the fence.

All that day, a pressure had been building in the forest.
Brother Longo had erected his branding iron by the bishop's
tent. By dusk his voice was hoarse with constant preaching,
and he had managed to baptize more than a thousand new
converts to the Cult of Loving Kindness. Only he had

changed the ceremony so that the temperature of the brand was lower, and so that the initiates did not receive the brand upon their dominant hand; he wanted them for fighting.

At nightfall he lit bonfires, and still the converts came. Miss Azimuth had laid out the bishop's body on a plastic tarpaulin, and for nine hours she labored over it. She drained out the blood. She cut small holes through the back of the bishop's nostrils and her mouth, and with a long silver hook she pulled out the heart, the brain, the lungs, the viscera. These she set aside for relics. Then she packed the body's empty case with cotton wadding soaked in tincture of formaldehyde. She rubbed the bishop's skin with a bicarbonate of soda, which she had mixed with perfume and with many astringent herbs. She worked far into the night, and pilgrims from every village in that sector of the forest came to watch her, came to admire the bishop's placid beauty. Many of them would not have crossed a rice field to see her when she was alive. Her dead body had a more compelling power than her words or her ambiguous self.

Rael had slept most of the morning. But in the afternoon he sat with the others, watching Miss Azimuth. He sat in the first circle, his face alternating between concentration and abstraction, and he watched the old woman stitch up Cassia's body under the bright sun. Occasionally he would wrinkle his nostrils as Miss Azimuth applied some new spice or herb or compress; he didn't speak. He seemed taken by a peculiar lethargy. Nor did he seem to notice that he also had excited some attention, and that the pilgrims were staring at him and whispering to each other.

In the evening Longo Starbridge came to sit beside him. He had been talking all day in his deep public voice, and it was all used up. Even though pilgrims sat close by, he spoke to Rael in a thin private tone. He put his curved palm up to Rael's ear and whispered into it. But he couldn't tell whether Rael understood; after a few minutes the boy raised up his hand. He made a brushing motion by his ear.

It was Longo Starbridge's intention to attack the sweet potato fields at the perimeter of Carbontown. All day he had been preaching to his soldiers. And as the hours wore on he had been preaching also to a growing crowd of pilgrims. They were unarmed but they were hopeful. All together they made an impressive sight—impressive enough, thought Longo Starbridge, who didn't anticipate much actual fighting.

It was his intention to attack the fence at dawn. He imagined the soldiers of Paradise led by two men carrying a bier, on which in awful splendor lay the body of the last bishop of Charn. For this reason he had asked Miss Azimuth to hurry with the process of embalming; though the old woman had been eager to start, she had been grumbling and complaining all day because her fingers were so stiff, because she did not have the correct tools, because she did not have the time to do a perfect job. Her small voice had buzzed around her as she worked, and by the time the lanterns and the bonfires were lit, she was almost finished. The plastic tarpaulin had disappeared under a bed of flowers, on which Cassia lay in state. She wore a golden wedding dress which had been donated by a rich shopkeeper from Cochinoor. Her skin was painted and her hair was carefully arranged. Two local cosmeticians had helped Miss Azimuth at the end, and they had combed out Cassia's tangled curls, and had arranged them in the latest syle around a rhinestone tiara. She wore a garter belt, silk stockings, and high-heeled shoes.

All the time that they were dressing her, Rael sat a few feet away, sometimes watching, sometimes not. Longo Starbridge, when he came to sit beside him, couldn't tell whether he understood what he was supposed to do—that he was supposed to be one of the two men who carried the bishop's bier in the attack.

Toward midnight when Miss Azimuth was finished, the Cult of Loving Kindness broke its camp. Carrying torches, they moved through the woods toward Carbontown, a disorganized and random crowd. In the middle of it moved

Cassia's body, and she was surrounded by a swell of voices and her litter moved like a small boat caught in a current—hesitating often, turning often to avoid small obstacles. A burly soldier carried the front end, and he was replaced every hour or so when he was tired. But Rael carried the back end; at the last moment he had come forward and had pushed aside the soldier—Longo Starbridge's alternative—who was spitting on his palms. Rael picked up the burden and refused to surrender it. Glowering, his face set in a mask of anger, he carried it throughout the night and in the morning too.

At six o'clock, in small dazed groups, the crowd began to come out of the wood, and they moved through the fields to Carbontown. Many stopped to dig the sweet potatoes from the ground, and some lit fires for breakfast. They had met no one in the forest, no one in the fields. The security battalion had withdrawn to the fence, and as the morning progressed there was some shooting. There were casualties. But from his position near the gate, Longo Starbridge could see through his binoculars a crowd of miners on the ridge beyond the fence. He could see the company office building surrounded by a mass of miners. They had climbed up into the scaffolding and had hung the colors of the UGM from the main catwalk.

The security battalion could see this too. At ten o'clock they surrendered their weapons and opened the gate, in return for certain guarantees. They turned over Benjamin Cathartes to a delegation of the union, led by Nanda Dev.

At ten-thirty the first relief arrived, a detachment of riot police on horseback, sent from the lumber farm at Cochinoor. They were commanded by an adjunct from the school of forestry, a man who favored direct action. He came riding up the road, and when he saw the banners of the Cult of Loving Kindness grouped around the bishop's bier, he gave an order to disperse the crowd. This order he rescinded as soon as he understood what was happening, but for about twenty minutes there was mayhem. A company of horsemen, carrying riot shields and dressed in plastic armor, charged across the field into a mass of unarmed pilgrims.

Longo Starbridge and the rest had already entered Carbontown. He had the skull of Angkhdt; at that moment he was standing in the guardhouse at the gate, the skull of Angkhdt between his big red hands. At that moment, only Miss Azimuth still accompanied the bishop's body—Miss Azimuth, four soldiers, and about three dozen women, for everyone else had moved forward to the gate. When she saw the horsemen coming toward her, she screamed. She hobbled away over the uncertain ground. The women and the soldiers scattered also, dropping their flags. The dog's head of Angkhdt, the shining sun of Abu Starbridge wafted to the ground, and over them rode the heavy horses, their hooves and claws impeded by the mud, impeded by the furrows. The riot police had nightsticks, and they chased the women back into the trees.

Rael watched them go. The soldier who had been supporting the front of the bier had fled with them, leaving him alone. The bier had collapsed forward, and Cassia's body had slid down the wooden ramp, pushing a mound of lilies, orchids, and white hyacinth off onto the ground. Rael stood with his arms aching, his hands still clasped around the poles. He was looking down at his feet. He was not paying much attention; the air was cool. Sounds seemed muffled to him. Clouds had covered over the sun. There had been people around him; now he was alone. Through the morning ground mist, which seemed to have persisted in this corner of the sweet potato field, he could see traces of erratic movement. He could hear shouts, and even a little gunfire. His arms were cramped and weak.

But he raised his head when he heard a new kind of noise. In front of him, ten feet away, stood an animal. It was four-legged, black, and huge.

Mr. Sarnath had owned a donkey once, when Rael and Cassia were very young. They had ridden on its back. And

Rael remembered horses from the towns where they had lived. But not like this. This one stood without moving. Its arched neck, its heavy head were higher than his own. Its horns, its beak were painted red, and the flesh around its eyes was painted also. Its wide strong back was loaded with bundles, loaded with bags behind its plastic saddle.

Its rider had fallen. Maybe he'd been shot. There was no sign of it; there was no mark. But he sat with his legs splayed in the mud, his round plastic helmet sunk upon his breastplate. He too made no motion.

Rael laid the bier upon the ground. He rubbed his elbows and his forearms for a moment, thinking, listening to the high, thin, airless breath of the animal, whistling through the slit in its beak.

A high, thin, creaking music, and it meant something. Rael let it seep into his mind, displacing thought. He used a technique that Mr. Sarnath had once shown him. Sarnath and Cassia—no. But that was gone. Instead he let his body move, and it seemed to him then that he was the only moving agent on that field. Other horsemen, other pilgrims had disappeared in the small mist.

And the plastic rider in front of him was sitting with his legs splayed out. He didn't even raise his head as Rael approached. He didn't even raise his head as Rael untied one of the bundles from the horse's back. It was a zippered duffel bag. Rael opened it and dumped out into the mud a primus stove, a dozen pots and pans. They clanged and banged and that too was a kind of music.

Cassia had fallen from the litter and was lying on her side. Flowers lay around her; he brought the duffel bag back to the bier and loaded it with flowers. He loaded Cassia in. Her body was lighter than he had remembered. He plucked off her high-heeled shoes and dropped them to the ground. He eased the zipper shut over her feet.

Now at the limit of his mind he could hear shouting. But he did not allow himself to hurry. He knew this was part of the myth also, how the antinomial took the bishop's body and disappeared with it into the wood, leading his horse north along the road, to Cochinoor and then beyond. In the story he was not pursued. The rider had not raised his head.

He tied the bag across the saddlebow. It sagged down on either side. He took the horse's bridle. By pulling it, he set the world in motion once again.

EPILOGUE

That summer, a new irregularity in the mechanism of the heavens brings Paradise within the reach of earth again, two hundred days after the bishop's death. On the night of December third, in the seventeenth phase of summer, it rises again over Mt. Nyangongo, whose crater is again filled with an expectant crowd. To them it seems to take up half the sky. It sheds a golden light.

In Carbontown the light touches the skeleton of the burnt-out office building. It touches the cold smokestacks. It finds the grave of Deccan Blendish by the fig tree. Benjamin Cathartes, taking supper in his cell in Cochinoor, sees it glow upon the window ledge. It casts a shadow of the grate.

In the forest, the light is soft, liquid, thick. It falls from leaf to leaf. Farther north where the trees falter in the chalky soil, the light seems harsher and more uniform, more a quality of the air.

The trees give out entirely on the bank of a shallow river.

On the night of the third, a horseman walks his horse over the stones.

The land rises quickly on the other side. The rider takes his horse along the gorge and then dismounts to lead it up through the thick grass. He is tired. It's been a hundred miles since he passed a town.

The grass at the top of the rise is full of insects and rodents, and the horse is distracted by small sudden noises. It is hungry. It pulls on the bridle. But the man is looking northward, to where the light of Paradise is breaking on the glaciers of a range of mountains.

He pulls himself back up into the saddle. They ride for a few hours. At midnight the land changes and they come out into a broad shallow bowl. The light is overhead now and it is underfoot, reflected from a circle of old concrete which lines the bottom of the bowl. It forms a flat expanse perhaps two thousand feet across, split apart in some places and in others still retaining vestiges of paint. Everywhere the moss has spread in complicated patterns, following the cracks.

The horse's hooves make a flat sound like the clapping of a hand. They pass by the remnants of three small buildings, surrounded by a rotten wire fence. Rael doesn't look at them, and he ignores also the four gigantic metal tubes—all broken, all fallen on their sides but one, which is still pointed like an arrow at the sky.

It doesn't take long for steel to crumble in this country. Even in summer, the wind is cold and harsh here. The rider doesn't feel it. He bloats his lungs with the cold air. It is like food to him, better food than the dried turnip which he gnaws without dismounting.

He is moving faster now. The duffel bag on his saddlebow knocks against the horse's shoulder. The bundle of wood which he collected in the forest knocks against the horse's rump. They have left the metal tower, left the tarmac an hour behind, and they are riding along a granite cliff. They are coming into shelter from the wind beside a stream which

runs down to Rangriver. The water is talking on the stones.
It is warmer. A line of gorse runs along the bottom of the
cliff, and some dead juniper trees. The rider draws rein here.
He dismounts.

He unloads the horse and sets it free to hunt. It goes down
to the stream to drink, then it moves off. The rider stands
with his bundles at his feet. He is listening to the wind, his
head cocked as if straining to hear something over the sound
of the water, but there is nothing. He sets to work.

With a thick-bladed knife he cuts down some dead trees,
and digs up some of the dead gorse. He drags it to the stream.
He breaks up the sticks that he brought from the forest and
on the dry grey strand he lays a bonfire—first the brush, then
the juniper, then the boughs of sandlewood. He builds it into
a six-foot cube. It takes him several hours to get it right.
Toward the end—it is the deep part of the night now, and
Paradise is down behind the cliff—he works slowly, resting
often.

When he is done, he goes down to the stream to smoke a
cigarette. He squats down by the water and takes out the
battered pack. He lights the cigarette with a plastic lighter.
The butane is almost gone.

When the cigarette is half-finished, he stands up. He walks
back to where he left the saddle. Holding the cigarette between his teeth, squinting at the smoke, he lifts the duffel
bag. It is lighter now than when he started this journey. Still,
he has to use both hands to hoist it to the top of the pyre.

Then he squats down again. He smokes the cigarette down
to the filter. When it is almost done, he holds it out into the
gorse. A few receding specks of red—he cups his hand and
blows at them until they make a flame.

There's a big rock a dozen feet away. He sits down on it
to watch. He is humming a bit under his breath—fragments
of tunes, fragments of words. It's not much of a ceremony;
the flame spreads slowly. Occasionally it flares up when it
hits a knot of pitch.

The smoke rises up into the sky. Light comes early to these latitudes.

Rael stamps his plastic boots against the stones. He stretches his hands out toward the fire, which has begun to roar now in its heart. The canvas duffel bag is smoking, and after a while it splits open. It burns back to reveal part of Cassia's arm, part of her hand, part of the sleeve of her gold dress. The herbs make a sweet smell.

Rael rubs his face with his hot hands. He gets up, and with a long stick of juniper he reaches in to pluck back the burning canvas from her face. Such is the embalmer's skill, for a moment it is recognizable.

The fire burns up bright and then it starts to fall apart. Rael watches it as it subsides, as the day gathers. He is still standing when the horse returns, nor does he look up when two more riders cross the stream. He pays no attention when they jump down barefoot on the stones, even though they sing soft words of interrogation. He goes back to his rock and he sits down.

In time, the men come to squat beside him. After half an hour one holds out a leather bottle. He is hungry, thirsty, and they give him things to eat and drink he's never had before.